Can she find a l...
perfect n...

For Christmas, Forever

Three enchanting Christmas romances from
three beloved Mills & Boon authors!

In December 2009 Mills & Boon bring
you two classic collections, each
featuring three favourite romances
by our bestselling authors

FOR CHRISTMAS, FOREVER

The Yuletide Engagement
by Carole Mortimer
The Doctor's Christmas Bride
by Sarah Morgan
Snowbound Reunion by Barbara McMahon

LITTLE CHRISTMAS MIRACLES

Her Christmas Wedding Wish
by Judy Christenberry
Christmas Gift: A Family
by Barbara Hannay
Christmas on the Children's Ward
by Carol Marinelli

For Christmas, Forever

CAROLE MORTIMER
SARAH MORGAN
BARBARA McMAHON

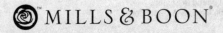

All the characters in this book have no existence outside the imagination of
the author, and have no relation whatsoever to anyone bearing the same name
or names. They are not even distantly inspired by any individual known or
unknown to the author, and all the incidents are pure invention.

First published in Great Britain 2009
Harlequin Mills & Boon Limited,
Eton House, 18-24 Paradise Road, Richmond, Surrey TW9 1SR

FOR CHRISTMAS, FOREVER
© by Harlequin Enterprises II B.V./S.à.r.l 2009

The Yuletide Engagement, The Doctor's Christmas Bride and *Snowbound
Reunion* were first published in Great Britain by Harlequin Mills & Boon
Limited in separate, single volumes.

The Yuletide Engagement © Carole Mortimer 2003
The Doctor's Christmas Bride © Sarah Morgan 2004
Snowbound Reunion © Barbara McMahon 2006

ISBN: 978 0 263 87144 9

05-1209

Printed and bound in Spain
by Litografia Rosés S.A., Barcelona

THE YULETIDE ENGAGEMENT

BY
CAROLE MORTIMER

Carole Mortimer was born in England, the youngest of three children. She began writing in 1978, and has now written over one hundred and fifty books for Mills & Boon. Carole has six sons, Matthew, Joshua, Timothy, Michael, David and Peter. She says, "I'm happily married to Peter senior; we're best friends as well as lovers, which is probably the best recipe for a successful relationship. We live in a lovely part of England."

For Peter

CHAPTER ONE

'CINDERS shall go to the ball!' Toby announced as he stood poised in the kitchen doorway, a look of triumph on his boyishly handsome face. 'Although the first person to call me the Fairy Godmother is going to get slapped!'

Ellie looked up from the newspaper she had been reading where she sat at the kitchen table, blue gaze narrowing as she took in the pleased flush on her brother's cheeks. 'Toby, did you call into the pub again on your way home from work?' she prompted suspiciously. His eyes looked overbright, and he wasn't making much sense, either!

'That's all the thanks I get for getting you out of a difficult situation—accusations of inebriation!' He grinned widely as he came fully into the kitchen, leaving the door open behind him, despite the fact that snow was forecast for later this evening.

Ellie gave an involuntary shiver as a cold blast of air followed her brother into the room. 'At least shut the door, Toby,' she reasoned with indulgent affection. 'You—'

'Didn't you hear me, Ellie?' He pulled her easily to her feet, swinging her round in the close confines of the kitchen.

'Something about Cinders and a ball.' She nodded, starting to feel slightly dizzy as the kitchen became a

5

giddy blur; maybe intoxication was infectious? 'Toby, will you please stop?' she gasped weakly.

He did, holding onto her hands as she swayed slightly. 'Ellie, I asked him and he said yes. Can you believe that?' he exclaimed happily. 'Didn't I tell you he's one of the good guys? He's even coming round later this evening to sort out the details,' he announced triumphantly. 'Isn't that just—?'

'Toby, will you just slow down and tell me who you have asked to do what?' Ellie cut in impatiently, but she already felt a terrible sense of foreboding as it slowly started to dawn on her exactly what Toby might have done. Surely he hadn't—he wouldn't have—? She had been joking, for goodness' sake!

Toby let go of her hands, grinning at her victoriously as he reached for an apple from the bowl in the middle of the kitchen table, biting down on its crispness with complete enjoyment.

'Toby!' Ellie said warningly. 'Will you just tell me exactly what it is you've done?' Although she had a feeling she already knew the answer to that!

Her brother returned her gaze with guileless blue eyes. 'I've asked Patrick to escort you to your company Christmas dinner, of course,' he dismissed with satisfaction.

'Patrick…?' she echoed faintly.

'Patrick McGrath. My boss,' her brother enlarged impatiently as she just stared at him. 'Remember? We were discussing the problem at the weekend and you said that what you really needed was someone high-powered like Patrick to accompany you. That way—'

'But I wasn't being serious, Toby,' she cut in incredulously, sinking back down onto the kitchen chair, staring disbelievingly at her brother. He was the younger by only a year, but sometimes—like now—it could feel like ten!

The company Christmas dinner was quickly looming, and this year, after Ellie's recent break-up with Gareth, a junior partner in the law firm they both worked for, it promised to be something of an ordeal for her. Not to go would give the impression she was too much of a coward to face Gareth and his new girlfriend, but to go on her own would make it look as if she were still pining for him. Which she most certainly was not!

Which was why, over the weekend, as she and Toby had lingered over their meal together on Sunday evening, she had drunk one glass of wine too many and suggested that she needed someone like Patrick McGrath, Toby's wealthy entrepreneurial boss, to go with her to the dinner—no one could possibly think she was still interested in Gareth when she was in the company of such a man.

Tall, dark, handsome and extremely successful, Patrick McGrath was the ideal man to allay any doubts anyone might have as to her having any lingering feelings for Gareth.

But she had thought Toby knew that it had only been that third glass of wine talking, that she hadn't really meant for it to happen!

She closed her eyes now in pained disbelief. 'Toby, please, please tell me you haven't really asked Patrick McGrath to take me out next week,' she groaned desperately.

Her brother paused in the act of taking another bite

of his apple. 'I haven't?' he said uncertainly, some of the look of triumph starting to fade from his face as he finally noticed Ellie's marked lack of enthusiasm.

'You haven't!' she repeated firmly.

She had met Toby's boss only once, five months ago. It had been enough. There was no doubting that Patrick McGrath was very rich, very self-assured, and very eligible. In fact, the very last person Ellie would ever want to ask her out!

Toby looked puzzled. 'But on Sunday night you said—'

'I had drunk too much wine, for goodness' sake,' Ellie stood up to pace the confines of the room. 'I wasn't being serious—I just thought of the most unlikely person ever to—I didn't really *mean* it when I said—'

'Patrick would make the perfect escort for your dinner a week on Friday,' Toby finished obligingly.

She winced as she remembered saying exactly that. But it was a situation that required an extreme solution for unusual circumstances. On Sunday evening she had run the gamut of them, and had suggested Patrick McGrath being the perfect escort as the most extreme of those extremes. She certainly hadn't expected Toby to act on it!

'Exactly,' she confirmed weakly. 'Toby, please tell me you didn't—'

'But I did,' Toby told her impatiently. 'I asked Patrick to accompany you. And as he said yes I can't see what your problem is.' He shook his head.

He couldn't see—! The problem was that Ellie felt

totally ridiculous and completely humiliated. She had no intention of—of—

'Toby, you can just call the man right now and tell him not to come here this evening—that you made a mistake, that your sister doesn't need an escort next Friday or any other time, and that if or when I do need an escort I'll find one of my own, thank you very much!' She glared her indignation at her irresponsible brother.

Blue eyes blazed at the thought of her humiliation if she should ever meet Patrick McGrath again. Her dark, shoulder-length hair seemed to crackle with the force of her anger, every inch of her five-foot-two-inch frame seeming to bristle with indignation.

'But—'

'Call him, Toby,' she repeated with cold fury. 'Call Patrick McGrath right now and tell him!'

'But—'

'Now, Toby!' she ground out forcefully.

'I think what your brother is trying to tell you—Ellie, isn't it?—is that there's no need for him to call and tell me anything—I'm already standing right here,' drawled a lazily amused voice from directly behind her.

Ellie had spun round at the first sound of that drawling voice, having to arch her neck back in order to look up into the confident face of Patrick McGrath.

If ever she had wanted the ground to open and swallow her up it was right now.

Patrick McGrath!

Tall—well over six feet. Dark—hair kept deliberately short as it looked inclined to curl. Handsome—grey eyes beneath arched dark brows, an arrogant slash of a nose, chiselled lips that were curved into a smile at the moment, an out-of-season tan darkening those distinctive features. Successful—even the casual clothes he was wearing this evening—a black silk shirt and faded denims—obviously bore a designer label, and the black leather shoes were no doubt hand-made.

'So, Ellie,' he drawled softly. 'What was it you wanted Toby to tell me?'

She was trying to speak, really she was; she just couldn't seem to get any words to come out of her throat!

'The details for next Friday, perhaps?' Patrick McGrath prompted interestedly, grey gaze lightly mocking.

How Ellie remembered that mocking gaze. How could she ever forget it? Toby still had no idea what had actually happened at her one and only other meeting with this man; Ellie hadn't told him, and as the days and weeks had passed, without Toby making any reference to it, it had eventually become obvious that Patrick McGrath wasn't going to tell her brother all the details of that meeting, either.

But Ellie was unlikely to ever forget them!

It had been an unusually hot summer this year, with everyone wearing the minimum of clothing, and Ellie, conscious of her impending summer holiday abroad and with a wish not to stand out like a sore thumb on the Majorcan beaches, had decided to spend one Saturday afternoon sunbathing in their secluded back garden.

Topless.

How could she have known that Patrick McGrath had been telephoning for over an hour, urgently trying to contact Toby? That he had decided to come over to the house in person when he'd received no reply? Or that he would stroll out into the garden when he found the house unlocked but seemingly deserted?

Ellie had made a mad scramble for her top when she'd realised she was no longer alone, but it hadn't been quick enough to prevent that piercing gaze from having a full view of her naked breasts.

Damn it, she was sure she could see the knowledge of that memory now, clearly gleaming in those mocking grey eyes.

Despite what she might have said on Sunday evening, warmed by the unaccustomed wine, Patrick McGrath was the last man she wanted to accompany her anywhere!

She drew in a deep breath. 'Toby has— He was mistaken when he asked—I'm sorry you've been troubled, Mr McGrath.' She spoke dismissively, her gaze fixed on the second button of his black silk shirt. 'I never meant—'

'Toby, why don't you make us all some coffee?' Patrick McGrath turned to the younger man authoritatively. 'While Ellie and I sort out whether or not I'm being stood up a week on Friday,' he added derisively.

Toby set about making the pot of coffee and Ellie looked up at Patrick McGrath reprovingly. He might find all this funny, but she certainly didn't. As if any woman would ever stand this man up!

But they did need to sort this mess out, and she would rather do it out of earshot of her well-meaning but unthinking younger brother.

'Let's go through to the sitting room, Mr McGrath,'

she suggested briskly, some of her normal self confidence returning as she led the way down the hallway to their lounge.

She was twenty-seven years old, had cared for Toby since their parents were killed in a car crash eight years ago, taking over the running of the family home as well as continuing her full-time job as secretary, eventually to one of the senior partners in a prestigious law firm. She was more than up to dealing with this situation.

Well…ordinarily she could be up to dealing with it, she conceded as Patrick McGrath stood in the middle of the sitting-room, looking at her with his laughing steely eyes.

How on earth did Toby cope with working for this man every day? she wondered frowningly. He had such presence, such confidence, that just being in the same room with him was a little overpowering. But she knew Toby thought the other man was wonderful, that her brother thoroughly enjoyed his job as this man's personal assistant.

Maybe it was only women who found Patrick McGrath overpowering…?

Well…one woman, Ellie conceded self-derisively. Maybe if she weren't so completely aware of the fact that this man had seen her sunbathing topless—

Stop that right now, Ellie, she told herself firmly. If she was going to sort this situation out at all then she had to put that embarrassing memory completely from her mind. Although it would help if Patrick McGrath were to do the same…

His next words didn't seem to imply that was the case!

'I don't believe the two of us have ever been formally

introduced,' he drawled softly, with an emphasis on the 'formally', it seemed to a slightly flustered Ellie. How could she possibly have formally introduced herself while at the same time clutching a top in front of her naked breasts?

'Probably not,' she conceded abruptly. 'But I'm sure you're aware that I'm Ellie Fairfax, Toby's older sister, and I am aware you're Patrick T. McGrath—Toby's boss.'

He gave an acknowledging inclination of his head. 'The T stands for Timothy, by the way. And Ellie is short for…?'

'Elizabeth,' she supplied dismissively. 'Although what—?'

'It may come up in conversation a week on Friday.' He shrugged broad shoulders.

'Mr McGrath, there isn't going to be any ''a week on Friday''.' She sighed frustratedly. 'I have no idea what my irresponsible brother may have told you, but—'

'He adores you, you know,' Patrick McGrath cut in softly.

She felt the warmth in her cheeks at this completely unexpected comment. 'I love him too.' She nodded. 'Although I don't really think that's relevant to our conversation.' She frowned.

'Ellie, do you think we could both sit down?' Patrick McGrath suggested gently. 'At the moment we look like two opponents about to face each other in the ring,' he added dryly.

Maybe because that was exactly how he made her feel—totally on the defensive! 'Please—do sit down,' she invited abruptly.

'After you,' he drawled politely.

Ellie looked at him impatiently, finding herself the focus of Patrick McGrath's cool grey gaze as he waited for her to be seated before he would sit down himself.

Old-fashioned good manners, as well as all those other attributes!

Ellie sat down abruptly, determinedly putting those 'other attributes' firmly from her mind. 'I accept that Toby meant well when he—when he spoke to you today—' she began huskily, stopping to look enquiringly at Patrick McGrath when he began to smile.

'Sorry.' He continued to smile. 'Toby is—he's one of the least selfish people I've ever met. As well as being completely honest, utterly trustworthy and totally candid.' He sobered slightly. 'You've done a lot for him, Ellie,' he told her admiringly.

The warmth deepened in her cheeks at this even more unexpected compliment. 'I'm pleased he's working out so well as your assistant.'

'I wasn't just talking about him as my assistant, Ellie,' Patrick McGrath cut in impatiently. 'Toby is an exceptional young man. And it's all thanks to you,' he added firmly.

She gave a rueful smile. 'I think my parents may have had something to do with it.'

'Your parents were killed when Toby was eighteen.' He shook his head. 'A very dangerous time for a young man to be left without guidance.'

Ellie frowned. 'You were right about Toby being candid!' It made her wonder exactly what else Toby had confided to Patrick McGrath about their private family affairs.

He looked at her quizzically. 'You should be proud of him, Ellie, not—'

'Here we are.' Toby was grinning widely as he kicked the door open with his foot and came in with the tray of coffee things.

Ellie looked up at him affectionately; she *was* proud of him—of the way he had carried on with his plans to go to university to study law after the accident that had killed their parents, of the way he had obtained a first-class degree, of the way he had worked doggedly in a law firm for the two years following, before applying and succeeding in getting this position with Patrick McGrath. Yes, she was very proud of him—she just wished that she had taught him to be a little less candid when it came to their own private affairs!

'All settled?' He sat back on his heels to look at them both expectantly after placing the tray down on the low table.

'Almost.' Patrick McGrath was the one to answer him dryly.

Almost nothing! Ellie was grateful to him for his praise of Toby and of the part she had played in helping to form him into the likeable young man he was—but that did not mean she was going to agree to this ridiculous plan for Patrick McGrath to accompany her to the company Christmas dinner!

'We just have to dot the ''i''s and cross the ''t''s,' Patrick McGrath assured the younger man.

'Really?' Toby looked pleased by the prospect as he stood up. 'I have a date later, so if neither of you mind I'll just go upstairs and change while you two chat. Be back in a couple of minutes,' he added, before leaving the room.

'You see what I mean,' Patrick McGrath murmured softly. 'He's like a puppy, or a little brother that you don't want to disappoint.'

'He happens to *be* a little brother,' Ellie reminded him frustratedly. 'And I'm afraid this time he's going to be very disappointed!'

'Why?' Patrick McGrath regarded her with cool eyes.

'Because—because, Mr McGrath—' she began impatiently.

'Patrick,' he invited smoothly.

'Very well—Patrick,' she bit out decisively.

'Has something changed since Toby spoke to me this afternoon?' he prompted interestedly. 'Have you and the ex-boyfriend managed to patch things up after all? Because if you have—'

'No, we haven't managed to "patch things up",' she cut in evenly, her frustration increasing by the minute as she felt this situation slipping more and more out of her grasp. 'And we never will,' she added firmly. 'But that does not mean—'

'You have to go to the dinner with me instead,' Patrick McGrath finished slowly. 'Do you have someone else in mind?'

'No. But—'

'Then where's your problem? I was asked; I said yes—'

'You're starting to sound like Toby now,' she interrupted weakly. 'Mr—Patrick,' she corrected as he raised his brows in silent rebuke, 'you can't seriously want to come to a boring company dinner as my escort!'

'Why can't I?'

'Because it will be *boring*!' she assured him heatedly. What was wrong with the man? Couldn't he see she didn't want him to go with her?

His mouth twisted into the semblance of a smile. 'Ellie, I think you underestimate yourself,' he drawled huskily.

'I wasn't—' She broke off, her cheeks fiery red. 'Look, Patrick, Toby shouldn't have told you any of those things about my personal life. Because they are personal. And, quite frankly—'

'A little embarassing?' he finished calmly, obviously having taken note of her red cheeks.

A little? This had to be the worst thing Toby had ever done to her. Honest and trustworthy were fine, candid she really needed to discuss with him!

'Yes, it's embarrassing.' Ellie sighed heavily. 'And, apart from the fact that you value Toby as your employee, I have no idea why you should even have listened to his suggestion, let alone actually contemplated going through with it.' She was totally exasperated with both men, and she didn't mind Patrick McGrath knowing it.

His eyes met her gaze unwaveringly for long seconds. 'Can't you?' he finally murmured softly.

Ellie frowned at him. Was that a smile she saw lurking on the edges of those sculptured lips? And was that a faint knowing gleam she detected in the depths of those grey eyes?

She had an instant flashback to that scene in the gar-

den five months ago, of her panicked grab for her top
when she realized she was no longer alone, her eyes
wide with dismay as she stared across the garden at the
stranger standing there watching her with amused grey
eyes.

The same amused grey eyes that were looking across
the sitting room at her right now!

'Besides, Ellie,' Patrick drawled huskily, 'why
should you be the one to feel embarrassed because
some man was too much of an idiot to appreciate what
he had?'

There was a compliment in there somewhere—if she
could only find it.

'That's isn't the reason I feel embarrassed,' she assured him dismissively. 'My broken relationship is—
was private. I just can't believe Toby has been so indiscreet as to ask you to be my dinner partner next
week.' She shook her head disgustedly.

'You were going to ask me yourself?'

'Of course not,' she answered impatiently.

What was wrong with these two men? Couldn't they
see that it was humiliating that either of them had
thought she was incapable of finding a dinner partner
for herself?

'Well, as I had no idea of the dinner until Toby told
me about it, I could hardly have been the one to do the
asking,' Patrick reasoned lightly.

As if he would have asked her anyway; it was obvious he had only agreed to the suggestion now for
Toby's sake.

'Look, Toby meant well,' Patrick insisted when he

could see she was about to protest once again. 'He's—
just concerned for your happiness,' he added evenly.

'But he has no reason to be,' she protested. 'I'm
twenty-seven, not twelve.'

His mouth quirked into a teasing smile. 'I don't think
anyone is disputing your maturity, Ellie,' he murmured
tauntingly.

So he did remember that afternoon in the garden as
well as she did!

'If anything,' he continued frowningly, 'it's the opposite, I think.'

Now it was Ellie's turn to frown. 'What do you
mean?'

'Nothing,' he dismissed abruptly, standing up. 'And
if you're absolutely sure about not needing an escort
next Friday...?'

'I'm sure,' she said firmly.

Much as she would have enjoyed sweeping into the
restaurant on the arm of this attractive and successful
man, if only to see the stunned look on Gareth's face,
she knew that she really couldn't do it under these circumstances.

'It isn't that I'm not grateful.' She grimaced.

'Just thanks but no thanks?' Patrick mused.

'Yes,' she sighed.

He nodded. 'Then I'm obviously wasting our time,'
he added briskly. 'I trust you'll explain the situation to
Toby when he comes down? Tell him that at least I
tried, hmm?'

'The coffee...' she reminded him lamely, belatedly

realizing she had made no effort to offer to pour him a cup.

He smiled humourlessly. 'We both know that was just a ploy to keep Toby busy while the two of us talked.'

'Yes.' Ellie sighed again, moving to accompany him from the room.

Patrick paused in the open doorway. 'Don't be too hard on Toby, hmm?' he encouraged softly. 'He feels a certain—responsibility where your happiness is concerned.'

'I'll try to bear that in mind,' she assured him dryly.

'Ellie…?'

She looked up, her breath catching in her throat as she found herself the focus of Patrick's McGrath's enigmatic grey gaze.

He really was the most gorgeous-looking man, she acknowledged weakly. All six foot two inches of him!

'You know where I am if you should change your mind…' he told her pointedly.

Yes, he was gorgeous, and there was no doubt that having him as her escort would have salvaged her damaged pride—just as there was no doubt she had no intention of taking him up on his offer!

'I won't,' she assured him with finality.

How could Ellie have known, how could she possibly have guessed, that something disastrous would occur during the following week—something that would necessitate her not only changing her mind, but having to go to Patrick McGrath herself and ask him if he would consider coming to the company dinner with her after all?

CHAPTER TWO

'How do I look?' She grimaced at Toby questioningly as she entered the kitchen where her brother sat eating the dinner she had prepared for him before getting ready for her evening out.

'You look great,' he assured her enthusiastically. 'New dress?' he observed teasingly.

Of course it was a new dress; she couldn't go out with Patrick McGrath wearing the old trusty little-black-dress that she had worn to last year's company Christmas dinner. No, as Patrick's dinner date she wanted to wear something much more stylish. And noticeable.

She had known as soon as she saw the knee-length figure-hugging red dress in the shop that it would ensure, once and for all, that Gareth was no longer under any misapprehension concerning her having fully got over him. Especially with Patrick McGrath as her dinner partner!

'Do you like it?' she asked her brother uncertainly.

Trying the dress on in the shop and actually putting it on at home were two different things, she had realised a few minutes ago. Seen in this homely setting, the dress was much more revealing than anything Ellie had ever worn before, clinging to her slenderness in a bright red swathe, the low neckline and sleeveless style show-

21

ing arms and throat still lightly tanned from her holiday
in the summer.

Her hair was swept up loosely from the slenderness
of her neck and secured with two gold combs. The
change in hairstyle seemed to enlarge her eyes and the
dark sweep of her lashes. Blusher highlighted her
cheeks, and the bright red gloss on her lips was the
same colour as the dress.

Ellie had noted all of this in her bedroom mirror a
few minutes ago, sweeping out of the room and down
the stairs before she had time for second thoughts and
settled for the familiar black dress after all.

'You look wonderful, sis,' Toby told her, sitting back
to look at her admiringly. 'You're going to knock him
off his feet!'

She frowned. 'Toby, the idea isn't for me to attract
Patrick McGrath—'

'I was referring to Gareth,' he murmured pointedly.

'Oh…Gareth,' she acknowledged weakly, feeling the
colour warming her cheeks at her mistake. In all honesty she had totally forgotten about Gareth as she prepared for her evening out. Which was ridiculous when
he was the reason she had gone to all this trouble in
the first place.

The reason she had swallowed her pride and gone to
Patrick, and told him she had changed her mind after
all!

To give the man his due, he hadn't batted an eyelid
when she had turned up at his office three days ago—
without an appointment—and asked him if he was still
agreeable to going out with her on Friday evening.

She had acted instinctively, knowing that if she gave

herself time to think about whether or not she should go and see him she would change her mind. Although she had been a little thrown by his opening comment!

'I've been expecting you.' He put his gold pen down on top of the papers on his desk before smiling across at her as she stood just inside his office, his secretary having closed the door behind her as she left.

'You have?' Ellie frowned; how could he possibly have been expecting her when until half an hour ago she hadn't expected to be here herself?

'Call it a hunch.' He nodded. 'You can sit down, you know, Ellie,' he added mockingly. 'There's no charge!'

He seemed different today, Ellie realized, more the thirty-eight-year-old successful businessman that he was. He was dressed formally too, in a dark grey suit with a white silk shirt, a light grey tie knotted meticulously at his throat.

She made no move to sit in the chair he indicated, knowing that she had made a mistake in coming here today, that she should have taken the time to think after all, that—

'I still have Friday evening free, if you're interested,' he told her huskily.

Her eyes widened. 'You do?'

He nodded. 'Are you interested?'

She swallowed hard, wishing she could say no but knowing that, after what she had learnt today, she badly needed this man's presence at her side on Friday evening—for moral support if nothing else.

'Ellie...?' he prompted at her continued silence.

'I'm interested,' she admitted abruptly.

'Has something happened?' he asked shrewdly.

Had something happened! Gareth, that selfish, un-thinking, uncaring—

'Something's happened,' Patrick acknowledged rue-fully, standing up to pour her a cup of coffee from the hot percolator that stood on the side. 'I'm sorry it's nothing stronger,' he apologised dryly as he handed her the cup and saucer. 'You look as if you could do with a double whisky!'

'I don't drink whisky,' she said vaguely, taking a sip of the hot coffee. Not because she thought it would make her feel any better, more for something to do with her shaking hands.

Cold hands, she realised belatedly as she wrapped them about the cup; the snow that had been threatening to fall all week had finally come tumbling down this morning. And in her agitation Ellie had completely for-gotten to collect her outer coat and gloves before leav-ing the office earlier.

'Is it anything I should know about?' Patrick gently urged.

'Anything...? It isn't Toby, if that's what you're worried about,' she hastened to reassure him.

'I didn't think for a moment that it was; as far as I'm aware Toby is in York today, with—with another of my employees,' Patrick dismissed lightly. 'I wish you would sit down, Ellie,' he said softly.

Of course. He wouldn't sit down if she didn't. Ellie sat, the cup rattling precariously in the saucer as she did so.

Patrick moved back to sit behind his desk. 'Take your

time,' he invited. 'I don't have any appointments for a couple of hours.'

'It isn't going to take me that long to—!' She broke off, her face pale as she brought herself under control. 'My ex-boyfriend intends announcing his engagement at the dinner on Friday evening,' she bit out reluctantly.

'Ah,' Patrick murmured comprehendingly.

Ellie looked across at him sharply. 'It doesn't bother me,' she assured him.

He raised dark brows. 'It doesn't?'

'Look, Mr—Patrick,' she amended as he raised those brows even higher. 'I don't know what Toby told you about the end of my relationship with Gareth, but—'

'Nothing at all, as it happens,' he assured her dryly. 'Toby can be discreet when he needs to be,' he added at her sceptical look. 'He wouldn't have lasted long as my assistant if he couldn't!'

'Yes. Well.' Ellie grimaced. 'I was the one to end my relationship with Gareth.'

Patrick frowned. 'Then why—?'

'He told everyone at the office that *he* was the one to end it,' Ellie recalled disgustedly. 'And when he was seen with someone else only a few days later...!' She shook her head. 'If I had tried to contradict his story then I would have just looked like "a woman scorned",' she reasoned heavily.

'Hmm. Just out of interest—why *did* you stop seeing him?' Patrick asked interestedly.

'Because—' She drew in a deep breath, shaking her head. 'I think that also comes under the heading of "Private",' she told him stiffly.

'Okay,' he conceded reluctantly. 'But if you aren't bothered by his engagement…?'

'I'm really not,' she insisted firmly. 'At least, only so far as… I have to work with all these people, Patrick.' She grimaced. 'Gareth informed me a couple of hours ago about the engagement announcement.'

'Big of him,' Patrick bit out scathingly.

It had been more out of spite, actually, but she was way past caring about anything Gareth did or said to her. 'If I turn up alone on Friday evening and the announcement is made—'

'All your work colleagues are going to end up feeling sorry for you,' Patrick acknowledged hardly.

Her eyes flashed deeply blue. 'Yes!' And the pity of people she worked with on a daily basis—even misplaced pity—was something she just couldn't bear to think about.

Even if it meant coming to this man and admitting she had made a mistake in so arbitrarily refusing his offer to act as her escort at the dinner!

'If you agree—if you're still willing—it will be a purely business arrangement if you consent to accompany me on Friday evening,' she told him coolly. 'I will, of course, be paying any expenses you may incur—including the petrol to get us there, any drinks we have to buy, the—'

'Stop right there, Ellie,' Patrick cut in firmly. 'When I take a woman out for the evening I do the paying. Okay?'

'No, it is not okay,' she came back, just as determinedly. 'I'm taking you out. That means I pay. What do you mean, no?' She frowned as he shook his head.

'I'll only agree to go if I take you. Otherwise the deal is off, Ellie,' he added decisively.

'But this isn't one of your business deals—' she broke off as she realised *she* had been the one to say Friday evening was to be treated on a businesslike footing.

Patrick laughed softly. 'Ellie, isn't the important thing here to show this Gareth that you're more than capable of attracting a man other than him? Which, of course, you obviously are,' he continued, his grey gaze sweeping over her with slow appreciation.

Ellie was dressed in one of the suits she wore to work, a fitted black one today, teamed with a blue blouse. Slightly damp from the snow still falling outside!

Ellie was under no illusions as regarded her looks; at best they could be called pleasant. She was neither fat nor too thin, and her hair—her one good feature as far as she was concerned—was always kept clean and well-styled. Her eyes were a clear blue, her lashes thick and dark, her skin smooth and creamy, but other than that her features were nondescript.

Which was why, when Gareth had joined the company six months ago—a blond Adonis with warm blue eyes and a charm that drew women to him like bees around honey—Ellie had been completely bowled over by his marked interest in her.

But she had definitely learnt her lesson where that sort of flattery and attention were concerned, which was why she knew that Patrick McGrath was just being polite now.

He was watching her with narrowed eyes. 'How long is it since the two of you broke up?'

'What does that have to do with anything?' she came back stiffly.

Patrick shrugged. 'I was merely wondering why you don't already have a new boyfriend.'

She gave a humourless smile. 'Because after my experience with Gareth I have no interest at the moment in finding myself a new boyfriend!'

'This gets more and more intriguing by the minute,' Patrick murmured interestedly.

Ellie shot him a reproving look. 'Believe me, it really isn't,' she assured him dismissively.

'So it's easier to ask me, a complete stranger, to go to your company dinner with you than it is to complicate matters with a genuine new boyfriend?' Patrick murmured consideringly. 'It makes a certain sense, I suppose.' He shrugged.

Ellie frowned. 'It does?' It sounded rather cold and contrived to her, but other than not going to the dinner at all—which was impossible now that Gareth had told her of the pending announcement of his engagement; she simply wouldn't give him the satisfaction of just not turning up!—she couldn't see any other way round the problem.

'It does,' he assured her enigmatically. 'Well, as I've already said, Ellie, I still have the evening free on Friday.'

She drew in a deep breath. 'Then you'll go to the Delacorte dinner with me?'

He gave a sudden grin, looking years younger, his grey eyes warm. 'I thought you would never ask!'

She wouldn't have done ordinarily, and they both knew it. But nothing about this situation was ordinary.

*　　*　　*

Which was why she was standing here, wearing a revealing red dress and more make-up than she had ever
worn before, feeling decidedly like the overdressed
Christmas tree that adorned their sitting room—waiting
for Patrick McGrath to arrive…

He was late.

It was already seven forty-five, and before Ellie had
left his office three days ago they had agreed that he
would pick her up at seven-thirty, in order for them to
drive to the restaurant and arrive a polite ten or fifteen
minutes late for pre-dinner drinks. At this rate they
would be lucky to arrive in time for the serving of the
first course!

'Is he always this unpunctual?' She frowned at Toby
as he cleared away his dinner things, before getting
ready to go out himself.

'He'll be here, sis,' Toby dismissed assuredly. 'But
I have to leave now.' He glanced up at the kitchen
clock. 'I told Tess I would pick her up just after eight,'
he added apologetically. He was going to the cinema
this evening with his girlfriend of the last two months.
'Do you want me to try reaching Patrick on his mobile
before I leave? Maybe the car broke down or something.'

'Do Mercedes break down?' Ellie came back dryly,
wondering if she was going to get to 'the ball', after
all!

'Mine doesn't,' drawled a familiar voice.

Ellie gasped, spinning round to face Patrick as he
stood in the doorway. She was glad she had already
gasped—otherwise she would have done so now; he
looked absolutely breathtaking in a dinner suit!

'I wish you wouldn't keep creeping up on me like that,' she complained, to cover up the confusion she felt at his appearance.

Was anyone supposed to be this handsome? This suavely sophisticated? This—this breathtaking? There really was no other word for Patrick's appearance this evening.

'Will I do?' He arched mocking brows at her as she continued to stare at him.

Would he do as what? As a more than adequate replacement for Gareth? Certainly. As a means for making every other woman in the room jealous of her good fortune in having him as her partner for the evening? Assuredly. As a calm and soothing balm to her already battered emotions? Definitely not!

He was a one-evening-only companion—just a shield for what promised to be a very difficult evening for her. He wasn't supposed to make her pulse flutter, her knees feel weak, her insides as if they were turning to jelly!

'Ellie is feeling a little—tense this evening, Patrick,' Toby excused her lightly, picking up his jacket from the back of the chair before walking over to the door. 'Have a good evening. Want me to wait up for you, Ellie?' he added mischievously, dark brows raised teasingly.

'No, thank you!' She shot him a reproving look as he ducked out of the doorway, grinning widely as he raised a hand in farewell before disappearing into the darkness.

'We aren't going to be late back this evening, are

we, Ellie?' Patrick looked down at her mockingly. 'Only I'm usually in bed by ten-thirty.'

Ellie would hazard a guess that the only reason this man would be in bed by ten-thirty at night would be because he wasn't there alone!

'You're late,' she told him sharply, more flustered that she had just had such a thought about Patrick's nocturnal habits than she actually was by his tardiness.

'Only a few minutes,' he dismissed unconcernedly. 'I stopped along the way to buy you this.'

'This' was a corsage, a single red rose, newly in bud, made even more beautiful by the melted snowflakes clinging to the dewy petals.

Ellie blinked hard before looking up at Patrick, hastily looking down again as he returned her gaze with slightly challenging eyes. Bringing her a rose, red or otherwise, was not very businesslike. And they both knew it. But then Patrick had warned her three days ago that he intended doing this his way...

'Thank you,' she accepted huskily, taking the rose and the pin he held out to her.

'Would you like me to—?'

'No! No, thank you.' She tried to refuse his offer of help less abruptly, at the same time giving him a sceptical glance. 'I can manage.' And to prove it she attached the rose to her dress at the first try.

'I thought you might,' he murmured ruefully. 'I suppose we should be on our way, then.'

'I suppose we should,' she echoed dryly, inwardly chiding herself for the fact that she was a little disappointed he hadn't mentioned her new dress, or anything else about her appearance.

Not that she had mentioned how gorgeous he looked either; it simply wasn't in keeping, she accepted, with their arrangement.

'What a pity,' Patrick murmured as he watched her pull on her long black winter coat. 'You look absolutely stunning in that dress; it's a shame to hide it beneath that coat,' he explained as Ellie looked up at him questioningly.

'Thank you.' She felt an inner glow now rather than the outer warmth of the coat.

'Hmm,' Patrick nodded as they went out to the car, opening the door for her to get in. 'Gareth can just eat his heart out,' he added with satisfaction.

'That's what Toby said!' She laughed to cover her flushed pleasure at his compliment.

'And, as we both know, Toby wouldn't tell you a lie,' he reminded her teasingly.

No, Toby wouldn't tell her a lie—at least, not a major one—but she had a feeling this man was more than capable of practising the subtle art of subterfuge if he thought the occasion warranted it. There was a steely edge to Patrick McGrath, a ruthlessness that obviously made him such a success in business.

But Ellie dismissed both Patrick's compliments and thoughts of that steely edge as they neared the restaurant where all the other Delacorte, Delacorte and Delacorte staff would already be gathered. No doubt all believing, with the lateness of the hour, that she had decided not to attend after all.

'Everything is going to be just fine, Ellie.' Patrick

reached out in the warm confines of the car and gave her restless hands a reassuring squeeze before returning his own hand to the steering wheel of his Mercedes sports car. 'Trust me, hmm?' he encouraged as she glanced at him with troubled eyes.

She wasn't sure, after Gareth's duplicity, that she would ever completely trust another man again. But Patrick wasn't asking her to trust him in that way...

'I don't believe I've ever thanked you for agreeing to help me out like this,' she murmured ruefully. Mainly because she had been too embarrassed by her need for him to be here to actually get around to thanking him!

'I believe you did mention the word gratitude once,' he drawled. 'But that was last week—when you were turning me down.'

Before she'd had to go back and tell him the situation had indeed changed!

'Ellie, why don't we wait until the end of the evening and see if you still want to thank me then, hmm?'

Ellie shot him a sharp look; that sounded a little ominous.

'Don't look so worried, Ellie.' He chuckled after a brief glance in her direction. 'I promise to be the soul of discretion this evening.'

'You do?' She eyed him doubtfully.

After all, what did she really know about this man? Only what Toby had told her. Which, now that she thought about it, really wasn't much. Maybe Toby *could* be discreet if he needed to be! At least as far as Patrick McGrath was concerned...

Thirty-eight. Extremely successful. Single—which was probably all she really needed to know. Except… For all she knew the man might be a terrible flirt, or become terribly loud after a couple of drinks. In which case having him as her escort could prove more of a liability than a plus!

'Of course, Ellie,' he answered blandly. 'I'll try very hard not to mention to anyone that you occasionally like to sunbathe topless in the back garden—weather permitting!' He grimaced as snow slowly began to fall on the windscreen.

'You—!' Ellie gasped, feeling the sudden heat in her cheeks as she turned to stare at him. 'Patrick—'

'Ah, here we are,' he informed her lightly, turning the Mercedes into the car park of the restaurant, parking it beside the green Rolls Royce owned by Ellie's boss before getting out of the car and coming round to open Ellie's door for her. 'Was it something I said?' he prompted innocently as she made no move to get out of the car.

He knew very well that it was!

'Come on, Ellie. I'm getting wet out here,' he encouraged briskly.

Of course he was; the snow was coming down in earnest now. Ellie wrapped her coat around her and pulled up the collar about her neck as they hurried over to the entrance to the restaurant.

'We'll leave this here, I think,' Patrick said firmly as they entered the foyer, removing Ellie's coat and handing it to the receptionist before Ellie even had time to realise what he was doing.

She suddenly felt self-conscious again as she looked

down at the eye-catching red dress. Maybe it was too much. After all, this was only a company Christmas dinner. Instead of looking eye-catching, as she had hoped, was she going to look ridiculously overdressed?

'Ellie, you look beautiful,' Patrick told her firmly—before his lips came down gently on hers and his arms moved about her waist to mould her body against the hardness of his.

The kiss was so unexpected that Ellie responded, her lips parting beneath his even as her arms moved up about his shoulders.

She totally forgot where they were, why they were there—who she was, even—as those warmly sensual lips continued to explore the softness of her own. The tip of Patrick's tongue was now moving erotically against her lower lip, turning her body to liquid fire, her legs to jelly.

His eyes were dark with query as he finally lifted his head to look into the flushed beauty of her face. 'Better.' He nodded, his thumb running lightly across her slightly swollen lips. 'Now you actually look like a woman out for the evening with her lover!' he added with satisfaction.

Of course. That was the reason Patrick had kissed her. The only reason.

'Perhaps next time you could give me some warning of what you're about to do,' she bit out abruptly, covering her confusion—and her blushes!—by opening her evening bag and searching through its contents. 'Lipstick,' she told him abruptly, and held out a tissue for him to wipe his mouth.

'You do it,' Patrick encouraged huskily. 'I can't see what I'm doing,' he reasoned before she protested.

She swallowed hard, willing her heart to stop pounding, her hand not to shake as she reached up to wipe the smears of lipstick that he now had on his mouth.

So engrossed was she in not betraying how shaken she felt that she didn't even see the man walking past, a dark scowl on his handsome features as he stopped to stare at the two of them.

'Ellie…?' he questioned uncertainly—as if he couldn't quite believe the woman in the red dress, a woman who had obviously just been very thoroughly kissed, was actually her.

She stiffened before looking at him. 'Gareth,' she greeted him distantly, feeling rather than seeing Patrick as he moved to stand beside her, his arm curving possessively about her waist. She glanced up at him, a shiver running down her spine as she saw the narrow-eyed look he was giving the younger man. 'Patrick, this is a work colleague—Gareth Davies,' she dismissed with deliberate lightness, glad of that lightness as she saw Gareth's scowl deepen. 'Gareth—Patrick McGrath,' she added economically, still too shaken by that kiss to think how to describe him to the other man.

'*The* Patrick McGrath?' Gareth questioned abruptly as he looked frowningly at the other man.

Patrick smiled—a smile that didn't reach the cold grey of his eyes. 'I very much doubt there's only one Patrick McGrath in the world,' he answered the other man tauntingly.

'We really should be going in, Patrick,' Ellie put in determinedly as she saw the light of challenge that had now appeared in both men's eyes. 'If you'll excuse us, Gareth?' she added dismissively, not giving him a second glance as she turned and walked in the direction of the main restaurant, Patrick at her side, his arm still firmly about her waist.

Not quite the way she had envisaged the evening beginning!

But then she hadn't expected Patrick to kiss her either...

Why on earth *had* he kissed her? Just for effect, as his words afterwards had seemed to imply? Well, he couldn't even begin to imagine the effect his unexpected behaviour had had on her!

She could still feel the sensuous touch of his lips against hers, still feel the hardness of his body as she moulded perfectly against him, the warmth that had coursed through her, that totally not-knowing-where-she-was-and-not-caring-either feeling.

As for Gareth! Amazingly, she had felt absolutely nothing as she'd looked at him just now. Except perhaps a vague disbelief that she had ever been taken in by his overt good looks and charm...

What did it all mean...?

But as they walked into the restaurant and Patrick was greeted effusively by her boss, George Delacorte, Senior Partner at Delacorte, Delacorte and Delacorte, Ellie knew she would have to get back to that particularly puzzling question later!

CHAPTER THREE

'I HAD no idea you were going to be here with Ellie this evening, Patrick.' The older man greeted him warmly and the two men shook hands. George Delacorte was a tall, distinguished-looking man with iron-grey hair and twinkling brown eyes that belied the shrewd trial lawyer he actually was. 'You should have told me, Ellie,' he chided teasingly.

Told him what? Until a few seconds ago she hadn't even known that he and Patrick were acquainted! Patrick certainly hadn't mentioned that he knew the older man.

'How are Anne and Thomas?' George smiled.

'Very well, thank you, sir,' Patrick replied smoothly, his arm still lightly about Ellie's waist, almost as if he weren't aware that she was staring up at him in amazement.

Why hadn't he told her he knew George Delacorte? It was obvious from the easy way he was talking with the older man that Patrick had been perfectly well aware that he would be seeing the other man this evening! In fact, she knew that he had; she had told him herself that it was the Delacorte Christmas dinner!

'And Teresa?' the older man continued lightly. 'Breaking hearts, as usual?'

Patrick shrugged. 'I think she might finally have met ''the one'',' he answered indulgently.

'Good for her.' George chuckled.

Who on earth were Anne and Thomas—let alone Teresa? Ellie realised she really should have asked Patrick for a few more personal details. And maybe she would have done if she had known they would be relevant to this evening!

'I must just go and tell Mary you're here; she'll be so pleased to see you,' George said happily. 'Sarah is here too—somewhere.' He frowned. 'You're coming to the family party tomorrow?' he prompted abruptly.

'Of course,' Patrick assured him.

'Bring Ellie, too,' George went on with a smile in her direction. 'If you would like to come, my dear?' he added gently.

She had no idea what party either of these two men were talking about!

'I'm not sure what Ellie's plans are for tomorrow.' Patrick was the one to answer smoothly. 'We'll let you know.'

'Of course,' George accepted briskly. 'I'll just go and find Mary.' He gave them another smile before going off in search of his wife.

'So that was the infamous Gareth,' Patrick murmured thoughtfully once the two of them were alone. 'I have to say, Ellie, I wasn't very impressed.' He shrugged.

'Never mind Gareth for now—who are Anne, Thomas and Teresa?' Ellie hissed explosively. 'And how is it that you know George Delacorte?'

'He's my uncle,' Patrick told her dismissively, at the same time looking interestedly at the forty or so other Delacorte staff in the room. 'As for Anne, Thomas and—'

'Your uncle?' Ellie spluttered incredulously, gaping up at him unbelievingly.

'By marriage.' Patrick nodded. 'Mary Delacorte is my father's sister.'

'Why on earth didn't you tell me?' she demanded indignantly.

Patrick turned to look at her, dark brows raised over slightly mocking grey eyes. 'I didn't think it was relevant.'

'You-didn't-think-it-was-relevant!' she repeated disgustedly.

'Ellie, why do you keep repeating everything I say?' he taunted derisively.

'Because I just can't believe this!' The colour was high in her cheeks, blue eyes sparkling. 'Is Toby aware that my boss is your uncle?' she asked suspiciously as that idea suddenly occurred to her.

'I'm really not sure.' Patrick shrugged. 'But I would have thought so. Do you think we ought to mingle?' he added consideringly. 'Several of your work colleagues have looked curiously across at us in the last few minutes.'

She didn't care who had looked at them in the last few minutes; she intended getting to the bottom of this if it took all night. If Toby knew that Patrick was related to George Delacorte, then he must also be aware—

'Patrick!'

Ellie turned just in time to see Sarah Delacorte, George's daughter and only child, throw herself into Patrick's arms, kissing him enthusiastically.

Ellie felt her heart plummet as she looked at the

beautiful young woman laughing up into Patrick's face, her pleasure at his presence obvious.

Sarah Delacorte was beautiful, there was no doubt about that, with her tall, slender figure—shown off to advantage now in a slinky black knee-length dress—her long silky blonde hair and delicate child-like features.

Unfortunately she was also the woman Gareth had been dating for the last six weeks and was about to announce his engagement to!

And she was, Ellie realised with dismay, Patrick's young cousin...

'What are you doing here?' Sarah demanded, still holding onto Patrick's hands as she gazed up at him in obvious delight.

Patrick looked no less pleased to see his cousin, grinning broadly. 'Ellie brought me,' he explained lightly, releasing one of his hands to turn and firmly clasp one of Ellie's, to bring her forward to stand at his side.

'Goodness, Ellie, I haven't seen you for ages!' Sarah greeted her warmly. 'You look wonderful!' she added with genuine warmth.

It was true the two women hadn't met for some time. Sarah had been in Paris for the last year, initially working with one of the fashion designers over there. But her career in modelling had taken a meteoric rise over the last six months, with her photograph appearing on the front page of all the popular women's magazines.

Sarah's absence abroad was also the reason she had no idea Ellie had still been dating Gareth until six weeks ago!

Ellie very much doubted that Gareth had told the

other woman anything about her, or the fact that they had still been dating after he and Sarah met. And Ellie certainly had no intention of telling the other woman any of that either. Although the fact that she now knew Patrick was the other woman's cousin certainly made things more than a little awkward in that direction!

'I understand congratulations are in order?' Patrick looked down teasingly at his young cousin.

Ellie noted that the warmth was no longer in his eyes, and his smile lacked some of its earlier spontaneity...

'Isn't it wonderful?' Sarah said dreamily, suddenly looking a very young twenty-one-year-old. 'One moment I was young and fancy-free, and the next—I was just swept off my feet the moment I looked at him!' She laughed self-consciously.

Patrick's hand tightened about Ellie's fingers as he felt her stiffen beside him, although his narrowed gaze remained fixed on his cousin's glowingly lovely face. 'Love at first sight, hmm?' he prompted dryly.

'Something like that.' Sarah gave another happy laugh. 'Wait until you meet him,' she enthused. 'You're going to love him!'

Considering what Patrick had said to Ellie about Gareth a few minutes earlier, she somehow doubted that very much!

Although how much of Patrick's opinion had been formed by what Ellie might have said or implied about the other man and what Patrick had actually decided for himself she had no idea!

Not that it mattered; this was just a very awkward situation all round.

What on earth had Toby been playing at when he

originally organised this date for her with Patrick? Because Toby, of all of them, was well aware of the connection of all the key players in what was turning out to be a fiasco!

Patrick gave a slight inclination of his head. 'I'm sure you'll have a chance to introduce the two of us later. For the moment, I think Ellie wants to introduce me to some of her friends,' he added lightly.

'Of course,' Sarah instantly accepted. 'It really is lovely to see you again, Ellie,' she added warmly. 'We must go out and have coffee together some time, like we used to.'

When Sarah, no doubt, would want to wax lyrical about Gareth! No, thank you!

It was true the two women had occasionally had coffee together before Sarah's departure for Paris, but they had lost touch with each other during the last year. In the present circumstances Ellie thought it better if it remained that way!

'We must,' Ellie agreed non-committally.

'Catch up with you later, Sarah,' Patrick told his cousin, before strolling away, Ellie very firmly pinned to his side. 'Save it for later, hmm?' he told her between barely moving lips.

'But—'

'Ellie, this is not the place to discuss it. Okay?' he prompted as she came to an abrupt halt in the middle of the crowded room.

No, it was not okay. She had no idea what was going on—how could she when the whole evening had been turned upside down by Patrick's family connection to the Delacortes?

He sighed at the mutinous expression on her face. 'I know how this must look to you—'

'You can have no *idea* how this looks to me,' she assured him derisively.

'Probably not,' Patrick conceded with a grimace. 'But we do have the rest of this evening to get through,' he reasoned. 'And your ex-boyfriend's engagement is still going to be announced before the end of it.'

'Gareth's engagement to *your cousin*,' Ellie bit out pointedly.

'Yes,' he acknowledged heavily. 'It probably escaped your notice earlier, but George isn't exactly thrilled at the prospect of having Gareth Davies as his son-in-law!'

Ellie blinked. 'He isn't?'

Of course George had known that Ellie was dating Gareth until a couple of months ago—everyone at Delacorte, Delacorte and Delacorte had been aware of it. But when the older man had approached the subject of Sarah's involvement with the other man with Ellie she had dismissed her own relationship with him as a mere friendship. After all, she did have her pride...

She hadn't realised that George was talking to her about Gareth because he didn't exactly trust the younger man's motives regarding his daughter!

'No,' Patrick confirmed grimly.

She frowned. 'Then why doesn't he do something about it?'

Patrick smile derisively. 'Such as what? Tell Sarah he's nothing but a fortune-hunter? Because he is, isn't he?' he drawled scathingly. 'A man with an eye to the main chance. A man who fancies the name Davies being added to the end of Delacorte, Delacorte and Delacorte!'

Yes, that was exactly what Gareth was. Handsome, charming—but totally mercenary. Ellie, as George's much-valued secretary, had seemed like a good prospect to him six months ago. But Gareth had dropped her like a hot coal when Sarah had returned from Paris and he'd realised George had a marriageable daughter.

'Yes,' Ellie confirmed miserably, feeling totally humiliated by her own past gullibility.

Patrick nodded abruptly. 'And how do you think Sarah is likely to react if anyone should tell her that about the man she believes herself madly in love with?'

How would Ellie have reacted if someone had told her those things about Gareth three months ago? Even two months ago? Would she have believed them if she weren't now the one with the knowledge of just how mercenary Gareth could be?

She gave a derisive grimace. 'She'll tell them to mind their own business!'

'In one.' Patrick nodded in mocking confirmation.

Ellie shook her head dismissively. 'But if George really distrusts his motives—'

'He does,' Patrick bit out grimly.

'Then why doesn't he just sack him?'

'For the same reason, wouldn't you think?' Patrick derided.

Yes, Ellie *did* think. It was obvious from Sarah's behaviour earlier, from the things she had said about Gareth, that the other woman was completely taken in by him.

As Ellie had once been...

But, as Ellie had learnt only too well—and obviously Patrick and his uncle knew too—Gareth's charm was all a front for his calculating brain, to create Delacorte, Delacorte, Delacorte, and Davies!

At only thirty-two Gareth had ambitions that he had no intention of working at if they could be achieved by a simpler route—such as marrying the senior partner's daughter!

It had taken Ellie almost two weeks to realise that Gareth was dating someone else besides herself—he hadn't wanted to give up on one option before making absolutely sure of the second one! Once she had realised what he was doing she had told him precisely what she thought of him. And what he could do with the relationship he had tried to offer her as consolation prize.

If she had thought he was genuinely in love with Sarah then it would have been a different matter; she would have just accepted the inevitable. But by that time her eyes had been wide open where Gareth was concerned, her illusions shattered.

But she still had no idea what Patrick was up to...

Because he was up to something. She was sure of it!

'So, Ellie, what do you think?' Patrick looked at her consideringly now. 'Do you want to help us prove to Sarah what an absolute bas—What a calculating mercenary her new fiancé actually is?' he amended harshly.

Ellie glanced across the room to where she could see Gareth, now talking to Sarah, a superior smile curving his lips as she looked up at him with absolute adoration, obviously enthralled by his every word.

A shudder ran down Ellie's spine. Had she once

looked and felt as Sarah so obviously did? She had been attracted to Gareth, of that she had no doubt—just as she had no doubt that she had been meant to feel attracted to him! She had been flattered by his interest too—what woman wouldn't be when he was so handsome and charming? But she was relieved to realise that if she had ever believed herself in love with him it had been short lived, because she felt nothing but disgust as she looked at him now.

She turned back to Patrick, her shoulders straightening with resolve. 'I have absolutely no idea how you intend going about that, but, yes, I'm willing to help. If I can,' she added uncertainly.

If Patrick and George, two very capable men, had no idea how to go about revealing Gareth in his true colours to the besotted Sarah, what could she possibly do to achieve that?

Simply telling Sarah what she thought of Gareth would do no good. She had thought of that once she'd become aware that Sarah was Gareth's latest target— her concern and liking for Sarah were completely genuine—but she had concluded that Sarah was very unlikely to believe anything she had to say about Gareth once he had told Sarah the 'woman scorned' story. Pity was the more probable emotion Sarah would feel on hearing it—for Ellie!

Patrick gave her hand a triumphant squeeze. 'I hoped my instinct about you was right, Ellie,' he told her warmly.

She eyed him uncertainly. 'What instinct?'

He grinned. 'I knew you were a fighter,' he said with satisfaction. 'You had to be, to have chosen and succeeded in taking on the responsibilities you did eight years ago. Any woman who could do that isn't going to let a man like Gareth Davies get away with anything—least of all gulling some other poor woman in the same way you were!'

Again, Ellie was sure there was a compliment in there somewhere—it was just buried beneath the insult that had followed it!

CHAPTER FOUR

'WHAT on earth do you think you're playing at?'

Ellie turned slowly to face Gareth, already knowing by the aggressive tone of his voice that his mood was ugly. She had briefly left the dinner table after dessert to go to the ladies' room. Gareth must have deliberately followed her.

Yes, she was right about Gareth's mood. He looked less than handsome in his anger, blue eyes glittering furiously as he strode purposefully towards her.

'I'm sorry?' she answered coolly, very aware of the fact they were completely alone in the foyer. The receptionist was inside, helping to serve drinks now, the Delacorte party having taken over the whole restaurant for the evening.

'You heard me, Ellie,' he snapped impatiently. 'What are you doing here with George's nephew?'

'Eating dinner, the same as everyone else,' she dismissed with a lightness she was far from feeling. She knew that physically there was nothing Gareth could do to her here—even if he did look as if he would like to wring her neck—but verbally he could rip her to shreds!

Gareth's mouth twisted frustratedly. 'Don't get clever with me, Ellie,' he scorned. 'Moving in rather exalted company nowadays, aren't you?' he added insultingly.

Deliberately so, Ellie knew. Although she refused to become angry. Or at least only with herself—that she could ever have been taken in by such a man. In fact, it was a pity Sarah couldn't see him in this mood—the younger woman would have no doubts about his duplicitous charms then!

But Ellie knew what he was referring to with that remark about 'exalted company'; ordinarily she would have been seated at one of the tables with other secretaries and their partners, but as the nephew of the senior partner was her guest for the evening, she and Patrick had been moved onto the top table with the other senior members of staff.

The same table as Gareth and Sarah...

Ellie coolly met Gareth's accusing gaze. 'Do you have some sort of problem with that?'

He gave a scornful laugh. 'Not at all. So if you were hoping to make me jealous—'

'Don't flatter yourself, Gareth!' she cut in derisively, feeling her anger starting to rise. Really, the conceit of the man...! 'The fact that Patrick and I are—friends has absolutely nothing to do with you.'

'Have you said anything to him about me?' Gareth rasped nastily, taking a painful grip of her arm. 'Because if you have—'

'Gareth, believe me, when I'm with Patrick I have better things to do with my time than discuss you,' she assured him hardly. 'Now, would you kindly let go of my arm?' she asked coldly.

He looked down at her with hard blue eyes, a humourless smile now curving his lips. 'No, I don't think I will,' he murmured slowly. 'You're looking rather beautiful tonight, Ellie,' he told her huskily. 'Rather sexy, in fact.'

Nausea welled up in her throat at this completely unwelcome compliment from a man she now despised, but the coldness of her gaze didn't waver from his. 'Patrick happens to like me in red,' she told him challengingly.

The angry glitter intensified in Gareth's eyes. 'Why, you little—'

'Everything all right, darling?' Patrick's voice suddenly interrupted pleasantly. 'You've been gone so long I thought there must be something wrong?' he added questioningly, and he strolled over to join them, much to Ellie's relief. She instantly felt the reassurance of his presence.

Gareth slowly released her arm, and Ellie resisted the impulse she had to wipe his touch from her flesh. Instead she shot Gareth a look of intense dislike before turning to smile her gratitude at Patrick. 'I was just directing Gareth to the men's room,' she dismissed lightly.

'Really?' Patrick turned cold grey eyes on the younger man. 'But I thought that was where you were going when we met earlier this evening?'

Gareth pulled himself together with obvious effort, even managing to give the other man a rueful smile. 'Actually, I was collecting Sarah's wrap that time,' he explained pleasantly.

No doubt Gareth was making an effort to be pleasant because he was very aware that Patrick was George's nephew, Ellie guessed shrewdly.

'Ah, yes. My cousin Sarah.' Patrick murmured coldly. 'I'm very fond of Sarah,' he added softly.

'She's a marvellous girl,' Gareth agreed heartily.

'That she is,' Patrick acknowledged evenly. 'I would hate to see her hurt in any way,' he added softly, a dangerous stillness surrounding him.

Ellie was watching Gareth as Patrick made this remark. The handsome face remained pleasantly smiling, but there was a certain wariness in the younger man's eyes.

She wasn't sure it was absolutely wise for Patrick to challenge the other man, even in this mild way—not when his cousin's happiness was at stake. But, as she was quickly learning, Patrick really did like to do things his own way.

Gareth gave an inclination of his head. 'We really should be getting back; George is going to announce our engagement as soon as the coffee has been served.'

'So I believe,' Patrick rasped, once again holding tightly to Ellie's arm as he felt her stiffen. 'You go ahead,' he encouraged the other man. 'I just want to— have a few minutes alone with Ellie,' he drawled dryly.

'I was just telling Ellie that she's a bit of a dark horse,' Gareth drawled teasingly. 'Who knows, Ellie? We may even be related to each other one day!' he added mockingly.

How Ellie wanted to smack that confident smile off his handsome face!

But instead she felt cold common sense come over her as she answered him. 'Somehow I doubt that very much,' she told him scathingly.

'I do hope your intentions are honourable, Patrick.' Gareth's smile didn't reach the hard glitter of his eyes. 'I should warn you George is extremely fond of Ellie—

treats her almost like another daughter. He will not be happy if he thinks you're trifling with her affections!'

She really would hit him in a minute, common sense notwithstanding!

George Delacorte *was* fond of her, and had taken her slightly under his parental wing after her parents had died. Which was what made this situation so difficult now; she would hate any inaction on her part to contribute to the unhappiness of George's only child. But at the same time, as Patrick had already pointed out, what could any of them do about it?

Patrick gave a confident smile as he released Ellie's arm and put his own arm about the slenderness of her waist. 'I don't think Ellie was referring to our own relationship when she cast doubt on the two of you ever being related,' he assured the other man derisively.

Gareth's gaze narrowed assessingly on the older man. 'I really wouldn't pay too much attention to second-hand opinions, if I were you, Patrick—especially when those opinions are biased, as Ellie's undoubtedly are,' he added, with a pitying glance in her direction.

Ellie would have hit him then, if Patrick's hand hadn't moved from her waist to take a firm grip of her arm once more. Gareth was making her sound like some twisted, lovesick, scorned woman, out to hurt him in any way that she could!

'I make a point of always forming my own opinions concerning other people,' Patrick told the other man smoothly. 'Which is why I'm here with Ellie this evening,' he added softly.

Gareth nodded. 'I know how much Ellie hated the thought of coming here on her own tonight.'

Why, the condescending—

'I can assure you, that was never an option,' Patrick told the other man derisively, turning to smile at Ellie, the hard glitter in his eyes telling her of his own—controlled—anger. 'There are plenty of other men who would willingly have taken my place tonight,' he assured Gareth hardly.

'Of course,' Gareth agreed sceptically. 'Well, I really should be getting back,' he added lightly. 'It wouldn't do for one half of the engaged couple not to be in the room when the announcement is made, now, would it?' He smiled before walking confidently back into the restaurant.

Ellie let out a deep breath, unaware until that moment that she had actually been holding it. The last few minutes had told her that Gareth was even more dangerous than she had thought he was. His vindictiveness where she was concerned was more than obvious—to the point that he had deliberately tried to belittle her in front of Patrick, to make her sound like a—

'Don't let him get to you, Ellie.' Patrick was looking down at her concernedly. 'He only behaved in the way he did because he's still not quite sure how much you've told me about him,' he added hardly.

Her main emotion at this moment was embarrassment. That she had been fooled by Gareth in the first place. That Patrick knew she had been fooled by him!

Because Patrick's opinion was important to her. And that had nothing to do with that pride she had been so desperately trying to hang onto for the last six weeks and everything to do with the fact that she did not want

Patrick to think of her as some poor, wounded woman, still in love with Gareth Davies.

Which, in turn, led her to wonder *why* Patrick's opinion of her was so important...

She gave a dismissive shake of her head; she couldn't think about that right now—had other things to deal with. 'I think Gareth could be a very dangerous man,' she said slowly.

'Not dangerous,' Patrick dismissed confidently. 'Irritating, yes. Extremely so as far as George is concerned. But I was watching Gareth Davies through dinner—and whenever he thought no one else was taking any notice he was watching you. The fact that he saw you go out of the room and followed you shows that he isn't quite as confident of the situation as he would like us to think he is,' he added shrewdly.

Ellie eyed him uncertainly. 'He isn't?' Gareth had seemed extremely confident to her! She hadn't been aware of the other man watching her as they all ate dinner either. But obviously Patrick had...

Patrick gave a slow shake of his head. 'You obviously bother Gareth Davies very much.'

'Somehow I doubt that,' she scorned disbelievingly.

'Oh, yes, you bother him, Ellie. At least, your being with me, Sarah's cousin, bothers him,' Patrick muttered, obviously deep in thought. 'In fact, we may not have to do anything other than produce you on a regular basis,' he added shrewdly.

Her eyes widened. 'What do you mean?'

Patrick grinned. 'You have him rattled, Ellie!' he said with satisfaction. 'All we have to do is keep up the pressure.'

Ellie wasn't sure she liked the sound of that! In exactly what way was Patrick proposing they 'keep up the pressure'…?

'Do you remember George mentioning a party earlier?' he reminded her.

'Tomorrow,' Ellie nodded slowly, eyeing him warily.

As far as she was concerned this evening was a one-off situation. Especially as it had turned out to be so much more complicated than she could ever have realised.

But Patrick seemed to have other ideas…

He nodded. 'The official engagement party.' He grimaced. 'I think it would be a good idea if you were to—'

'No,' Ellie cut in firmly, at the same time shaking her head in protest. 'The answer is no, Patrick,' she insisted determinedly as his expression turned cajoling. 'As far as I've been able to ascertain you accompanied me this evening under false pretences,' she told him accusingly. 'Admittedly you were doing me a favour, but as circumstances have turned out I think that favour has more than been returned. After all, George is your uncle; you knew that the engagement announcement I told you about was actually between Gareth and your cousin—that's why you weren't surprised when I arrived in your office earlier in the week!' Her eyes sparkled accusingly as that realisation finally dawned on her too.

'Ellie—'

'No, Patrick.' She firmly resisted his teasing tone. 'This evening has been awful. I have no wish to repeat it.'

'Awful, Ellie?' Patrick repeated softly, suddenly standing much closer than was comfortable. For her peace of mind! 'All of it?' he prompted huskily.

No, as it happened, not all of it. The kiss the two of them had shared earlier had been more pleasurable than she cared to think about. Certainly more disturbing than she cared to admit!

'All of it,' she insisted forcefully. 'I am absolutely, definitely not going to the party with you tomorrow!'

He looked at her consideringly. 'Not even for Sarah's sake?'

'Not even for— That's emotional blackmail, Patrick!' she snapped irritably as her resolve began to sway at the mention of Sarah.

She and Sarah had been good friends in the past, and she knew the other girl to be bubbly, loving, completely carefree. Marriage to Gareth, once Gareth had shown just how ruthless he could be—and there was no doubting that he *would* show himself in his true colours one day—promised to ruin all that.

'I don't want to go to this party with you, Patrick,' she protested.

And it sounded weak, even to her own ears.

'I have nothing to wear!' she added inconsequentially when he made no reply.

Which sounded even weaker!

As evidenced by the fact that Patrick laughed, eyes twinkling warmly, his teeth showing whitely in his mouth—that mouth that only two hours ago, on this very spot, had very thoroughly kissed hers!

It was a mistake to think of that kiss…

Because she wanted very badly for Patrick to repeat it!

Something of that desire must have shown in her face, because Patrick took her very firmly by the shoulders and held her away from him at arm's length. 'No, Ellie,' he murmured regretfully. 'I'm not going to be accused of seduction as well as emotional blackmail!' He grimaced.

Ellie felt warmth enter her cheeks at her emotions being that transparent. Maybe it was the way her gaze had gone to his mouth—and stayed there. Or maybe it was just an expression of longing on her face. Either way, it wasn't very sophisticated of her to allow her emotions to be so easily gauged.

'Very well, Patrick,' she bit out abruptly. 'I'll come to the party with you—'

'I knew you wouldn't let me down!' Patrick beamed, seeming to forget his resolve as he pulled her into his arms to hug her.

Ellie pulled back, looking up at him warningly. 'I'm not doing this for you,' she reminded him firmly.

'No, of course you aren't,' he accepted lightly, but he still grinned broadly, looking far too attractive for Ellie's peace of mind. For the sudden rapid beat of her heart. For the heated longing that coursed through her body. For the way she wanted to just throw caution to the winds and kiss him if he wasn't about to kiss her!

She really would have to get a grip on her emotions where Patrick McGrath was concerned. Because to fall in love with him wouldn't only be ill-advised—it would be pure madness!

THE WORKAHOLIC

slightly. 'You really should have told me, Toby,' she made her final protest.

'Stubborn! It wouldn't have done one to the trouble I am. Actually, what a brother I am—And that would have been a way?'

CHAPTER FIVE

'Not a word,' Ellie cautioned Toby when he looked up from reading the Saturday newspaper as she came into the kitchen, dressed warmly for going out, needing only to pull her coat on when the time came. 'Not one word, Toby,' she repeated as he continued to look at her. 'You aren't my favourite person at the moment,' she added, and dropped down onto one of the kitchen chairs to wait.

Toby returned her gaze with too-innocent blue eyes. 'I can't imagine why you're in such a bad mood, sis.' He shrugged unconcernedly. 'You know how you love shopping.'

Ordinarily she did. But today wasn't ordinary. As Toby very well knew.

She glared across the table at her brother. 'I think working for Patrick is having a bad effect on you,' she muttered bad-temperedly. 'You're becoming as sneaky as he is!'

Toby chuckled softly. 'You forgot "underhand", "secretive", and—"manipulative", wasn't it?' he prompted lightly.

They were all the names she had called her brother this morning, after he had asked her how the previous evening had gone!

'You forgot "too clever for your own good",' she reminded him heavily, but her mood began to thaw slightly. 'You really should have told me, Toby.' She shook her head disgustedly.

'But then you wouldn't have gone to the dinner last night. At least, not with Patrick,' he reasoned. 'And that would have been a pity.'

Ellie eyed him suspiciously. 'Why?'

'Hey, look, Ellie, in case you've forgotten Patrick and I are two of the good guys,' Toby pointed out protestingly. 'Gareth is the bad guy—remember?'

Oh, yes, she remembered. She also remembered that look of triumph on Gareth's face the previous evening when George had stood up to announce the younger man's engagement to his daughter, Sarah.

'He doesn't deserve Sarah, Ellie—let alone you!' Patrick had muttered disgustedly at her side.

Which was why, when the Delacorte family—and Ellie—had all been chatting together at the end of the evening, Patrick had been only to happy to suggest that Ellie accompany Sarah the following day, when she shopped for a new dress to wear to the party tomorrow evening!

'Ellie has just been complaining that she has nothing to wear either,' Patrick had told his young cousin happily.

Ellie glared up at him; she might have said something along those lines, but as Patrick must know only too well Sarah was the last person she wanted to go shopping with.

'I don't mind coming with you, Sarah,' Gareth put in—rather hastily, it seemed to Ellie. A brief glance at Patrick, his expression knowingly satisfied, showed her that he thought so too.

'It's very sweet of you, darling.' Sarah gave her new
fiancé's arm a grateful hug, the emerald and diamond
engagement ring twinkling brightly on her left hand.
'But you know how you hate shopping. Besides, I want
the dress I'm wearing tomorrow evening to be a surprise.'

'I thought it was the wedding dress I wasn't supposed
to see until the day?' Gareth frowned.

'It is, silly.' Sarah laughed huskily. 'I just—wait and
see,' she dismissed excitedly, before turning to Ellie. 'I
think it would be lovely for the two of us to go shopping together tomorrow, don't you?'

It was obvious from Sarah's completely confident expression that she didn't expect Ellie to refuse. And, with
Patrick looking at Ellie with the same expectation, what
choice did she have? Absolutely none.

Which was why she was sitting here now, dressed
warmly in jeans and a thick sweater, waiting for Sarah
to pick her up so they could drive into town together.

'I remember,' she answered Toby heavily. 'Until
Patrick told me last night I had no idea how worried
George and Mary are by the relationship.' She shook
her head.

'Strange how these things come around in circles,
isn't it?' Toby said ruefully. 'Your dastardly ex-
boyfriend engaged to Patrick's cousin,' he explained, at
Ellie's questioning look.

Ellie winced at having Gareth described as her ex-
boyfriend; she just wanted to forget she had ever known
him. Which was impossible in the present situation.

Although she had felt slightly warmed by Patrick's
comment last night— 'He doesn't deserve Sarah,

Ellie—let alone you!' Quite what he had meant by that she wasn't sure, but again it had sounded as if there might be a compliment in there somewhere.

A compliment she would be wise to ignore, if she had any sense. And, after her recent disappointment over Gareth, she ought to have a lot of sense!

Except...

She had felt quite shy as Patrick had driven her home last night, wondering exactly how they were going to say goodnight to each other. Not that they had been out on a genuine date or anything—even less so than she had initially realised!—but Patrick *had* kissed her earlier in the evening.

She hadn't known whether to be disappointed or relieved when, having walked her to the door, he'd bent to kiss her lightly on the cheek before telling her he would call for her at eight o'clock the following evening.

'There's no point in getting there too early,' he had added grimly.

'None at all,' she agreed with a grimace.

'And don't worry about the shopping expedition with Sarah tomorrow,' he told her with a grin. 'Just be yourself and nothing can go wrong.'

Which was okay for Patrick to say—but Ellie did not relish the thought of having to listen to several hours of Sarah telling her how wonderful Gareth was. It promised to be a very trying afternoon.

'Buy something blue, Ellie,' Patrick had added huskily. 'The same blue as your eyes.'

Once again Ellie felt warmed by the fact that he had even noticed what colour her eyes were!

'Oh, and by the way—' he turned before getting into his car '—Anne and Thomas are my parents; Teresa's my younger sister.'

Oh, great. She was going to meet all of Patrick's family tomorrow evening, too.

'That dress is perfect on you, Ellie,' Sarah told her admiringly as Ellie came out of the changing room.

It might be, but a brief glance at the label whilst in the changing room had shown Ellie that the price was perfect too—for bankrupting her!

She should have known the other woman would want to go to a designer shop for her own outfit. In fact, Sarah had already picked out a gown—an emerald-green sheath that perfectly matched the emerald in her engagement ring—and had only returned to try the dress on after alterations.

The dress she had persuaded Ellie to try on was indeed the blue that Patrick had suggested, its material pure silk, with a fitted, mandarin-style collar and short sleeves.

'With your dark hair swept up like it was last night, and some kohl around your eyes, you'll look positively exotic, Ellie,' Sarah enthused.

The gown was beautiful, it was also more glamorous than anything Ellie had ever worn before. Dared she buy it?

'Patrick is going to be bowled over when he sees you in this,' Sarah added encouragingly.

She wasn't sure she wanted Patrick 'bowled over' when he saw her. Where could any relationship between the two of them ever go? Nowhere, came the resounding answer. And yet a part of her so wanted the dress—if only to see if she *could* bowl Patrick over…!

'Why don't you think about it while the two of us have a cup of coffee?' Sarah proposed as she saw Ellie's uncertainty.

'Good idea,' Ellie accepted with a certain amount of relief.

Although she wasn't so sure it *had* been a good idea once the two women were seated in a coffee-shop further down the street and the conversation naturally turned to Sarah's engagement!

'It was all a bit—sudden, wasn't it?' Ellie suggested lightly as she stirred sweetener into her coffee.

'Mmm,' Sarah acknowledged thoughtfully. 'I've quite enjoyed this last year—the modelling and having my photograph on the cover of magazines but you know, Ellie, it's a very lonely sort of life too. I missed my friends, the family,' she added wistfully. 'Most of all the family. Marriage, the possibility of having my own family, suddenly seemed the right option.'

But, as Ellie knew only too well, Gareth most certainly wasn't the right man to share that option!

'You're only twenty-one, Sarah,' she teased. 'There's plenty of time for that once you've done all the other things you want to do with your life. Didn't you once mention that you wanted to do some fashion designing of your own?'

'I've already done some,' Sarah told her excitedly. 'I had totally forgotten in the excitement of the last few weeks,' she went on ruefully, 'but I'm waiting for Jacques, the designer I worked with in Paris, to tell me what he thinks of them.'

Ah. So Sarah hadn't completely given up on her life in Paris after all...

'That sounds interesting,' Ellie encouraged. 'Do you think that will affect your engagement to Gareth?'

Sarah looked startled. 'I must admit I hadn't given that much thought.' She grimaced. 'This being engaged and having to think of another person is all new to me,' she added self-derisively. 'But I would really like to follow it through if Jacques thinks I have any talent at all.'

Again, this was encouraging, Ellie thought; it showed the other woman wasn't yet quite so tied up in her relationship with Gareth that she had given up on her own ambitions.

'I'm sure Gareth will understand if we have to wait a while before getting married,' Sarah added dismissively.

Ellie thought the other woman was being slightly optimistic concerning Gareth's patience in that direction— after all, the sooner Sarah was his wife, the sooner his position at Delacorte, Delacorte and Delacorte was secured—but wisely she didn't voice any of those doubts to Sarah.

She did, however, relay the conversation to Patrick when he arrived to collect her that evening.

'You look wonderful, Ellie.' He stood back to look at her appreciatively.

Ellie felt warmth in her cheeks at his praise. 'Patrick, didn't you hear what I said? Sarah—'

'Still has plans to become a fashion designer,' he finished dismissively. 'That's great. But—'

'Just "great"?' Ellie persisted frowningly. 'Don't

you realise this could be the way to drive a rift between her and Gareth?'

'Well, of course I realise that,' he confirmed lightly. 'He isn't going to like the idea of a delayed marriage at all.'

'Exactly,' Ellie said with satisfaction. 'Which is good—isn't it…?' she added uncertainly when Patrick didn't look as thrilled by the news as she had been earlier.

'Very good.' He nodded. 'But at the moment I'm more interested in the way you look, Ellie. That dress is—you look wonderful,' he said again.

Ellie had given in to impulse and gone back to the shop to buy the blue silk gown, aware that it was costing a small fortune but for the moment not caring. She had also swept up her hair and applied kohl to her eyes, as Sarah had suggested. The finished effect was pretty good, even if she did say so herself. And it was also good that Patrick liked the way she looked this evening. Wasn't it…?

That was the particular problem she had at the moment. There was no denying that she was attracted to Patrick, that she more than liked being in his company, but at the same time she was still very much aware that their relationship was nothing but a sham. It certainly wouldn't do for either of them to forget that. Because once this situation had been sorted out she and Patrick would go back to being strangers—perhaps occasionally mentioned to each other by Toby, but other than that strangers.

The fact that Patrick was once again dressed in evening clothes, and it made her heart flutter just to look at him, was not something Ellie could allow herself to dwell on!

There was also the matter of the large flat white box he had carried in under his arm...

'You told me off yesterday evening for repeating things,' she reminded him dryly.

'Telling you how beautiful you look in that dress deserves to be repeated,' he said unrepentantly, his gaze still appreciative. 'It's blue too,' he added with satisfaction.

'Shouldn't we be going?' Ellie prompted sharply, after a glance at her wristwatch, not particularly wanting to get into a conversation about why she had chosen this particular gown. 'After all, there's politely late and then there's just bad manners!'

Patrick laughed softly. 'You sound like my mother!'

Great! Just the person she wanted to be likened to!

'Oh, no, you don't.' Patrick removed the heavy winter coat from her hand as she would have put it on, throwing it back over a chair before laying the white box on the kitchen table and removing the lid. 'I bought you a present today,' he told her lightly, folding back the tissue paper in the box.

'A present?' Ellie gaped. 'For me? But—'

'For you,' Patrick repeated firmly, taking something black and woollen out of the box. 'It's a pashmina. It's made from the soft wool of goats in Northern India—'

'I know what it's made from,' Ellie cut in dazedly, staring at the soft woollen shawl. She also knew that it was very expensive! 'Patrick, you really shouldn't have—'

'I really should,' he told her firmly, shaking out the long shawl to drape it decorously about her shoulders. 'You deserve something in the way of thanks for what you're doing. Think of it as an early Christmas present. Besides,' he added as she would have protested again, 'that black coat does absolutely nothing for you,' he told her dryly.

Or for the image of the woman who was to be his partner for the evening, Ellie realized ruefully.

Not that he wasn't right about her long black winter coat; it had been bought more for warmth rather than as any sort of fashion statement. It was just the fact of Patrick having bought her a gift—an expensive one at that—that was so disturbing. And it might be Christmas in just over a week's time, but Patrick wouldn't have been buying her a present anyway...

But the shawl did feel so warm, and it had such panache—its front drape fell to just above her knees; the other drape was thrown stylishly across one shoulder by Patrick. She didn't want to refuse it!

Patrick's hands moved up to cradle either side of her face as he looked down at her intently. 'Just say, "Thank you, Patrick", politely,' he told her dryly. 'Give me a kiss for good measure. And then we'll be on our way.'

She tried to swallow, knowing which part of those instructions had suddenly caused this obstruction in her throat. Verbally thanking him would be no problem -

'Too difficult?' he teased mockingly. 'Okay, just kiss me and we'll forget all about saying thank you!'

That was the part that was bothering her! And Patrick knew it too. The light of challenge burned in those otherwise enigmatic grey eyes.

The problem was, if she 'just' kissed him, as he suggested, would either of them be able to forget about that? Ellie knew that she wouldn't!

'Don't take too long deciding, Ellie,' Patrick told her dryly. 'Or the party will be over before we even get there!'

Which, to Ellie's mind, wouldn't be a bad thing!

But she was prevaricating. She knew she was. Patrick knew she was, too. Why not just kiss him and get it over with?

'Thank you for my present, Patrick.' She stood on tiptoe and kissed him lightly on the mouth. 'But you shouldn't have—'

Patrick put silencing fingertips over her lips. 'Don't ruin it, Ellie,' he told her huskily. 'And do you call that a kiss?' he added derisively. 'Sarah shows me more enthusiasm than you just did!'

Sarah was his cousin, and perfectly free to kiss him as enthusiastically as she chose. Ellie—who wasn't quite sure what she was to him—felt rather more constrained.

'How about you try again, hmm?' Patrick encouraged throatily.

He was suddenly very close. Ellie was able to feel the warmth of his body, smell his spicy aftershave, and as she looked up into his eyes she could see that his pupils were dilated, so that only a ring of grey showed about the eyes.

'Patrick...!' She groaned huskily, before she once again rose on tiptoe, her mouth soft and pliant against his as she kissed him with all the pent-up longing inside her.

Patrick's arms moved about her waist as he pulled her in against his body, although he let Ellie continue to control the kiss.

If you could call it control when she just wanted to melt against him and give in to the languorous yearning of her body!

'Wow!' he breathed slowly when Ellie broke the kiss, lightly resting his forehead against hers. 'Now, that's what I call a kiss. You have hidden talents, Miss Fairfax,' he added warmly.

Ellie swallowed hard. 'I—'

'Will I do?' Toby burst unceremoniously into the kitchen, coming to an abrupt halt as he saw how close Ellie and Patrick were standing to each other. 'Sorry.' He grimaced self-consciously. 'I had no idea— I mean—'

'You'll do, Toby,' the older man told him dryly as he stepped away from Ellie. 'I was just telling your sister how beautiful she looks this evening,' he prompted pointedly.

'Er—yes, sis, you look great,' Toby said, a perplexed frown on his brow. He still sounded slightly flustered— as well he might; the last thing he had expected was to see Ellie and Patrick in what must have looked like a clinch!

Ellie was a little puzzled as to why Toby was dressed in a black dinner suit and white shirt...

Patrick shot the younger man a searching look, and whatever he saw there in Toby's face caused him to give an impatient shake of his head. 'Did I forget to mention that Toby is coming with us this evening?' he said blandly, turning to pick up his car keys from where he had left them on the table earlier.

Not only had he forgotten to mention it—but so had Toby!

CHAPTER SIX

ELLIE still had no idea, seated beside Patrick in the front of the car as he drove competently through the busy streets, why her brother should be accompanying them.

Obviously he was Patrick's assistant, but this was a family party, to celebrate—or commiserate!—with Sarah on her engagement to Gareth. Admittedly, Toby obviously knew much more of the Delacorte family than Ellie had at first realised, but what possible place did he have amongst such a gathering?

She gave a dismissive shake of her head, giving up on trying to work that one out; she already had enough to think about this evening without worrying about why her brother should have been invited too.

Patrick's present, for one thing...

Even now Ellie snuggled down into the warmth of the shawl, loving the feel of the soft wool against her arms. And Patrick had obviously been out and bought the gift himself. Which made it doubly precious.

That kiss, for another thing...

Given enough opportunity, she could quite get used to kissing Patrick. In fact, she couldn't think of anything she enjoyed more, could still feel the sensuous warmth of his lips against hers...

Stop it, she instantly ordered herself exasperatedly. There was no point in getting used to Patrick kissing her. In fact, it might never happen again, so she had better get used to that!

The Delacorte house was ablaze with lights as Patrick parked the car outside. Over twenty cars were already parked in the long driveway—Jaguars, Mercedes, Rolls Royces and the occasional Range Rover, Ellie noted with a self-conscious grimace.

As Gareth had quickly realized when he'd come to work for Delacorte, Delacorte and Delacorte, Ellie was quite a favourite with George Delacorte, but she had never actually been to George and Mary's house before. She now found a butler opening the door to their ring, a maid taking their coats and wraps. The luxurious décor and furnishings of the house were all a bit overwhelming.

Did Patrick's parents have a house like this one too?

Probably, she acknowledged heavily. Even if, as she vaguely remembered Toby once telling her, as a bachelor of thirty-eight Patrick lived in an apartment of his own in town.

All this luxury made their own little house seem positively minute in comparison!

But then there was no point in comparison; the obvious wealth of Patrick's relatives only served to emphasise the differences between the two of them. Differences she would do well to remember.

There was the sound of voices and laughter coming from a sitting room that led off to the right of the huge reception hall, and it was to this room that Patrick took them, his hand lightly under Ellie's elbow. Almost as if he knew that what she really wanted to do was turn tail and run!

'My family doesn't bite, Ellie,' Patrick told her mockingly now. 'At least not on first acquaintance!' he added tauntingly.

'How reassuring,' Ellie drawled, taking a glass of champagne from the circulating waiter.

'If the two of you will excuse me...?' Toby muttered distractedly, before disappearing into the throng of people already crowded into the room.

Ellie watched his departure with puzzlement. 'What—?'

'Let's go and say hello to George and Mary,' Patrick suggested lightly. 'You had better hold my hand.' He held it out to her. 'I would hate to lose you in the crush.'

Ellie would hate to lose him too; she hadn't recognised a single face in the room so far, apart from George and Mary Delacorte where they stood over by the huge fireplace, chatting to another middle-aged couple.

It was undoubtedly a large room, seeming to run the entire width of the house, with a huge bay window at one end and doors out into the garden at the other, but with fifty or so people in it there was barely room to move.

'We have a large family,' Patrick told Ellie ruefully as he managed to push his way through in the direction of the fireplace.

Ellie and Toby had several aunts, uncles and cousins too, but they would be hard pushed to fill even their small sitting room with the dozen or so that made up their family.

It didn't help her nervousness when she instantly saw

the likeness between Mary Delacorte and the tall dark-haired man who made up half of the other couple the Delacortes were chatting to. She knew she was right in the conclusion she had come to as the man gave a light laugh; his likeness to Patrick was unmistakeable.

Saying good evening to George and Mary was one thing, meeting Patrick's parents was something else entirely!

Ellie came to an abrupt halt before they reached the foursome, giving Patrick an accusing glare when he looked down at her questioningly. 'I don't think that's a good idea, Patrick,' she bit out tautly.

He gave her a considering look. 'Ellie, introducing you to my parents is not tantamount to making a declaration about our relationship,' he finally drawled teasingly.

'No, Patrick.' She gave a firm shake of her head. 'Helping out with this situation concerning Gareth is one thing, but I won't complicate things by meeting your parents.' She determinedly released her hand from his. 'You go and say hello to them. I'll go and find the ladies' room.'

He frowned darkly. 'But—'

'I said no, Patrick.' Her gaze met his unwaveringly. 'I'll be standing over by the bay window when you've finished talking to them.'

'Wearing a pink carnation in your lapel?' he returned, with obvious impatience at her determination.

She gave the ghost of a smile. 'I don't have a lapel.'

Patrick shook his head as he looked down at her frustratedly. 'You are undoubtedly the most stubborn woman I've ever met!'

Her smile was more genuine this time. 'Nice to know I have the distinction of being something,' she returned unconcernedly.

His expression lightened. 'Oh, you're a lot more than that, Ellie,' he assured her dryly, before sighing resignedly. 'Okay, no introduction to my parents. But try not to get lost, hmm?' he encouraged.

As it happened, despite directions from the busy maid in the hallway, she did get lost—several times— and it was almost fifteen minutes later when she came back down the stairs. Only to walk straight into Gareth—literally—as he began walking up them.

The words of apology died on his lips as he looked up and recognised her. The boyish smile turned to one of derision. 'I thought you had decided not to come to the party after all when I saw your boyfriend was in there alone,' he bit out caustically.

Ellie straightened her shoulders, her hand tightly gripping her evening bag; Gareth was the last person she'd wanted to find herself alone with! 'Obviously you thought wrong,' she returned, non-committal—about the 'boyfriend' or the fact that she was there!

'Obviously,' Gareth acknowledged hardly. 'I don't know what you're hoping to achieve by all this, Ellie, but—'

'I have no idea what you're talking about,' she interrupted firmly, glancing over his shoulder in the hope that Patrick or Toby might see her predicament and come to her rescue; neither of them was in sight.

He grimaced. 'I realise that you're in love with me, Ellie, but—'

'You realise no such thing!' Ellie interrupted heatedly, knowing that briefly she might have thought herself in love with this man. But it had only been briefly. She was most certainly over whatever she had once felt for him! 'If I'm in love with anyone, it most certainly isn't you,' she added scathingly.

Gareth's gaze narrowed. 'McGrath?'

She didn't know what she felt for Patrick—had spent most of the last twenty-four hours determinedly not giving herself time to even think along those lines.

Her chin rose challengingly. 'And what if it is?'

He gave a pitying shake of his head. 'Then you're wasting your time there more than you were with me,' he scorned. 'Delusions of grandeur!' he added nastily.

'And what about you?' Ellie flushed angrily—more so because she knew what he said was true. 'Isn't Sarah Delacorte just as much out of your league as Patrick is out of mine?'

'Ah, but I've already succeeded with Sarah,' he reminded her confidently.

'Not for long, if I have my way,' Ellie snapped furiously. 'You— Let go of my arm, Gareth!' she gasped as he grasped her painfully on exactly the same spot he had the previous evening. And she had the bruises to prove it!

He ignored her, maintaining his grip, his face very close to hers now, his eyes glittering angrily. 'Don't try and mess this up for me, Ellie,' he warned softly. 'Because if you do—'

'Everything all right, Ellie?'

It was Toby who came to Ellie's rescue this time. Gareth released her in time for her to turn and see her brother strolling across the hallway to join them.

'Davies,' he greeted the other man coolly before turning to look at Ellie concernedly.

Ellie had a good idea what he would see too; she was both shocked and dismayed by Gareth's verbal attack on her, and the bruises on her arm were hurting.

'Ellie, Patrick was looking for you so that you can go into the buffet together,' Toby said softly. 'I think you should go and join him,' he added firmly.

She didn't want to rejoin Patrick; she just wanted to leave, to go home and lick her wounds—literally. Her arm really was throbbing, adding to the discomfort of the bruises already there.

'I'll just stay here and have a few quiet words with Gareth,' Toby continued lightly, before turning to the other man. 'I don't think I've congratulated you on your engagement yet, have I?'

Ellie left them to it. These confrontations with Gareth were unpleasant as well as nerve-shattering. Although Patrick seemed to be right in his surmise that she only needed to appear in order to upset Gareth's self-confidence. She just wasn't sure she was up to the effect these meetings were having on her own self-confidence!

Patrick was frowning darkly as she joined him by the window. 'Where on earth have you been?' he snapped. 'I finished talking to my parents long ago. I— What is it?' he probed concernedly when Ellie's eyes misted over with tears. 'Ellie…?' He lightly clasped her arm.

Ellie gasped at this added pressure on a spot that already felt black and blue, biting her bottom lip as her tears became tears of pain.

Patrick instantly released her when he realised he was

hurting her. 'Ellie, where have you been?' he asked slowly. 'And why does your arm hurt?'

She shook her head, desperately blinking back the tears; she didn't want to make a complete fool of herself—and Patrick—in front of his family. 'I bumped into Gareth in the hallway—'

'That's how you hurt your arm?' he ground out suspiciously, eyes narrowed to steely slits.

'Not exactly,' she conceded awkwardly. 'You see, I still have bruises there from last night, when he grabbed me, and—'

'Davies hurt you?' Patrick bit out, dangerously soft.

'I don't suppose he meant to,' she lied—knowing from the expression on Gareth's face earlier that he would greatly enjoy strangling her for what he saw as her interference! 'You see—'

'Yes, I do see, Ellie,' Patrick ground out harshly, his narrowed gaze searching as he looked across the room towards the door. 'Here's Toby,' he rasped. 'I want you to stay here with him—while I go and have a few words with my so-called future cousin-in-law!'

'Patrick, no—' But she was too late. He had already left her side, muttering a few words to her brother in passing before going out into the hallway himself.

This was awful! She deplored Sarah's choice of future husband, knew Gareth for exactly what he was, but the last thing Ellie wanted was to cause trouble at Sarah's engagement party. And she was pretty sure, from the grim expression on Patrick's face as he'd left her side, that there was going to be trouble!

Toby smiled as he reached her. 'Patrick wants me to

take you in to the buffet; he's going to join us in a few minutes.'

Maybe this was the reason Toby had accompanied them to the party—this way Patrick had ensured that she was never left alone. Except she had been...

'Toby, Patrick is going to find Gareth and, from the looks of him, hit him,' she said agitatedly, staring anxiously towards the direction in which Patrick had so recently disappeared.

'So?' Toby prompted unconcernedly.

'Toby—'

'Ellie,' he cut in firmly. 'I would have hit the man myself if I hadn't thought the bruises might show, but I had to settle for a few choice words instead. And talking of bruises...' He looked down at her searchingly. 'Patrick said something about Gareth having hurt you just now?'

She sighed her impatience, wishing she hadn't given away the fact that her arm was bruised beneath the sleeve of her dress. 'It doesn't matter,' she dismissed. 'What matters is that Patrick is going to make a scene.' Her eyes were wide with distress at the thought.

Toby gave a confident shake of his head. 'Patrick never makes a scene,' her brother assured her dryly.

No, he probably didn't—could probably get his point over by talking in that softly dangerous voice she had heard him use just now. But, nevertheless, she doubted Gareth would just meekly stand there and take whatever Patrick had to say to him.

'Come on, sis,' Toby encouraged lightly. 'Let's go through to the other room and get some food.'

The last thing Ellie felt like doing was eating! How

could she even think about food when Patrick and Gareth might even now be at each other's throats?

She hung back. 'I just want to go home, Toby.' She sighed. 'In fact, after tonight I need to rethink my whole life,' she added frowningly.

After tonight she wasn't even sure she could go on working in the same building with Gareth, let alone anything else. If Gareth could be this threatening in the midst of his future in-laws, what possible chance did she stand of avoiding his wrath at the office?

She had worked for Delacorte, Delacorte and Delacorte since leaving school at eighteen, had been steadily promoted through the firm, until she'd become George's personal secretary four years ago. It was a job she greatly enjoyed. At least, she had. The last couple of months, with the chance of bumping into Gareth around every corner, hadn't been quite so much fun. And after this evening it promised to get worse!

Toby frowned. 'I don't think you need to do anything drastic just yet, Ellie,' he cautioned. 'Give Patrick a bit more time to resolve the situation, hmm?'

She gave a wry smile. 'You have great confidence in your employer!'

Her brother gave a rueful shrug. 'I've never seen Patrick at the losing end of a fight yet.'

No, she could believe that; Patrick had the air of a man completely confident in his own abilities. But this situation was too personal, too close to home, to be dealt with like the business deals he was usually involved with.

'Hello, Ellie,' Sarah greeted her brightly, looking exceptionally beautiful in the green dress she had bought earlier that afternoon. 'You don't happen to have seen my fiancé about anywhere, do you?' she added ruefully.

Ellie felt the colour drain from her cheeks. 'Er—'

'He was outside talking to Patrick when I last saw him.' Toby was the one to answer. 'I'm Ellie's brother Toby, by the way,' he added lightly, holding out his hand in friendly greeting.

'Sarah Delacorte.' She gave Toby a considering look as she shook his hand. 'Yes, I can see the likeness.' She smiled warmly. 'You work with Patrick, don't you?'

'For him, actually,' Toby corrected dryly.

Sarah's smile widened. 'Of course. Well, it's very nice to meet you,' she added sincerely. 'I hope you'll both excuse me while I go and find Gareth?'

Ellie looked up impatiently at Toby once they were alone. 'Shouldn't you go and warn Patrick?'

Her brother shrugged unconcernedly. 'One thing I've learnt from working for Patrick—he's quite capable of taking care of himself. Now, let's go and get some food; I'm starving!' With his hand under her elbow he guided her through to the dining room.

Toby had learnt something else from working for Patrick, Ellie realized: how to take charge of a situation with the same arrogance!

Somewhere along the way, she realised dazedly as she put food on her plate without even noticing what she had chosen, her little brother had grown up...

She had spent so long thinking of him as her younger brother, that she just hadn't noticed him grow into a man almost as confident as the one he worked for.

He was a handsome man too, Ellie had to acknowledge as a girl of about twenty who stood helping herself to the buffet—probably yet another relative of Patrick's—gave him more than a cursory glance from beneath lowered dark lashes.

At twenty-six and over six feet tall, with short dark hair, laughing blue eyes, a pleasantly handsome face and a healthily fit body from his visits to the gym several times a week, her brother wasn't the boy she had always thought him; he was a man who was obviously attractive to women.

When had that happened? She—

'You aren't eating, Ellie.'

She turned sharply to find Patrick standing at her side, and quickly checked his face for signs of a fight. Thankfully she didn't find any.

'How was I supposed to eat when for all I knew you might have been lying unconscious in the hallway?' she came back, her sharpness due to her worry concerning his welfare.

Like a mother when her child came back to her unharmed after doing something she considered dangerous? Or like a woman worried about the man she loved…?

Patrick's reply didn't exactly calm her impatient anger. 'Not very likely,' he drawled confidently.

Ellie's eyes sparkled angrily. 'That's okay for you to say, but—'

'Ellie!' Toby cut in laughingly. 'I told you that Patrick is more than capable of taking care of himself.'

She glared at them both—Toby laughing, Patrick amused, one dark brow raised mockingly. 'Men!' she finally muttered frustratedly, turning away to pile more food haphazardly onto her plate.

'Are you sure you're going to eat all that?' Patrick murmured close beside her. 'Maybe we should just share the plate,' he added teasingly.

Ellie turned to find that she and Patrick were alone. Toby had wandered off, was now standing across the dining room chatting to the dark-haired girl who had given him such an admiring look a few minutes ago. He hadn't wasted much time!

She looked up at Patrick, some of her anger abating in the face of his teasing look. 'I had visions of a brawl in the hallway,' she admitted ruefully.

He shrugged. 'I very rarely resort to violence, Ellie. Although in Davies's case,' he added hardly, his expression becoming grim, 'I could be willing to make an exception. As it is, I've made it very clear what I will do to him if he so much as comes near you again, let alone touches you.'

Ellie raised dark brows. 'Oh?'

Patrick nodded abruptly. 'I think we need to discuss your continued involvement in all this.'

Ellie felt her heart stop for a moment. What did he mean? Was he suggesting that it was no longer necessary for her to be involved?

She might have decided minutes ago that she needed to rethink her life, to perhaps consider giving up her position at Delacorte, Delacorte and Delacorte as a way of avoiding accidentally bumping into Gareth any more. But she hadn't included not seeing Patrick any more in that rethinking... The very thought of that filled her with desolation.

A week ago Patrick had just been her brother Toby's boss—a man she had once shared an embarrassing experience with—but he was now so much more than that. How much more she still didn't want to admit to herself. She just knew she couldn't bear the thought of not seeing Patrick again!

Her mouth tightened. 'You can manage without me now—is that it?' She was waspish in her disappointment.

'I didn't say that.' Patrick gave her a reproving look. 'I just think that it might be better for you—'

'I'll decide what's best for me, if you don't mind,' Ellie told him shortly. 'And while I can still be of any help in preventing Sarah making a terrible mistake I intend staying very much in Gareth's face!' she announced firmly—in complete contradiction of what she had decided minutes ago!

But the only way she could continue to see Patrick was to remain a thorn in Gareth's side.

And she very much wanted to continue seeing Patrick…

CHAPTER SEVEN

'I'M SORRY, how did you say Toby was getting home?' Ellie yawned tiredly as Patrick drove her home a couple of hours later.

He shrugged dismissively. 'Someone he met at the party is driving him back later, I believe.'

Ellie would take a bet on it being that pretty dark-haired girl who had looked at him so interestedly as they stood at the buffet table; she certainly hadn't seen much of her brother during the rest of the evening.

Oh, well, good luck to him, Ellie thought slightly enviously. She had spent the whole evening with Patrick glued to her side—but for completely the wrong reason!

'I felt so sorry for George and Mary this evening.' She sighed heavily. The older couple's unhappiness at their daughter's choice of future husband had been perfectly obvious to Ellie as they'd looked at Sarah so wistfully. She frowned. 'Does Sarah really have no idea how they feel about Gareth?'

'George has voiced his—reservations concerning the speed of the engagement.' Patrick grimaced. 'Anything else is sure to just make her all the more determined to have her own way.'

Ellie turned to smile at him in the semi-darkness of the illuminated streets they were driving through. 'Runs in the family, does it?' she teased.

He gave a slight smile. 'Something like that.'

She could believe it. They were certainly an attractive family, but stubbornness seemed to be one of their less endearing characteristics.

'Gareth is going to cling like a leech,' Ellie warned heavily.

Patrick's mouth tightened. 'I agree. He's a parasite.'

How embarrassing it was for her that she had been the previous woman taken in by Gareth's charm! In fact, she would rather not talk about Gareth at all.

'So what's the next move?' she prompted briskly.

'Dinner on Tuesday, I thought,' Patrick came back lightly.

Ellie turned to him frowningly. 'What's happening on Tuesday evening?'

'I just said—dinner,' he dismissed.

'Yes, but—what's it for?'

He shot her a sideways glance. 'So we don't starve?'

'Yes, but—'

'You're repeating yourself again, Ellie,' he mused teasingly. 'I'm inviting you out to dinner on Tuesday evening,' he explained lightly.

Ellie's frown deepened. 'But—'

'Ellie, will you or will you not have dinner with me on Tuesday evening?' Patrick cut in patiently.

'Well, of course. I've already told you I'll do everything I can to help—'

'This is dinner with me, Ellie.' He parked the car in the driveway and turned in his seat to look at her. 'No one else. Well...I suppose there will be other people in the restaurant. But they will have nothing to do with us. Have I made myself clear now?'

If she understood this correctly, Patrick had just invited her out on a date!

He gave a smile at her perplexed expression. 'I believe it's usual to invite your escort in for coffee at the end of the evening.'

Ellie was still so dazed by his invitation out to dinner on Tuesday that she did ask him in, getting out of the car to unlock the front door of the house and lead the way in to the kitchen.

'Leave that for a minute,' Patrick murmured softly, and he took the coffee pot out of her hand, turning her to face him. 'I want to see the bruises on your arms,' he told her grimly as he removed the wrap from her shoulders.

She felt the colour warm her cheeks as he turned the sleeves back on her dress. There was a huge thumb-print-size bruise on the front of each arm, one already turning a sickly yellow, the new one a blue-black. Ellie stood still as Patrick walked around to look at the back of her arm, hearing the angry hiss that followed.

'I should have hit him while I had the chance,' Patrick snapped angrily. 'Damn it—I've a good mind to go back to the party right now and hit him anyway!' he bit out harshly.

Ellie shook her head as she pulled the sleeves back down over her arms. 'He really isn't important.'

'No, he isn't,' Patrick agreed abruptly as he moved to stand beside her, his eyes gleaming metallic grey. 'But I have no intention of just standing by while he hurts you.'

She gave a self-derisive laugh. 'You're a little late in the day to prevent him doing that!'

Patrick stepped back, watching her with hooded eyes as she prepared the coffee. 'Did you love him very much?'

'Not at all,' she answered with complete honesty. 'Oh, I may have thought I did for a while. But I was just—flattered by his attention, I suppose. Believe it or not, he can be very charming when he wants to be.' Besides, she already knew that the way Patrick made her feel, just by being in the same room as her, was far deeper than anything she might have thought she felt for Gareth!

'I'm sure he can,' Patrick dismissed scathingly.

'No—really.' She gave a self-conscious laugh.

It was strangely intimate in the quiet of the kitchen— the muted light under the kitchen cupboards the only illumination, the only sound the drip, drip of the coffee percolator.

Patrick's eyes were mesmerizing now as he looked down at her, obliquely black, ringed with silver. 'Dinner on Tuesday?' he prompted huskily.

'Er—Well—Yes,' she agreed awkwardly, still unsure as to the reason for his invitation. 'Although—'

'Just a yes will do,' Patrick assured her mockingly, his arms moving lightly about her waist. 'I would like to see you relaxed and enjoying yourself for a change,' he added frowningly.

If he thought she was going to be relaxed in his company then he was mistaken! Although she *would* enjoy spending the evening with him. If she knew the reason for it...

But he was standing so close now she couldn't even think straight, let alone try to rationalise his dinner invitation. Her heart was beating erratically, her breathing shallow as she looked up into the handsome ruggedness of his face.

'You look extremely lovely tonight, Ellie,' he told her huskily.

'You said that earlier,' she reminded him breathlessly.

He smiled, his eyes crinkling warmly at the corners. 'Some things need to be repeated.' His hands linked at the base of her spine and he moulded her body lightly against his, his head bending slightly as his lips moved teasingly across hers.

She had forgotten to breathe again, felt as if time itself were standing still. Only her hands resting on the broadness of Patrick's shoulders prevented her from actually falling down.

'You have a very kissable mouth, Ellie Fairfax,' Patrick murmured huskily as he took little sips from her lips. 'A very sensuous neck,' he whispered as his lips moved down the silky column of her throat. 'Divine breasts—'

'I think perhaps you should stop there, Patrick, don't you?' Ellie moved awkwardly in his arms, very aware of the sudden pertness of those 'divine breasts', the nipples hard against the silky material of her dress.

He straightened, his head tilted to one side as he regarded her quizzically. 'Why do I get the impression you're an innocent?' he murmured ruefully.

'Probably because I am!' Ellie admitted uncomfortably as she extricated herself from his arms, at the same time looking up at him irritably. 'There's nothing wrong with that,' she added sharply.

Patrick's smile deepened. 'Did I say there was?'

'You looked as if there was,' she snapped defensively.

He shook his head, still smiling. 'I don't think so, Ellie.'

Well...okay, maybe he hadn't. But he certainly seemed surprised to meet a twenty-seven-year-old virgin!

Maybe it *was* odd at that; Ellie really wouldn't know. It wasn't something she had ever discussed with any of the women she worked with.

She had been out with several boys of her own age up to the age of nineteen, but after her parents had died she had been too busy trying to keep a home for Toby and herself—hadn't really had much time to think about relationships. Which was probably the reason she had fallen for Gareth's charm six months ago!

But in the face of Patrick's sophistication, his obvious experience when it came to women, she must seem rather gauche and naïve.

Well, tough! She had no intention of pretending an experience she just didn't have. And that included appearing sophisticated in the face of Patrick's appreciative comments on her body!

'Coffee, Ellie,' he reminded her lightly, moving to sit down at the kitchen table.

'Of course.' She moved economically about the kitchen, getting out the cups, cream and sugar, all the time avoiding Patrick's gaze, but knowing it followed her every movement.

'Did Davies—? Steady,' Patrick soothed as a spoon

landed on the floor with a clatter when Ellie just dropped it.

She bent to pick it up, her face averted so that he shouldn't see the heated colour in her cheeks.

'Ellie?'

Just that. Her name. Nothing else. But it was said compellingly enough for Ellie to know he wanted her to look across at him. And she did exactly that. The steadiness of his gaze as he looked at her wordlessly was as forceful as Ellie had known it would be.

'What do you want to know, Patrick?' she snapped impatiently, picking up the tray of coffee things only to put it down noisily on the kitchen table. 'Whether Gareth and I came close to being lovers?' she bit out sarcastically. 'What business is it of yours if we did?' she added challengingly, blue eyes bright with anger as she glared down at him.

'Black, no sugar,' he told her economically. 'My preference for coffee,' he explained mildly at her blank look.

'Oh. Fine,' she muttered, sitting down abruptly to concentrate all her attention on pouring the coffee. She didn't want to think about anything else!

'You're quite right, Ellie,' Patrick began softly, 'it is none of my business just how—intimate your relationship was with Davies. Except...'

She looked up sharply. 'Yes?'

His gaze was intense on the paleness of her face. 'Did he hurt you, Ellie?'

She felt the blood drain completely from her cheeks, her hand shook as she held the coffee pot poised over one of the cups.

'Ellie?'

She drew in a deep breath, swallowed hard, willing herself to carry on pouring the coffee without spilling it. No, Gareth hadn't hurt her, he had humiliated her. But it wasn't an incident she particularly wanted to relate to Patrick. It was the reason she knew she had meant absolutely nothing to Gareth—the reason she knew what sort of man he really was...

She gave an over-bright smile, her gaze not quite meeting Patrick's as she handed him his cup of coffee. 'It isn't important, Patrick,' she dismissed lightly. 'We're all agreed that he isn't a nice person.'

Patrick reached out, his hand covering hers as it rested on the tabletop. 'Tell me what happened,' he encouraged huskily.

She closed her eyes, wishing she could shut out the memory of that last time she had been with Gareth but at the same time knowing that she couldn't.

Gareth called into her office as she was finishing work, suggesting that he drive her home. Things had been rather strained between them the last couple of weeks— forgotten telephone calls, cancelled dates—and she had welcomed this chance to talk to him alone for a while.

Toby was still at work when they arrived back at the house, and almost before Ellie and Gareth were in the door, it seemed, Gareth began to kiss her. But as the kiss deepened, with Gareth's hands roaming more freely over her body than ever before, Ellie began to pull away from him.

'Don't,' she told him frowningly, at the same time

pushing ineffectually at his painful hold about her waist.

He smiled then—a smile like no other Ellie had seen him give, a smile so scornful it made her cringe. 'That's always been the trouble with you, Ellie,' he told her scathingly as he released her so abruptly she staggered slightly. 'Maybe if you hadn't been so frigid I wouldn't have needed to find someone else. As it is…'

Ellie stared at him. She had suspected something; of course she had. Gareth had been far too elusive these last two weeks for her not to have realised that something had gone seriously wrong with their relationship.

Gareth raised blond brows at her stricken expression. 'Of course, it isn't too late,' he drawled suggestively. 'I could still be persuaded into continuing our relationship. If you were to—'

'You conceited—!' Ellie broke off angrily, glaring up at him disgustedly. 'Let me get this right, Gareth,' she said evenly, eyes narrowed now. 'If I'll agree to go to bed with you then you'll consider breaking off your other—relationship?'

The fact that he had another relationship had come as a complete shock to her. But she would think about that later. Once Gareth had left. Because he *was* leaving. Soon!

He smiled. 'Well, I wouldn't go quite that far,' he mocked.

Her eyes widened. 'You're suggesting that I become part of some harem?'

'Of course not, Ellie.' He chuckled. 'If everything goes according to plan, I should be getting married soon. But that's no reason for us to break off our relationship. If things were different between us,' he added pointedly.

If everything went according to plan! What plan?

She swallowed hard. 'If the two of us were lovers, you mean?' she clarified icily.

Gareth shrugged. 'Well, it would hardly be worth the risk otherwise, now, would it?'

'Get out,' Ellie told him shakily, her hand on the table beside her for support; her legs felt so shaky she thought she might fall over otherwise.

'Now, Ellie, there's no reason to be like that,' he cajoled huskily, taking a step towards her.

She straightened, her chin raised challengingly. 'I said, get out, Gareth, and I meant it. And God help the poor woman you're planning to marry,' she added disgustedly.

He had come to a halt some distance away from her. 'Frigid,' he repeated scornfully.

Her eyes glazed coldly. 'You'll never know,' she bit out forcefully.

He smiled. 'But I already do know, Ellie,' he assured her derisively. 'Oh, well.' He shrugged in the face of her stony expression. 'I made the offer. See you around.' He raised a hand in farewell before letting himself out of the house.

She turned to Patrick now, having no intention of relating any of that conversation to him. It was bad enough that she still remembered every painfully humiliating word of it, without sharing it with anyone else. Least of all Patrick!

She gave him a dismissive smile. 'It isn't important

what happened, Patrick,' she told him lightly. 'Gareth hurt me with words, that's all. And as my mother always said, ''sticks and stones may break my bones, but words can never hurt me''', she quoted ruefully.

Patrick looked unconvinced. 'Bones heal; words can never be forgotten.'

How true that was. She hadn't forgotten a single word Gareth had said to her six weeks ago, whereas a broken finger or wrist would have healed and been dismissed by now.

'Surely it's Gareth's problem if he considers that any woman who doesn't want to sleep with him must be frigid.' She shrugged.

Grey eyes widened. 'He actually said that? To *you*?' Patrick sounded incredulous.

Ellie gave him a disgruntled frown. 'Yes, he said that to me,' she repeated irritably.

Patrick chuckled softly. 'You're right, Ellie.' He gave a rueful shake of his head. 'He isn't important,' he explained at her questioning look. 'He obviously didn't get to know you very well at all, did he?' he added derisively.

'Exactly what do you mean by that remark?' she demanded defensively.

He looked at her consideringly before answering. 'Ellie, you are one of the warmest, most responsive women I have ever had the pleasure to meet.'

Her cheeks coloured hotly. It was no good denying what he said; her response to him whenever he touched her was undeniable.

'I'll tell you something else,' Patrick added huskily as he stood up to move round the table and pull her unresistingly to her feet. 'I'm glad Davies never got close enough to you to discover that for himself,' he murmured throatily, before bending to lightly brush Ellie's lips with his own.

So was she.

She hadn't always felt that way, had wondered in the days and then weeks that had followed Gareth's abrupt departure from her life whether she could indeed be frigid. But she only had to be in the same room with Patrick to be completely aware of him, and when she was actually in his arms like this...!

No, she wasn't frigid. She was just a woman who only responded to the right man. The right man for her. Because, although he was unsuitable in every other way—rich, powerful, successful, completely removed from her own lifestyle—she knew she had fallen in love with Patrick McGrath.

She had been fighting that knowledge for some time now, refusing to allow the thought to even enter her head. But alone here with him in the silence of her kitchen, held in his arms, their two bodies moulded perfectly together, she could no longer deny how she felt about him.

To herself, at least.

To Patrick it was another matter!

'Well, I'm relieved to hear it,' she told him lightly, at the same time moving determinedly out of his arms. 'Maybe there's hope for me after all,' she added with deliberate self-derision.

Patrick's gaze followed her frowningly. 'Ellie—'

'I just heard a car in the driveway, so I think Toby

must be home,' she told him with a certain amount of relief.

Her mother used to say something else to her, about 'jumping from the frying pan into the fire'. Well, she had certainly done that where Patrick was concerned; he was a more unsuitable man for her to have fallen in love with than Gareth had ever been!

CHAPTER EIGHT

'DID you enjoy yourself on Saturday?'

Ellie gave a startled glance towards the open door of her office, her gaze narrowing as she focused on Gareth standing in the doorway, looking incredibly cheerful. As well as self-confident.

The latter instantly made Ellie more wary than she would normally have been in his unwanted presence, and she glanced towards the door that connected hers to George's, to make sure it was firmly shut, before replying. 'The Delacortes gave you and Sarah a wonderful engagement party,' she answered non-committally.

Gareth grinned, coming fully into the room before closing the door behind him. 'That didn't exactly answer my question, now, did it?' he reproved derisively, moving to sit on the edge of her desk as he looked down at her with mocking blue eyes.

Ellie sighed. 'I didn't think it really needed an answer,' she dismissed, still eyeing him warily, sure his pleasantness wouldn't last for long; nowadays it usually didn't.

Besides, she remembered all too well his nastiness on Saturday evening. Still had the bruises to prove how angry he had been then.

He shrugged. 'Thanks for the cut-glass crystal vase, by the way. Sarah will be writing to everyone formally, of course, but I thought I would come and thank you personally.'

Cut-glass crystal vase? Ellie had been aware that Patrick had carried a gift-wrapped present into the house on Saturday evening, of course, but even if it had been a cut class crystal vase, what did it have to do with her...?

'"Congratulations, love from Patrick and Ellie",' Gareth continued tauntingly. 'You've been "Patrick and Ellie" for how long?' he added scathingly.

A matter of days. Except they weren't 'Patrick and Ellie' at all.

She'd had no idea that Patrick had put her name beside his on the gift card that had accompanied the engagement present he'd given to his cousin on Saturday. She realised why he had done it, of course, but he might have warned her!

She gave Gareth a stony look. 'Gareth, I have no idea why you should be in the least interested,' she scorned.

'I'm not. Not really.' He still looked incredibly pleased with himself. 'It will be quite a coup for the Fairfax family if you and Toby manage to pull this off.' He gave her an admiring look. 'I must say, Ellie, you're something of a surprise. Especially after your holier-than-thou attitude before.' He shook his head. 'Those people in glass houses shouldn't throw stones, you know.'

Ellie gave him a suspicious look. Could he possibly have been drinking? Admittedly it was only eleven-thirty in the morning, but she couldn't think of any other explanation for the fact that what he was saying made absolutely no sense to her.

She shook her head, not wanting to prolong this unwanted conversation any further by asking him for an explanation. 'I'll bear your advice in mind, Gareth,' she dismissed. 'Now, if you wouldn't mind, I have some work to do...?' She gave a pointed look at where he sat on some of the papers on her desk.

Gareth grinned, making no effort to move. 'Don't you see, Ellie? There's no longer any need to be all coy with me. The truth is, you and I are more alike than I would ever have guessed.'

She stiffened defensively. 'I don't think so!' she snapped distastefully.

'But of course we are,' he contradicted happily. 'It's a pity you came on so prim and proper six weeks ago; you and I would have made a great team. And Toby, of course.'

He *had* been drinking; there was no other explanation for this completely puzzling conversation!

'What on earth does Toby have to do with any of this?' She looked at him impatiently.

The two men had met on several occasions, when Gareth had come to call for her at the house, but as far as she was aware Toby hadn't particularly taken to the other man then, and he certainly didn't like him now. As for Gareth, he hadn't seemed particularly interested in Toby either.

Gareth grinned. 'You can stop the pretence now, Ellie,' he teased. 'The game is up, so to speak. Maybe the three of us should form some sort of club? We could call it—'

'Gareth, I have no idea what you're talking about.' Ellie lost all patience with him. 'Besides which, you're sitting on my desk when I want to get on with some work. Now, would you please go?' She glared at him.

He stood up slowly. But looked no less confident. 'Okay, play it that way if you want to.' He shrugged. 'But just remember that if you keep my little secret then I'll keep yours. And Toby's, of course,' he added enigmatically. 'Fair's fair, after all.'

'Gareth—'

'Ellie, I'm just going across to—Gareth...?' George came to a halt in the doorway that connected his office to Ellie's, his gaze narrowing suspiciously on the younger man as he saw him standing there.

Gareth looked completely unconcerned by the interruption. 'I just popped in to tell Ellie how much Sarah and I loved the crystal vase she and Patrick gave us for an engagement present,' he told his future father-in-law lightly.

'Well, now you've told her might I suggest you leave her to get on with her work?' George nodded abruptly, continuing to look at the younger man with narrowed eyes.

'Of course,' Gareth accepted smoothly, moving unhurriedly to the door. 'I believe I'm seeing you and Mary for dinner this evening,' he added with a smile.

'I believe you are,' George acknowledged noncommittally.

'See you later, Ellie,' came Gareth's parting shot.

Not if she saw him first! She had found him obnoxious enough before. Now she not only disliked him intensely, she didn't understand a word he said!

George gave a shuddering sigh. 'No matter how hard

I try, I simply can't bring myself to like that young man.' He shook his head sadly.

Ellie gave a wan smile. 'I wouldn't worry about it, George; you're in the majority rather than the minority!'

He grimaced. 'I wouldn't worry about it at all if Sarah hadn't decided to marry the man! I had just about decided that he wasn't suitable for Delacorte, Delacorte and Delacorte when Sarah dropped the bombshell of her engagement to the man. Her mother and I simply don't know what to do for the best,' he added heavily.

Ellie gave him a sympathetic smile. 'I think the two of you are doing very well. Very often seeming to do nothing is the right thing to do,' she added encouragingly.

George gave her a grateful smile. 'A word of advice, Ellie. Never have daughters; it plays the very devil with your heart.'

She felt so sorry for him. Especially as there was nothing she could say or do to make him feel any better.

He straightened, seeming to shake off his despondency as he glanced down at the file he held in his hand. 'I'm just going across to Gerald's office for a few minutes. My next appointment is at twelve-thirty?'

Ellie nodded after a brief glimpse at the appointment book on her desk, breathing a sigh of relief when she was finally left alone in her office.

Gareth's conversation was still a complete puzzle to her. But then, the man himself was a complete enigma to her; how could he possibly be contemplating marrying someone he so obviously didn't love? As beautiful as Sarah was.

And how could she be in love with a man when she stood absolutely no chance of him ever feeling the same way about her?

Ellie had pondered that question several times over the weekend, and she still had no answer. Only knew that she was counting the hours until she saw Patrick again!

'Oh, good, you got the message and aren't dressed up,' Patrick said with relief as Ellie opened the door to him at eight o'clock on Tuesday evening.

She raised dark brows. 'It would serve you right if I said that I was dressed up.' She opened the door wider to let him in, wearing a fitted blue jumper with faded denims.

He shook his head, grinning. 'I knew Toby wouldn't let me down!'

Her brother had dutifully passed on Patrick's message earlier that they were going to eat at a pizzeria, and Ellie had dressed accordingly. Although Patrick looked as ruggedly handsome as ever in the black sweater and black denims that he wore.

'We always seem to be going somewhere formal,' Patrick dismissed. 'I thought it would be nice if we could completely relax this evening.'

There was also no possibility of them running into anyone Patrick knew in some out-of-the-way pizzeria!

Ellie had had plenty of time to think once Toby had passed on Patrick's message to dress casually because they were going to eat informally. Patrick had never said, and she hadn't liked to ask Toby, but there was always the possibility that Patrick actually had a woman in his life at the moment. Perhaps not someone he had wanted to introduce to his family, as in accompanying him to the party on Saturday evening, but that didn't mean he wasn't involved in a relationship. She had never thought to ask…

But she wanted to ask now—wanted to know everything there was to know about Patrick McGrath. Especially if there was already a woman in his life!

Not that Ellie didn't already know she was wasting her time feeling about him as she did; she just didn't like the idea of Patrick having to explain these dates with her to another woman. In fact, she just didn't like the thought of there being another woman at all!

'I hope you like Italian food?' Patrick prompted ruefully.

'I like it fine.' Ellie nodded, picking up her fleecy blue jacket from the kitchen chair—if only to show him that she didn't always wear the unattractive long black coat.

The beautiful pashmina Patrick had bought for her on Saturday was now carefully folded and placed back in its tissue paper inside the box, stashed away at the back of her wardrobe. Ellie knew she might never find the opportunity to wear such a glamorous item again.

'Shall we go?' she prompted lightly once she had shrugged into the jacket.

Patrick looked at her consideringly. 'Is everything okay? Has Davies been bothering you again?' he added hardly.

Ellie frowned. 'Apart from a very strange conversation with him yesterday morning, no.'

'Tell me about it while we eat,' Patrick suggested,

opening the door for her. 'Unless you think it will give us both indigestion?' He grimaced as he moved to unlock the car door.

It was warm and cosy as she settled inside the car, which smelt vaguely of the aftershave Patrick favoured. 'No more than any other subject would, I don't suppose,' she answered Patrick dismissively as he got in beside her.

He gave her a sideways glance. 'What's that supposed to mean?'

Ellie sighed. 'I still don't know what this evening is about—'

Patrick shrugged. 'How about it's a thank-you for all the—inconvenience you're having to go through on my family's behalf?'

'What about the inconvenience you're now having to go to on my behalf?' she came back dismissively.

He frowned his puzzlement as he drove. 'What inconvenience would that be?'

She gave a self-derisive smile. 'Taking me out.'

He smiled ruefully. 'I have no idea what you're talking about, Ellie.'

She grimaced. 'It must be the week for it!'

'Forget Davies for the moment,' Patrick bit out impatiently. 'I want to know what you meant by that remark just now.'

Seeing the determination on his face, Ellie wished she had never made the remark in the first place. She was just feeling sorry for herself because she had fallen in love with a man who was completely unobtainable. Which was absolutely no reason to try and make life difficult for him on the rare occasions she saw him!

'Forget it,' she advised self-derisively. 'It's just pre-Christmas tension, I expect. It's very kind of you to take me out—'

'Ellie, I know you haven't known me very long,' he interrupted evenly, his expression grim, 'but when you do know me better you'll realise that, although I'm not a cruel man, neither am I someone who takes a woman out—namely you—because I am simply being kind!'

She had seen Patrick in many moods over the last couple of weeks—amused, attentive, charming, angry when it came to Gareth—but he had never been annoyed or angry with her before. At the moment he appeared to be both!

'I'm sorry if I've mistaken the situation—'

'And don't start apologising,' he cut in impatiently. 'You have done nothing to apologise for. I appear to be the one who hasn't made myself clear. A fact I am about to change right now,' he assured her determinedly, and he turned the car into a deserted private car park on the edge of town.

'What are you doing?' Ellie looked about them dazedly as Patrick parked the car in the middle of the dimly lit area.

He released his seat belt before turning in his seat to face her. 'I'm about to convince you that I asked you out this evening for one reason and one reason only. You can let me know afterwards if I've succeeded or not,' he added firmly, before reaching out to pull her into his arms, his mouth coming down forcefully on hers.

Ellie was so stunned by the suddenness of the kiss that for a moment she lay acquiescent in his arms, but then the magical thrill of his lips thoroughly exploring hers warmed her body in that familiar way, and her arms moved up about his shoulders as she returned the kiss with all the pent-up longing inside her.

Patrick's hands moved caressingly along the length of her spine, sending ripples of pleasure through her whole body. Her neck arched as his lips moved from her mouth to her cheek, and then down the creamy column of her throat, his tongue doing amazing things to the tiny hollow he discovered there.

Ellie's eyes were closed, her head back against the car seat, her fingers entwined the thick darkness of Patrick's hair as she held him against her.

'Are you wearing anything underneath this jumper, Ellie Fairfax?' Patrick murmured throatily as his thumb moved across the tip of one hardened nipple.

'What do you think, Patrick McGrath?' she came back huskily.

'I think perhaps I should find out,' he said softly.

Ellie gasped at the first touch of his hands on her nakedness. They were cool as they cupped the warmth of her breasts, the moistness of his tongue against the hardened tips causing her back to arch instinctively, and she moaned low in her throat at the pleasure that swept heatedly through her body.

She felt mindless, every bone in her body fluid as the warmth of Patrick's mouth closed erotically over one hardened nipple. Her own hands moved restlessly up and down the long length of his back as she wished the pleasure to go on for ever.

Patrick's hands encircled her waist as he held her against him, his lips travelling down the flat slope of her midriff now, pausing to explore the dip of her navel revealed by the low-waisted denims.

Even that felt wonderful, Ellie realised with a surprised gasp, leading her to wonder what other parts of her body would respond to Patrick's slightest touch.

Patrick raised his head to look at her, his eyes bright in the semi-darkness. 'I'm not hurting you?'

'Oh, no,' she breathed weakly, feeling as if she must have died and gone to heaven.

'And do you know now why I invited you out to dinner?' he prompted huskily.

'Er—yes, I think so.' She nodded; it was a little disconcerting looking at him over her bared breasts!

'You only *think* so?' he murmured teasingly, eyes glinting with intent. 'Perhaps I wasn't convincing enough—'

'Oh, yes—you were!' She reached down and raised his head as he would have commenced kissing her breasts again. 'Patrick—'

'I know.' He grimaced self-derisively as he gently pulled her jumper down to cover her nakedness. 'This isn't the ideal place for lovemaking. In fact—' he straightened, running his hand restlessly through hair already tousled by Ellie's own hands '—I think I'm a little old to be making love in a car park. But later, Ellie, when I get you home…!'

'Promises, promises,' she teased self-consciously.

'Be warned, Ellie,' he told her decisively, 'I always keep my promises.'

Had Patrick really just made love to her? Had he really just paid homage to her body as if he found her beautiful and desirable?

He most certainly had!

And, what was more, he'd said he was going to do it all over again once they returned from their evening out!

The rest of the evening—the Italian restaurant, the delicious food they ate there, the easy flow of conversation—all passed in a dream for Ellie.

She learnt that Patrick had gone to university, eventually leaving with a first class degree in Business Studies, and that instead of going into industry working for someone else had put his knowledge to use on a personal basis, building up a varied and successful business over the last fifteen years. It was a challenge he obviously still enjoyed.

She also learnt that his was a very close family, that his sister Teresa was fourteen years younger than his thirty-eight, also that she was the cherished baby of the family.

What Ellie still hadn't established by the time Patrick drove her home was whether or not he had a woman in his life; it didn't seem the sort of thing she should ask him after their intimacy earlier this evening!

'Damn,' he muttered as they arrived at Ellie's home and saw Toby's car was already parked in the driveway.

Ellie felt warmth in her cheeks as she guessed the reason for his irritation: Toby's presence meant that they wouldn't be able to carry on where they had left off earlier after all.

Patrick turned to look at her ruefully after parking the car behind Toby's. 'Have you never thought of getting a home of your own?' he said dryly.

Until this moment, quite honestly, no. It had always

seemed the natural thing for her and Toby to continue living together after their parents' death. But at this moment Ellie had to admit she was disappointed that they weren't to be alone again, too.

'Never mind.' She squeezed Patrick's arm lightly. 'It can't be helped,' she added ruefully.

'You're right. There will be other occasions.' He nodded before getting agilely out of the car to come round and open her door for her.

Ellie felt as if she were floating on air as they walked over to the house; Patrick had said there would be other occasions. That must mean he was going to ask to see her again.

To her surprise, Toby was nowhere to be found once they were inside the house.

'He must have gone to bed.' Ellie shrugged dismissively.

Patrick moved so that he was standing very close to her. 'Does that mean we're alone after all?'

'I suppose it must do. I—' Ellie broke off as she heard the sound of feet descending the stairs. 'Perhaps not,' she added ruefully, turning expectantly towards the doorway that led out into the hallway.

Except it wasn't Toby who came into the kitchen!

But Ellie had no trouble placing the other woman as the one who had looked so interestedly at Toby at the party on Saturday evening. And if she had been upstairs with Toby…!

'Thank goodness you're here,' the other woman burst out agitatedly.

Although it wasn't to Ellie that she spoke…

'What is it?' Patrick was instantly alert and left

Ellie's side to go to the other woman, the languid intimacy that had existed between the two of them all evening instantly broken.

'Toby,' the woman choked emotionally. 'I think it must be something he's eaten—I had to drive him here. He felt too ill even to drive home.' She looked distraught. 'Oh, Patrick, I'm so worried about him!' She launched herself into Patrick's arms, the tears starting to fall down her creamy cheeks.

Ellie looked at the two of them in total stupefaction. The other woman appeared to have spent the evening with Toby, and yet she and Patrick obviously knew each other rather well too. Of course, this woman had been at the party on Saturday evening, so the two might be related. Even so…

But for the moment she was too concerned about Toby herself to try to puzzle this one out, turning wordlessly to hurriedly leave the room and run upstairs to her brother's bedroom.

Toby looked awful. He lay weakly back against the pillows, his face waxen, his eyes dull with discomfort and pain as he looked up at Ellie.

'I'm going to call the doctor,' she told him decisively.

'Fine,' he nodded. 'Tell him to bring something with him to put me out of my misery!' he called after her as she hurried from the room.

Ellie turned to give a strained smile at his attempt to joke. At least, she hoped he was joking! 'I'll tell him.' She nodded before running down the stairs again. The fact that her brother hadn't argued about her calling in the doctor told her just how ill he must feel; Toby, like most men, absolutely hated the necessity of ever seeing a doctor.

'Food poisoning, do you think?' Patrick prompted economically as he came out into the hallway where she stood telephoning.

'I think so.' She nodded, frowning as she waited for her call to be answered. 'I—perhaps you could make some coffee for all of us?' she suggested distractedly.

'Teresa is already doing that,' he informed her grimly. 'Who are you calling?' he added frowningly.

Ellie stared him speechlessly. Teresa? The young woman who was at this very moment making coffee in the kitchen, the woman Toby had obviously spent the evening with, was Patrick's young *sister*, Teresa?

What—?

'Ellie, who are you telephoning?' Patrick repeated firmly.

'The doctor—' She broke off as Patrick shook his head grimly.

'I'll ring my own doctor and get him to come out.' He took the receiver from her hand, disconnecting her call and putting through one of his own.

Ellie could only stand by dazedly as Patrick spoke decisively with whoever had answered his call, not *asking* the doctor to come out and see Toby, but giving him the directions to do so.

The young woman in the kitchen—the same woman who had looked so interestedly at Toby on Saturday evening—was Patrick's sister, Teresa. Teresa? Tess...? That was a shortened version of the name Teresa, wasn't it? Could Patrick's sister possibly be the Tess that Toby had told Ellie he'd been dating the last couple of months?

And, if she was, why hadn't Toby ever told her that it was Patrick's sister he was dating?

Why hadn't Patrick told her?

Because she was absolutely positive, from the fact that Patrick hadn't looked in the least surprised to see his sister here, that he had known about the relationship before this evening!

What did it all mean?

CHAPTER NINE

'WOULD you like one or both of us to stay with you for the rest of the night?' Patrick asked Ellie some time later. The doctor had been to see Toby, and diagnosed—as they had all suspected he might—that her brother had food poisoning.

It had been an extremely traumatic couple of hours for Ellie, worried about Toby and completely puzzled by his relationship with Teresa/Tess.

But the idea of either Patrick or his sister staying for the rest of the night did not appeal to her. It also wasn't necessary. The doctor had given Toby an injection to stop him vomiting, and although her brother was still pale, he was now fast asleep.

'That won't be necessary,' Ellie answered Patrick distantly. None of the tension she had felt earlier, at discovering Toby's girlfriend Tess was in fact Patrick's sister Teresa, had evaporated.

In fact, if anything it was worse, all sorts of suspicions and conclusions having popped into Ellie's head over the last couple of hours. Most of them too depressing to contemplate for long!

'I'm very grateful for your help in getting a doctor here so promptly,' she added as she realised she probably sounded less than polite.

'But now you want us to leave?' Patrick guessed ruefully.

It was almost one o'clock in the morning. She was incredibly weary from the worry over Toby, and her head ached from the circles her thoughts were going round and round in. So, yes, she wanted him—and his sister—to leave now.

She glanced at the younger woman, Teresa, sitting dejectedly at the kitchen table staring into a cup of cold coffee, her face pale.

Ellie could see a faint family resemblance between the brother and sister now—both were dark, with those magnetic grey eyes—but where Patrick's face was all ruggedly sharp angles Teresa's was softened into gamine beauty.

Why hadn't she seen that resemblance on Saturday evening?

Because she hadn't been looking for it! Because no one had told her that Toby's girlfriend Tess *was* Patrick's young sister!

That was what really bothered Ellie about all this; why had no one told her of the relationship?

Until she had the answer to that, she felt the more distance she put between Patrick and herself the better.

'If you don't mind,' she answered Patrick evenly. 'I wouldn't expect Toby in to work tomorrow either, if I were you,' she added dryly; she doubted her brother would be strong enough to get out of bed in the morning, let alone anything else!

'I wasn't,' Patrick dismissed impatiently, looking down at her frowningly. 'Ellie—'

'Patrick, I don't think now is either the right time or place for the two of us to talk,' she bit out abruptly, moving sharply away from him, at the same time giving a pointed look in the direction of his sister.

Not that Teresa looked as if she were taking any notice of their conversation. She was completely wrapped up in the misery of her worry over Toby. Which probably meant that the affection Toby obviously felt for 'Tess' was reciprocated.

Why had no one told her that Toby was dating Patrick's sister?

But perhaps someone had, Ellie realised slowly, as she recalled Gareth's enigmatic conversation of yesterday...

Gareth had seemed to be under the impression that Toby, as well as herself, was no better than he was. Because he believed them both to be dating the McGrath brother and sister for the same reasons he had become engaged to Sarah—wealth and ambition? He was totally wrong, of course—on both counts. But—

'Ellie?'

She looked up to find Patrick watching her concernedly. 'Perhaps you should take your sister home now,' she suggested stiffly. 'She looks as if she's had enough for one evening,' she added, with a rueful glance at the younger woman.

'I think we all have.' Patrick nodded grimly. 'I'll call in tomorrow and see how Toby is.'

And continue this conversation, his words seemed to imply. Well, Ellie needed time and space to form her tangled thoughts into some sort of order. She wasn't sure twelve hours was long enough for that!

'Of course,' she accepted smoothly. 'Now, it really is late...'

He gave her another searching look before turning abruptly to his sister. 'It's time to go, Teresa,' he told her briskly. 'I'm sure Ellie will call us if she needs us,' he added as Teresa looked about to protest.

Considering the only telephone number she had for Patrick was his business one, that wouldn't really do a lot of good. Although Toby would have Patrick's mobile number.

'Of course I will,' Ellie assured the younger woman as Teresa gave her a distressed look.

Teresa stood up, very tall and slender. 'I'm really sorry we've had to meet for the first time under these circumstances.' She grimaced.

Yes, it might have been better—it definitely *would* have been better for Ellie!—if the two of them had met before now.

'I don't suppose Toby will feel like this for long, and then perhaps he can bring you here for a drink one evening,' she consoled.

Once he had given Ellie an explanation as to exactly what was going on! Because something *was* going on— Ellie was just too tired at this moment to be able to make sense of it all.

'Maybe the four of us could go out to dinner together at the weekend,' Patrick put in smoothly.

Ellie turned to give him a cool look. 'I think it would be better if we took one step at a time. Besides,' she added firmly as she saw Patrick was about to argue the point, 'I doubt Toby will feel up to eating anything for several days.' It was a valid point—one she could see Patrick would have a problem arguing with.

Thank goodness. She didn't want to tie herself down

to a definite time for seeing Patrick again. Not until she had some answers to a few pertinent questions. Answers that only her brother could give her.

'I'll ring you in the morning, if that's okay,' Teresa McGrath told her a few minutes later as she stood in the doorway preparing to leave.

'Of course,' Ellie accepted, deliberately avoiding looking at Patrick as he stood at his sister's side. 'Brr, it's cold out here.' She shivered from the icy wind blowing around them.

'Yes, it does seem to have turned a little icy,' Patrick murmured softly.

Ellie looked at him sharply as she sensed his double meaning, and those raised dark brows told her she hadn't been mistaken. 'The forecast is for snow,' she returned, deliberately meeting his gaze.

'Luckily it never settles for long in our climate,' he came back, just as deliberately.

Ellie shrugged. 'The forecast is for a long-term cold front.' Two could play at this game. And, until she knew exactly what was going on, a cold front was exactly what she intended showing Patrick McGrath.

He shrugged broad shoulders. 'Ice and snow eventually melt.'

'Eventually,' she echoed evenly.

'Patrick, you can discuss the weather another time; we really should go, and let Ellie get back inside out of this biting wind,' Teresa prompted her brother, obviously having no idea of the double-edged conversation that had been taking place between her brother and Ellie.

To Ellie they had sounded like a couple of secret

agents in a B-rated movie, talking in a code only the two of them understood!

'So we should.' Patrick nodded abruptly before bending his head and lightly brushing Ellie's mouth with his own. 'But I will be back in the morning, Ellie.'

A threat if ever she had heard one, Ellie decided irritably. Well, if, as the doctor had implied, Toby was better by the morning, Patrick would arrive here to find Toby recovering on his own and Ellie at work!

But not before she had spoken to Toby herself...

'I have no idea what you're talking about, sis.' Toby shook his head, his face still very pale as he lay back on the pillows. He had slept well through what had been left of the night, and the nausea seemed to have completely abated, although he had been left with a severe headache.

Join the club, Ellie thought, and gave a deep sigh before sitting on the side of her brother's bed. 'Okay, let's start this off simply: why did you omit to tell me that the Tess you have been dating the last few months is actually Teresa McGrath, Patrick's young sister?'

'I—'

'Please, don't tell me that you didn't think it was important,' Ellie advised him dryly—she sensed he was about to tell her exactly that. 'Because you know very well that it is. That it always was. That it still is,' she concluded pointedly.

'I'm not sure you should be badgering a sick man in this overly strident way.' Toby shook his head before lying back to close his eyes, having just risked consuming a cup of weak tea and a dry piece of toast, both of which seemed—so far—to have stayed down.

'It could get worse, Toby,' she warned him. 'If what I suspect is true, I could actually end up strangling this "sick man"—and so put *everyone* out of their misery!' Her eyes glittered dangerously.

She had had plenty of time to think during a rather sleepless night—and some of the conclusions she had come to had been less than reassuring!

Toby opened one eye to look at her with obvious reluctance. 'Why don't you tell me what you suspect— and then I'll tell you if it's right or not?'

'There's little point in doing that if you aren't going to answer me honestly!' she bit out sharply.

Both Toby's eyes opened innocently wide now. 'My big sister taught me to always tell the truth.'

'Very funny!' Ellie gave a humourless smile, getting up from the side of the bed to move impatiently about the room, her narrowed gaze fixed on her brother the whole time she did so. Finally she gave a heavy sigh. 'Are you and Teresa McGrath serious about each other?'

'Yes,' Toby answered unhesitatingly.

Ellie nodded; it was the answer she had expected. 'Why did Patrick McGrath agree to take me to the company Christmas dinner?'

Her brother frowned his puzzlement at this sudden change of subject. 'I told you—'

'I know what you told me, Toby,' she cut in impatiently. 'But now I want the real reason.'

He shook his head, wincing as it obviously caused him a certain amount of discomfort. 'But that *was* the real reason. Wasn't it?' he added uncertainly as Ellie looked unconvinced.

To Ellie's relief, her brother's answer told her one thing at least; whatever Patrick McGrath had been up to this last couple of weeks, Toby had obviously played no part in it. Which meant it had all been Patrick McGrath's own doing!

She had thought about several of the puzzling remarks Patrick had made this last week, about how much Toby cared for her, how her young brother felt a responsibility towards her, and all those questions about why she didn't have someone else in her life after Gareth—questions that all seemed to lead to the same unpleasant conclusion.

She was even more convinced about it now she knew from Toby that his relationship with Teresa McGrath was a serious one: Patrick was desperately trying to clear the way—clear Ellie out of the way, if only temporarily—in order to secure his young sister's happiness with Toby.

'Toby, why didn't you just tell me about Tess?' she prompted gently.

'But I did tell you about her,' he answered evasively.

Ellie shook her head. 'Only when the two of you were going out. Nothing else about her. Certainly not that the two of you are in love with each other. Why was that?'

Toby drew in a ragged breath. 'I'm sure that was just what you wanted to hear two months ago!' he bit out disgustedly.

Two months ago? When she had suspected that Gareth was seeing someone else behind her back—six weeks ago when she had finally found out the truth and stopped seeing him?

'Oh, Toby!' she cried emotionally, tears misting her eyes now. 'I would be pleased to hear of your happiness at any time. Any time at all!' she repeated with affectionate exasperation.

Instead of which Toby had kept the seriousness of his relationship with Tess a secret in an effort not to hurt Ellie.

Patrick McGrath, it seemed, was the one who had taken it a step further than that!

She sat back on the side of the bed, taking her brother's hand in her own. 'Are you and Tess going to get married?'

Toby gave a start at the directness of the question, his gaze not quite meeting Ellie's searching one. 'Maybe—in time,' he answered evasively.

It was just as she had thought!

Toby and Tess *were* serious about each other, and until six weeks ago it must have looked as if Ellie was in a serious relationship too. But that had all come crashing down around her ears, leaving Toby feeling the responsibility towards her that Patrick had mentioned.

She could see exactly what had happened now—knew that Toby, despite numerous protestations on her part, felt he owed her an emotional debt for taking care of him after their parents died. The fact that her relationship with Gareth had fallen apart under unpleasant circumstances had triggered Toby into putting his own relationship with Teresa McGrath on hold.

Except Patrick obviously had other ideas where his sister's happiness was concerned...

So much for what Ellie had thought—hoped—was developing between the two of them!

'No "maybe", Toby,' she told her brother firmly now, standing up. 'No "in time" either,' she added decisively. 'If you love the girl, and she loves you, then you should ask her to marry you.'

Toby grimaced sheepishly. 'I already have.'

'When?' Ellie prompted sharply.

'Eight weeks ago,' he admitted reluctantly.

Ellie raised dark brows. 'And?'

The grimace turned to a self-conscious smile. 'She said yes.'

Ellie gave an emotional laugh. 'You are an idiot, Toby,' she told him affectionately. 'You've asked her; she's said yes. The next move is to buy her a ring. Then arrange the wedding. I'll be there to dance at it,' she promised. 'Am I making myself clear, Toby?' she teased.

He grinned widely. 'Very.'

'Good.' She nodded her satisfaction. 'I'll just have to learn to cope with having the arrogant Patrick McGrath as some sort of relative.' She frowned.

Toby frowned too. 'But I thought you liked him?'

Too much!

She swallowed hard, straightening determinedly; after all, there was such a thing as pride involved here— her own! 'He's your boss, Toby; of course I had to be pleasant to him. Now that he's going to be your brother-in-law too, I'll just have to continue being pleasant to him. It shouldn't be that difficult; with any luck I'll see very little of him,' she dismissed scathingly, turning to leave the bedroom—and finding herself face to face with a stricken Teresa McGrath!

Ellie looked at the other woman searchingly, knowing by her unhappy expression that she had heard every word of Ellie's last statement…

CHAPTER TEN

'I KNOW I said I was going to telephone, but— I did knock on the kitchen door when I arrived, and when no one answered I let myself in,' Teresa explained awkwardly. 'I hope you don't mind?' she added with a self-conscious grimace.

Mind? Of course Ellie didn't mind the younger woman letting herself in—it was the remarks that Teresa had overheard her making about her brother that Ellie minded! It was one thing to say those things about Patrick to Toby—completely out of defence for her heart—quite another for a member of the McGrath family to have actually heard her saying them...

'Tess...?' Toby called hopefully from inside the bedroom.

Teresa's face visibly brightened. 'He's feeling better?'

'Much,' Ellie assured her warmly. 'I'll go down and make some coffee and leave the two of you to have a chat.' And, hopefully, regain some of her lost composure!

What she really wanted to happen was for the ground to open and swallow her up!

Ellie was shaking by the time she reached the sanctuary of the kitchen, sitting down weakly in one of the kitchen chairs before burying her face in her hands with a groan of self-disgust.

125

All she had wanted to do with those remarks she'd made to Toby was regain some of her damaged pride—and what she had succeeded in doing was probably alienating her future sister-in-law!

How could she explain that to Teresa without giving away the fact that she had fallen completely in love with Patrick?

Her groan of self-disgust turned to one of pain. She had fallen in love with Patrick, and all he had been doing was keeping her romantically occupied long enough to ensure that Toby announced his engagement to Teresa.

She was sure now that was all Patrick had been doing this last week or so. She was the one who had been stupid enough to take his attention seriously. To fall in love with him!

How to extricate herself without Patrick ever being aware of that fact, without completely losing her self-respect? That was the problem!

Out of the frying pan into the fire, once again sprang to mind.

She had thought her infatuation with the fickle Gareth was the worst thing she had ever done in her life, but falling in love with Patrick had to be so much worse. Because he wasn't fickle. The love she felt for him wouldn't be as easily shrugged off as her feelings for Gareth had been.

It was because she truly loved Patrick that she was now able to see her previous feelings for Gareth for exactly what they were!

But this time she would come out of it with at least

her pride intact, Ellie decided as she straightened determinedly. She had to!

The coffee was fresh in the pot, and cups, cream and sugar placed on the kitchen table by the time Teresa came downstairs ten minutes later. The smile on Ellie's face was warm and friendly.

'He's much better, isn't he?' she told Teresa lightly.

'Much.' The younger woman nodded, her expression slightly reserved.

Was that so surprising, when minutes ago Teresa had walked in on a conversation where Ellie had been totally dismissing any need for her to like this woman's brother?

Ellie drew in a ragged breath, deciding it was probably better to jump in at the deep end. 'Look, concerning what you overheard me saying about Patrick earlier—'

'Please,' Teresa cut in with an awkward wave of her hand. 'I know how—how Patrick can be sometimes. He really doesn't mean anything by it. He's just—well, he's used to being in charge.' She grimaced. 'Not that he's in the least arrogant about it.' She hastened to defend her brother. 'Usually he just charms people into submission!'

Ellie knew just how true that was!

She shook her head. 'That was still no reason for me to—to—Well, I'm sorry you overheard my remarks,' she concluded heavily.

Great, Ellie, she instantly chided herself. That was really apologising for being so rude earlier about Teresa's brother!

'Would you like some coffee?' she offered briskly.

Teresa turned to look at the things laid out on the kitchen table before glancing back at Ellie. 'That would be lovely, thank you.' She smiled before sitting down.

Somehow Ellie very much doubted this young woman was any more used to sitting down in a kitchen drinking coffee than Patrick was; it would most likely be served to them in the drawing room, by staff as efficient as George's had been on Saturday evening.

Which posed the disheartening thought: where did Toby fit into all this?

No doubt he and Teresa were in love—that was only too easy to see after last night!—but how would the two of them fare being married to each other when their backgrounds were so different? Toby, as Patrick's assistant, earned a very good wage, but he certainly couldn't keep Teresa in the life to which she was accustomed...

'I'm an interior designer.'

Ellie looked up from pouring the coffee to find Teresa McGrath smiling at her ruefully.

Had her thoughts been so obvious? Or was it just that Teresa had the same ability as Patrick to be able to read her thoughts in particular? After Ellie's earlier remarks about Patrick, that was a disquieting thought.

Ellie shook her head. 'I didn't mean—'

'I know.' The other woman reached out to give Ellie's hand a reassuring squeeze, giving a shake of her head as she chuckled huskily. 'It's only that I've already had all those particular conversations with Toby,' she admitted affectionately. 'He has this terrible dread that people will think he's only interested in me for my money.'

In the same way that Gareth was interested in Sarah!

'I know that he isn't,' Ellie said firmly.

'Of course he isn't.' Teresa's chuckle deepened. 'If you only knew the trouble I had getting Toby to go out with me in the first place…!' She gave a shake of her head, dark hair silky on her shoulders. 'He seemed to think that as Patrick's sister I came under the heading of "untouchable."'

Ellie could well imagine that he had. In the same way she thought that Patrick was unobtainable to her…

'But you obviously managed to charm him into submission?' Ellie returned lightly.

'Not exactly.' Teresa smiled wistfully. 'I told Patrick how I felt about Toby, and he—well, he arranged for me to be around rather a lot—redesigning the offices he has here, and some new ones he's acquired in York.'

York…? Hadn't Patrick said something the other day about Toby being in York with another of his employees? Employee, indeed; his younger sister hardly came under that heading! And, no matter what Teresa might say to the contrary, the role of matchmaker that Patrick had adopted for himself was arrogance personified!

'I see.' Ellie nodded.

'Ellie—may I call you, Ellie?' Teresa paused politely.

'Of course,' she instantly acknowledged.

'Tess,' the other woman invited lightly. 'The family always calls me Teresa, but I prefer friends to call me Tess. And I do hope the two of us are going to be friends, Ellie…?'

For Toby's sake they would have to be. Although Ellie had to admit the McGrath family were very difficult to dislike, having a warm charm that drew like a magnet.

'Of course,' Ellie said again, wondering exactly where this conversation was leading.

Tess nodded, her expression intent now. 'I'm really not some little-rich-girl who saw something she wanted and instantly had her wish granted by an over-indulgent older brother. I love Toby very much, and those differences between us that you were thinking of earlier are totally unimportant.'

'Now,' Ellie felt compelled to point out.

Tess gave a definite shake of her head. 'Ever. Yes, my parents are rich. Yes, my brother is successful, and also rich. But we were both brought up with the belief that we had to make our own way in the world, to earn our own living. We were never going to just sit around waiting to inherit. I know how awful that sounds—' Tess grimaced as Ellie gave a surprised choking noise '—but it's exactly the way a lot of children of wealthy parents behave nowadays.'

'I wouldn't know.' Ellie laughed incredulously.

Once again Tess reached out and squeezed her hand. 'You don't need to—the closeness you and Toby have makes you so much richer than a wealth of money could ever do. I hope you will allow me to become part of that closeness…?' She gave Ellie a wistful look.

How could she resist this charming young woman? How could Toby have resisted her? Obviously he couldn't!

And if Toby and Tess's marriage meant that she would have to see more of Patrick than was comfortable, then she would have to learn to live with that.

Because she had no intention of taking anything away from the love Tess and Toby had found together.

Ellie gave the other woman a warm smile. 'I can't wait to dance at your wedding,' she assured her—and instantly wished she hadn't. That was exactly the remark she had made earlier—before coming out with her insulting remark about Patrick!

A remark Tess remembered all too well if her teasing smile was anything to go by. 'So you said.' She nodded.

Ellie felt the colour warm her cheeks. 'I really wish you hadn't overheard those remarks.' She grimaced.

Tess chuckled, grey eyes warm with humour. 'I wouldn't worry about it, Ellie; I'm sure Patrick has had much worse said to his face!'

'But not from his future—I'm not quite sure what the relationship is between the brother and sister of the bride and groom!' Ellie frowned.

'Neither am I.' Tess grinned. 'But, as I said, don't worry about it; if need be, Patrick is perfectly capable of standing up for himself.'

'And *do* I need to?'

Ellie swung round guiltily at the sound of Patrick's voice behind her, the colour in her cheeks fiery-red now as she saw the narrow-eyed way he was looking at her.

'I heard the two of you talking and decided not to disturb you by knocking on the door.' He shrugged, coming fully into the kitchen to close the door behind him.

Not to disturb her! Patrick disturbed Ellie every time she so much as looked at him! Did no one in this family ever knock?

She stood up abruptly. 'We were just having a cup of coffee. Would you like one?' she invited awkwardly.

'No, thanks,' he dismissed. 'What I would really like—'

'Toby is much better today,' Tess cut in brightly. 'He was asleep earlier, but I'm sure he will want to see you.' She stood up, a slight figure in fitted denims and a thick black sweater.

Patrick's gaze hadn't wavered from Ellie's stricken face. 'You go up; I'll join you in a moment,' he told his sister slowly.

'Oh, but—'

'I'll come upstairs once I've spoken to Ellie,' Patrick told Tess firmly.

Tess gave Ellie a sympathetic glance before leaving the kitchen, both women knowing that when Patrick spoke in that tone of voice there was no point in arguing with him.

The very air seemed to crackle with tension once Ellie and Patrick had been left alone in the kitchen. Ellie busied herself clearing the used cups from the table to put them in the dishwasher. At least that way she didn't have to look at Patrick!

But she was very aware of him standing behind her, of every magnetic inch of him, his dark hair, that aristocratic face, the business suit, white shirt and grey tie that in no way detracted from the powerful body beneath.

Was it always going to be like this? Ellie wondered in dismay. Would she still feel this complete awareness of him, this love for him, in all the years to come?

Years when he would probably marry and have children of his own? She hoped not!

'What's going on, Ellie?'

She drew in a controlling breath before turning to face him, a brightly meaningless smile curving her lips. 'I have no idea what you mean.' She kept her tone deliberately light. 'I like Tess, by the way,' she added—before he could tell her exactly what he had meant by that earlier remark! 'I'm sure she and Toby are going to be very happy together.'

'No doubt.' He nodded uninterestedly, eyes still narrowed as he looked at her searchingly. 'Look, I'm sorry you had to find out about the two of them in the way that you did—'

'Don't be silly, Patrick,' she said derisively. 'In fact, I have no idea what the big secret was in the first place,' she continued hardly, her head back challengingly. 'Toby is twenty-six and I'm twenty-seven; it's well past time one of us moved on.'

She couldn't pretend—to herself, at least—that it wouldn't be a little strange, no longer having Toby's less than peaceful presence around the house—that she wouldn't miss the way he never shut a door behind him, left the bathroom in a shocking mess every morning and more often than not forgot to put his washing in the wash-basket, but she had never been under any illusion that the status quo would continue indefinitely. Her brother was a handsome young man, for goodness' sake; Ellie had never doubted that he would eventually find someone he loved and wanted to marry.

The fact that the woman Toby loved was the sister of the man Ellie had been stupid enough to fall in love

with herself was just something she would have to learn
to live with!

'Ellie—'

'Patrick,' she cut in firmly, blue eyes flashing a warning now. 'I'm aware that you've been acting as—as
some sort of ambassador for Toby and Tess this last
ten days or so, but there really was no need!'

Patrick's mouth tightened now, a nerve pulsing in his
jaw. 'Is that really what you think has been happening
this last week?'

'Of course,' she dismissed scathingly, desperately
hoping that none of the aching love she felt for him
showed in her face or eyes. 'Not that I don't appreciate
the fact that you came to the company dinner with me.
It's nice to finally know that it was actually an attempt
on your part to further family relations.'

Patrick took a step towards her. 'You think that's the
only reason I agreed to accompany you to that dinner?'
he murmured huskily.

Ellie stood her ground, even though every particle of
her cried out for her to move away from her complete
physical awareness of him. 'Of course,' she said again.
'Oh, I'm aware there was also a curiosity on your part
to meet your cousin's fiancée on neutral territory, but
other than that—' she shrugged '—it must have been
quite a chore for you.'

His eyes suddenly glittered silver. 'Exactly what is
going on, Ellie?' he rasped. 'Last night—'

She gave a dismissive laugh. 'Last night I think the
two of us may have got a little carried away by the
roles we've been playing—'

'Last night I didn't think we were playing any roles.
I thought we went out to dinner together for no other

reason than I asked you and you accepted!' Patrick insisted harshly.

And she shouldn't have done! Shouldn't ever have allowed herself the luxury of believing there was any future in a relationship between Patrick and herself. In fact, now that she was aware of the reason behind Patrick's attentions, she knew very well that there wasn't a future in it!

She forced another rueful laugh. 'Then you thought wrong,' she bit out derisively.

He took another step towards her, so close now Ellie could feel the heat of his body against her sensitised skin. 'I didn't imagine your response to me last night.' He spoke gruffly now.

'Or your own to me,' she came back, with a defensive arch of her brows. 'I'm not denying there's an attraction between us—it would be silly to even try. As I said, I think we both got a little carried away with the moment. But it really wouldn't do—in the circumstances,' she continued, determined though Patrick would have interrupted once again, 'for the two of us to indulge in a meaningless affair.'

Patrick's mouth tightened. 'Meaningless...?' he repeated softly. Dangerously, to Ellie's ears.

But what did he expect from her? What did he want from her? She had already had one disastrous relationship this last year—and a relationship with Patrick promised to be even more catastrophic than that had turned out to be!

She shook her head. 'Patrick, I think, for Tess and Toby's sake, that we shouldn't pursue this attraction. After all,' she continued brightly, 'once the two of them are married, the two of us will be related too. Which could prove a little embarrassing if we've been silly enough to indulge in an affair.'

Patrick looked down at her searchingly, the silver gaze seeming to see deep into her soul.

Ellie stood that probing gaze for as long as she could—precisely thirty seconds!—before giving a lightly dismissive laugh. 'Patrick, isn't it already bad enough that I find going to work extremely uncomfortable, in case I have to see or speak to Gareth, without having that same discomfort concerning any necessity to see Toby's future in-laws?' She arched dark brows at him.

'You do care for him after all? Is that it?' Patrick rasped.

Care for Gareth? Absolutely not. Ellie could see him for exactly what he was now—and the knowledge was extremely unpleasant. As well as embarrassing.

But wasn't Patrick's suggestion giving her the perfect let-out for what promised to be an even more unacceptable situation…?

'I'm not sure what I feel any more.' She shrugged, though actually claiming to feel anything but contempt for Gareth was lodging in her throat and staying there. 'About anything,' she added firmly.

'I see.' Patrick's expression became unreadable and he moved away from her.

Did he? Somehow Ellie doubted that very much. But it was better this way, she told herself firmly. For all of them.

Except…the thought of not knowing when she would see Patrick again gave her a feeling of heaviness in her chest. She rushed into awkward speech 'Of course, I understand there's still a problem concerning Sarah's engagement to Gareth. And if there's anything more I can do to help—'

'Like winning Davies back yourself, for example?' Patrick rasped scathingly.

Ellie drew in a sharp breath at what she guessed was a deliberate insult. 'Somehow I don't think so,' she came back evenly; if she lost her temper she might just say things she would be better keeping to herself! Totally damning things, like how could she even *think* of looking at another man when she was desperately in love with Patrick?

'Then I think we've probably imposed on your good nature enough already,' Patrick assured her distantly, every haughty inch the successful businessman he was.

That heaviness in Ellie's chest instantly got heavier. Well, she had wanted to distance herself from this man, to keep her pride intact, and it appeared she had succeeded. Only too well!

But there was nothing more she could say or do now, without backing down from the stand she had made concerning any sort of a relationship between Patrick and herself.

She glanced at her wristwatch. 'If you'll excuse me? I really have to be going now. Toby is so much better, and I promised George I would try to get into the office before lunch,' she explained briskly.

Patrick nodded tersely. 'Teresa will probably want to stay with Toby for most of the day anyway.'

'Of course,' she accepted evenly, reluctant to go even after claiming that she had to. Reluctant to part from Patrick not knowing when she would see him again.

Oh, she knew she would see him again some time, at Toby and Tess's engagement and at their wedding, but they would be occasions crowded with lots of other people, when Patrick wouldn't even need to speak to her if he didn't want to. And after today she accepted he probably wouldn't want to.

Patrick gave her another searching glance before nodding abruptly. 'I'll go up and see Toby now.'

'Yes.' Ellie looked up at him, hoping all the aching longing she felt in her heart for him to hold her, to kiss her, wasn't evident in her eyes.

'I'll say goodbye, then.' He turned sharply on his heels and left the room, his back stiff with disapproval.

Proving to Ellie she was a better actress than she would have given herself credit for!

Not that that helped in the least now that she was left alone with her feelings. Part of her wanted to run after Patrick, to tell him that she had made a mistake, that it hadn't been an act on her part at all, that she wanted him with a desperation that made her shake with longing, in any sort of relationship he cared to choose.

But she did none of those things. Slowly she collected her coat from the closet, able to hear the murmur of voices upstairs—Tess's lightly teasing one, Patrick deep baritone—as she let herself out of the house.

It was beginning already, she realised as she drove numbly through the busy streets, totally immune to the Christmas gaiety in the shops around her. Toby was moving away to become a part of the McGrath family, to be enveloped in their warmth.

Something that, after today, Ellie knew she would never be…

CHAPTER ELEVEN

'It's official, sis,' Toby announced happily as he came into the house Friday evening, throwing his outer coat over a chair as usual. 'Tess and I went out and bought the ring at lunchtime today,' he explained brightly as Ellie turned from cooking their evening meal to give him a questioning look.

She had been expecting it, had thought she had prepared herself for it, but as the sinking feeling increased in her stomach Ellie knew that she hadn't been ready for it at all.

It was all happening so quickly now that the decision had been made. Toby had dined with Thomas and Anne McGrath the previous evening, in order to ask Tess's father's permission for the two of them to marry. In view of Patrick's favourable opinion of Toby Ellie had known there would be no objection to the request, and there hadn't been. The McGraths were absolutely thrilled for their daughter, welcoming Toby into their family as if he were another son. Which, indeed, he would be.

Whereas Ellie still hadn't quite come to terms with the fact that she wasn't so much losing a brother as gaining the McGrath family. One member of the McGrath family in particular!

As she had expected, after their last conversation she had heard nothing from Patrick since they'd parted so abruptly on Wednesday morning. It had been a very long three days!

'The engagement party is going to be at the McGraths' on Christmas Eve,' Toby continued chattily, as he uncorked the bottle of champagne he had brought in with him and took three glasses out of the cupboard.

The engagement party...!

Ellie was filled with a mass of contradictions at the thought of seeing Patrick again. Happiness, because she ached to see him, and despair, because seeing him again would do nothing to alleviate that ache. Besides, he might actually be at the party with someone!

'That's wonderful, Toby.' She pushed aside her own feelings to give her brother a congratulatory hug. 'I'm really pleased for you both,' she added with total sincerity, taking the glass of pink champagne her brother handed her. 'To you and Tess,' she toasted warmly.

Toby took a sip of the champagne before lifting up his own glass. 'To the best Christmas ever,' he returned with feeling.

Ellie took another sip of her drink. Christmas. Despite knowing that it was quickly looming, she hadn't really given it much thought. But now that Toby was engaged to Tess it posed the problem of whether she and Toby would actually even celebrate Christmas together this year.

Christmas always tended to be rather a quiet affair for the two of them anyway, with them having no really close relatives. It promised to be even quieter than usual for Ellie this year!

'We're both invited to spend Christmas with the

McGraths too,' Toby informed her as he turned to pick up the bottle of champagne and replenish their glasses.

Ellie was relieved that her brother was actually turning away as he made this announcement, otherwise he wouldn't have failed to notice the look of complete dismay that she wasn't quick enough to hide.

Christmas with the McGraths. With Patrick.

Much as Ellie longed to see him, to be with him, she hated the thought of being invited to spend Christmas with his family as if she were some sort of charity case!

'It's very nice of them to ask me, Toby,' she said slowly, at the same time shaking her head. 'But I really don't think—'

'If you don't go, sis, then neither do I,' her brother told her with a frown.

Blackmail. Of the emotional kind. But not deviously so; Ellie knew it was only that Toby just wouldn't be happy leaving her here on her own over the Christmas period. Even if she would have preferred it!

She drew in a controlling breath. 'Perhaps for Christmas lunch,' she conceded reluctantly.

'I understand the invitation is for the whole of the Christmas period,' drawled an all too familiar voice from behind her.

Ellie turned sharply to look at Patrick as he stood in the doorway. She really would have to get a lock put on that door, one that came into effect automatically as it closed. In fact several of them, just to be sure!

'We were just drinking a toast to Tess and our engagement.' Toby felt none of the dismay at Patrick's presence that Ellie did, turning to pour some of the bubbly champagne into the third glass he had put out on the work surface.

Three glasses. Which meant Toby had already been aware that the other man was about to join them...

'Cheers.' Patrick toasted the younger man before sipping the champagne. But his gaze, enigmatic over the rim of his glass, remained firmly fixed on Ellie. Who just continued to stare back at him. Toby had obviously known the other man was coming here this evening, but for what reason?

Toby put his empty glass down on the worktop. 'I'm just going upstairs to change; I won't be long.'

'Not exactly subtle, is he?' Patrick drawled ruefully once Toby could be heard going up the stairs two at a time. Patrick was wearing a dark overcoat over the suit he had obviously worn to work, flecks of the gentle snow falling outside had settled on his shoulders and in the darkness of his hair.

Ellie had recovered from some of her shock at Patrick being here, although she was still slightly puzzled as to why he was there at all. 'Does he need to be?' she said guardedly, feeling decidedly casual in her worn denims and sloppy old blue jumper. Patrick gave a shrug. 'I thought I would come and add my—voice to my parents' invitation for you to spend Christmas with all of us.'

His voice? What did that mean, exactly?

He sighed, putting down his glass, the champagne only half drunk. 'Ellie, I realise that you probably don't want to spend Christmas with me, of all people, but if I try to keep my presence down to a minimum will you at least think about it?'

'There's really no need—' She swallowed hard, touched by his offer in spite of the fact that he had it all wrong—he was exactly the person she would love to spend Christmas with! Just not under these circumstances. 'It's very kind of your parents to make the offer,' she said non-committally.

His mouth twisted into a humourless smile. 'They really do want to meet you, Ellie,' he assured her dryly.

She shrugged. 'I'm sure there will be plenty of opportunity for that at the engagement party.'

'Hmm,' Patrick conceded slowly. 'Ellie, about the engagement party…'

She looked up at him sharply, tensing defensively as she guessed by his guarded expression that he was about to say something she wasn't going to like. 'Yes?' she prompted warily.

'Look, would you mind if I took my coat off? It's very warm in here,' he added, even as he shrugged out of the thick outer coat.

Ellie's wariness deepened. Obviously Patrick wasn't in any particular hurry to leave this evening, and dinner was quite obviously cooking away quite happily on top of the stove, a roast chicken was in the oven; the last thing she wanted was to feel compelled by good manners to ask him to join them for dinner. She would probably choke on the chicken!

'You were saying?' she prompted sharply.

Patrick picked up his champagne glass, emptying it in one swallow before looking across at her once more. 'It's going to be a big family party.' He grimaced. 'Brothers, sisters, aunts, uncles—and cousins,' he added pointedly.

Meaning Sarah and Gareth would undoubtedly be there...

'What I'm trying to say, Ellie,' Patrick continued impatiently, 'is do you think you could bury your hostility for one evening and come to the party as my partner?'

'Hostility...?' she echoed faintly, knowing exactly why he had made the invitation, but knowing a sense of inner excitement anyway. If he were inviting her to be his partner on Christmas Eve, then he obviously wasn't taking anyone else...

But did he really think she viewed him with hostility? When it was taking every ounce of will power she possessed not to throw herself into his arms and kiss him until they were both senseless? It was a weakness she had no intention of giving in to!

'I don't feel in the least hostile towards you, Patrick,' she told him crisply, at the same time giving a firm shake of her head. 'I have no idea why you should even think that I do.' Unless...? Tess wouldn't have told her brother of those remarks of Ellie's she had overheard, would she? She knew that the brother and sister were close, but it would be rather silly of her future sister-in-law if she had; it certainly wasn't guaranteed to further the smooth running of inter-family relations.

Patrick's mouth twisted into a self-derisive grimace. 'You were pretty—forceful in expressing your feelings towards me the other morning.'

But surely not to the point where he'd thought she felt hostility towards him?

She frowned. 'I believe I admitted to there being a certain—attraction between us—'

Patrick nodded. 'At the same time as you told me you still have feelings for Davies!' he bit out harshly.

Well…yes, she had hinted at something like that. But what else could she have done, in the circumstances? She still felt battered and bruised from Gareth's totally mercenary betrayal two months ago; wasn't she allowed a little self-pride now?

'Let's leave Gareth out of this,' she suggested abruptly.

'I would be pleased never even to hear the man's name again,' Patrick assured her harshly, his face set in grim lines. 'Unfortunately, that isn't yet possible. He and Sarah will be at the party on Christmas Eve; there's absolutely no doubt about that. In the circumstances, I think it would be—politically correct if you were there as my partner.' His eyes was narrowed on her compellingly.

Politically correct. How Ellie hated the phrase that seemed to have become so popular over the last few years. But in this case she could see how adequately it described the situation they found themselves in.

Her mouth twisted ruefully. 'Not the most gracious invitation I've ever received,' she mocked lightly. 'But if you think it will be of any help, of course I'll come as your partner.' It wasn't a completely unselfish decision; she hadn't particularly relished the idea of being at the party on her own anyway.

The tension seemed to ease out of Patrick's shoulders, his expression relaxing into a self-derisive smile. 'Not the most gracious acceptance of an invitation *I've* ever received either—but I suppose it will have to do,' he added dryly.

Ellie eyed him uncertainly, not quite knowing what to say next. Patrick seemed to be having the same problem, and the air of tension deepened between the two of them, with only the sound of the saucepans boiling on the stove to breach the silence.

Pointedly so, it seemed to Ellie, and if it were anyone else but Patrick she would already have invited them to stay to dinner…

Thankfully Toby chose that moment to come bouncing back into the kitchen, changed now into an Aran sweater and a pair of black denims. But he seemed to lose some of his bounce as he noticed the food cooking.

'Did I forget to mention that Tess and I are going out to dinner at a Chinese restaurant this evening?' He grimaced guiltily.

No, Ellie instantly realised with dismay, Toby hadn't forgotten to mention it at all—she was the one who was so muddle-headed at the moment that she had forgotten he had ever told her!

Going to work had become a nightmare, never knowing whether or not she might accidentally bump into Gareth and so be a victim of more of his veiled threats, and life at home didn't feel much better at the moment—she was either pining because she wasn't seeing Patrick, or a trembling mass of nerves when she did. Not a good inducement to remembering anything that was said to her.

Toby glanced at the bubbling saucepans. 'Perhaps Patrick—'

'Go, Toby,' his boss and future brother-in-law cut in decisively.

'But—'

'If your sister wants to invite me to share her evening meal, then I'm sure she will do so.' Patrick sharply interrupted Toby once again. 'Don't bully her into it, okay?' he added, more gently.

'Okay.' Toby shrugged, as if he couldn't quite see what the problem was but didn't have the time right now to try and find out. 'I'll see you later, then, sis.' He moved to kiss her lightly on the cheek. 'I really am sorry about the meal.' He grimaced again in apology, raising a hand in parting to Patrick before hurrying out of the house.

The silence after his departure was even more tense. Except for those bubbling saucepans, Ellie acknowledged impatiently.

'I had better—'

'Would you—?'

They both began talking at once, both breaking off at the same time too.

'After you,' Ellie invited with a rueful shrug.

'Ladies first,' Patrick insisted.

She didn't want to go first, positive that Patrick had been about to say he had better be leaving, whereas she—through sheer good manners—had been about to invite him to share her evening meal. Something she was sure Patrick was well aware of, which was why he was suggesting she go first! Although why on earth he should want to stay and have dinner with her Ellie had no idea...

She drew in a deep breath. 'I was about to suggest that you join me for dinner. It seems a pity to waste the roast chicken,' she added dismissively.

Patrick continued to look at her for several seconds.

Then his mouth began to twitch, and finally he burst out laughing. He finally sobered enough to speak, eyes sparkling with humour. 'You know, Ellie, you do absolutely nothing for my ego. ''It seems a pity to waste the roast chicken'',' he repeated incredulously, before he began to laugh again. Ellie looked at him frowningly for several seconds, before she also saw the funny side of it. She had sounded distinctly uninterested in his answer, to the point of rudeness. In fact, it was to Patrick's credit that he could laugh about it.

'I'll try again, shall I?' she decided self-derisively. 'Patrick, I would like it very much if you would join me for dinner,' she amended ruefully.

Patrick sobered, but his eyes still laughed as he looked across at her. 'Truthfully?' he prompted sceptically.

'Truthfully,' she echoed huskily.

It might be a mistake on her part, a self-indulgence that she would later regret, but at this moment, after several days of not seeing or hearing from him, she could think of nothing she wanted more than to spend the evening with Patrick. Anything to stop him leaving just yet.

'Then I accept.' He nodded teasingly. 'The roast chicken smells wonderful,' he added. 'Much better than the frozen lasagna I was going to put in the microwave when I got home!'

Ellie moved to take the vegetables off the cooker. 'Do you cater for yourself a lot?' she prompted interestedly, relieved to have an innocuous subject to talk about. Although, no matter how hard she tried, she couldn't quite see Patrick wandering round a super-market buying his weekly groceries!

'Sometimes.' Patrick nodded. 'Is there anything I can do to help?' he offered as she began to serve the meal.

She opened her mouth to refuse, and then thought better of it; a busy Patrick wouldn't be able to sit and watch her as she carved the chicken and served the vegetables. 'There's knives and forks in the drawer un-der the table. Salt and pepper in the cupboard over there,' she accepted lightly.

It was strangely intimate, moving about the kitchen together, with Patrick pouring some more of the cham-pagne to accompany their meal once he had set the kitchen table.

Something else Ellie was sure Patrick didn't nor-mally do. No doubt he usually ate in the dining room in his own home. Well, they didn't have a dining room as such—the house wasn't big enough for such a lux-ury.

'This reminds me of when I was a child,' Patrick told her happily as they sat down to eat their meal. 'My nanny used to serve tea in the nursery when I was home from boarding school,' he explained at Ellie's question-ing look. 'I was less than pleased when I reached the age of twelve and my parents decided I was grown up enough to eat in the formal dining room with them. No fun at all,' he added with a grimace.

Ellie eyed him interestedly. 'Did you enjoy going to boarding school?' Their lives, their upbringing, really had been so different.

'Not particularly,' he dismissed. 'It was just the done thing, I suppose.' He shrugged. 'My father and grandfather went there before me—that sort of thing.' He frowned. 'That particular tradition will end with my own children, I'm afraid; I have no intention of educating them away from home.'

His children. He spoke about having them so easily that he must have given the subject some thought.

Whereas Ellie found the thought of Patrick's children—children he would have with some as yet unnamed other woman—highly displeasing!

'Mmm, Ellie, this food is delicious!' Patrick broke enthusiastically into her disturbing thoughts, having just tasted the roast chicken. 'Where on earth did you learn to cook like this?' he complimented warmly.

Her cheeks became flushed with pleasure at the obvious sincerity of his compliments. 'My mother and my grandmother before me, I suppose,' she returned lightly.

'Thank you, Mother and Grandmother!' He raised his glass in a toast. 'When Toby moves out, can I move in?' he added hopefully.

He was only joking, Ellie knew he was, and yet just the thought of it deepened the blush in her cheeks. What would it be like, living with Patrick all the time? Talking with him, laughing with him, making love with him? Heaven, she decided wistfully.

And just as quickly pushed the thought very firmly from her mind!

'Wouldn't it be easier to just hire yourself a cook?' she suggested derisively.

'It might,' he conceded slowly. 'But, again, not as much fun,' he added with a smile.

Ellie eyed him interestedly. 'You seem to put great store on having fun…?'

Patrick shrugged. 'If you aren't enjoying what you're doing, or who you're with, there doesn't seem to be much point in pursuing it. Does there?' he reasoned huskily.

Did that mean he enjoyed being with her? That he wouldn't be here at all, wouldn't have accepted her invitation, if that weren't the case?

That did seem to be what he was saying. But Ellie knew she must try to keep remembering that Patrick's only interest in her lay in ensuring the happiness of his much younger sister...

Besides, he could just be warning her of how stupid she was to continue to have feelings for Gareth!

How she wished she had never made that claim! It had seemed the only thing to do at the time, had been done completely out of self-defence. But a part of her still wished Patrick hadn't believed the outright lie...

'Not everyone has the luxury of such choices,' she told him hardly.

Patrick gave her a considering look. 'Is working at Delacorte, Delacorte and Delacorte still proving difficult?'

Impossible would probably better describe this last week. In fact, she was seriously thinking of changing her job. Maybe it was time she moved on anyway; she had worked for the same company for almost ten years now. Her home life would be changing radically when Toby and Tess were married and her brother moved away from home, so maybe it was time for her to move on too?

She turned away from Patrick's probing eyes. 'I'm sure you can have no real interest in hearing about my problems,' she dismissed lightly. 'Your food is getting cold,' she reminded him as he would have spoken.

Patrick continued to look at her wordlessly for several long seconds before giving an abrupt inclination of his head. 'So it is.'

The silence that followed as they began to eat— Patrick with obvious enjoyment, Ellie less than enthusiastically—was no more reassuring than his probing questions had been.

She could sense there was still so much Patrick would have liked to say to her, but didn't. And it was the content of what he had left unsaid that troubled her now.

'That was excellent, Ellie,' Patrick told her warmly as he finished his meal.

She stood up to clear the plates; Patrick's was completely empty, her own food was only half eaten. 'I'm afraid we don't usually bother with dessert,' she explained with a grimace.

'I don't eat them, anyway.' He sat back in his chair to look across at her. 'Ellie, do you think—?' He broke off as a knock sounded on the back door, his body tensing, his eyes narrowing coldly as Gareth opened the door and entered the kitchen.

Ellie stared at the other man in total disbelief.

What on earth was Gareth doing here?

CHAPTER TWELVE

GARETH didn't look surprised to see the other man sitting in the kitchen with Ellie, and she quickly realised that was because he must have seen the Mercedes parked outside in the driveway and drawn his own conclusions as to its owner being Patrick.

Which posed the question: why had Gareth come here, knowing that Patrick was already there?

In fact, why had Gareth come here at all?

Not that the why really mattered; one look at the suspicion that now narrowed Patrick's eyes, the disgusted twist on his lips as he slowly stood up, was enough to tell Ellie that he had drawn his own conclusions as to the reason Gareth was here.

Ellie felt her heart plummet at the realisation. It was one thing for her to actually claim—falsely!—to have residual feelings towards Gareth, something else entirely for Gareth to come here and so give Patrick the impression that there might be more to it than that.

Gareth gave a confident smile. 'Patrick,' he greeted him lightly. 'Ellie,' he added warmly.

With Patrick's broodingly disapproving attention all focused on the other man, Ellie felt free to glare her resentment across the kitchen at Gareth. He looked so completely unconcerned at her obvious lack of welcome, so sure of himself, that a part of her just wanted to wipe that slightly mocking smile off his too-handsome face!

He raised mocking brows at her obviously glowering expression. 'I didn't have a chance to see you before you left the office earlier, so I just popped in to wish you a merry Christmas,' he told her with a challenging smile.

A merry—! What on earth was Gareth up to? With Christmas just under a week away, Delacorte, Delacorte and Delacorte had finished for a two-week Christmas holiday at five o'clock this evening. Ellie had decided to give the usual impromptu office party a miss this year, mainly in an effort to avoid seeing Gareth and so completely ruining her day. With his arrival here instead, she realised she might as well have saved herself the bother!

'You could have done that on Christmas Eve.' Patrick was the one to answer the other man harshly. 'My parents are having a party that evening to celebrate my sister Teresa's engagement to Ellie's brother Toby; you and Sarah are obviously invited,' he explained scathingly.

Uncertainty flickered briefly in Gareth's eyes at what was obviously news to him, to be quickly masked as he once again smiled confidently. 'Of course,' he said smoothly. 'But parties can be so impersonal, can't they? And Ellie and I used to be such close friends,' he added pointedly.

Not *that* sort of 'close friends'! Thank goodness. This situation would be even more humiliating if she and Gareth *had* ever been lovers!

'Champagne?' Gareth's gaze narrowed as he noticed

the empty bottle standing on one of the worktops. 'The two of *you* wouldn't have something to celebrate too, would you?' he added, with a conspiratorially knowing look in Ellie's direction.

He really believed that she and Toby were no better than he was, she realised angrily. 'Only Toby and Teresa's engagement,' she snapped coldly.

'Of course,' Gareth acknowledged smoothly.

Too smoothly for Ellie's liking. Why didn't he just go? He had obviously succeeded in what he'd come here to do, namely create a difficult situation for Ellie where Patrick was concerned, so why didn't he just leave? Surely there wasn't more to come…?

'Looks like we're all going to be one big happy family, doesn't it,' Gareth continued pleasantly.

'Two out of the three, perhaps,' Patrick rasped icily. 'And in your case I wouldn't be too sure about the third one either!' He gave the young man a scathing glance.

Gareth looked at Patrick consideringly. 'I get the distinct feeling that you don't particularly like me…' he murmured slowly, at the same time somehow managing to sound like a hurt little boy.

Not that Patrick looked particularly impressed by the latter, Ellie noted ruefully.

What she really wanted now was for both men to just leave. Her nerves were stretched to breaking point after the last hour or so, and Gareth's arrival a few minutes ago was doing nothing to help that situation. In fact, she was starting to feel decidedly ill, not knowing from one moment to the next what Gareth was going to say. Patrick either, for that matter. The two men looked like a pair of gladiators, facing each other across the arena!

'I've never liked men who feel the need to beat up women,' said Patrick disgustedly, hands clenched into fists at his sides as he glared at the other man.

'Beat—? Ellie?' Gareth scowled as he turned to look at her. 'What on earth have you been telling Patrick about me?' He looked slightly less confident now.

'She didn't need to tell me anything,' Patrick assured him coldly. 'I've seen the bruises you inflicted on her the night of the company dinner, and at my aunt and uncle's house the following evening! Next time you feel like threatening someone, come and see me, hmm?' He looked challengingly at the younger man.

As far as Ellie was concerned, this situation was rapidly spiralling out of control; if she didn't put a stop to it right now she had a feeling the two of them might actually start fighting in the middle of her kitchen!

She stepped forward, effectively standing between the two men. 'You've said what you came here to say, Gareth,' she rasped—done what he wanted to do! 'Now I suggest you leave.'

He continued to hold Patrick's gaze for several more long seconds, before giving a slight inclination of his head. 'I'll look forward to seeing you both on Christmas Eve, then.' he shrugged dismissively.

'Don't hold your breath on that one either,' Patrick bit out harshly as the other man left.

Gareth paused to turn in the doorway and look back at them. 'Sarah and I have set our wedding date for Easter weekend,' he drawled mockingly.

'A lot can happen in three and a half months,' Patrick replied calmly.

Gareth gave a derisive grin. 'Who knows? Maybe

you and Ellie will decide to make it a double wedding!' he taunted, his smile one of satisfaction as he saw Ellie's embarrassed dismay at the outrageous suggestion. 'See you,' he added lightly, before letting himself out.

If she had thought the situation tense before Gareth's arrival, Ellie now felt as if she could cut the atmosphere with a knife. Gareth was nothing but an arrogant, troublemaking—

Patrick spoke forcefully into that tense silence. 'I will never—never, *ever*,' he continued with feeling, 'understand what either Sarah or you see in that man!' His mouth twisted with distaste, his eyes still cold with the dislike he didn't even attempt to hide.

As far as Ellie was concerned, she saw Gareth exactly as Patrick did. But she knew she would just be wasting her time to try and tell him that now—could see by the scorn on his face that he wouldn't believe her.

Patrick gave an impatient shake of his head. 'I think I should leave now,' he rasped, taking his overcoat from the back of the chair. 'Do you want me to collect you on Christmas Eve, or will you drive over with Toby?' he added uninterestedly.

What Ellie most wanted to do right now was sit down and have a good cry. And once Patrick had gone that was exactly what she was going to do. In fact, if he didn't soon leave she might just break down and cry in front of him!

'I'll come over with Toby,' she answered quietly, looking down at the tiled floor in preference to Patrick's scornful expression.

'Fine,' he snapped harshly. 'I— Thanks for dinner,' he added, with a slight softening of his tone.

That slight relenting on Patrick's part was her undoing. The tears started to fall hotly down her cheeks, a sob catching in the back of her throat as those tears threatened to choke her.

'Hey,' Patrick murmured gently as he saw those tears, throwing his overcoat back down on the chair to come over stand in front of Ellie. 'He isn't worth it, you know,' he added dismissively, his hand moving to lift her chin and raise her face so that he could look at her.

The tears fell more rapidly because she knew he had misunderstood the reason for them, but also knew she couldn't correct him without losing all the ground she had gained in the last few days; it would be just too humiliating if Patrick were to realise her tears were because she was in love with him, and not Gareth, as he supposed!

'Why is it that nice women seem to fall in love with bastards?' Patrick rasped, with a disgusted shake of his head.

She shrugged. 'Sarah is still very young—'

'I was referring to you!' Patrick cut in harshly, grey eyes glittering coldly.

Ellie blinked, looking up at him uncertainly. 'Am I a nice woman…?'

'Of course you are,' he confirmed impatiently. 'One of the nicest I've ever met,' he assured her hardly. 'In fact, the only thing that's wrong with you is this tendency you have to be in love with the wrong man!'

She gave a choked laugh. 'The only thing…?'

Patrick gave an impatient snort. 'Ridiculous, isn't it?' he dismissed disgustedly. 'But I'll tell you one thing, Ellie,' he snapped decisively. 'After speaking to the man this evening, I'm even more convinced that Gareth Davies marries Sarah over my dead body!'

Ellie looked up at him searchingly. What about her? How would he feel about *her* marrying Gareth? Not that it was even a possibility, but she couldn't help noticing Patrick's omission where she was concerned…

Patrick returned her gaze for several long minutes, finally releasing her chin to take a step away from her. 'Once I've sorted that particular situation out,' he said grimly, pulling on his overcoat, 'I'm going to do everything in my power to ensure *you* don't marry him either!'

She swallowed hard. 'You are?'

'Most definitely,' he assured her determinedly. 'There is absolutely no way that man is going to become part of my family—even by marriage!'

Oh. Patrick's vehemence had nothing to do with her personally. He just wanted to ensure Gareth had nothing to do with the McGrath family.

She grimaced. 'You'll have more trouble convincing Sarah of that than me!'

'We'll see,' he came back enigmatically. 'You're sure you don't want me to pick you up on Christmas Eve?'

'Positive,' she assured him with feeling.

He nodded impatiently. 'I'll see you in a few days, then?'

'Yes,' she confirmed.

Why didn't he just go now? He had made it more

than plain exactly what his interest was in her and her supposed feelings for Gareth, so why didn't he just leave?

Before she started to cry again!

Patrick shook his head frustratedly as he continued looked down at her tear-stained face. 'I could kiss you until you're senseless!' he muttered harshly.

Ellie's eyes widened. 'What would that achieve?' she finally murmured huskily.

'Absolutely nothing,' he accepted impatiently. 'But it would make me feel a whole lot better!'

And it would reduce her to a complete emotional puddle!

She straightened defensively. 'I don't think so, thank you, Patrick,' she told him evenly.

His mouth twisted humourlessly. 'No, neither do I.' He sighed, turning without another word and letting himself out of the house, closing the door gently behind him as he left.

Ellie's shoulders slumped once she was alone.

How much more of this would she have to take? How much more of this could she be expected to take?

CHAPTER THIRTEEN

'Toby, could you zip me up—?' Ellie's words came to an abrupt halt as she entered the sitting room and found not Toby sitting there, as she had expected, but Patrick. She quickly turned fully to face him, clutching the front of her black dress to her chest. 'I thought Toby was in here…' she murmured self-consciously.

When had Patrick arrived? She hadn't heard the doorbell ring. Although, come to think of it, he hadn't rung the doorbell the last few times he'd arrived here unexpectedly either!

'He was, but he had to leave early so that he can be at the house with Teresa when the first guests arrive.' Patrick put down the magazine he had been idly flicking through when Ellie entered the room and stood up. 'You mentioned you have a zip that needs fastening…?' he prompted expectantly, once again suave and sophisticated himself, in a black dinner suit and snowy white shirt.

That had been before she'd realised it was Patrick in the room and not Toby!

'I'll manage,' she frowned. 'Okay, I understand about Toby, but what exactly are you doing here?' If Toby had told her he had to be at the McGraths earlier than arranged then she could quite easily have been ready in time to go with him. She was also quite capable of calling herself a taxi.

Patrick shrugged dismissively. 'I told you. It was decided that Toby should be with Teresa when the first guests arrive—'

'I understood that bit,' Ellie dismissed impatiently. 'I'm just not sure who decided you should be here.' She frowned.

'Does it matter?' Patrick dismissed uninterestedly.

Ellie gave a puzzled shake of her head; this present arrangement really didn't make much sense.

'Turn around and let me do up your zip,' Patrick instructed dryly.

Her hand tightened on the material she held up in front of her. It was yet another new dress, a figure-hugging black tube that seemed to cling to her body magnetically, having neither shoulder straps nor sleeves to keep it in place, leaving her legs long and shapely beneath its knee length.

'I said turn around, Ellie,' he repeated encouragingly.

She wore neither bra nor slip beneath the dress, just a pair of black lace panties, the top of which would be clearly visible if she turned around, as the zip unfastened down the whole length of her spine.

But she could see by Patrick's face that he wasn't about to be fobbed off with an excuse, and sighed heavily as she slowly turned her back towards him.

Nothing happened for several long seconds. Ellie finally looked back over her shoulder to see what the problem was.

Patrick was looking across at her with dark eyes, his expression remotely unreadable, but a nerve pulsing erratically in his tightly clenched jaw.

Ellie turned quickly away again. 'We're going to be

late ourselves if we don't leave soon,' she encouraged huskily, finding she was trembling slightly now, unsure what to make of that look on Patrick's face. In any other man she would have said it was—But Patrick was like no other man she had ever met!

She gave a sensitive start as she felt the light touch of his fingers on the base of her spine, her back stiffening defensively at her unbidden response.

His fingertips slowly travelled the length of her spine, Ellie's skin seeming to burn where he touched, stopping as they reached the sensitised arch between her shoulderblades.

What was he doing? Ellie wondered with a mixture of pleasure and dismay. Pleasure because she liked his touch upon her naked flesh, dismay because the involuntary arching of her body must have told him how much she liked it!

His hands lightly gripped the tops of her shoulders, his thumbtips now moving in a slow caress against her spine and up the silky length of her neck.

Ellie swallowed hard, not sure how much more of this she could stand without turning in his arms and kissing him. Which would nullify everything she had done this last week to put a certain amount of distance between them.

'The zip, Patrick,' she reminded him determinedly, her jaw clenched in tight control now.

'Your skin feels so wonderful to the touch,' he murmured admiringly, seeming not to have heard her. Or, if he had, choosing to ignore her! 'But then I always knew that it would,' he continued gruffly. 'When I saw you in the garden, that day in the summer—'

'Never mind. I'll do the zip up myself!' Ellie said sharply, and she moved abruptly away to turn and glare at him. 'I think it's decidedly ungentlemanly of you to even mention seeing me that day in the garden!' she told him indignantly, eyes glowing deeply blue, her cheeks fiery-red with embarrassment.

Why, oh, why, couldn't Patrick just pretend not to remember seeing her sunbathing topless? It certainly wasn't the first time he had mentioned it!

She gave a low groan in her throat. 'I'll be back down in a few minutes!' She turned and fled the room before Patrick could even think of preventing her.

This was awful. Just awful. And it was only the beginning of the Christmas holiday—a holiday she had finally allowed Toby to persuade her into spending with the McGrath family. What choice did she have when Toby had refused to go if she didn't?

But it was going to be three days of hell if Patrick didn't hold to his promise to keep his distance!

'Ready?' he prompted lightly when she rejoined him downstairs a few minutes later.

Ellie eyed him warily, the black pashmina he had bought for her now brought back out of its box at the back of her wardrobe, draped about the nakedness of her shoulders. 'There's just my case and that bag to take with us,' she answered slowly, nodding in the direction of the two pieces of luggage she had brought down with her and left in the hallway.

Patrick bent down and picked up Ellie's case and the bag containing the impersonal Christmas presents she had bought for the McGrath family, straightening to grin at her. 'This feels almost indiscreet, don't you think?' He quirked dark brows. 'Almost as if the two of us are sneaking off somewhere together for the weekend,' he explained teasingly at her frowning look.

The warmth in her cheeks seemed to be becoming a permanent fixture! 'I really wouldn't know anything about that,' Ellie told him sharply; he probably had more experience with clandestine weekends away than she did. How could he not? Her own experience in that direction was precisely nil! 'I just need to check round the house once more before I leave to make sure I've switched everything off.' It really wouldn't do for the house to burn down in her three-day absence!

Patrick nodded. 'I'll put your things in the car while you do that.'

Ellie breathed more easily once he had left the room, moving slowly to double-check that she had switched off all the Christmas lights. As usual the tree looked starkly gaudy without its glittering lights. Ellie gazed up at it sadly as she accepted that by the time she returned to the house in three days' time Christmas would effectively be over.

It was strange to think—

What on earth was that?

She could hear raised voices outside, and they certainly didn't sound like the happy revellers she had been hearing the last few evenings; these voices sounded distinctly angry.

They also, she realised incredulously, sounded like Patrick and Gareth!

Ellie hurried from the sitting room, through the kitchen and out onto the driveway—arriving just in time to see Patrick punch Gareth on the chin!

She came to an abrupt halt, staring in horrified fascination as Gareth reeled from the blow but remained standing on his feet, only to swing his own fist up and land a punch in Patrick's right eye.

What on earth—?

Patrick also remained standing on his feet, his expression cold with fury as his arm swung once again.

'Patrick!' Ellie cried out in alarm. The sound of her voice caught both men off-guard and they turned to look at her.

But not quickly enough to stop Patrick's fist once again making contact with Gareth's chin. And this time he went down, falling heavily onto the concreted driveway, despite the thin layer of snow that still partially covered it.

'What do you think you're doing?' She hurried over to both men. The air seemed to pulse with their fury as she looked from one to the other of them.

Gareth still sat on the driveway, his hand raised to his bruised chin as he glared up balefully at the other man. Patrick was standing over him, his hands clenched into fists at his sides.

Ellie drew in a ragged breath, still not quite able to believe this was happening. 'I said—'

'Don't try and pretend you aren't as much a part of this as your boyfriend!' Gareth scorned, getting slowly to his feet now, dusting the snow from his denims as he did so.

'Leave Ellie out of it,' Patrick rasped harshly. 'In fact, why don't you just leave?' he added scathingly.

Gareth shook his head, his eyes narrowed with dis-

like as he looked at the older man. 'I'm not going anywhere,' he said slowly.

'No, you're not, are you?' Patrick acknowledged
with satisfaction.

Ellie looked at both men as she felt the tension rising
between them once more; any minute now they were
going to start hitting each other again! 'Would someone
please tell me exactly what is going on?' she demanded
determinedly.

Gareth's mouth twisted derisively. 'Did the two of
you think I would just take this lying down? Because,
if you did, I can assure you—'

'You seemed to be doing a fair imitation of doing
exactly that a few seconds ago!'

Patrick was antagonizing him. Almost as if, Ellie
realised dazedly, he *wanted* the other man to take another swing at him—just so that he had a good excuse
to hit Gareth again!

An angry red tide of colour moved into Gareth's
cheeks. 'You—'

'Will you both stop this?' Ellie ordered impatiently.
'This happens to be my home. And, if nothing else,
you're giving my neighbours something to gossip about
all over Christmas!'

She had already seen the curtains twitching in the
house opposite, the couple that lived there no doubt
alerted to the fight outside by the sound of raised
voices. As she had been...

'If you really must continue this—argument,' she bit
out caustically, 'then at least come inside and do it. But
don't even think about hitting each other again once

we're in the house,' she warned as she turned to go inside. 'I don't want anything of mine broken!'

Anything *else* of hers broken; her heart was already in pieces!

She still had no idea what had caused this flare-up in the ongoing dislike the two men had of each other, but she certainly intended getting an explanation—from one of them!—before the evening was over.

Thankfully the two men followed her into the house, and Ellie looked at them frowningly once they all stood in the sitting room. Gareth's expression was belligerent as he glared at the other man; Patrick's was one of quiet satisfaction. It was that latter expression that roused Ellie's curiosity the most... But it was to Gareth she expressed her next remark.

'What are you doing here?'

Even if she and Patrick left for the party right now they were going to arrive well past the given time of eight o'clock; Gareth, wearing denims and a thick Aran jumper, wasn't even dressed to go out for the evening yet.

'Letting your boyfriend know that as far as I'm concerned this is far from over,' Gareth answered, his jaw clenched.

Ellie really wished he would stop referring to Patrick as her boyfriend...!

Patrick eyed the younger man derisively. 'In what way is it not over, Davies?' he prompted challengingly. 'Unless I'm mistaken, George has given you three months' notice at Delacorte, Delacorte and Delacorte. Notice he has waived in lieu of never having to set eyes on you again! I believe your engagement to Sarah is likewise terminated. Permanently!'

His satisfaction was no longer quiet!

Ellie's eyes widened. When on earth had all this happened? Four days ago Gareth had definitely still been a junior partner with Delacorte, Delacorte and Delacorte, and his engagement to Sarah had seemed unshakeable too...

But there was no mistaking the fact that Gareth certainly wasn't wearing the right sort of clothes to attend Toby and Teresa's engagement party this evening...

Gareth's mouth twisted contemptuously. 'You both think you've been so clever, don't you? Did you really think I would just go quietly?' he scorned, shaking his head. 'For one thing, George has no reason to dismiss me other than a personal one, which in a court of law—'

'He doesn't need one,' Patrick cut in confidently. 'I'm surprised at you, Davies; you really should have read the small print on your contract of employment,' he taunted. 'It clearly states that three months' notice can be given, on either side, without prejudice, during your first year of employment. You've been with Delacorte, Delacorte and Delacorte how long now...?' he prompted pointedly.

Ellie could see by Gareth's stunned expression that he really *hadn't* been aware of that particular clause in his contract of employment.

'As for your engagement to Sarah,' Patrick continued derisively, 'I believe it's a woman's prerogative to change her mind?'

Gareth's expression was ugly now. 'With a lot of help from her interfering family!' he rasped.

'Maybe.' Patrick shrugged unconcernedly. 'It doesn't change the fact that Sarah *has* changed her mind.'

The relief Ellie felt on hearing this completely dispelled any doubts she might have had about having the two men fighting in her driveway in full view of her neighbours. She didn't care how Patrick had achieved it. All that mattered was that Sarah had escaped Gareth's mercenary clutches!

But Gareth's feelings about the broken engagement were obviously different, and as he turned on the other man. 'You self-satisfied—'

'I said there would be no fighting in here, Gareth!' Ellie told him firmly as he took a threatening step towards Patrick.

Gareth turned a furious blue gaze on her. 'As for you—'

'I believe I told you to leave Ellie out of this,' Patrick reminded him in a dangerously soft voice.

The younger man's hands were clenched into fists at his sides. 'From what I can tell she's already in this up to her pretty neck!' Gareth rasped, his gaze raking over her scathingly. 'I hope you realise he'll never marry you, Ellie,' he taunted with hard derision. 'The McGraths and the Delacortes believe themselves far too good for the likes of you and me!' he added bitterly.

Ellie swallowed hard as she felt the colour drain from her cheeks, at the same time desperately hoping that neither of these men had seen just how much Gareth's last remark had hurt her. Of course Patrick would never consider marrying her; it wasn't even a possibility. But she could well have done without having that fact thrown in her face. Especially by a man she so utterly despised.

'How do you work that one out, Davies?' Patrick was the one to answer the other man scornfully. 'Tonight we're celebrating the engagement of Ellie's brother and my sister!'

'An engagement isn't a marriage,' the other man came back derisively, before turning to look pityingly at Ellie once again. 'An affair even less so,' he warned her mockingly.

'Get out,' she told Gareth shakily.

'Oh, I'm going,' he assured her, raising a hand to his bruised jaw. 'But I'll be back,' he added softly.

'In that case, make sure it's me you come back at; come near Ellie again and you'll find out how it feels to be on the wrong side in a court of law,' Patrick warned him coldly. 'Which I don't think would do a great deal for the furtherance of your legal career,' he added challengingly.

Gareth's cheeks flushed angrily. 'Don't threaten me, McGrath,' he rasped.

But his tone held little conviction, Ellie noted; the possibility of ending up as the defendant in a court of law rather than the prosecuting lawyer—for what charge was anybody's guess!—obviously didn't appeal to Gareth one little bit, if the suddenly wary expression on his face was anything to go by.

A fact which, by his next comment, Patrick had obviously noticed too. 'Davies, I think the best thing for everyone is for you to just disappear back down whatever sewer you came out of,' he advised dismissively.

The ugly flush deepened in Gareth's cheeks as he turned to direct his next insult at Ellie. 'Give me a call when he's finished with you—you never know; I just might be interested in continuing where we left off!' With one last contemptuous glare in Patrick's direction he exited the room, the back door slamming noisily behind him seconds later as he left the house.

The awkward silence that followed his abrupt exit made Ellie squirm...!

What must Patrick think of her now?

CHAPTER FOURTEEN

'Is IT my imagination, or does Patrick have what looks to be the beginnings of a very black eye?'

Ellie turned sharply at the sound of Sarah's voice. She had been looking at Patrick herself until that moment, as he stood across the room talking with one of his numerous aunts; Ellie had quickly learnt, on their arrival at the party an hour ago, that the McGrath family was a large one, and Patrick a particular favourite with all of them.

She looked up warily at Sarah now. 'Sorry?' she prompted guardedly.

Sarah's smile was a little strained, but other than that she looked as beautiful as ever in a short, figure-hugging red dress. 'Don't look so apprehensive about seeing me, please, Ellie.' She reached out and gave Ellie's arm a reassuring squeeze. 'After all, I believe we've both recently made a very lucky escape?' She quirked self-derisive brows.

Ellie grimaced. The problem was, she still didn't really have any idea what had happened to end Sarah's engagement to Gareth. It had been well after eight o'clock by the time Gareth made his furious exit from her house, and, other than pausing briefly to collect an ice-pack to place on Patrick's rapidly bruising eye, the two of them had come straight to the engagement party. Although, as Sarah had so astutely noticed, the ice pack

173

didn't seem to have worked too well; Patrick definitely had the start of bruising that would be a very black eye!

'Yes,' she confirmed huskily. 'And, yes, Patrick does have a black eye.' She grimaced. In fact, by tomorrow, it would probably rival the bruises on her arm for all the colours of the rainbow! Gareth, when thwarted, really was a very violent man.

Sarah frowned across at her cousin. 'I suppose it's too much to hope that Gareth had nothing to do with it?'

Ellie sighed. 'I'm afraid it is.' She nodded.

Sarah shook her head, her gaze troubled as she looked at Ellie. 'How could two such accomplished women as us ever have been so stupid where Gareth was concerned?' she muttered disgustedly.

Ellie couldn't help it; she laughed. And, after several stunned seconds, so did Sarah, the two women falling weakly into each others arms as they laughed together.

'"Two such accomplished women as us"?' Ellie repeated as she finally straightened, aware that their laughter had a slightly hysterical edge to it. Also aware that they were attracting a certain amount of attention.

Sarah took two glasses of champagne from a passing waiter, handing one to Ellie. 'To liberation,' she toasted determinedly.

Whatever had happened to cause Sarah to break her engagement, Ellie was pleased to see that on the surface at least Sarah seemed to be recovering rapidly from the disappointment.

She couldn't help admiring the younger woman; it couldn't have been easy for Sarah to come here this evening. The announcement of her own engagement had only been made days ago—an engagement that had now been abruptly terminated.

'Liberation,' Ellie echoed just as firmly, before taking a sip of the bubbly wine. 'Sarah—'

'It really is all right, Ellie,' Sarah assured her with a smile that didn't quite light up her eyes. 'I'm still a little shell-shocked, obviously, but I'll get over it. How about you?'

Ellie shuddered. 'I got over Gareth months ago!' Only to fall irrevocably in love with Patrick!

'Hmm,' Sarah nodded ruefully. 'I believe I was mostly to blame for what happened to you—for—for—'

'Gareth dumping me?' Ellie finished dismissively. 'Yes, you were—thank goodness.' She gave a shake of her head. 'Gareth didn't—he didn't hurt you in any way, did he?' She frowned her concern.

The younger woman gave a humourless laugh. 'My pride,' she grimaced. 'I can't believe now that I ever thought he was so wonderful! Boy, did his true colours come out when I told him about the designs I had sent Jacques, and that I would like to delay the wedding for a while so that I could return to Paris for six months.' She gave a disgusted shake of her head. 'He seemed to think that you and Patrick had had a hand in it somewhere, which I found extremely puzzling to start with. But he kept going on about "a woman scorned"—that you would say and do anything to try and break the two of us up. The penny finally dropped, and I realised that you and he must have been dating until I came back to England a couple of months ago. Why didn't you tell me, Ellie?' she chided gently. 'In your shoes,

I would have wanted to scratch the other woman's eyes out!'

Ellie gave a shake of her head. 'I knew what Gareth was really like by then, and if anything I wanted to try and warn you off him.'

Sarah took a sip of her champagne. 'So why didn't you?' she prompted curiously.

She glanced across to where Patrick was now in conversation with his parents. 'Patrick convinced me that you probably wouldn't believe me.' She grimaced.

'He did?' Sarah looked across at her cousin, blonde brows raised speculatively.

'Mmm,' Ellie nodded. 'So what did happen to—to change your mind about Gareth?'

Sarah gave another grimace. 'Well, I wasn't too happy with the things he said about you and Patrick. As you've probably realized, Patrick is a particular favourite with me, and, although we haven't seen a lot of each other this last year, you and I have been friends for a long time too,' she said. 'The things he said about the two of you were bad enough, but it was when he started insulting my father that I took exception!'

Ellie looked up at her disbelievingly. 'Your father?' Was Gareth completely stupid? Or, more to the point, so arrogant he didn't realise when he was stepping on dangerous ground?

Sarah gave a rueful smile. 'Never, ever insult the girl's father ought to be the first rule any man should learn about courtship!' She gave a self-conscious shake of her head. 'Ellie, I adore my father—'

'It's reciprocated,' she confirmed affectionately.

Sarah nodded. 'Gareth was obviously too stupid to

realise that,' she dismissed hardly. 'And all because he couldn't have his own way about the wedding!'

'You do realize why now, though?' Ellie prompted cautiously.

'Oh, yes,' Sarah acknowledged self-disgustedly. 'Don't worry, Ellie, my eyes are wide open now where Gareth Davies is concerned!'

'I'm very glad to hear it!' Patrick announced with satisfaction as he joined the two of them.

Ellie gave a nervous start, having been completely unaware of his approach. She looked up at him as he came to stand beside her. Yes, his eye was now turning a rather nice shade of purple.

He returned her gaze unblinkingly. 'How about you, Ellie, are your eyes wide open now too?'

About Gareth? Or did he mean something else…?

'I think we should put some raw steak on that eye,' she answered instead.

Sarah winced as she looked at him. 'Does it hurt?'

Patrick shrugged. 'Not as much as Davies's jaw, I expect,' he said with satisfaction.

His young cousin laughed. 'I hope you gave him a punch from me!'

Patrick grimaced. 'I think he may have a little trouble eating for a few days.'

'Good,' Sarah bit out firmly, before turning to Ellie and lightly squeezing her arm. 'I'm really glad the two of us have had this little chat together. But now, if the two of you will excuse me, I think I'll go over and tell my father how wonderful he is!' She gave a glowing smile.

'I'm sure Uncle George will be pleased about that,' Patrick encouraged huskily.

'I hope so.' Sarah laughed softly. 'I'll see you both later.'

There was a silence after Sarah had left to weave her way through the crowd to where her father stood talking to Patrick's parents. Although it wasn't a particularly awkward silence. More, Ellie decided, an expectant one…

'I'm sure there will be something in the fridge in the kitchen that I can put on this eye.' Patrick finally spoke huskily at Ellie's side. 'Care to come with me?'

Why not? The engagement had already been announced, and Toby and Teresa were the centre of attention as everyone stood around laughing and talking. The buffet supper was to be served in an hour's time.

'If you think I can be of help,' Ellie agreed.

Patrick gave her a considering look. 'I'm not really sure you're ready to hear what I'm thinking right now, Ellie.'

She looked up at him searchingly. Could she be mistaken, or had there been a wistful note in his voice just now?

She drew in a deep breath, swallowing hard before speaking. 'Patrick, exactly why did you come to my house this evening?'

He shrugged. 'Because I knew, once I was made aware that Sarah had finished things with Davies, that his next move would be to pay you a call.'

She had already worked that part out for herself! 'And?' she prompted huskily.

'Ellie, do you think we could get out of this crush of

people before I answer that?' he asked impatiently, not waiting for her answer but taking a firm hold of her arm to guide her out of the sitting room, through the hallway—beautifully decorated with boughs of holly and red ribbons—into the kitchen at the back of the house.

As Ellie had expected, the McGrath house was equally as grand as the Delacortes'. The huge kitchen was of mellow oak, with a dozen or more copper saucepans hanging from the rack over the work table in the centre of the room, and a green Aga giving the room its warmth.

Patrick grimaced as he saw there were several members of the household staff bustling around the room, preparing the last of the buffet supper. 'Is there nowhere in this house that we can be alone?'

He scowled his displeasure, whereas Ellie felt heartened by the fact that he wanted to talk to her alone!

'They've almost finished, Patrick,' she soothed lightly, giving one of the maids a sympathetic look as she glanced at them curiously. 'Why don't you see if there's any red meat in the fridge we can put on your eye?'

'Damn my eye!' he dismissed impatiently, grasping hold of her hand to pull her out of the room, back down the corridor and into another room off the hallway. 'Ah,' he said with satisfaction as he saw this room— probably his father's study, judging by the desk and book-lined walls—was empty. He closed the door behind them decisively, and the two of them were instantly surrounded by blessed silence.

Ellie eyed Patrick quizzically for several seconds. 'And?' she finally reminded him huskily.

He grimaced. 'I came over to your house this evening because—because—'

'Yes?' Ellie prompted breathlessly, a cautious excitement starting to build up inside her.

Patrick drew in a harsh breath. 'Because if Davies had come over to see you with the intention of hurting you in any way I intended stopping him,' he bit out determinedly, grimacing as Ellie continued to look at him wordlessly. 'Because if he'd come to see you with any intention of persuading you into taking him back into your life I intended stopping him from doing that too! As I told you I would,' he concluded impatiently, grey gaze challenging.

It was a challenge Ellie had no intention of answering. A hope was welling up inside her now, so intense that she could barely breathe, let alone speak.

'Ellie, don't you want to know the reason why?' Patrick finally asked harshly.

She thought—hoped!—she knew the reason why. But she wasn't sure...

'Ellie, will you please say something?' Patrick demanded at her continued silence.

Was there a time and place to lose that pride she had been trying so desperately to hang on to? And was this the time and place?

'For days now I've had trouble stopping you from saying things I *didn't* want to hear, and now I want you to say something—anything—you've been struck dumb!' he muttered frustratedly. 'Ellie, I'm tired of waiting for you to come to your senses. And I swear, if you don't soon say something I'm going to pick up my father's favourite whisky decanter and throw it out the window!'

Once again Ellie couldn't help it; she laughed. 'And what good will that do?' she finally sobered enough to ask. 'Except break a perfectly beautiful decanter and let in all the frosty air from outside!'

'It's preferable to the overwhelming urge I have right now to wring your beautiful neck!' Patrick rasped.

Tears filled her eyes now. But they were tears of joy, not sadness. 'Patrick—Oh, Patrick—' It was no good. She couldn't talk through the emotion that choked her.

His expression softened slightly before he moved to wrap her fiercely in his arms. 'Ellie, I can't stand this any more! I love you,' he told her forcefully. 'I've loved you for so long, it seems—since the moment I called at your house in the summer, walked round to the garden and saw you lying there—'

'Patrick!' she protested as once again he reminded her of the embarrassment of being caught out bathing topless. Only to become very still in his arms as his words fully penetrated her heightened emotions. 'I— Patrick, did you just say that you love me?' She stared up at him unbelievingly.

He nodded, his mouth twisting into a smile as he looked down at her. 'For all the good it's done me!' He sighed heavily. 'I was always under the impression that falling in love would be a joyful experience—not make me feel as if I had been pole-axed!' he muttered disgustedly. 'Of course it might have helped if the woman I fell in love with felt the same way about me, but as it is—'

'Oh, but she does,' Ellie cut in eagerly, her hands tightly gripping his arms as she gazed up at him, a feeling of such joy welling up inside her she felt as if she might burst. 'I mean—I do,' she corrected awkwardly.

'You do?' Patrick repeated slowly.

She smiled shyly. 'I do,' she confirmed huskily.

He looked at her uncertainly now. 'But the other night, when Davies left so abruptly, you were crying—'

'Because of the way he'd kept belittling me in front of you—making me sound like—! Patrick, I only told you that I still cared about Gareth to try and cover up the fact that I've fallen in love with you,' she added softly.

'And all this time I've been going quietly insane with jealousy!' he groaned. 'Ellie, do you love me enough to walk down the aisle to me with Toby at your side, to stand next to me in front of a vicar, with all our family and friends looking on and wishing us well as we make our vows to each other?' he said slowly.

Was Patrick asking her to marry him? It certainly sounded like it!

'A "meaningless affair",' he muttered disgustedly, before Ellie could answer him. 'As if that's what I ever wanted from you!' He moved back slightly, holding her away from him as he looked down at her. 'I love you, Elizabeth Fairfax. Will you marry me?'

She swallowed the tears, gazing up at him adoringly. 'Oh, yes!' she answered joyfully.

His eyes widened. 'You will...?'

'I will,' she confirmed emotionally.

He closed his eyes briefly, as if he couldn't quite

believe what he had just heard, and then those eyes gleamed silver as he looked at her once again.

'Darling Patrick.' Ellie raised a hand to gently touch the hardness of his cheek, making no effort to hide her love for him now, knowing by the sudden glow of emotion in his eyes how deeply affected he was just by the touch of her hand. 'Why did you never tell me before—show me that you felt this way about me?' she choked.

'Because when I first began to feel this way about you I very quickly learnt from Toby that you were involved with Gareth Davies, and had been for several months.' He scowled at the memory. 'Not the best news I'd ever had in my life. Patience is not exactly one of my virtues,' he admitted self-derisively, 'but I decided, when it came to you, I didn't have much choice in the matter; no one else would do for me once I had seen you.'

Ellie could hardly believe all this; Patrick had been in love with her for months and she had had no idea!

She frowned. 'But I stopped seeing Gareth two months ago...'

Patrick nodded. 'And I'm sure having me turn up on the doorstep with every intention of sweeping you off your feet would have been exactly what you wanted immediately after that!' he drawled. 'No, I decided I had to leave things for a while, give you a chance to get over—whatever.' He scowled again, just at the thought of her ever having felt anything for Gareth. 'It was all I could do to stop myself getting up and hugging Toby when he came to me three weeks ago and asked if I would mind taking you to the Delacorte dinner!' he revealed happily. 'Mind?' he repeated mockingly. 'I ''minded'' so much I followed Toby home that very evening just for the opportunity of seeing you again!'

Ellie winced as she remembered that evening. 'At which time I said thanks, but no thanks. I'm so sorry, Patrick.' She groaned in remorse. 'I really had no idea.'

No idea that he had loved her for months. No idea that all this time she had been fighting her feelings for him he had already been in love with her.

'It doesn't matter.' He shook his head. 'None of that matters if you really do love me.' He still looked as if he couldn't quite believe it was true.

And no wonder, when she had been pushing him away at every opportunity, to the point where she had even claimed to still have feelings for Gareth!

'Patrick, I thought—' She gave a heavy sigh. 'When I found out about Toby and Teresa that evening we came back from dinner, I thought you had just been taking me out to give them enough of a breathing space to convince Toby into announcing their engagement. You were so—definite about Toby's sense of loyalty, how fond he was of me, how he felt a responsibility—'

'But not to the point of my deceiving you in that way!' he instantly protested. 'Was that the reason you suddenly cooled towards me? Another reason you told me that you were still in love with Davies?' he added hopefully.

'Yes,' she confirmed with a grimace.

'Ellie, by saying those things about Toby I was just letting you know that, when the time came I'd fully approve of Toby as my sister's future husband, listing the qualities he had that made me feel that way. I never—' Patrick broke off, shaking his head. 'Ellie, I only ever went out with you because I'm so deeply in love with you I can't think straight half the time! Do you believe me?' He looked down at her intently.

She gave a tremulous smile. 'As long as you tell me that the children you're going to educate from home will be my children too!'

The tension left him and he gathered her close in his arms. 'They were never going to be anyone else's,' he assured her huskily.

Her arms tightened about his waist as she told him fiercely, 'I love you so much, Patrick.'

'I love you, Ellie.' His words were muffled in the dark thickness of her hair. 'Would you mind very much if we were married as soon as it can be arranged? I really don't think I can wait too much longer to make you completely mine,' he owned longingly.

She didn't want to wait either—wanted to be Patrick's wife as much as he wanted to be her husband.

'I don't mind at all,' she assured him huskily. 'But perhaps we should wait until you no longer have a black eye; at the moment you most resemble a panda bear!' she added teasingly.

'As long as you become *Mrs* Panda Bear, who the hell cares?' he dismissed happily.

Certainly not Ellie!

How different everything was now from her unhappiness when the evening had begun. She loved Patrick. He loved her in return. They were going to be married. To each other.

Toby was right; this was going to be the best Christmas ever.

And it was only the start of what promised to be the best years of her life.

Of their life together.

Patrick and Ellie.

How wonderful that sounded!

THE DOCTOR'S
CHRISTMAS BRIDE

BY
SARAH MORGAN

Sarah Morgan trained as a nurse and has since worked in a variety of health-related jobs. Married to a gorgeous businessman, who still makes her knees knock, she spends most of her time trying to keep up with their two little boys, but manages to sneak off occasionally to indulge her passion for writing romance. Sarah loves outdoor life and is an enthusiastic skier and walker. Whatever she is doing, her head is full of new characters and she is addicted to happy endings.

PROLOGUE

'MUMMY, I've written my letter to Santa.'

Bryony tucked the duvet round her daughter and clicked on the pink bedside light. A warm glow spread across the room, illuminating a small mountain of soft toys and dressing-up clothes. 'Sweetheart, it's only just November. Don't you think it's a little early to be writing to Santa?'

'All the decorations are in the shops. I saw them with Grandma.'

Bryony picked up a fairy outfit that had been abandoned in a heap on the floor. 'Shops are different, Lizzie.' She slipped the dress onto a hanger and put it safely in the wardrobe. 'They always start selling things early. It's still ages until Christmas.'

'But I know what I want, so I thought I might as well write to him now.' Lizzie reached for the stuffed mermaid that she always slept with. 'And anyway, this present is special so he might need some time to find exactly the right one.'

'Special?' Bryony gave a groan and picked up the book they'd been reading all week. 'Go on.' Her tone was indulgent. 'Hit me with it, Lizzie. What is it this time—a horse?' She toed off her shoes and curled up on the end of her daughter's bed with a smile. This was the best time of the day. Just the two of them, and Lizzie all warm and cuddly in her pink pyjamas. She smelt of shampoo and innocence, and when she

5

was tucked up in bed she seemed younger somehow, less like a seven-year-old who was growing up too fast.

'Not a horse.' Lizzie snuggled down, her blonde curls framing her pretty face. 'Bigger.'

'Bigger than a *horse*?' Bryony's eyes twinkled. 'You're scaring me, Lizzie. What if Santa can't find this special present?'

'He will.' Lizzie spoke with the conviction of youth. 'You said that Santa always gives you what you ask for if you're good.'

'Ah—did I say that?' Bryony took a deep breath and made a mental note to concentrate more when she answered her daughter's questions in future. 'Well, it does depend on what you ask for,' she hedged, and Lizzie's face fell.

'You said he *always* gives you what you ask for if you're good.'

'Well, he certainly does his best,' Bryony said finally, compromising slightly and hoping that the request wasn't going to be too outlandish. Her doctor's salary was generous, but she was a single mother and she had to watch her expenditures. 'Do you want to show me this letter?'

'I've sent it already.'

'You've sent it?' Bryony looked at her daughter in surprise. 'Where did you post it?'

'I went into the post office with Grandma and they said that if I posted it there it would go all the way to Santa in Lapland.'

'Oh.' Bryony smiled weakly, her heart sinking. 'So it's gone, then.'

Which meant that there would be no chance to talk

Lizzie out of whatever it was that she'd chosen that was obviously going to cost a fortune and be impossible to find in the wilds of the Lake District.

Bryony sensed a trip to London coming on. Unless the internet could oblige.

'Uh-huh.' Lizzie nodded. 'And he's got until Christmas to sort it out.'

'Right. Are you going to give me a clue?'

'You'll like it, I know you will.'

'Is it something messy?'

'Nope.'

'Something pink?' Everything in her daughter's life was pink so it was a fairly safe bet that whatever was top of her Christmas list would be pink.

Lizzie shook her head and her eyes shone. 'Not pink.'

Not pink?

Feeling distinctly uneasy, Bryony hoped that her mother had managed to sneak a look at the letter before it was 'posted' otherwise none of them were going to have the first clue what Lizzie wanted for Christmas.

'I'd really like to know, sweetheart,' she said casually, flipping through the pages of the book until she found where they'd left off the night before. She wondered whether the post office had binned the letter. At this rate she was going to have to go and ask for it back.

'OK. I'll tell you, because it's sort of for you, too.'

Bryony held her breath, hoping desperately that it wasn't a pet. Her life was so frantic she absolutely didn't have time to care for an animal on top of everything else. A full-time job and single parenthood was the most she could manage and sometimes she struggled with that.

A pet would be the final straw.

But then she looked at Lizzie's sweet face and felt totally overwhelmed by love. More than anything she wanted her daughter to be happy and if that meant cleaning out a rabbit…

'Whatever it is you want,' Bryony said softly, reaching out and stroking her daughter's silken curls with a gentle hand, 'I'm sure Santa will get it for you. You're such a good girl and I love you.'

'I love you, too, Mummy.' Lizzie reached up and hugged her and Bryony felt a lump building in her throat.

'OK.' She extracted herself and gave her daughter a bright smile. 'So, what is it you want for Christmas?'

Lizzie lay back on the pillow, a contented smile spreading across her face. 'A daddy,' she breathed happily. 'For Christmas this year, I really, *really* want a daddy. And I *know* that Santa is going to bring me one.'

CHAPTER ONE

'Six-month-old baby coming in with breathing difficulties.' Bryony replaced the phone that connected the accident and emergency department direct to Ambulance Control and turned to the A and E sister. 'That's the third one today, Nicky.'

'Welcome to A and E in November.' The other woman pulled a face and slipped her pen back in her pocket. 'One respiratory virus after another. Wait until the weather gets really cold. Then everyone falls over on the ice. Last year we had forty-two wrist fractures in one day.'

Bryony laughed. 'Truly?'

'Truly. And you wouldn't laugh if you'd been working here then,' Nicky said dryly as they walked towards the ambulance bay together. 'It was unbelievable. I wanted to go out with a loudhailer and tell everyone to stay at home.'

As she finished speaking they heard the shriek of an ambulance siren, and seconds later the doors to the department crashed open and the paramedics hurried in with the baby.

'Take her straight into Resus,' Bryony ordered, taking one look at the baby and deciding that she was going to need help on this one. 'What's the story?'

'She's had a cold and a runny nose for a couple of days,' the paramedic told her. 'Temperature going up and down, and then all of a sudden she stopped taking

9

any fluids and tonight the mother said she stopped breathing. Mother came with us in the ambulance—she's giving the baby's details to Reception.'

'Did she call the GP?'

'Yes, but he advised her to call 999.'

'Right.' Bryony glanced at Nicky. 'Let's get her undressed so that I can examine her properly. I want her on a cardiac monitor and a pulse oximeter—I need to check her oxygen saturation.'

'She's breathing very fast,' Nicky murmured as she undid the poppers on the baby's sleepsuit. 'Poor little mite, she's really struggling. I suppose we ought to call Jack—even though calling him will massage his ego.'

Bryony looked at the baby, saw the bluish tinge around her lips and heard the faint grunting sound as she breathed.

'Call him,' she said firmly. 'This baby is sick.'

Very sick.

She didn't care if they massaged Jack's ego. She trusted his opinion more than anyone else's and not just because he was the consultant and she was a casualty officer with only four months' A and E experience behind her. Jack Rothwell was an incredibly talented doctor.

Nicky finished undressing the baby and then picked up the phone on the wall and dialled, leaving Bryony to carry out her examination. She watched the baby breathing for a moment and then placed her stethoscope in her ears, strands of blonde hair falling forward as she bent and listened to the child's chest.

When she finally unhooked the stethoscope from her ears, Jack was standing opposite, looking at her with that lazy, half-bored expression in his blue eyes that always drove women crazy.

And she was no exception.

She'd known him for twenty-two years and still her knees went weak when he walked into a room. She'd often tried to work out why. Was it the sexy smile? The wicked blue eyes that crinkled at the corners when he smiled? The glossy dark hair? The broad shoulders? Or was it his sense of humour, which had her smiling almost all the time? Eventually she'd come to the conclusion that it was everything. The whole drop-dead-gorgeous, confident masculine package that was Jack Rothwell.

When she'd started working in A and E in the summer, she'd been worried about how it would feel to work with a man she'd known all her life. She was worried that finally working together would feel odd. But it didn't.

She'd fast discovered that Jack at work was the same as Jack not at work. Clever, confident and wickedly sexy.

'So, Blondie,' his deep masculine tones were loaded with humour. 'You need some help?'

Blondie…

Bryony grinned. He'd called her 'Blondie' when she'd been five years old, and now she was twenty-seven he was still calling her 'Blondie'. She'd even had a brush with being brunette at one point in her teens but it had made no difference. He'd still called her 'Blondie'. It was one of the things she loved about their friendship. The way he teased her. It made her feel special. And, anyway, it meant that she could tease him back.

'This baby's sick.'

'Which is presumably why she's in hospital,' Jack drawled, leaning across and reaching for her stethoscope, the fabric of his shirt moulding lovingly to the hard muscle of his shoulders. Despite his teasing words his eyes were on the baby, looking, assessing, mentally cataloguing his findings.

Bryony watched him with admiration and more than a touch of envy. His instincts were so good. If anyone she loved ever ended up in A and E, the doctor she'd want them to see would be Jack. He had a brilliant brain and an amazing ability to identify medical problems based on seemingly scanty information. And she'd learned more from him in her four months in A and E than she had from any other doctor in her career so far.

'So what did you notice, Blondie? Apart from the fact that there's a little patient on the trolley?'

He stood back while Nicky attached leads to the baby's chest and connected them to the monitor.

'She's cyanosed, has intercostal recession and she's grunting,' Bryony said immediately, her eyes on the baby. 'Her resps are 60 per minute and she's becoming exhausted.'

Jack nodded, his eyes flickering to the monitor, which was now operational and giving them further clues to the baby's condition.

'She has acute bronchiolitis. We need to get a line in this baby fast,' he ordered softly, holding out a hand to Nicky who immediately proffered the necessary equipment. He handed it to Bryony. 'Go on. Impress me.'

'You want me to do it?' Bryony looked at those

tiny arms and legs and shook her head. 'I'd rather you did it.'

She could see how ill the baby was and she didn't have the confidence that she'd get the line in first time. She knew Jack could. And with the baby that sick, his skill was more important than her need to practise.

His eyes narrowed and his gaze was suddenly serious. 'Don't doubt yourself,' he said softly, his blue eyes searching as he read her mind. 'Do it.'

He was still holding out the equipment and Bryony sucked in a breath. 'Jack, I—'

'Can do it,' he said calmly, those wicked blue eyes locking on hers. 'In three months' time you're going to be working on the paediatric ward and you're going to be taking blood all the time. You need the practise. Go for it.'

Bryony hesitated and Jack lifted an eyebrow, his blue eyes mocking.

'You want me to hold your hand?' His voice was a lazy drawl and Bryony blushed. How could he be so relaxed? But she knew the answer to that, of course. During her time in the A and E department she'd learned that panic did nothing to improve a tense situation and she'd also learned that Jack's totally laid-back attitude to everything rubbed off on the rest of the staff. As a result, they operated as a smooth, efficient team.

Looking at the baby, Bryony bit her lip and lifted the child's tiny wrist.

'Relax. Take your time.' Jack closed long, strong fingers around the baby's wrist and squeezed. 'OK.

Here's one for you. What do you call a blonde with half a brain?'

Bryony was concentrating on the baby's wrist. She found a tiny, thready vein and wondered how she was ever going to hit such a tiny target. It seemed almost impossible.

'Gifted,' Jack said cheerfully, squinting down at the baby's hand. 'You'll be fine. She's got good veins. Stop dithering and just do it.'

So she did and the needle slid smoothly into the tiny vein on her first attempt.

Relief and delight flooded through her.

'I did it.' She looked up, unable to hide her pride, and Jack smiled, his eyes creasing at the corners.

'As I said. Gifted. Now you just need the confidence to go with it. You're a good doctor. Believe in yourself.' His eyes held hers for a moment and then he looked at Nicky. 'OK, we need a full blood count, U and Es, BMG, blood culture and viral titres. And Nicky, let's give the child some humidified oxygen.'

Believe in yourself.

Well, she did believe in herself. Sort of. It was just that she was afraid of making a mistake and Jack Rothwell never seemed to be afraid of anything. He just did it. And it turned out right every time.

Bryony busied herself taking the necessary samples. 'Should I do arterial blood gases?'

'They can do them on the ward,' Jack said immediately. 'Nicky, can you call Paeds and get them up here? This little one is going to need admitting. She's a poorly baby.'

Bryony looked at him. 'You think it's bronchiolitis?'

'Without a doubt.' He smothered a yawn and looked at her apologetically. 'Sorry. I was up half the night.'

It was Bryony's turn to look mocking. 'Was she nice?'

'She was gorgeous.' He grinned, that wonderful slightly lopsided grin that affected her knees so acutely. 'She was also eighty-four and had a fractured hip.'

'You love older women.'

'True.' He checked the monitor again. 'But generally I like them mobile. OK, Blondie. What's the likely causative organism here? Exercise your brain cell and impress me twice in one evening.'

'RSV,' Bryony said immediately. 'Respiratory syncytial virus causes 75 per cent of cases of bronchiolitis.'

He inclined his head, his expression mocking. 'All right, you've impressed me. And you've obviously been studying your textbook again. Now we'll do some maths. What's two plus two?' His eyes were dancing. 'No need to answer immediately and you can use your fingers if you need to. Take your time—I know it's tricky.'

'No idea,' Bryony returned blithely, batting her eyelashes in a parody of a dumb blonde and handing the bottles to Nicky for labelling. 'Jack, should we pass a nasogastric tube?'

'No. Not yet.' He shook his head, his gaze flickering over the baby. 'When you've finished taking the samples we'll set up an IV and get her to the ward. I've got a bad feeling about this little one. She's going to end up being ventilated.'

'I hope not,' Bryony murmured, but she knew that Jack was always right in his predictions. If he thought the baby was going to need ventilating, then it was almost certain that she would.

He looked at her quizzically. 'Is the mother around?'

As he asked the question the doors to Resus opened and the paramedics came back in, escorting a tall woman wrapped in a wool coat. Her face was pale and her hair was uncombed.

'Ella?' She hurried over to the trolley, her face lined with anxiety, and then she looked at Jack.

Bryony didn't mind that. She was used to it. Women always looked at Jack.

Even before they knew he was the consultant, they looked at him.

And it wasn't just because he was staggeringly, movie-star handsome. It was because he was charming and had an air of casual self-assurance that attracted women like magnets. You just knew that Jack would know what to do in any situation.

'I'm Dr Rothwell.' He extended a hand and gave her that reassuring smile that always seemed to calm the most frantic relative. 'I've been caring for Ella, along with Dr Hunter here.'

The woman didn't even glance at Bryony. Her gaze stayed firmly fixed on Jack. 'She's been ill for days but I thought it was just a cold and then suddenly today she seemed to go downhill.' She lifted a shaking hand to her throat. 'She wouldn't take her bottle and she was *so* hot and then tonight she stopped breathing properly and I was *terrified*.'

Jack nodded, his blue eyes warm and understanding. 'It's always frightening when a baby of this size is ill because their airways are so small,' he explained calmly. 'Ella has picked up a nasty virus and it is affecting her breathing.'

The woman blanched and stared at the tiny figure on the trolley. 'But she's going to be OK?'

'We need to admit her to hospital,' Jack said, glancing up as the paediatrician walked into the room. 'This is Dr Armstrong, the paediatric registrar. He's going to take a look at her now and then we'll take her along to the ward.'

'Will I be able to stay with her?'

'Absolutely.' Jack nodded, his gaze reassuring. 'You can have a bed next to her cot.'

Deciding that Jack was never going to be able to extricate himself from the mother, Bryony briefed Dr Armstrong on the baby's condition.

She liked David Armstrong. He was warm and kind and he'd asked her out on several occasions.

And she'd refused of course. Because she always refused.

She *never* went on dates.

Bryony bit her lip, remembering Lizzie's letter to Santa. She wanted a daddy for Christmas. A pretty tall order for a woman who didn't date men, she thought dryly, picking up the baby's charts and handing them to David.

Dragging her mind back, she finished handing over and watched while David examined the baby himself.

A thoroughly nice man, she decided wistfully. So why couldn't she just accept his invitation to take their friendship a step further?

And then Jack strolled back to the trolley, tall,

broad-shouldered, confident and so shockingly hand-some that it made her gasp, and she remembered the reason why she didn't date men.

She didn't date men because she'd been in love with Jack since she'd been five years old. And apart from her one disastrous attempt to forget about him, which had resulted in Lizzie, she hadn't even *noticed* another man for her entire adult life.

Which just went to show how stupid she was, she reflected crossly, infuriated by her own stupidity.

Jack might be a brilliant doctor but he was also the most totally unsuitable man any woman could fall for. Women had affairs with Jack. They didn't fall in love with him. Not if they had any sense, because Jack had no intention of ever falling in love or settling down.

But, of course, she didn't have any sense.

It was fortunate that she'd got used to hiding the way she felt about him. He didn't have a clue that he'd featured in every daydream she'd had since she'd been a child. When other little girls had dreamed about faceless princes in fairy-tales, she'd dreamed about Jack. When her teenage friends had developed crushes on the boys at school, she'd still dreamed about Jack. And when she'd finally matured into a woman, she'd carried on dreaming about Jack.

Finally the baby was stable enough to be trans-ferred to the ward and Nicky pushed the trolley, ac-companied by the paediatric SHO, who had arrived to help, and the baby's mother.

Bryony started to tidy up Resus, ready for the next arrival, her mind elsewhere.

'Are you all right?' David Armstrong gave her a curious look. 'You're miles away.'

'Sorry.' She smiled. 'Just thinking.'

'Hard work, that, for a blonde,' Jack said mildly, and Bryony gave him a sunny smile, relaxed now that the baby was no longer her responsibility.

'Why are men like bank accounts?' she asked sweetly, ditching some papers in the bin. 'Because without a lot of money they don't generate much interest.'

David looked startled but Jack threw back his head and laughed.

'Then it's fortunate for me that I have a lot of money,' he said strolling across the room to her and looping her stethoscope back round her neck.

For a moment he stood there, looking down at her, his eyes laughing into hers as he kept hold of the ends of the stethoscope. Bryony looked back at him, hypnotised by the dark shadow visible on his hard jaw and the tiny muscle that worked in his cheek. He was so close she could almost touch him, but she'd never been allowed to do that.

Not properly.

He was her best friend.

They talked, they laughed and they spent huge amounts of time together. But they never crossed that line of friendship.

Jack's pager sounded and he let go of the stethoscope and reached into his pocket. 'Duty calls. If you're sure you can cope without me, I'll be off.'

'I'll struggle on,' Bryony said sarcastically, and he gave her that lazy wink that always reduced her legs to jelly.

'You do that. I'll see you later, then. Are you join-ing the team at the Drunken Fox tonight?'

'Yes. Mum's babysitting.'

The whole of the local mountain rescue team were meeting for a drink to celebrate her brother's birthday.

'Good.' He gave a nod. 'See you there, then.'

And with that he strolled out of the room with his usual easy confidence, letting the door swing closed behind him.

David stared after him. 'Don't you mind the blonde jokes and the fact that he calls you Blondie?'

Bryony shot him an amused look. 'He's called me that for twenty-two years.' She fiddled with the stethoscope that Jack had looped round her neck. 'He's just teasing.'

'You've known him for *twenty-two years*?'

'Amazing that I'm still sane, isn't it?' Bryony said lightly. 'Jack was at school with my two brothers but he spent more time in our house than his own.' *Mainly because his parents had been going through a particularly acrimonious divorce.*

'He's practically family. He and my brothers were at medical school together.'

Nicky entered the room in time to hear that last remark. 'I bet the three of them were lethal.'

'They certainly were.'

David looked at her in surprise. 'Of course—why didn't I realise before? Tom Hunter, the consultant obstetrician—he's your brother?'

Bryony smiled. 'That's right. And my other brother, Oliver, is a GP. When I've finished my ro-tation I'm going to join him in his practice. He's the reason for the trip to the pub—it's his birthday today.'

Not that they needed an excuse for a trip to the pub. Most of the mountain rescue team members lived in the pub when they weren't working, training or on a callout.

David looked at her. 'I can't believe that I didn't click sooner that Tom Hunter is your brother.'

Bryony shrugged. 'Well, we don't know each other that well.'

'And whose fault is that?' David said in an undertone. 'I keep asking you out.'

And she kept refusing.

Conscious that Nicky was within earshot, Bryony handed David the last of the charts. 'Here you go. Everything you need on baby Ella. I hope she does OK.'

'Thanks.' He hesitated and then gave her a smile as he walked out of Resus.

'That man fancies you,' Nicky said dryly, and Bryony sighed.

'Yes, I know.'

'Don't tell me, you're in love with Jack, the same as every other woman on the planet.'

Bryony looked at her, carefully keeping her expression casual. She'd never admitted to *anyone* how she felt about Jack, and she wasn't going to start now. 'Jack's my best friend. I know him far too well to ever fall in love with him.'

'Then you're more sensible than the rest of the female population,' Nicky said happily. 'Every woman I know is in love with Jack Rothwell. He's rich, single and sexy as sin. And most of us could scratch your eyes out for being so close to him. According to rumour, he spends half his life hanging around your kitchen.'

Bryony smiled. When she'd lived at home Jack had always been there, and when she'd moved into her own cottage he'd taken to dropping round so often that he was almost part of the furniture. 'Don't get the wrong idea. Usually he's telling me about his latest girlfriend. He's my brothers' closest friend, he's my daughter's godfather and we've been in the mountain rescue team together for years. I can assure you there's nothing romantic about our relationship.'

Unfortunately.

Nicky sighed. 'Well, it sounds pretty good to me. I'd love to have him in my kitchen, if only for his decorative qualities. The guy is sublime.'

'Nicky, you're married.'

Nicky grinned. 'I know. But my hormones are still alive and kicking.'

Bryony busied herself restocking one of the equipment trays. Strictly speaking it wasn't her job but she didn't want to look at Nicky in case she gave herself away.

Her relationship with Jack was good.

They had a fantastic friendship.

But even the most fantastic friendship didn't soothe the ache in her heart.

She was about to say something else to Nicky when the doors to Resus opened again and one of the paramedics stuck his head round.

'Has the baby been transferred to the ward? Only I've got her father here.'

'I'll speak to him,' Bryony said immediately, glad

to be given an excuse to get away from the subject of Jack. She followed the paramedic out of the room.

A tall man in a suit was hovering anxiously in the corridor, his face white with strain.

'I'm Dr Hunter,' Bryony said, holding out her hand. 'I've been looking after Ella.'

'Oh, God…' he breathed out slowly, obviously trying to calm himself down. 'I came as soon as Pam called me but I was at a meeting in Penrith and the traffic was awful.'

Bryony gave an understanding smile and slowly outlined Ella's condition, careful to be realistic without painting too grim a picture.

'So she's on the ward?' He ran a hand over the back of his neck and gave a shuddering sigh. 'Sorry. I know I'm panicking like mad but she's my baby and—'

'It's OK,' Bryony said gently, putting a hand on his arm. 'You're her father and you're entitled to be worried.'

His shoulders sagged and he looked exhausted. 'You don't know what worry is until you have kids, do you?'

Bryony thought of Lizzie and shook her head. 'No,' she agreed softly, 'you certainly don't.'

'Do you have children yourself, Doctor?'

'I have a little girl.'

They shared a smile of mutual understanding. 'And the bond between a little girl and her daddy is so special, isn't it?'

Bryony tensed and then she smiled. 'It certainly is,' she croaked, feeling as though she'd been showered with cold water. 'Very special.'

She directed the man to the children's ward and stared after him, feeling sick inside.

She loved Lizzie so fiercely that she rarely thought about the fact that her little girl didn't have a father. She had plenty of father figures—her two brothers and Jack, and she'd always consoled herself that they were enough. But Lizzie obviously didn't think so or why would she have asked for a father for Christmas?

Lizzie wanted the real thing. She wanted a father to tuck her up at night. A father who would read to her and play with her. *A father who would panic and leave a meeting because she was sick.*

Bryony gave a groan and covered her face with her hands. How was she ever going to satisfy Lizzie's Christmas wish this year?

How was she going to produce a father when she didn't even date men and hadn't since Lizzie had been conceived? And not even then, really.

Bryony let her hands drop to her sides, torn with guilt at how selfish she'd been. Because of the way she felt about Jack, she'd shut men out of her life, never thinking about the long-term effect that would have on Lizzie.

It was true that she didn't want a man in her life, but it was also true that Lizzie needed and wanted a father.

And suddenly Bryony made a decision.

She was going to stop dreaming about Jack Rothwell. She was going to stop noticing his broad shoulders. She was going to stop noticing the way his cheeks creased when he smiled. She was going to stop thinking about what he looked like with his shirt off.

In fact, she was going to stop thinking about him altogether and start dating other men.

Finally she was going to get a life.

And Lizzie was going to get a daddy.

CHAPTER TWO

BRYONY paused outside the entrance to the pub, her breath clouding the freezing air. She could hear the muffled sounds of laughter and music coming from inside, and she lifted her chin and pushed open the door.

They were all there. The whole of the mountain rescue team, most of whom she'd known for years, crowding the bar and laughing together. In one corner of the bar a log fire crackled and the room was warm and welcoming.

'It's Blondie!'

There were good-natured catcalls from the moment they spotted her and Toby, the equipment officer, slipped off his stool and offered it to her with a flourish.

'Hi, guys.' She settled herself on the stool and smiled at the barman. 'Hi, Geoff. The usual, please.'

He reached for a bottle of grapefruit juice. 'On the hard stuff, Bryony?'

'That's me.' Bryony nodded her thanks and lifted the glass in a salute. 'Cheers, everyone. And happy birthday, Oliver.'

Her brother grinned. 'Thanks, babe. You OK?'

'I'm fine.' In fact, she was better than fine. She was brilliant. And she was finally going to restart her life.

As if to test that resolve, Jack strolled over to her and dropped a kiss on her cheek.

'What did the blonde say when she walked into the bar?'

'Ouch,' Bryony answered wearily, rolling her eyes in exasperation. 'And, Jack, you really need some new jokes. You're recycling them.'

He yawned. 'Well, I've been telling them for twenty-two years—what do you expect?'

'A bit of originality would be nice,' she said mildly, taking another sip of her drink and making a point of not looking at him. She wasn't going to notice Jack any more. There were plenty of men out there with good bodies. He wasn't the only one. 'Maybe I should dye my hair brown to help you out.'

'Brown? Don't you dare.' Jack's voice was husky and enticingly male. 'If you dyed your hair brown, you'd ruin all my jokes. We love you the way you are.'

Bryony took a gulp of her drink. He didn't love her. And he never would love her. Or, at least, not in the way she wanted him to love her.

'Bry, are you free on Thursday or Friday?' Oliver leaned across the bar and grabbed a handful of nuts. 'Mum wants to cook me a birthday dinner, whole family and Jack in attendance.'

Bryony put her glass down on the bar. 'Can't do Thursday.'

Jack frowned. 'You're on an early shift. Why can't you do it?'

Bryony hesitated. 'Because I have a date,' she said finally, and Oliver lifted his eyebrows.

'A date? You have *a date*?'

Jack's smile vanished like the sun behind a cloud. 'What do you mean, you have a date?' His voice was surprisingly frosty. 'Since when did you go on dates?'

Bryony took a deep breath and decided she may as well tell all. 'Since I saw Lizzie's Christmas list.'

At the mention of Lizzie, Jack's expression regained some of its warmth. 'She's made her list already?'

'She has indeed.'

'Don't tell me.' His voice was indulgent. 'She wants something pink. A new pair of pink wings for her fairy costume?'

'Nope.'

Oliver looked at her searchingly. 'Well? We're all dying to hear what she asked for. And what's it got to do with you going on a date?'

Bryony sat still for a moment, studying her empty glass. 'I'm going on a date,' she said slowly, 'because Lizzie wants a daddy.' She looked up and gave them a bland smile. 'Lizzie has asked for a daddy for Christmas.'

There was a long silence around the bar and the men exchanged looks.

It was Jack who eventually spoke first. 'Does she realise that they're not all they're cracked up to be?'

There was bitterness in his tone and Bryony frowned slightly. She knew that his parents had divorced when he'd been eight and she also knew that it had been a hideously painful experience for Jack.

But it was unlike him to ever mention it.

Like most men, Jack Rothwell didn't talk about his feelings.

'A *daddy*?' Oliver cleared his throat and exchanged looks with Tom. 'Does she have anyone in particular in mind?'

Bryony shook her head. 'No. She's leaving the choice up to Santa, but Mum gave me the letter and she's listed the qualities she's looking for.'

'She has?' Oliver gave an amazed laugh and glanced round at the others. 'And what are they?'

Bryony delved into her pocket and pulled out a rumpled piece of paper. She cleared her throat and started to read. 'I want a daddy who is strong so that he can swing me in the garden. I want a daddy who is funny and makes jokes. I want a daddy who lets me watch television before school and who won't make me eat sprouts because I hate them and I want a daddy who will meet me at the school gate and give me a hug like the other daddies sometimes do.' Bryony broke off at that point and swallowed hard, aware of the stunned silence around her. 'But most of all I want a daddy who will hug my mummy and stay with us for ever.'

No one spoke and Bryony gave a small shrug. 'That's it.'

She folded the paper carefully and put it back in her pocket, and Jack frowned.

'I never knew she wanted someone to pick her up from school,' he said gruffly, glancing between Oliver and Tom. 'We could do something about that, guys.'

'Sure.' Tom nodded agreement immediately and Bryony lifted a hand.

'Thank you, but no. That isn't what she wants. In fact, that would probably make it worse because the person who is picking her up isn't her daddy.'

Oliver frowned and rubbed a hand over the back of his neck. 'So where did it come from, this daddy business?'

'I don't know.' Bryony shrugged. 'I suppose she's just getting to that age where children notice differences between themselves and others. Most of the kids in her class are in traditional families.'

'You've been reading her too many fairy stories,' Jack said darkly, and she shrugged.

'She's a little girl, Jack. Little girls dream of weddings.'

Oliver grinned at Tom. 'Some big girls dream of weddings, too. I find it terrifying.'

'Stop it.' Bryony frowned in mock disapproval. 'How my daughter has ever grown up to be remotely normal with you three around her is a mystery to me. She's always asking me why none of you are married.'

'Did you tell her that we're too busy having fun?' Tom drawled, and Bryony rolled her eyes.

'Actually, I tell her that none of you have met the right woman yet, but that it's bound to happen soon.'

'Is it?' Oliver gave a shudder, his expression comical. 'I hope not.'

'You're awful. All three of you.'

Tom lifted an eyebrow in her direction. 'Well, you're not exactly an advert for relationships yourself, little sister. You haven't been on a date since Lizzie was born.'

'I know that. But that's all going to change.'
Bryony lifted her chin. 'I've decided that Lizzie needs
a daddy.'

'So what are you saying?' Jack was staring at her,
all traces of humour gone from his handsome face.
'You're going to go out there and marry the first guy
you meet just so that she can have a daddy?'

'Don't be ridiculous. Of course not.' Bryony lifted
her chin and looked around her, her voice quiet but
firm. 'I'm just saying that I'm going to start dating
again.'

Oliver glanced at Tom and shrugged. 'Well, good
for you.'

'Yeah.' Tom nodded and smiled at his sister. 'I
think it's great. You've locked yourself up in a cupboard long enough. Get yourself out there, I say. Paint
the town red. Or pink, if you're using Lizzie's colour
scheme.'

Some of the other men in the team clapped her on
the back and one or two made jokes about joining the
queue to take her out.

Only Jack was silent, studying her with a brooding
expression on his handsome face, his usual teasing
smile notably absent. 'You really think you can find
her a *daddy*?'

'I don't know.' Bryony gave a little shrug. 'Maybe
not. But if I don't at least go on dates, it definitely
won't happen.'

When he finally spoke his tone was chilly. 'So
who's your date with on Thursday?'

Bryony looked at him in confusion, thinking that
she'd never heard Jack use that tone before. He

sounded…*angry*. But why would he be angry? The others actually seemed pleased for her. But not Jack.

'I'm not sure it's any of your business,' she teased him gently, trying to nudge their relationship back onto its usual platform, but on this occasion there was no answering smile.

'I'm Lizzie's godfather,' he reminded her, his blue eyes glittering in the firelight and a muscle working in his jaw. 'Who you choose as a *daddy* is very much my business.'

'You want to interview the guys I date, Jack?' She was still smiling, trying to keep it light, but he was glaring at her.

'Maybe.'

Bryony gave a disbelieving laugh, her own smile fading rapidly. 'You can't be serious.'

'You know absolutely nothing about the opposite sex, Blondie,' he said coldly. 'You've always refused to tell us who Lizzie's father was but he isn't around now which says quite a lot about your choice of men.'

Bryony gasped in shock. Lizzie's father wasn't a topic she discussed with anyone and Jack had never spoken to her like that before. He'd always been totally supportive of her status as a single mother.

'I don't know why you're looking so disapproving,' she said softly, aware that all the others had long since returned to their conversations and were no longer listening. Suddenly it was just the two of them and the tension in the atmosphere was increasing by the minute. 'You date all the time.'

His mouth tightened. 'I don't have a seven-year-old daughter.'

'But it's because of her that I'm doing this!'

Jack picked up his glass from the bar, a muscle flickering in his darkened jaw. 'That's ridiculous. You think you can just get out there and produce a happy family like magic?'

She sighed, knowing what was behind his words. 'No, I don't think that, Jack. But I think that it's time to see if I could maybe meet someone who seemed right for Lizzie and me.'

'Your life runs very smoothly,' he pointed out. 'Why complicate things?'

'Because Lizzie needs something more...' She hesitated. 'And I need something more, too, Jack. I've been on my own long enough.'

His mouth tightened. 'So basically you've suddenly decided to get out there and have fun.'

'And so what if I have?' Bryony looked at him, confused and exasperated. 'I just don't understand your attitude! You and my brothers have practically worked your way through most of the females in Cumbria.'

Streaks of colour touched his incredible cheekbones. 'That's different.'

Suddenly Bryony decided she'd had enough. 'Because you're a man and I'm a woman?'

'No.' His fingers tightened on his glass. 'Because I don't have any responsibilities.'

'No. You've made sure of that. And there's no need to remind me of my responsibilities to Lizzie. That's what started this, remember?' She glared at him, suddenly angry with him for being so judgmental. 'Lizzie wants a daddy and it's my job to find her one. And

I'm more than happy to try and find someone I can live with because frankly I'm sick and tired of being on my own, too.'

How could she have been so stupid as to put herself on ice for so long? She should have realised just how deep-rooted his fear of commitment was. Should have realised that Jack Rothwell would never settle down with anyone, let alone her.

It was definitely time to move on.

'I'm going home,' she said coldly, slipping off the barstool and avoiding his gaze. 'I'll see you at work tomorrow.'

She heard his sharp intake of breath and knew that he was going to try and stop her, but she virtually ran to the door, giving him no opportunity to intercept her.

She didn't want to talk to him. Didn't want to hear all the reasons why she shouldn't have a boyfriend when he dated a non-stop string of beautiful women.

She'd call Oliver later and apologise for ducking out without saying goodbye, but she knew he wouldn't mind. They were a close family and she adored her brothers. At least they'd been encouraging.

Which was more than could be said for Jack.

Why had he acted like that? All right, he was absolutely against marriage, but it wasn't *his* marriage they were talking about. It was *hers*, and Jack was usually warm and supportive of everything she did. They *never* argued. They were best friends.

She unlocked her car quickly, feeling tears prick her eyes.

Well, if dating other men meant losing Jack as a

friend, then so be it. She'd wasted enough time on him. He didn't even notice her, for goodness' sake!

And if she'd needed confirmation that it was time to move on, she had it now.

Jack banged his empty glass down on the bar and cursed under his breath.

'Nice one, Jack,' Oliver said mildly, clapping him on the shoulder and glancing towards the door. 'I thought the three of us agreed that we weren't going to bring up the thorny subject of Lizzie's father.'

Jack groaned and ran a hand over his face. 'I know, I know.' He let out a long breath. 'It's just that she knows *nothing* about men—'

'She's twenty-seven.'

'So?' Jack glared at Oliver. 'And we know that she hasn't been out with a man since Lizzie was conceived. That guy broke her heart! I don't want her making the same mistake again. She's obviously never got over him. What if she picks someone on the rebound?'

Tom joined them. 'I'm not sure you can rebound after seven years,' he said mildly, and Jack's mouth tightened.

'So why does Lizzie never date, then?'

Tom looked at him steadily. 'I don't know…'

'Yes you do.' Jack's eyes narrowed as he studied his friend. 'You think you know. I can tell.'

Tom shook his head and drained his glass. 'No. I don't know.' He studied his empty glass. 'But I can guess.'

Jack frowned. 'So what's your guess?'

Tom gave a funny smile and looked at Oliver. 'My guess is that she has a particular guy on her mind,' he drawled casually, 'and until she gets over him, she can't move on.'

'Precisely what I said,' Jack said smugly. 'She needs to get over Lizzie's father.'

And with that he grabbed his jacket and strode out of the pub after her.

Oliver looked at Tom. 'I always thought he was a bright guy. How did he ever come top in all those exams?'

Tom gave a faint smile. 'He'll get there in the end.'

'Unless Bry meets someone else.'

'Bryony has been in love with Jack for twenty-two years,' Tom said calmly, glancing at the barman and waggling his glass. 'She's never going to fall in love with anyone else.'

'So what happens now?'

Tom reached for his wallet. 'I think we're in for a very interesting few weeks. Happy birthday, bro. This one's on me.'

Damn.

Jack strode out to the car park, cursing himself for being so tactless. He couldn't believe he'd argued with Bryony. He *never* argued with Bryony. Or, at least, not seriously. Bryony was the nearest he had to family and their relationship was all banter and teasing and a great deal of confiding. Well, on his part at least. He told her everything about his relationships and she was always giving him little suggestions. And that was one of the things he loved about their friendship. Unlike the women he dated, Bryony never tried to change him or lecture him. She just accepted him as he was. He was more comfortable in her kitchen than any other place in the world. And now he'd upset her.

What the hell had come over him?

He looked round the car park, part of him hoping that she was still there, but of course she was long gone. He just hoped she wasn't driving too quickly. The air was freezing and the roads would be icy.

He gritted his teeth and swore under his breath. She'd been really upset by his comments and there was a very strong chance that he'd made her cry. Despite the fact that she rarely let him see it, he knew she was soft-hearted. He'd known her since she was five, for goodness' sake, and he knew her better than anyone.

Realising that he had a big apology to make, he ran a hand over his face and strolled to his car, pressing the remote control on his keyring.

He could drive over to her cottage now, of course, but she'd still be mad with him and anyway her mother would be there so they wouldn't be able to talk properly.

No. The apology was best left until they could be alone.

If he'd been dating her he would have sent her flowers, but he'd never sent Bryony flowers in his life, and if he did she'd think he'd gone mad.

He slid into his sports car and dropped his head back against the seat.

No doubt, now that word was out that she was going to start dating, flowers would be arriving for her thick and fast.

He growled low in his throat, tension rising in him as he contemplated the impact that her announcement had made.

Why had she chosen to tell the whole pub? Didn't she know that all the guys lusted after her? That with her long silken blonde hair and her fabulous curvy body, she couldn't walk across a room without stopping conversations? And he felt every bit as protective towards her as he knew her brothers did.

And now some sleazy guy would come along and take advantage of her, and she was so trusting and inexperienced with men she wouldn't even notice until it was too late.

Jack reversed the car out of its space, crunching the gears viciously. Well, *not* while he was available to prevent it happening.

She'd become pregnant in her second year at medical school and neither he nor her brothers had been around to sort the guy out. Damn it, she hadn't even told them who he was. Just mumbled something about the whole thing being a mistake and refused to even discuss it even though Tom and Oliver had pumped her for hours.

Well, there wasn't going to be another mistake, Jack thought grimly, his strong hands tightening on the wheel. Because now there was Lizzie's happiness to think of, too. No one was going to hurt either one of his girls.

From now on, if any guy so much as *looked* at

Bryony the wrong way, if there was even a *scent* of someone messing her around, he'd step in and floor them.

Satisfied that he was back in control of the situation, he stopped trying to pulverise his precious car and slowed his pace.

All he needed to do now was plan. He needed to know exactly whom she was dating so that he could issue a warning.

Bryony let herself into the house and found her mother in the kitchen. 'Is she asleep?'

'Fast asleep.' Her mother dried her hands on a towel. 'You're back early, darling. Is something wrong?'

'No.' Bryony unwrapped the scarf from around her neck and tossed it onto the chair. Her coat followed.

'Bryony, I'm your mother. I can tell when something is wrong.'

Bryony glared at her, her eyes sparkling with unshed tears. 'Jack Rothwell, that's what's wrong!'

'Ah.' Her mother gave a smile and turned to put the kettle on. 'Tea?'

'I suppose so.' Bryony slumped into the nearest chair and sighed. 'He is the most infuriating man.'

'Is he?'

'You know he is.'

Her mother reached for the tea bags. 'I know that you two have been very close for almost the whole of your lives,' she said mildly. 'I'm sure that whatever it is you've quarrelled about will go away.'

'The man dates every woman on the planet,' Bryony said, still outraged by his attitude, 'but when

I announce that I'm going to start going out with men, he's suddenly disapproving. And he had the nerve to lecture me on my responsibilities to Lizzie!'

'Did he?' Her mother looked thoughtful. 'That's very interesting.'

'Interesting?' Bryony shot her mother an incredulous look. 'Irritating, you mean. And hypocritical. How many girlfriends has Jack Rothwell had since I first met him?'

Her mother poured the tea. 'Quite a few, I should think.'

'Half the planet,' Bryony said flatly. 'He certainly isn't in a position to lecture me about morals.'

'I imagine he thought he was protecting Lizzie.'

Bryony stared at her. 'From what?'

Her mother put two mugs on the table and sat down opposite her. 'Jack hasn't had a very positive experience of marriage, sweetheart.'

'You mean because of his parents?'

Her mother's mouth tightened with disapproval. 'Well, you know my opinion on that. They were grown-ups. He was a child. They should have sorted out their differences amicably. After his father walked out, Jack spent most of his childhood at our house and I don't think his mother even noticed he wasn't at home. She was too busy enjoying herself to remember that she had a child.'

Bryony bit her lip, suddenly realising why Jack might have been so sensitive about her dating. 'But I wouldn't do that. That isn't what this is about.'

'I know. But you understand Jack better than anyone,' her mother said calmly. 'He wasn't thinking about you, darling. He was thinking about his own experiences.'

Bryony bit her lip. 'Do you think I should start dating, Mum?'

'Certainly I think you should date,' her mother replied calmly. 'I've always thought you should date, but you've always been too crazy about Jack to notice anyone else.'

Bryony stared at her, opened her mouth to deny it and then caught the look in her mother's eye and closed it again. 'You know that?'

'I'm your mother. Of course I know that.'

'He doesn't notice me.'

'You're a huge part of Jack's life,' her mother said mildly. 'He virtually lives here. But that's going to have to change if you really are going to date other men.'

Bryony curled her hands round her mug. 'But I don't want it to change my friendship with Jack.'

'One day you'll get married again,' her mother said quietly, 'and I can't see any man wanting to see Jack lounging in your kitchen every time he comes home from work. Of course your friendship is going to change.'

Bryony stared into her mug, a hollow feeling inside her. She didn't want things to change. Despite their row, she couldn't imagine not having Jack in her life.

But she couldn't carry on the way she was now, for Lizzie's sake.

'Then I suppose I'll just have to get used to that,' she said, raising her mug in the air. 'Cheers. To my future.'

Her mother lifted her mug in response. 'May it turn out the way you want it to,' she said cryptically, and Bryony let out a long breath.

She wasn't really sure what *she* wanted.

But she knew Lizzie needed a daddy.

The next morning she was woken by her pager.

'Is that a callout?' Lizzie was by her bed in a flash, her eyes huge. 'Is someone in trouble on the mountain?'

Bryony picked up her pager and was reading the message when the phone rang. Lizzie grabbed it immediately.

'Hunter household, Elizabeth Hunter speaking,' she said formally, the angle of her chin suggesting that she was very proud of herself. She listened for a moment and then a smile spread across her face. 'Hello, Jack! Yes, Mummy's right here... I'll tell her. Will I see you later?'

Bryony pulled on her clothes and sprinted to the bathroom to clean her teeth. By the time she'd finished, Lizzie was off the phone.

'There's a party of Duke of Edinburgh Award boys overdue,' she said importantly. 'They're sending out the whole team but Sean wants you and Jack to be an advance party. Jack is picking you up in five minutes.'

'Five minutes.' Bryony hurried through to the kitchen, grabbed an apple from the fruit bowl and dropped some bread in the toaster. 'Get your school things, sweetheart. Jack and I will drop you at

Grandma's on the way past and she can take you to school.'

Lizzie sprinted off and Bryony sent up a silent prayer of thanks that she had her mother close by. How did single parents manage without mothers?

By the time Jack hammered on the door, Lizzie was dressed and was standing by the door with her school-bag, munching toast.

She stood on tiptoe and opened the door.

'Hi, there.' Jack stooped and swung her into his arms, squeezing her tightly. 'Are we dropping you with Grandma?'

'We certainly are.' Bryony walked into the hall and picked up her rucksack and the other bits and pieces that she'd piled by the door, avoiding Jack's gaze. She was grateful that Lizzie was there. At least it prevented her from having to continue the conversation from the night before.

She was still hurt and angry by Jack's response to her announcement that she was going to start dating.

They piled into the mountain rescue vehicle and Jack drove down the lane that led to Bryony's cottage and turned onto the main road.

'So what's the story?' Bryony twisted her blonde hair into a ponytail and pushed it under a woolly hat. Then she rummaged in her bag for her gloves.

Jack kept his eyes on the road. 'Two boys have been reported overdue. They should have been back down last night but they didn't appear.'

Bryony frowned. 'So why did no one call the team last night?'

'They were camping and didn't leave their plans

with anyone so no one noticed until their friends stumbled into camp this morning and raised the alarm. The weather was foul last night, which is doubtless why Sean is worried.'

Lizzie stared at him, her eyes huge. 'Have they called the helicopter?'

'Yes, sweetheart.' Jack glanced at her with a smile. 'But the weather is pretty awful so Sean, the MRT leader, wants your mum and me to get going up that mountain in case we can help.'

'Why do you and Mummy always go together?'

Jack turned his attention back to the road and pulled the vehicle up outside Bryony's mother's house. 'Because your mum and I have always worked together in the mountain rescue team,' he said lightly. 'When your mum trained, I was her buddy. I looked after her.'

'And you still look after her,' Lizzie said happily, jumping down from the vehicle and grabbing her school-bag.

'I don't need looking after,' Bryony said crossly, glaring at Jack and calling after Lizzie, 'Sweetheart, ask Grandma to give you some more breakfast. I'll see you later.'

They waited until Bryony's mother opened the door and then Jack gave a wave and hit the accelerator.

Suddenly Bryony was very aware that it was just the two of them and she stared out of the window, for the first time in her life not knowing what to say.

'We think we know where they are,' Jack told her, flicking the indicator and turning down a narrow road.

'It's just a question of what state they'll be in when we get there.'

Which was why Sean had sent them as the advance party, Bryony thought. He wanted doctors. Which meant that he was anticipating trouble.

She picked up the map. 'What's the grid reference?'

He told her and she traced it with her finger. 'They're in the ghyll?'

'Sounds like it.'

Bryony looked at him in concern. 'But the water level is terribly high after all that rain we've had…'

'That's right.' Jack's voice was even and he brought the vehicle to a halt. 'Which is why we need to get a move on. Personally I doubt they'll be able to fly a helicopter in this. Sean has called the whole team out, but we're going on ahead.'

He sprang out of the vehicle and reached for the equipment that they'd need. They worked quickly and quietly, each knowing what the other was doing.

'You ready?' Jack lifted an eyebrow in her direction and she nodded.

'Let's go.'

Jack set off at a fast pace and Bryony followed, knowing that speed was important. After a night out in the open in the wet and temperatures below freezing, the boys would be in serious trouble.

They had to reach them fast.

The path grew steeper, the mist came down and Jack shook his head. 'It's November, it's freezing cold and the visibility is zero.' He hitched his rucksack more comfortably on his broad shoulders and squinted into the mist. 'Who the hell chooses to climb mountains at this time of year?'

'You do it all the time,' Bryony pointed out, checking her compass again. 'One of these days we're going to be out here rescuing you.'

'Never.' He winked and gave her a sexy grin. 'I am invincible.'

Bryony rolled her eyes. 'And arrogant.' She stopped dead and he looked at her questioningly.

'Why have you stopped?'

'Because your ego is blocking my path.'

Jack laughed and then the laughter faded. 'Listen, Blondie, about last night—'

'Not now,' Bryony said hastily. She really didn't want to tackle the subject again so soon, especially not halfway up a mountain.

'I just wanted to apologise,' he said softly. 'I was out of line. You're a brilliant mother and I know you'll do what's right for Lizzie.'

Stunned by his apology, Bryony lost her ability to speak. She'd never heard Jack apologise for anything before.

'Let's forget it,' she mumbled, and Jack nodded, his blue eyes studying her closely.

'All right. We'll talk about it later.' He glanced up the path and frowned. 'There is no way that helicopter is going to fly in this.'

'So we evacuate them down the mountain.'

He nodded and then turned to her, his eyes twinkling wickedly. 'Why did the blonde stare at the can of frozen orange juice?' He leaned forward and tucked a strand of hair back under her hat. 'Because it said "concentrate".'

Bryony tipped her head on one side and stared back at him. 'Why are men like government bonds?' He lifted an eyebrow, his eyes dancing, and she smiled sweetly. 'Because they take for ever to mature. Now, can we get on with this rescue?'

They stuck to the path and the mist grew thicker. Jack's radio crackled to life and he paused and had a quick conversation with Sean back at base.

'They're sending out the whole team,' he told her when he came off the radio, 'but I reckon we must be nearly at the place where they were last seen.'

Bryony stood still, listening, but all she could hear was the rush of water. The freezing air snaked through her clothing and she shivered.

'If they didn't have any protection last night, they won't have stood a chance,' she muttered, and Jack nodded, his handsome face serious.

'Better find them, fast.'

He started up the track again and then stopped, squinting down into the ghyll. 'Do you see something?'

'What?' Bryony stepped towards the edge but Jack reached out a strong arm and clamped her against him.

'If it's all the same to you, I'd rather you didn't go over the edge, too,' he said dryly, keeping his arm round her as he peered through the mist into the ghyll again.

Bryony held her breath, painfully conscious of his hard body pressed against hers.

'I don't see anything.' She wondered when he was going to let her go and was about to ask when she spotted a flash of red below them. 'OK, I see something.'

'Me, too.' Jack released her. 'There's a path here but it's narrow and slippery. Think you can manage, Blondie? You have to put one leg in front of the other and not fall over.'

'It'll be a struggle, but I'll do my best,' Bryony assured him earnestly, relieved that their relationship seemed to have restored itself to its usual level. 'What about you? Think you can find your way without asking for directions?'

They kept up the banter as they picked their way down the path, and finally they reached the bottom and immediately saw the boys huddled together by a boulder.

Jack closed the distance in seconds and dropped to his haunches, his expression concerned. 'Hi, there— nice day for a stroll in the mountains.'

'We thought no one was ever coming,' the boy whispered, his teeth chattering as he spoke. 'Martyn keeps falling asleep and leaving me on my own.'

'Right. Put a bivouac tent over them.' Jerking his head to indicate that Bryony should deal with the conscious child, Jack shifted his position so that he could examine the other boy.

He was lying still, moaning quietly, his cheeks pale and his lips blue.

Jack spoke to him quietly and checked his pulse while Bryony checked the other boy for injuries. Once she was satisfied that he was just cold and shaken, she erected the tent and helped him to scramble inside a casualty bag.

'What's your name?'

'Sam.'

'Well, Sam, that will keep you warm until we can get you off this mountain,' she assured him, and he gave a little sob.

'Martyn fell. His leg is awful. I saw bone.'

Bryony slipped an arm round him and gave him a hug. 'Don't you worry about that now,' she said softly. 'We'll sort him out and get you both home. I'm going to pour you a hot drink and that will warm you up.'

She grabbed the flask that she'd packed and poured thick creamy chocolate into a mug.

'Here—drink this. I'll be back in a sec.' Aware that Jack was going to need her help, she slid out of the tent and moved over to him.

'Sam says that his friend fell.'

Jack nodded, still checking the child over. 'He's got a compound fracture of his tib and fib and he's bleeding a lot. We need to get a line in, Blondie, and then splint that leg.'

Bryony reached for the rucksack and found what they needed, aware that Jack was on the radio again, updating Sean on their position and the condition of the boys.

By the time he'd finished on the radio Bryony had a line in. 'Do you want to give him fluid?'

Jack nodded. 'And then we need to splint that leg. It will help the pain and reduce blood loss.' He leaned over the boy, talking quietly, explaining what they were doing, and Bryony gave a sigh. He was so good when anyone was in trouble. A rock. And he always knew what to do. Her confidence came from being with him.

She covered the wound on the leg with a sterile saline-soaked dressing while Jack carefully removed the boy's boot.

He placed his fingers on Martyn's foot, feeling for a pulse. 'That's fine—let's splint this leg. We're just going to give you something for the pain, Martyn, and then we're going to put your leg in a splint. Then we're going to warm you up and get you off this mountain.'

Bryony gave a shiver. The temperature was dropping fast and even in her top-quality gear she could feel the cold.

By the time they'd splinted the boy's leg, Sean had arrived with the rest of the mountain rescue team.

'Nice day for a walk,' he drawled, glancing around him at the thick mist. 'The views are fantastic.'

Bryony smiled. 'Absolutely fantastic,' she said sarcastically. 'Enjoy your stroll, did you?'

Sean grinned in appreciation. 'Didn't want to rush things,' he said, lifting an eyebrow in Jack's direction. 'Well?'

'We need a helicopter but I don't suppose there's any chance of that.'

'You suppose correctly.'

Jack sighed and checked the pulses on the boy's foot again. 'So we'd better carry them off, then. Good. I needed a workout.'

It seemed to take ages to organise both boys onto

stretchers but eventually they managed to carry them out of the ghyll and started down the mountain.

By the time they reached the valley floor the mist had cleared and it was a sunny day.

'I don't believe this,' Bryony muttered, tugging off her hat and shaking her hair loose. 'What is it with our weather?'

Both boys were loaded into the mountain rescue team ambulance and then transferred to hospital under Sean's supervision while Jack and Bryony followed behind.

'Are you working today?' Jack glanced across at her and she nodded.

'Yes. I'm on a late. Why?'

He returned his attention to the road. 'I thought you had a date.'

Bryony looked at him warily. 'That's tomorrow, but I don't know if I'm going because Mum has to go and visit someone in Kendal so I don't think she can babysit.'

'I'll babysit for you.'

Bryony stared at him. 'You?'

'Why not?' His eyes were fixed on the road. 'I often babysit for you. It gives me a chance to talk to my godchild. I like it.'

Bryony looked at him suspiciously. 'But last night…' She broke off and bit her lip, not really wanting to bring the subject up in case it rocked the peace that had resumed between them. 'Last night you said that you didn't think I should be dating.'

'And I've already apologised for that,' he said, flicking the indicator and turning into the road that led to the hospital. 'And to make up for it, I'll babysit for you. What time do you want me?'

Still feeling uneasy about the whole thing but not knowing why, Bryony gave a shrug. 'Seven-thirty?'

'Seven-thirty is perfect. There's just one thing…' He pulled up in the ambulance bay and yanked on the handbrake. 'You haven't told me who you're going out with.'

There was something in his smooth tones that made her glance at him warily but his handsome face was impassive.

She paused with her hand on the door. 'David.'

'David Armstrong? The paediatrician?' Jack's expression didn't change but she sensed something that made her uneasy.

'Look, Jack—'

'I'll be there at seven-thirty. Now, let's get on. I need to get antibiotics into Martyn and call the surgeons. That wound is going to need some attention.'

And with that he sprang out of the vehicle, leaving her staring after him.

Jack was going to babysit while she went on a date?

It seemed harmless enough, generous even, so why did she have such a strong feeling that something wasn't quite right?

CHAPTER THREE

'Mummy, you look pretty.'

'Do you think so?' Bryony surveyed her reflection in the mirror, wondering whether the dress was right for the evening that David had in mind. He'd said dinner in a smart restaurant, but she never went to smart restaurants so she wasn't that sure what to wear.

In the end she'd settled for the little black dress that her mother had given her three Christmases ago and which she'd never worn.

She'd fastened her hair on top of her head, found a pair of pretty, dangly earrings and dabbed perfume over her body.

And she had to admit that she was looking forward to going out with a man.

So much so that when the doorbell rang she opened the door with a wide smile.

'Hi, Jack.' Her face glowed and she stood to one side to let him in. 'There's a casserole in the oven. I assumed you wouldn't have eaten—'

'I haven't eaten.' His eyes slid down her body and he frowned, his expression suddenly hostile.

Bryony felt the confidence ooze out of her. She'd thought that she looked good but, judging from the look on Jack's face, she obviously didn't.

'Come through to the kitchen,' she said quickly, suddenly wishing that she'd worn something different. Obviously the black dress didn't suit her. 'We've got time for a quick drink before David gets here. He was held up in clinic.'

Jack's mouth tightened with disapproval. 'So he's going to be late, then.'

'Well, only because a child with asthma was admitted at the last minute,' Bryony said mildly, tugging open the fridge and reaching for a bottle of wine. 'You know how it is.'

'Do I?'

Instead of settling himself at her kitchen table as he usually did, he prowled round the room, his eyes constantly flickering back to her dress.

Trying to ignore his intense scrutiny, Bryony poured two glasses of wine and handed him one. 'Here you are. Cheers.'

He took the wine and put it on the table, his eyes fixed on her legs.

Bryony felt her whole body warm with embarrassment. She hardly ever showed her legs. She usually wore trousers for work because they were more practical, and when she went to the pub with the rest of the mountain rescue team she wore trousers, too.

But tonight, for the first time in ages, she'd put on a pair of sheer, black stockings and she was beginning to wish she hadn't.

'You hate it, don't you?' she croaked, and his eyes lifted and welded to hers.

'Hate what?'

She swallowed. 'The way I look. My dress. Me. You're staring and staring.'

Jack let out a breath. 'That's because I don't think you should be going out with a man dressed like that,' he said tightly. 'It sends out all the wrong messages.'

She frowned at him, totally confused. 'What messages?'

He tensed. 'Well—that you're available.'

'Jack,' she said patiently, 'I *am* available. That is the message I want to send out.'

'So you wear a skirt that's up to your bottom?' He glared at her and she stared back helplessly, totally confused by his attitude.

She'd met some of the girls that he'd dated and they were almost all blondes with skirts up round their bottoms.

'Jack, my skirt is just above the knee,' she pointed out, glancing down at herself to check that half her dress hadn't fallen off without her knowledge. 'It is nowhere near my bottom.'

'Well, it's definitely too low in the front,' he said hoarsely, reaching across the kitchen table, yanking a flower out of a vase and snapping it halfway up the stem. 'Try this.'

He walked up to her and slipped the flower down the neckline of her dress and stood back with a frown.

'That's a bit better.'

'Jack—'

Before she could say anything, Lizzie came running into the room wearing a pink gauze fairy dress and wearing wings. 'Jack, Jack!' She flung herself into his arms and he picked her up and gave her a kiss on the cheek.

'Hello, beautiful. Shouldn't you be in bed?'

'I was waiting for you.' Lizzie curled her legs round his waist and waggled her finger at him. 'Look. I'm wearing three rings. They're sweets really, but aren't they great?'

Jack dutifully studied her finger. 'Really great. And if you get hungry in the night you can eat them.'

Lizzie beamed. 'Can we play a game, Jack?'

'Sure.' Jack put her down gently and smiled indulgently. 'Any game you like. Just name it.'

'Weddings.'

Jack's smile vanished. *'Weddings?'*

Lizzie nodded happily. 'Yes, you know. You're the boy and I'm the girl and we get married.'

Jack gave a shudder. 'I don't know the rules, sweetheart.'

Bryony covered her hand with her mouth to hide her smile. Jack was brilliant at playing with her daughter but 'Weddings' was the one game guaranteed to bring him out in a rash.

'It's easy,' Lizzie assured him happily. 'We hold hands and then we get married.'

Jack ran a hand over the back of his neck and looked at Bryony for help, but she simply smiled.

'Weddings, Jack,' she said softly, her eyes dancing as she looked at him. 'That well-known game enjoyed by men and women the world over.'

His eyes shot daggers at her but he turned to Lizzie with a resigned sigh. 'All right, peanut, tell me what I have to do.'

'Well, first I have to go and dress up.' Lizzie shot out of the room and Jack turned on Bryony.

'She's playing *weddings*?'

'She's a girl, Jack,' Bryony said mildly. 'Girls play weddings.'

'I'm breaking out in a sweat here,' he muttered dryly, and she grinned unsympathetically.

'She's seven years old. I think you can cope. Great practice for when you do the real thing.'

His gaze locked on hers, his blue eyes mocking. 'You know I'm never doing the real thing.'

'Well, don't tell my daughter that. I don't want her saddled with your prejudices about relationships.'

'I should be teaching her about reality.'

Before Bryony could answer, Lizzie danced back into the room, this time wearing a full-length sparkly dress complete with glittering tiara.

Jack blinked. 'Wow…' He cleared his throat. 'I didn't know you had a tiara.'

'I've got seven,' Lizzie said proudly, and Bryony smiled cheerfully.

'A girl can never have too many tiaras, can she, Lizzie?'

'Come on, Jack.' Lizzie grabbed his hand. 'First we have to hold hands and walk across the carpet. Mummy can video us.'

Jack glanced at Bryony who could barely stand up she was laughing so much. 'Great idea, Lizzie,' she choked. 'It would make great viewing at the MRT Christmas party. Jack finally getting married.'

Jack scowled, but his eyes were dancing. 'Revenge is going to be sweet, Blondie,' he warned softly, but he was laughing too and shaking his head as Lizzie dragged him into the sitting room and Bryony reached for the video camera.

To give him his due, Jack treated the whole occasion with the appropriate amount of solemnity, sweeping Lizzie's hand to his lips as if she were a princess.

At first Bryony was laughing so much that she

could hardly keep the camera steady, but as she watched Jack playing his role to perfection and saw the delight on her little girl's face, her smile faded and she felt an ache growing inside her. Jack was so brilliant with Lizzie. And although he couldn't see it himself, he'd make a wonderful father.

She was reminding herself firmly that she wasn't going to think that way any more when the doorbell rang and she realised that her date had arrived.

She answered the door and David stood on the doorstep, flourishing a bunch of flowers.

'Are they for me? They're beautiful, thank you.' She smiled at him and was wondering whether she ought to kiss him when she heard Jack clear his throat behind her.

'You'll need a coat, Blondie,' he said coolly, the humour gone from his eyes as he held out the long woollen coat that she always wore to work and which covered her from her neck to her ankles.

'I was going to take my pashmina,' Bryony began, but Jack walked up behind her and draped the coat over her shoulders, pulling it closed at the front so that not one single inch of her was visible.

'It's too cold for a pashmina,' he grated. 'You don't want to get hypothermia over dinner.' He stood back and gave David a nod. 'She needs to be home at eleven.'

'What?' Bryony gaped at him and then gave an embarrassed laugh. They hadn't even discussed what time he wanted her home but she'd assumed that she could be as late as she liked. She knew Jack well enough to know that he didn't go to bed early himself.

And invariably he slept in her spare room. So why was he saying that she needed to be in by eleven?

David gave an awkward smile. 'Eleven is fine.'

Bryony scowled, less than impressed that he hadn't stood up to Jack. Surely he should have said that he'd bring her home when he was ready, or some such thing. She knew for sure that if someone had told Jack that he should bring a girl home by eleven he would have kept her out for the whole night just to prove a point.

But she'd promised herself that she wasn't going to think about Jack, she reminded herself hastily, taking the flowers through to the kitchen and putting them in water.

When she arrived back at the door the two men were staring at each other. David looked mildly embarrassed and Jack was standing, feet planted firmly apart, very much the dominant male and not in the slightest bit embarrassed.

Deciding that Jack had definitely gone mad, Bryony held out a hand to David and smiled. 'Shall we go?'

'Jack.' Lizzie tugged his arm and frowned at him. 'You're skipping bits.'

Jack shook himself and stared down at the book he was supposed to be reading. 'Am I?'

'Yes.' Lizzie grabbed the book from him and went back two pages. 'You didn't read this page at all. And you've got a funny look on your face.'

'Have I?'

Jack tried to concentrate on the pink fairy flying across the page of the book but all he could see was

Bryony in that dress. He hadn't seen her legs since she'd been in the netball team at school and he and her brothers had gone to matches to cheer her on, but he now realised that his best friend had sensational legs.

And if she was going to start showing them, how the hell was he going to protect her?

And it wasn't just her legs, of course...

He closed his eyes, trying to forget the shadowy dip between her full breasts revealed by the cut of her dress.

Right now they were in the restaurant and David was probably sitting opposite her, staring into paradise.

With a soft curse he stood up and the book fell to the floor.

'You said a rude word, Jack,' Lizzie said mildly, leaning over and retrieving the book.

'Sorry.' Suddenly seized by inspiration, he gave Lizzie a smile. 'How would you like to call your mother and say goodnight?'

'Now?'

'Sure, why not?' Before Dr Armstrong had time to get too hot and over-eager. Suddenly driven by an urgency that he couldn't explain, Jack grabbed Lizzie's hand and dragged her into the kitchen. 'We'll ring her mobile.'

Lizzie looked at him uncertainly. 'Grandma says we only ring if there's an emergency.'

Jack was already pressing the keys. 'Trust me, this is an emergency,' he assured her, his mind still mentally on Bryony's creamy breasts. His mouth tightened. 'A big emergency. Her baby girl wants to say goodnight.'

Trying to ignore the fact that Lizzie was looking at him as though he was slightly mad, Jack held the receiver and waited for Bryony to answer.

As the phone rang and rang, his heart started to thud in his chest.

Why the hell wasn't she answering?

Unless she wasn't at dinner after all. What if the rat had taken one look at that dress and whisked Bryony back to his flat?

'Uncle Jack, you're breathing really fast,' Lizzie said, climbing onto a kitchen stool, her fairy wings still attached to her back. 'And you look weird.'

He felt weird.

Why wasn't she answering?

David sat back in his chair. 'Is that your phone?'

Bryony looked at him, startled, and then picked up her bag. 'Oh, my goodness, yes.' She fumbled in her handbag, her stomach turning over. 'I hope nothing is wrong with Lizzie. I don't usually get phoned...'

She delved amongst tissues, make-up, notebooks and various pink hairbands that belonged to her daughter and eventually found the phone.

Feeling distinctly nervous, she answered it. 'Jack?' She cast an apologetic look at David. 'Is something wrong?'

She listened for a moment and then frowned. 'I'm in the restaurant, Jack. Where did you think I was? Well, I couldn't find my phone.'

At that moment the waiter delivered their starter and Bryony smiled her thanks, trying to ignore his look of disapproval. She knew that mobile phones were banned from lots of restaurants but she refused to turn hers off in case Lizzie needed her.

But it seemed that all Lizzie wanted was to say goodnight. Strange, Bryony thought as she spoke to her daughter and then ended the call. Lizzie was normally fine. Especially when she was with Jack. She loved being with Jack.

'Everything OK?' David looked at her quizzically and she smiled.

'Fine. Sorry about that.'

She picked up her fork and tucked into her starter, determined to relax. Part of her mind was still dwelling on the fact that Jack had hated her dress, but she ignored it. David seemed to think she looked nice and that was all that mattered.

They chattered about work and the mountain rescue team and they were just tucking into their main course when her phone rang again.

This time Bryony heard it immediately and stopped the ringing before the waiter had time to glare at her.

It was Jack again, this time telling her that Lizzie was refusing to take her fairy wings off.

Bryony frowned. This was a guy who could save a life halfway up a mountain in a howling gale with nothing more than a penknife and a piece of string.

And he was calling her about *fairy wings*?

'Just take them off when she's asleep, Jack,' she muttered, smiling apologetically at David as she slipped the phone back into her bag.

She tried valiantly to resume the conversation but when Jack called for the third time, David raised his hand and gestured to the waiter.

'I think I'll take you home,' he said dryly. 'Then you can answer Jack's questions in person and he won't have to keep calling you.'

'Sorry.' Bryony blushed slightly. As a first date it had been less than perfect. 'I honestly don't know what's the matter with him. He and Lizzie are normally fine together.'

David drove her home and then walked her up the path to her cottage. At the front door he paused, his expression thoughtful as he looked down at her.

Bryony stared back, feeling slightly awkward. Was he going to kiss her?

Suddenly she felt a flash of panic. She wasn't actually sure that she wanted him to kiss her.

His head was bending towards hers when the front door was jerked open and Jack stood there, broad-shouldered and imposing.

'You're home. Great.'

Bryony looked at David. 'Would you like to come in for coffee?'

'He needs to get going,' Jack said coldly, his face unsmiling. 'The roads are icy tonight and they're forecasting snow.'

David was silent for a moment, his eyes on Jack. 'Right. In that case I'd better make a move.'

'OK, then.' Secretly relieved by the decision, Bryony stood on tiptoe and kissed his cheek. 'Thanks for tonight. I enjoyed it.'

'Me, too.' David was still looking at Jack and then he gave a funny smile and turned to Bryony. 'I'll see you at work.'

With that he turned the collar of his coat up and strolled back down her path towards his car.

Bryony followed Jack into the cottage and slipped her coat off.

'I'm sorry Lizzie was such hard work tonight, Jack.' She strolled into the kitchen and flipped the kettle on. 'She never normally wants to call me. And she doesn't normally care if she's lost the book she was reading—she'll just pick another one. It doesn't sound as though you managed to relax at all.'

'I managed.' Jack sank onto one of the kitchen chairs and put his feet on the table in his usual pose. 'I expect she was just a bit unsettled by the thought of you going out with a strange man.'

Bryony frowned slightly. It was Lizzie who had suggested this whole daddy business, so why would she be unsettled? On the other hand, perhaps she hadn't really thought the whole thing through. It was certainly true that Lizzie wasn't used to seeing strange men in her life. She saw Jack and her two uncles and that was about it.

'She'll get used to it.'

'Maybe.' Jack sounded noncommittal. 'So—did you have a good evening?'

There was something in his tone that she couldn't interpret and Bryony lifted two mugs out of the cupboard, not sure how to answer. Had she had a good evening? If she was honest, she didn't really feel she'd had a chance to talk to David. Every time they'd begun a conversation the phone had rung.

Poor Lizzie.

She'd talk to her tomorrow and see how she felt about the whole thing. She certainly didn't want to go on dates if it was going to upset her daughter.

'I had a nice evening,' she said finally, not wanting

to admit to Jack that it had been anything less than perfect. 'It's a shame David wouldn't come in for coffee.'

'It's not a shame. It was a lucky escape.' Jack swung his legs off the table and glared at her. '*Never* invite a man in for coffee.'

Bryony looked at him in astonishment. 'I was being polite.'

He lifted an eyebrow. 'Offering to have sex with a man is being polite?'

Bryony gaped at him, stunned. 'I did not offer to have sex with him, I offered him *coffee*.'

'It's the same thing.' A muscle flickered in his jaw, rough with stubble so late in the evening. He looked dark and dangerous and Bryony felt her stomach flip.

Why couldn't she find David even *half* as attractive? She'd been less than enthusiastic at the possibility of him kissing her, but if it had been Jack who'd been on the doorstep with her...

Reminding herself that she wasn't supposed to be noticing Jack, Bryony picked up the coffee-jar.

'Coffee is the same as sex?' She twisted the jar in her hand, looking at it with a mocking expression. 'Full of caffeine and sold in supermarkets. I don't think so.'

Jack glared at her. 'You can joke about it, but do you really think a man wants to sit around, drinking your coffee?'

'You're sitting around, drinking my coffee,' Bryony pointed out logically, and his mouth hardened.

'That's different. I'm not trying to get you into my bed.'

More's the pity, Bryony thought wistfully, putting the coffee down on the side. If Jack ever tried to get her into his bed she'd be there like a flash.

'Jack, I'm sure David didn't have anything immoral on his mind.'

'Which just shows how little you know about men,' Jack said tightly. 'Do you know the average man thinks about sex every six seconds?'

'So presumably that's why they say men are like photocopiers,' Bryony said dryly. 'Good for reproduction but not much else.'

For once Jack didn't laugh and she sighed inwardly. There was obviously something about the idea of her dating that short-circuited his sense of humour.

Suddenly she wanted the old Jack back. The Jack that called her Blondie and teased her unmercifully. The Jack with the wicked smile and the sexiest wink known to woman.

'Jack.' Her tone was patient. 'I invited David in for coffee because I was being polite. I had no intention of having sex with him.'

'And what if he'd decided to have sex with you?'

She looked at him in exasperation. 'Well, despite the colour of my hair I do have a brain and a mouth,' she said tartly. 'I can think no and say no. At the same time. Amazing really. If I concentrate really hard I can add two and two. Jack, *what is the matter with you?*'

'I just think you're being naïve.'

'Inviting a guy in for coffee?' Bryony gritted her teeth and shook her head. 'You've gone crazy, do you know that?'

There was a long silence and streaks of colour touched his hard cheekbones. 'Maybe I have,' he said shortly, putting his half-full mug on the table and rising to his feet in a fluid movement. 'I'd better get home.'

'Fine. Thank you for babysitting.'

'You're welcome.'

As a farewell it had none of its usual warmth and Bryony turned away and poured the rest of her coffee down the sink, boiling with frustration and feeling confused and upset.

She heard Jack stride to her front door, heard him pick up his jacket and car keys and then the front door slammed behind him.

Bryony winced and let out a long breath.

Just what was going on with Jack?

Bryony was nervous about working with Jack the next day but he seemed back to his usual self, relaxed and good-humoured as they sat in the staffroom and discussed the shifts for Bonfire Night.

'It's my turn.' Sean Nicholson, one of the other consultants, looked at Jack with a resigned expression on his face. 'You deserve a year off from Bonfire Night. You've had a bad few years.'

Jack rolled his eyes. 'I won't know what to do with myself,' he drawled, and Bryony gave him a sympathetic smile.

'You hate this time of year, don't you?'

'I've just seen too many kids with burns after handling fireworks,' he said grimly, scribbling something on his pad. 'OK, so Blondie and I are officially off that night, but if you need us you can call us.' He looked at Bryony. 'Would you be able to come in that night if we needed you?'

Bryony nodded. 'After eight. I'm taking Lizzie to her bonfire party.'

Jack stared at her, his body suddenly unnaturally still. 'What bonfire party?'

'Her friend is having a few sparklers in the garden. Nothing dramatic,' Bryony assured him, but he shook his head.

'No way.' His jaw was tense. 'She shouldn't be going.'

Bryony sighed. 'She's seven, Jack. She wants to be with her friends.'

'So? Invite them all out for a hamburger.'

'It's just a few fireworks and drinks for the parents. It will be over by eight.'

He let out a breath. 'All right. But I'm coming with you.'

'Jack—'

'I'm off and I'm bored.' His blue eyes glittered dangerously. 'It's that or she doesn't go.'

'You're not her father, Jack!' Suddenly remembering that Sean was still in the room, Bryony coloured with embarrassment and shot them an apologetic look. 'Sorry, you guys.'

'No problem,' Sean said easily, 'and I'm sure we won't need you here so just go and have a good time.'

'Great. That's what we'll do, then.'

Jack ran through the rest of the rota and Sean left the room.

Bryony looked at him. 'So what are you planning to do? Bring the fire brigade?'

'When you've spent as long working in A and E

as I have, you won't let your daughter go to domestic firework parties,' he said tightly. 'It's fine. I'll come, too. And you can tell Lizzie's friend's mother that I want a bucket of sand and another bucket of water handy.'

'Why don't we just have an ambulance on standby, just in case?' Bryony suggested tartly. 'Anne's mother will think I've gone barmy.'

'Better barmy than burned.' Jack strode to the door. 'What time does it start?'

'We're getting there at five-thirty for tea and then fireworks,' Bryony said wearily, and Jack nodded.

'Right. I'll pick you both up at five-fifteen. And I want Lizzie in gloves. She's not touching a sparkler with her bare hands.'

Bryony stood up and followed him out of the staff-room, wanting to argue but knowing that he was only being cautious.

He had dealt with a huge number of burns on Bonfire Night, all of which could have been avoided.

And he did adore Lizzie.

Deciding that she should be grateful that he was so protective of her daughter, she picked up a set of notes and called the next patient from the waiting room.

And secretly part of her was excited at spending an evening with Jack. Even if it was in the company of half a dozen parents and their offspring.

It would be lovely to have him there, even though nothing was going to happen.

Reminding herself that Jack was not the man she was dating, she sat down in her chair and waited for the patient to arrive.

CHAPTER FOUR

THE NIGHT of the bonfire party was freezing cold and Bryony pulled on her jeans and thickest jumper and wore her long black coat.

Lizzie was wearing a bright pink hat, pink tights and a pink fleece, and Jack blinked when he arrived to pick them up.

'How are my girls?' He picked Lizzie up and planted a kiss on her cheek. 'You're looking very pink, angel.' He spoke in that lazy drawl that sent butterflies flitting through Bryony's stomach. 'Do you have any pink gloves to go with that outfit, sweetheart?'

'Somewhere.'

Jack smiled and put her back down. 'Find them for me, there's a good girl.' He looked at Bryony and she smiled, determined to have a nice evening.

'Is my dress decent enough for you, Jack?'

For a moment he didn't react and then he laughed. 'Exactly the way I like it. None of you showing.'

Bryony rolled her eyes and tried not to be offended that he didn't actually want to see any of her body. Obviously she was lacking in something, or he would have pounced on her long ago.

Lizzie came back into the hall, holding her gloves, and Jack nodded.

'Good girl.' He opened the front door and led them towards his car. 'Now, Lizzie, tonight when the fireworks start, I want you to stay by me. The whole time. OK?'

'But what if I want to play with my friends?'

'You can play with them before and after,' he said firmly, strapping her into her seat. 'But during the fireworks, you stay with me.'

Lizzie's eyes were huge and solemn. 'Are you very afraid of them, Jack? Will I need to hold your hand?'

Bryony smothered a giggle but Jack's expression didn't flicker. 'I'm terrified of them, angel. And I'm relying on you to be beside me.'

'I'll be there the whole time,' Lizzie assured him, and Bryony rolled her eyes as she slid into the passenger seat, knowing that Jack had got his own way.

Lizzie's friend Anne lived in a house with a huge garden and they arrived to find that the trees had been decorated with fairy lights and everyone was gathered round, laughing and waiting for sausages to cook.

It felt wintry and cold, and delicious smells wafted through the freezing air.

'Hello, Lizzie.' Anne's mother greeted them warmly and drew them into the garden, introducing them to people they didn't know.

'Where have you stored the fireworks?' was Jack's first question, and Bryony put a hand on his arm and smiled at Anne's mother.

'Jack is a consultant in A and E,' she explained hastily, 'and we doctors are always a bit nervous of fireworks. Take no notice.'

'Anne's father has it all under control,' the woman assured them, waving a hand towards the bottom of the garden. 'The children won't be allowed near them. Apart from the sparklers, of course.'

Bryony saw Jack's mouth open and quickly spoke before he did. 'That's great,' she said cheerfully, her fingers biting into his arm like a vice. 'Those sausages smell fantastic.'

'Well, we're just about ready to eat.' Anne's mother led them to a table loaded with food. 'Grab yourself a roll and some ketchup and tuck in!'

She walked away and Jack scowled at Bryony. 'You just made holes in my arm.'

'I was trying to stop you embarrassing Lizzie,' she hissed, smiling sweetly at one of the mothers who passed. 'Now, eat something and relax. Try and remember that you only see the disasters in A and E. You don't see the normal, happy bonfire parties that everyone enjoys.'

There was a long silence and then, to her surprise, Jack sucked in a breath and gave her a lopsided smile. 'You're right,' he said dryly, running a hand through his cropped dark hair. 'I'm being an idiot. It's just that I love Lizzie so much.'

Bryony's face softened. 'I know you do.' On impulse she stood on tiptoe and kissed his cheek, feeling the roughness of stubble against her lips and smelling the sexy male smell that was Jack.

He looked startled. 'What was that for?'

'For being you.' Deciding that, for a girl who was supposed to be forgetting about Jack, she wasn't actually doing that well, Bryony left him by the bread rolls and went and found Lizzie.

'You kissed Jack.' Lizzie was looking at her curiously and Bryony felt herself blush.

'Just on the cheek,' she said hastily, and Lizzie tipped her head on one side.

'Jack would make a cool dad.'

Pretending that she hadn't heard that remark, Bryony turned to chat to one of the mothers that she knew vaguely, trying not to look at Jack who was now deep in conversation with one of the prettiest mothers in the school. He looked broad-shouldered and powerful with his back to her, and her stomach twisted as she saw the woman laughing up at him flirtatiously.

Reminding herself that she was supposed to be getting a life and forgetting about Jack, Bryony joined in with the others, handing food to the children, topping up drinks and wiping ketchup from faces.

Anne's father lit the bonfire and the flames licked towards the dark sky, suddenly illuminating the massive garden.

'You kids stay here,' he ordered cheerfully. 'I'm going to start the show.'

'Mummy, can I have another drink?' Lizzie tugged at her sleeve, her cheeks pink from the cold, and Bryony took her hand and led her over to the table.

'What do you want?' She picked up some empty cartons and then found a full one. 'Apple juice OK?'

'Great.' Lizzie took the cup and looked around her happily. 'Isn't this great, Mummy? You, me and Jack together.'

Bryony swallowed. 'Well, er, we're not exactly…' Then she smiled weakly. 'Yes, sweetheart, it's great.'

There were shrieks of excitement from the other children as they played closer to the fire and Bryony felt a stab of unease.

They were too close…

Opening her mouth to caution them, she noticed

the other parents laughing, totally relaxed, and closed her mouth again. She really must try and act like a normal parent and not like a doctor, seeing accidents everywhere.

'Can I go and play, Mummy?' Lizzie put her drink down and moved towards the other children, but Bryony grabbed her arm, struck by a premonition so powerful that it made her gasp. 'No, Lizzie. I think—'

Before she could even finish her sentence there was a series of horrific screams from Annie, and Bryony saw flames engulfing her little body with frightening speed.

'Oh, my God—*Jack*!' Bryony screamed his name at the top of her voice and ran forward, dragging off her coat as she ran.

Jack was there before her, knocking the girl to the ground and covering her with his jacket. 'Cold water—get me cold water *now*!' His voice was harsh and everyone ran to do as he said while Bryony stood there, so shocked she could hardly move.

All Jack's attention was on the injured girl. 'It's going to be all right, sweetheart. You're going to be fine.' Jack lifted his head and looked straight at one of the fathers. 'Call the paramedics and get me a hosepipe and cling film. Blondie, I need your help with her clothes.'

Bryony still didn't move.

'Dr Hunter.' His voice was sharp. 'I need your help here.'

His sharp reminder of her profession brought her back to reality. She nodded and breathed deeply, trying to forget that it was Annie lying on the ground.

Her daughter's friend.

Annie's mother was screaming hysterically and clinging to the other mothers while two of the fathers had fortunately listened to Jack's orders and rolled out a hosepipe.

'OK, sweetheart, you're going to be fine.' Jack carried on talking to Annie, his voice gentle and reassuring as he removed his jacket from the injured girl and took the end of the hosepipe.

Bryony dropped on her knees beside him. 'What do you want me to do?'

She felt physically sick but as usual Jack was rock-solid and totally calm.

'Her clothes are smouldering. If they're not actually stuck to her body, I want them off.'

He turned the hose onto Annie's body, the cold water taking the heat away from the burn as Bryony struggled to remove the clothing.

'Get me scissors.'

Someone quickly produced a pair and she cut the clothing away as gently as she could, careful not to disturb any that actually adhered to the burn.

'It's all below her waist,' Jack said softly, his eyes assessing the area of the burn. 'It's the skirt area. Her skirt caught fire. Has someone called the ambulance?'

'I did, Jack,' Lizzie said in a shaky voice from right beside them. 'They said they'd be here in two minutes.'

'Good girl.' Jack gave her a nod of approval. 'Sweetheart, I need some clingfilm. The stuff you wrap round food in the kitchen. The women over there are too upset to help and the men seem to have forgotten. Can you find it for me, angel?'

Lizzie nodded and shot down the garden towards the house, legs and arms pumping. She was back in less than a minute with a long, thin box.

'That's my girl. Now open it up for me,' Jack ordered, and Lizzie fished it out awkwardly and struggled to find the end.

'How much do you want?'

'I'll do it, Lizzie.' Bryony took it from her, worried about her daughter seeing her friend so badly injured. 'You can go into the house with the other children.'

'I want to help.'

They heard the sound of an ambulance approaching and Jack looked at Lizzie. 'Go and meet them. Tell them I want oxygen, two large-bore cannulae, IV fluids and morphine. Have you got that?'

Lizzie nodded and Bryony glanced at him.

'She won't remember that, Jack, she's only seven.'

'She'll remember,' Jack said firmly, his eyes fixed on Lizzie. 'Oxygen, two large-bore cannulae, IV fluids and morphine. Go, angel.'

Lizzie sped back down the garden to meet the ambulance, leaving Jack and Bryony to wrap the exposed burns.

'Can you get us clean sheets?' Bryony addressed one of the fathers who was hovering by helplessly.

'And someone put that bonfire out,' Jack added, checking Annie's pulse and breathing.

She'd stopped screaming and was lying shivering, sobbing quietly, her father by her side.

Annie's mother was still hysterical at the far side of the garden.

Seconds later the paramedics arrived with Lizzie,

complete with all the equipment that Jack had asked for.

As Bryony grabbed the oxygen and fitted the mask gently to Annie's face, Jack smiled at Lizzie, his blue eyes showering her with approval and warmth.

'Good girl.'

Despite the stress of the situation Lizzie returned the smile bravely and Jack gave a nod.

'All right, I'm going to need your help here, Lizzie. Annie needs some fluid and we're going to put a line in and give her fluid through her arm. Then we're going to take her to hospital. I want you to hold this for me.'

Bryony looked at him uncertainly, still not sure that her young daughter should be exposed to the harsh realities of immediate care, but Jack seemed determined to involve her and Lizzie was frowning with concentration as she listened carefully to Jack's instructions and did as he asked.

Too worried about little Annie to argue, Bryony turned her attention back to the little girl, following Jack's instructions to the letter.

'Shall I give her morphine?'

'We're going to give it IV.' Jack murmured, picking up a cannula and searching for a vein. 'Can you squeeze for me?'

Bryony took Annie's little arm and squeezed, praying that Jack would find a vein first time.

He did, of course, and she breathed a sigh of relief.

'Give her the morphine and cyclizine in there and then we'll put a line in the other arm, too,' Jack said, holding out a hand for the syringe that the paramedic was holding ready. 'OK, sweetheart.' He looked down at Annie, his eyes gentle. 'This is going to make you feel better, I promise. And then we're going to take you to hospital. You're doing fine. You're brilliant.'

He gave the morphine and then put a cannula into the other arm and looked at Bryony. 'OK, let's get some fluid into her and get her covered or she'll get hypothermia from the cold water.'

He and Bryony worked together, each anticipating the other's needs, until finally the little girl was stabilised and in the ambulance.

'I'll go with her,' Jack said. 'Meet me at the hospital when you've dropped Lizzie at your mother's.'

'I want to come, too,' Lizzie said firmly, and Bryony shook her head.

'Sweetheart, no.'

'Bring her,' Jack said firmly. 'I'll run her home later. She can wait in the staffroom.'

He dug in his pocket and produced his car keys, a wry smile playing around his firm mouth. 'If you prang my car, Blondie, you're history.' Handing the keys to Lizzie, he jerked his head towards the front of the house. 'Go and wait for your mother by the car, sweetheart.'

Lizzie did as she was told and Jack took Bryony by the shoulders, forcing her to look at him. 'She's just seen her best friend horribly burned,' he said quietly. 'That is going to stay with her a long time and will be easier to bear if she knows she did something to help. Trust me on this one. She's tough, our Lizzie. She'll be fine. But do it my way.'

Bryony swallowed and nodded, knowing that whatever they did now the trauma had already happened for Lizzie. Maybe it was best for her to be involved.

Anne's parents came over, her mother clinging to her husband, her face streaked with tears.

'Can we go in the ambulance with her?'

Jack exchanged glances with one of the paramedics and then nodded. 'Of course. But try and be calm. I know it's a terrible shock but she needs you to be strong. If she sees you panicking, then she'll panic, and I don't want her any more scared than she is already.'

Bryony waited while they loaded Annie into the ambulance and then she joined Lizzie by Jack's car.

She pressed the remote to unlock the door and gave a short laugh. Now she knew it was an emergency. There was no other reason that Jack would have let her near his precious sports car—he never let anyone drive it.

She strapped Lizzie in the front seat and slid into the driver's seat, telling herself that it was only a car. Exactly like her car really, except that it was capable of ridiculous speed and cost about fifteen times as much.

She started the engine and flinched as the car gave a throaty growl. 'Boys with toys,' she muttered disparagingly, finding first gear and carefully pulling out of the driveway onto the road. She just hoped she didn't meet any other traffic on the way to hospital.

When she arrived she settled Lizzie in the staff-room, promising to come back and update her as soon as possible.

Jack was already in Resus, along with Sean

Nicholson and a full team of staff. Jack was barking out instructions as he worked to stabilise Annie.

'Can someone check her weight with her parents?'

'I've just done it.' Bryony hurried into the room and reached in her pocket for a calculator. 'I've worked out 4 mils of fluid per kilogram multiplied by the percentage of the burn. Do you have that yet?'

'Just doing it. My estimate is twenty-two per cent,' Jack said, glancing up at her. 'Are you OK?'

Bryony nodded and studied the Lund and Browder charts that helped them to assess the area of the burn according to age. 'You're about right, Jack,' she said lightly, feeding the numbers into her calculator. 'I make it twenty-two per cent.'

She worked out the volume of fluid and showed her calculation to Jack.

'Right.' He gave a nod. 'So she needs that in twenty-four hours, but we need to give her half in the first eight hours and monitor her urine output. I want her to have a combination of crystalloid and colloid.'

'Catheter is in,' Nicky said quickly, 'and I've started a chart.'

'Great. Can you test her urine? And, Bryony, we need to take some bloods before she's transferred. Cross-matching, FBC, COHb, U and Es, glucose and coagulation.'

Bryony reached for the appropriate bottles. 'You're sending her to the burns unit?'

Jack nodded. 'The helicopter is waiting to take her as soon as we give the word. I've spoken to the consultant, he's waiting for her.'

Bryony took the samples and then went to talk to

Annie. The little girl was drifting in and out of sleep, hardly aware of what was going on around her.

'I gave her some sedation,' Jack said softly, covering the last of the burns and then giving Nicky a nod. 'OK. Let's go.'

'Are you going with her?'

He nodded. 'Take Lizzie home in my car. I'll see you later.'

'How will you get home?'

'I'll get the paramedics to drop me at your place, or I'll grab a taxi.' He shrugged, totally unconcerned, and she nodded.

'Fine. I'll see you later. Do you want me to talk to Annie's parents?'

'I'll do it,' Sean said immediately. 'That way you can get home with your little girl and Jack can get loaded into the helicopter.'

Bryony was tucking Lizzie into bed when she heard the doorbell. 'That will be Jack.'

She dropped a kiss on Lizzie's forehead and went to answer the door, praying that Annie's condition hadn't worsened during the transfer.

'How is she?'

Jack strolled into her house and gave a shiver, and it was only then that she remembered that he'd used his jacket to put out the flames and that he'd been working only in a jumper. He must be freezing.

'Come and sit by the fire,' she urged, and he did as she'd suggested, stretching out his hands towards the flames.

'It's nice and warm in here.' He looked at her. 'Is my girl asleep?'

Bryony shook her head, her expression troubled. 'No. She's very upset by it all.'

'Of course she is.' His jaw tightened. 'I'll talk to her.'

They both walked towards Lizzie's bedroom and Jack strolled in and settled himself on the edge of the bed.

'Hi, there.' His voice was soft and Lizzie stared up at him, her eyes huge in her pretty face.

'Hi, Jack.' Her smile was shaky. 'Annie is very badly hurt, isn't she?'

Jack hesitated. 'She is pretty badly hurt,' he agreed, and Bryony mentally thanked him for not lying. She knew that Annie's condition was serious and if anything happened to the little girl, she didn't want Lizzie to feel that they'd been dishonest.

'Is she going to die?' Lizzie's voice trembled and Jack shook his head.

'No, sweetheart. I'm sure she isn't going to die. I've just taken her to a special hospital where they know all about burns.'

'Can I go and see her there?'

'Sure,' Jack said immediately. 'We'll go together.'

Tears suddenly welled up in Lizzie's eyes and Jack immediately leaned forward and lifted the little girl onto his lap.

'Don't cry, baby,' he said roughly, stroking her hair with his strong hand and exchanging an agonised look with Bryony. 'You were brilliant. My little star. All those grown-ups were panicking and you were cool as ice cream.'

Lizzie gave a sniff and pulled away from him, but her little hands still clutched at his jumper. 'I told the paramedics everything you wanted, just like you said.'

'I know you did.' Jack smiled down at her, pride in his eyes. 'You were unbelievable. And I was so proud of you. You really helped save Annie.'

'I helped?' Lizzie's face brightened slightly. 'Really?'

'Really.' Jack nodded, his handsome face serious. 'You see, you did all the right things. Everyone was scared and I bet you were, too, but you didn't let being scared stop you from doing what needed to be done. And that makes you a very special person.'

'It does?'

'Certainly. I don't know many grown-ups who would have been as calm as you and remembered all those things and done what you did.' Jack lifted a hand and stroked Lizzie's blonde curls away from her face. 'One day, if you wanted to, I think you could be a very important doctor.'

Bryony swallowed down a lump in her throat and Lizzie's eyes widened. 'Like you and Mummy?'

Jack grinned. 'Maybe not quite as important as me,' he said teasingly, winking at Bryony who smiled back weakly. 'But important, just the same.'

Lizzie gave a gurgle of laughter and punched him on the shoulder. 'That's boasting, Jack,' she said reprovingly, and wound her arms round his neck. 'I'm glad you and Mummy were there.'

For a brief moment Jack squeezed his eyes shut, his jaw tense, and Bryony knew exactly what was going through his mind. He'd been imagining a scene where he hadn't been there, a scene where there hadn't been a doctor on site to administer first aid, a scene where Lizzie might have been the one near the bonfire.

She gave a little shudder, imagining the same scene, and Jack's eyes opened and locked on hers for a meaningful second.

'Time for you to go to bed now, angel,' he said softly, lifting Lizzie off his lap and tucking her under the covers with her mermaid. He leaned across and switched her little pink lamp on. 'Your mum and I will just be eating some supper in the kitchen. Shout if you want anything.'

'I don't want you to go home tonight.'

'I'm not going,' Jack said immediately, sounding rock-solid, dependable and altogether too male for Bryony's piece of mind. 'Tonight I'm sleeping in your spare room.'

Lizzie gave a smile and they were just tiptoeing to the door when she spoke again.

'Jack?' Lizzie's voice was a little-girl whisper and Bryony saw Jack's face soften.

'Yes, angel.'

'Tomorrow when we wake up, will you play with me?'

Jack grinned. 'Absolutely.'

'Can we play Weddings?'

'My favourite game,' Jack said softly, walking back across the room and bending down to kiss her one more time. 'Now, get some sleep. I can't marry you with black rings under your eyes.'

Lizzie chuckled, sounding much happier. 'Mummy, will you leave the door open?'

'Of course, sweetheart. And I'll pop my head in later.'

Jack followed Bryony out of the room.

'Thank you for that,' she said quietly, walking
through to the kitchen and opening the fridge. 'You
said all the right things. In fact, you did all the right
things, too. My instincts were to just get her out of
there.'

'That would have been my instinct, too, if she
hadn't already seen her friend engulfed by flames,'
Jack said wearily, sinking down on one of her kitchen
chairs with a groan. 'To be honest, I was mostly concentrating on Annie, but I did think that if Lizzie
knew she'd helped, she might feel better.'

'Which she did.' Bryony removed a bottle of wine
from the fridge and handed it to him along with a
corkscrew. 'I just hope she doesn't have nightmares.'

'She's a tough kid,' Jack said, yanking the cork out
and setting the bottle down on the table. 'She'll be
fine. As soon as Annie is a bit better we can take
Lizzie along to see her.'

We.

Listening to him talking as if they were a family,
Bryony found it harder and harder to remember that
she was supposed to not be thinking of Jack in *that*
way any more.

Remembering how skilled he'd been with Annie
brought a lump to her throat. 'You're amazing, do
you know that?' She reached into the cupboard for
two glasses, trying to keep her tone light. 'You never
lose your cool, no matter what. I just saw Annie on
fire and I froze.'

'Only for about three seconds,' Jack said easily,
stretching out a hand for the glasses and filling them
both to the top. 'And working in a well-equipped

A and E department is very different from immediate care, as you know. Here. Have a drink. I think we both need it.'

'I should cook some supper first.'

'Forget cooking.' Jack took a mouthful of wine and gave a groan of pleasure. 'That's good. Let's send out for pizza or something.'

Bryony giggled. 'I can't do that. Lizzie will find the boxes in the morning and she'll kill me. Pizza is her treat.'

Jack shrugged. 'All right. Indian, then. I left a menu by your phone last time I was here.'

'It would be nice not to cook,' Bryony agreed, and Jack stood up.

'That's decided, then. Indian it is. What do you want?'

Bryony shrugged. 'You choose.'

So he did and the food arrived half an hour later and was wonderful.

They were well into the bottle of wine when they heard Lizzie's screams.

Both of them sprinted to her bedroom to find her sobbing and clutching her mermaid, her face blotched with tears.

'I keep thinking of Annie.'

Bryony cuddled her close, rocking her gently. 'Well, of course you do, darling. Annie is your friend. She's going to be fine, Lizzie.'

As she said the words she prayed that she was right. If anything happened to Annie...

Eventually Lizzie calmed down and fell asleep again and the two of them tiptoed back to the kitchen.

Bryony felt totally stressed and she was seriously

worried about the effect of the accident on her daughter. As Jack had rightly said, she'd actually seen it happen. What sort of impact would that have on her in the long term?

She desperately wanted to lean on Jack but she couldn't bring herself to ask him for the hug she so badly needed.

And then he looked at her and she knew he felt the same way. 'I hate Bonfire Night.'

His voice was hoarse and for the first time Bryony caught a glimpse of the strain he must have been under.

She gave a little frown. 'We forget about you, Jack,' she said softly, stepping up to him and looking at him with concern in her eyes. 'You always seem so strong—so much the one in charge. Everyone else is panicking and flapping and you're so calm. It's easy to forget that you can be affected by things, too.'

'Hey.' He gave a sexy grin that belied the strain in his eyes. 'I'm Mr Tough.'

She smiled. 'Well, would Mr Tough like a cup of coffee?'

'As I'm not driving, I'd rather finish the wine,' he admitted ruefully, reaching for his glass. 'Do you mind me staying?'

'Of course not,' she said blithely, wondering why her heart was thumping so hard. Jack had stayed in her cottage on numerous occasions. Why did this time feel different?

'I'll get you some stuff ready,' she said formally, and he reached out and grabbed her arm.

'Don't bother. I don't wear anything in bed anyway.'

Bryony swallowed hard, trying to dispel the mental image of Jack naked in her spare room.

For a woman who was not supposed to be thinking about Jack Rothwell, she was failing dismally.

'Jack…'

'What I really need is a hug.' Without waiting for a response, he hauled her against him and she went into his arms, feeling the softness of his jumper covering the hard muscle of his chest and the strength of his arms as he held her. He gave a groan and tightened his hold, burying his face in her hair.

Bryony could hardly breathe. She felt the steady thud of his heart against her flushed cheek, felt her whole body tingle in response to the feel of his body against hers. He felt strong and safe and deliciously male.

They stood like that for a moment and she closed her eyes, wishing that it could last for ever. Wishing that it could lead to something more.

And then gradually his grip on her loosened and his hands slid slowly up her arms. His strong fingers curled into her shoulders and he looked down at her, his blue eyes suddenly intent on her face.

A warmth spread slowly through her pelvis and her whole body melted with longing.

She felt his fingers tighten, saw something flicker in his eyes and then his head lowered towards hers.

He was going to kiss her.

Finally, after so many years of dreaming about exactly that, Jack was going to kiss her.

Dizzy with excitement, Bryony stared up at him, breathless with anticipation.

And then suddenly his hands fell away from her

shoulders and he stepped back, his handsome face blank of expression.

'We should probably get some sleep, Blondie.' His tone was light and he glanced at the clock on the wall. 'It's getting late.'

Bryony tried to smile but it was a poor effort. She felt swamped with a disappointment so powerful that it was almost a physical pain. *She'd been so sure that he was going to kiss her.*

But why would Jack kiss her?

She gritted her teeth, furious with herself. She was doing it again. Fantasising about Jack.

So much for her campaign to date other men. So far she'd been on one date that had been an utter disaster and she was still noticing Jack.

She had less than two months to find Lizzie a daddy, or at least someone who looked as though he had potential. It was time she made more effort.

She needed to kiss someone and see if that helped.

She needed to stop comparing everyone with Jack.

There must be another man who looked good in jeans. There must be another man who always knew exactly what to do when everyone around them was panicking. There must be another man who would make her knees wobble every time he walked into a room.

And she was going to find him.

CHAPTER FIVE

THE rest of November flew past and Annie's condition gradually improved.

'The burns are almost all round her skirt area,' Jack told Bryony one day as they snatched a quick cup of coffee during a late shift. 'I talked to the consultant last night. She's going to need extensive skin grafts.'

'Poor mite.' Bryony pulled a face at the thought of the number of hospital stays Annie was going to have to endure. 'It's going to be so hard for her.'

Jack nodded. 'But at least she's alive. And Lizzie seems to have bounced back amazingly well.'

'Yes.' Bryony smiled. 'I was worried about that but she's doing fine. We're visiting Annie a lot, which helps, and Lizzie has made it her mission to act as the link between Annie and the school. She's been taking her all sorts of books and things to do and generally keeping her in touch with the gossip.'

'She's a great girl.' Jack drained his coffee and sat back in his chair with a yawn, long legs stretched out in front of him. 'So, Blondie. December the first tomorrow.'

Bryony stared gloomily into her coffee. 'Don't remind me. I now have less than a month to sort out Lizzie's Christmas present, and I'm fast coming to the conclusion that it's an impossible task.'

Jack looked at her quizzically, a strange light in his

eyes. 'So, is the romance with David Armstrong not working?'

Romance?

Bryony looked at him. 'We've been on two dates. The first one we barely had time to talk because you kept calling—not that it was your fault that Lizzie was demanding that night,' she added hastily, hoping that he didn't think that she was complaining, 'and the second date was disturbed because you called him back to the hospital to see a child. And that wasn't your fault either.'

Jack looked at her, his expression inscrutable. 'And he hasn't asked you out since?'

'Well, funnily enough, he rang me this morning,' Bryony confided, 'and he's taking me to dinner at The Peacock on Saturday. Neither of us is on call and Lizzie is sleeping at my mother's so this time there should be absolutely no interruptions.'

And this time she was going to kiss him.

She'd made up her mind that she was going to kiss him.

She was utterly convinced that kissing another man would cure her obsession with Jack.

David was a good-looking guy. She knew that lots of the nurses lusted after him secretly. He must know how to kiss.

And it was going to happen on Saturday. She was going to invite him in for coffee and she was going to kiss him.

The next day was incredibly busy.

'It's the roads,' Sean said wearily as they snatched a five-minute coffee-break in the middle of a long and intensive shift. 'They're so icy and people drive too fast. I predict a nasty pile-up before the end of the evening.'

His prediction proved correct.

At seven o'clock the ambulance hotline rang. Bryony answered it and when she finally put the phone down both Sean and Jack were watching her expectantly.

'Are you clairvoyant?' She looked at Sean who shrugged.

'Black ice. It was inevitable. What are the details?'

'Twenty-two-year-old female, conscious but shocked and complaining of chest pains.'

She'd barely finished repeating what Ambulance Control had told her when the doors slammed open and the paramedics hurried in with the trolley.

'Straight into Resus,' Jack ordered and they transferred the woman onto the trolley as smoothly as possible. While the rest of the team moved quickly into action he questioned the paramedics about the accident.

'It was a side impact,' the paramedic told him. 'She was driving and the other vehicle went straight into her side. Her passenger walked away virtually unharmed. He's giving her details to Reception now.'

Jack nodded and turned his attention back to the young woman, a frown on his face. 'She has a neck haematoma. I want a chest X-ray, fast,' he murmured, and looked at Bryony. 'Have you got a line in?'

She nodded. 'One.'

'Put in another one,' he ordered, 'but hold the fluid. And cross-match ten units of blood.'

Bryony's eyes widened. 'Why?'

'Just a feeling. Nicky, I want a BP from both arms,' he said, gesturing to the staff to stand back while the radiographer took the chest film.

'Her blood pressure is different in each arm,' Nicky said quickly, and Jack nodded.

'I thought it might be. She's only slightly hypotensive so I want minimal fluid replacement for now.'

Bryony looked at him, waiting for a blonde joke or one of his usual quips that would ease the tension, but this time his eyes were fixed on the patient.

'Fast-bleep the surgeons,' he ordered, 'and let's take a look at that chest X-ray.'

They walked across to look at the chest X-ray and Bryony looked at him, able to talk now that they were away from the patient. 'Why did you cross-match so much blood?'

'Because I think she's ruptured her aorta.'

Bryony's eyes widened. 'But a ruptured aorta has a 90 per cent mortality rate. She'd be dead.'

He squinted at the X-ray. 'Unless the bleed is contained by the aortic adventitia. Then she'd be alive. But at risk of haemorrhage.'

Bryony stared at the X-ray, too, and Jack lifted an eyebrow.

'OK, Blondie—impress me. What do you see?'

'The mediastinum is widened.'

'And is that significant?'

Bryony chewed her lip and delved into her brain. 'On its own, possibly not,' she said, remembering something she'd read, 'but taken with other factors…'

'Such as?'

Bryony looked again, determined not to miss anything. 'The trachea is deviated to the right. The aortic outline is blurred and the aortic knuckle is obliterated.'

'What else?'

'It's cloudy.' She peered closer at the X-ray. 'I haven't seen that before. Is it a haemothorax?'

'Full marks.' He gave her a lazy smile but his eyes glittered with admiration. 'She has a right-sided haemothorax caused by a traumatic rupture of the thoracic aorta, which is currently contained. In this case we can see it clearly on the X-ray, but not always.'

Bryony looked at him and felt her heart thud harder. The patient was lucky to be alive. 'So what happens now?'

'She needs urgent surgical repair. In the meantime, we need to give fluid cautiously, otherwise the adventitia could rupture and she'll have a fatal haemorrhage.'

'So presumably we also need to give her good pain relief so that her blood pressure doesn't go up?'

His eyes rested on her shiny blonde hair and he shook his head solemnly. 'Amazing.'

She poked her tongue out discreetly and he gave her a sexy smile that made her knees wobble.

Fortunately, at that moment the surgeons walked into the room and provided a distraction. They all conferred, agreeing to take the woman to Theatre right away for surgical repair.

'So what exactly do they do?' Bryony asked Jack after the woman had been safely handed over to the surgeons and they were left to deal with the debris in Resus.

'Depends.' He ripped off his gloves and dropped them into the bin. 'They'll attempt a surgical repair.'

'And if they can't repair it?'

'Then they'll do a vascular graft.'

Bryony helped Nicky to clean the trolley. 'But what made you suspect an aortic rupture? I always thought patients died at the scene of the accident.'

'Well, if they're alive it basically suggests a partial injury,' he told her. 'It's often hard to diagnose on X-ray. A widened mediastinum doesn't necessarily indicate an abnormality. But in her case there were other classic chest X-ray signs and she had clinical signs too. The neck haematoma, asymmetric BP and chest pain.'

'And if the X-ray hadn't been clear?'

'I would have talked to the consultant radiologist and we would have done a multi-slice CT scan. It's worth finding out as much as you can about the details of the accident. The paramedic told us her car had been hit on the driver's side. A significant number of blunt traumatic aortic ruptures are caused by side impact.'

Bryony stared at him in fascination. 'What's the pathology?'

'Basically a sudden deceleration such as a fall from a height or an RTA allows the mobile parts of the aorta to keep moving. It usually tears where the aorta is tethered to the pulmonary vein—'

'The ligamentum arteriosum,' Bryony intervened, and he rolled his eyes.

'If there's one thing I can't stand, it's a brainy blonde,' he drawled, and she clucked sympathetically.

'If I'm threatening your ego then just let me know.'

'My ego is shivering,' he assured her, his blue eyes twinkling as looked down at her. 'What do you get when you give a blonde a penny for her thoughts?'

'Change,' Bryony said immediately, tilting her head to one side. 'Why is a man like a vintage wine?'

Jack's eyes narrowed and his mouth twitched. 'Go on…'

'Because they all start out like grapes,' Bryony said cheerfully, 'and it's a woman's job to tread all over them and keep them in the dark until they mature into something you'd like to have dinner with.'

Nicky gave a snort of amusement from the corner of the room and Jack grinned.

'That's shockingly sexist, Blondie.'

'Just giving as good as I get.'

Jack's smile faded. 'And talking about having dinner, haven't you got a date tomorrow night?'

'Yes.' Bryony frowned as she remembered that she had all of three weeks to find a man who might make a good father for Lizzie. By anyone's standards it was a tall order.

But at least she had another date with David so he must be fairly keen.

And he was a really nice man. Her eyes slid to Jack's face and then away again. She wasn't going to compare him to Jack. All right, so Jack was staggeringly handsome and he was clever and he had a great sense of humour— She cut herself off before the list grew too long. Jack didn't do commitment. And Jack didn't notice her. Which ruled him out as a potential partner.

At least David noticed her.

And she was going to start noticing him, she told

herself firmly, leaving the room so that she wouldn't be tempted to continually look at Jack.

'I'm really looking forward to tonight.' Bryony slid into David's car and gave him a smile. 'The food is meant to be great and Lizzie is at my mother's so we are guaranteed no interruptions.'

David waited while she fastened her seat belt and then pulled out of her drive. 'Let's hope not.'

They walked into the restaurant ten minutes later and Bryony gave a gasp of delight as she saw the Christmas tree sparkling by the log fire. 'Oh—it's lovely.'

And romantic.

How could she and David fail to further their relationship in this atmosphere?

It was made for lovers.

She handed over her coat, feeling David's eyes slide over her.

'You look great,' he said quietly, and she smiled shyly, pleased that she'd bought the red dress she'd seen on a shopping expedition a week earlier.

'So do you.'

And he did. He was wearing a dark, well-cut suit and she saw several female heads turn towards him as they were shown to their table.

All right, so he didn't make her knees wobble but that was a good thing surely. With Jack she actually felt physically sick every time he walked into a room, which was utterly ridiculous. She couldn't concentrate and she couldn't breathe. All she was aware of was him. And that wasn't what she wanted in a stable, long-term relationship.

At least being with David didn't make her feel sick with excitement.

They ordered their food and then David picked up his glass and raised it. 'To an uninterrupted evening.'

She smiled and lifted her glass in response but before she could speak she gave a gasp of surprise. 'Oh—it's Jack!'

David's jaw tightened and he put his glass carefully down on the table. *'Jack?'*

'Jack Rothwell. He's just walked in with some blonde.'

Bryony felt a flash of jealousy as she studied Jack's companion. She was his usual type. Endless legs, silvery blonde hair and a skirt that barely covered her bottom. She wore a very low-cut top and Bryony glanced at Jack to see signs of disapproval, but he seemed perfectly relaxed, his eyes twinkling flirtatiously as he laughed at something the girl had said.

By contrast, David was glowering, his earlier good humour seemingly gone as he reached for his wine.

'Well…' Bryony made a determined effort not to look at Jack and not to mind that he didn't appear to have noticed her anyway. 'That's a coincidence.'

'Is it?' David's eyes glittered ominously and he sat back in his chair as the waiter poured more wine into his glass. 'Aren't you beginning to wonder why it is that Jack Rothwell would want to sabotage every date we have?'

'Sabotage?' Bryony looked at him in astonishment and gave a puzzled laugh. 'Jack has nothing to do with the fact that our last two dates haven't worked out that well.'

'No?'

'Well, he's certainly not sabotaging tonight,' Bryony said reasonably. 'I mean, he hasn't even noticed we're here. He's with a woman himself.'

She glanced across the restaurant again and immediately wished she hadn't. Jack was leaning forward, his attention totally focused on his beautiful companion.

Bryony looked away quickly, trying not to mind. Knowing that she had no right to mind.

And, anyway, she was with David.

But he was looking at her with an odd expression on his face. 'He knows you're here,' he said quietly, 'and no man could fail to notice you, Bryony.'

She blushed at the compliment. 'Well, that's very kind of you, but I can assure you that Jack certainly doesn't notice me in the way you're suggesting.'

In fact, he didn't seem to notice her as a woman at all. Until she wore something that he disapproved of, she thought gloomily. Goodness knew how he would have reacted had she been the one dressed like his date. He probably would have had her locked up. But evidently the girl staring into his eyes at that precise moment was allowed to dress however she pleased.

Realising that she was staring again, Bryony turned her attention back to David but the atmosphere had changed. She made a valiant attempt to keep up lively conversation but it seemed like hard work.

In the end they ate their starter in virtual silence and Bryony's gaze flickered surreptitiously to Jack yet again.

Immediately their eyes locked and she swallowed hard, aware that he must have been looking at her.

His eyes held hers and everything and everyone else in the room gradually faded into the background. For Bryony there was just Jack and he seemed as reluctant to break the contact as she was.

Her heart banged against her ribs with rhythmic force and the sick feeling started in her stomach.

And still Jack's eyes held hers.

They might have stared at each other for ever if the waiter hadn't chosen that moment to deliver their next course, walking across their line of vision.

Staring down at her plate, Bryony realised that suddenly she wasn't hungry any more. Her insides felt totally jumbled up.

Why had Jack been staring at her like that?

Did he disapprove of her seeing David? Did he think that she was dating the wrong man?

She pushed her food around her plate, miserably aware that David had finished his main course and was now watching her in silence.

Finally he spoke. 'You don't seem hungry.'

'Not very.' She put her fork down and smiled at him apologetically. 'I'm so sorry.'

'It doesn't matter.'

She bit her lip, embarrassed that the evening was going so badly. 'I'm just a bit tired—it's been a pretty busy week.'

'Do you want to go home?'

She hesitated and then nodded. 'Yes. If that's all right with you.'

'Shall we have coffee first?'

She remembered her resolution to kiss him. 'No,' she croaked. 'Let's have coffee at my house.'

He looked at her thoughtfully and seemed to relax

slightly. Then he nodded and rose to his feet. 'Good idea. Come on. I'll settle the bill while they get our coats.'

'If you've finished, I'll take her home.' Jack's deep voice came from right beside her, his eyes fixed on her face. 'It's on my way.'

The two men stared at each other with ill-disguised hostility.

'She's my date,' David said tightly, and Jack smiled.

'You've had your date,' he drawled softly, 'and now I'm taking her home.'

Realising that everyone in the restaurant was staring at them, Bryony flushed scarlet and tugged Jack's arm.

'For goodness' sake, Jack! Everyone's looking at us.'

Jack gave a dismissive shrug that indicated just how little he was bothered by other people's opinions and then he smiled as his date for the evening joined them. 'Nina, this is David. He's offered to take you home.'

Nina gave Jack a longing look that left no one in any doubt as to how she felt about him. And then she sighed and shot David a dazzling smile. 'If you're sure it's no trouble...'

Wondering why Nina was giving up so easily, Bryony watched as David's eyes dropped to the neckline of Nina's dress which revealed a hypnotic amount of female flesh.

He stared in blatant fascination and then finally cleared his throat and dragged his gaze up to Nina's.

'It's no trouble at all,' he said hoarsely and Bryony resisted the temptation to scream with frustration.

Men were just so pathetic!

Boiling with anger, she said goodnight to David and Nina and followed Jack across the car park.

He unlocked the car and opened the door for her and she slid inside and yanked at the seat belt.

As Jack settled himself in the driver's seat, she let rip.

'David was my date! You had no right to interfere.'

Jack reversed out of his parking space. 'I merely offered to take you home.'

'You didn't offer, Jack,' she said caustically, 'you insisted. David was taking me home and he was ready to argue until your Nina thrust her chest in his face.'

Jack grinned, maddeningly unperturbed by her outburst. 'Impressive, isn't she? I thought as I was taking you away from him, I ought to offer him something in compensation.'

'So I suppose she was the *booby* prize?' Bryony's voice dripped sarcasm and Jack's grin widened.

'Booby prize.' He repeated her words and chuckled with appreciation. 'I admit I hadn't thought of it in exactly those terms, but now you mention it...'

Bryony ground her teeth in frustration. 'You are so hypocritical, do you know that? You have the nerve to criticise my black dress and then you go out with a girl who has a cleavage the size of the Grand Canyon and shows it off to the entire population. I didn't notice you covering *her* up with a coat.'

Jack glanced across at her and in the semi-darkness she could see his eyes twinkling wickedly. 'It would have had to be a big coat and it seemed a shame to deprive everyone of the view,' he drawled, and she felt fury mix with a very different emotion.

Hurt.

When Nina wore a low-cut dress, Jack obviously thought she looked incredibly attractive. But when *she* wore one he thought she looked awful and tried to cover her up.

David had said that she looked nice but, thanks to Jack, David was now with Nina and was doubtless enjoying the view as much as all the other men in the restaurant.

And she was with a man who didn't find her attractive and never would.

'There are times when I hate you, Jack Rothwell,' she muttered, and he gave a soft laugh.

'I don't know what you're getting so worked up about, Blondie.'

For once his use of her nickname irritated her. 'He was my date, Jack. *My date.* And you ruined it.'

To her utter humiliation she felt a lump starting in her throat. She wasn't going to cry in front of Jack.

But fortunately Jack had his eyes fixed on the road. 'How did I ruin it?'

'You really need to ask that question?' She stared at him incredulously. 'I was spending the evening with a man and you suddenly dived in and insisted on taking me home. And I really don't understand why.'

In the moonlight she saw the muscle in his jaw flicker. 'The roads are icy. I didn't want him driving you.'

Her jaw fell open. 'You think you're the only man who can drive on ice?'

'No.' His tone was calm. 'But I've never seen David Armstrong drive on ice and until I do, he's not driving you.'

'Jack, you're being ridiculous!' She looked at him in exasperation. 'And what about Nina? You were perfectly happy for him to drive Nina.'

'Nina can look after herself.'

Bryony slumped back in her seat and gritted her teeth. 'And I can't?'

'You know nothing about men.'

'I thought we were talking about ice?'

'Amongst other things.'

'Oh, right. So we're back to the fact that I haven't dated anyone for ages. It doesn't make me stupid, Jack.'

'And it doesn't make you experienced.'

'Well, it's obvious that I'm never going to get any experience while I'm living in the same town as you!' She glared at him and he gave a shrug.

'I don't know why you're making such a fuss. You had your date. You spent the evening together. Was it good, by the way?'

She opened her mouth to tell him that, no, it had not been good because she'd been staring at him all night, but she realised in time just how much that would reveal about her feelings and stopped herself.

'It was fine,' she lied, 'but it hadn't finished. I wanted *him* to take me home.' And she'd wanted him to kiss her just to see whether it was possible for another man to take her mind off Jack.

'You wanted him to take you home?' There was a tense silence and she saw Jack's fingers tighten on the wheel. 'Why?' His voice was suddenly harsh. 'Or was that where the date was supposed to begin? Keen to make up for lost time, were you?'

His tone was frosty and she gave an exclamation of disgust. 'And so what if it was? What I do with my life is none of your business. I don't need you to look out for me, Jack.'

It was only when he stopped the car and switched off the engine that she realised that they were outside her home. The house was in darkness and suddenly she felt utterly depressed and lonely. Maybe Lizzie was right, she thought miserably. It would be great to walk into her house, knowing that someone was waiting for her. It would be great to have someone to hug her at night. She'd been without a man for almost all her life and suddenly she wanted someone special. Someone who cared whether she came home or not.

But so far her quest for a man had been a disaster.

And suddenly she just wanted to be on her own.

'Well, thanks, Jack. Thanks for ruining my evening.' She undid her seat belt and reached down to pick up her bag. 'I would invite you in for coffee but, seeing as you think that's a euphemism for sex, naturally I wouldn't dream of it. And anyway I'm sure you're dying to get back to Nina.'

'Nina is just a friend.'

'I really couldn't care less, Jack,' she lied, 'because your love life isn't any of my business, just as my love life is none of your business. A whole month has gone past since Lizzie sent her letter to Santa and so far I haven't even managed to get a man to kiss me.'

'You want a man to kiss you?' Jack's voice was a deep growl and without waiting for her answer he slid a hand round her head and brought his mouth down on hers with punishing force. His long fingers bit into her scalp and he lifted his other hand and curved it around her cheek, holding her face still for his kiss.

Utterly shocked, Bryony lifted a hand to his chest, intending to push him away, but instead her traitorous fingers curled into his shirt, then loosened a button and slid inside. Her fingers felt the roughness of his chest hair, warm skin and solid muscle and she felt his grip on her head tighten as his kiss gentled and his tongue traced the seam of her mouth, coaxing her to open for him.

And then he was really kissing her.

Kissing her in the way that she'd always known only he could.

And it felt like magic. How could one person make another feel so different unless it was magic? She was trembling and shivering, overwhelmed by an excitement so intense that she didn't know where it was leading or how it would end. She only knew that she wanted to get closer to him, to crawl all over him but the seats in the car didn't exactly encourage that type of contact. So instead she leaned into him, sliding her hand around his body and trying to draw him closer.

His tongue teased hers gently and then dipped deeper, exploring the interior of her mouth with a lazy expertise that was so erotic it set her entire body on fire. With a maddening degree of self-control, he slid the backs of his fingers over her cheek and down to her neck, trailing his fingers tantalisingly close to her aching breasts before stopping just short of his target. Bryony whimpered with frustration. Longing for his touch, she arched against him but he didn't move his hand. Instead, he continued to kiss her with increasing intensity until none of her senses were under her control.

And then finally, just when she thought her entire body would explode with frustration, he touched her. His strong hand cupped one breast through the silken fabric of her dress and then he drew his thumb over her nipple, creating an agony of sensation so powerful that she gasped against his mouth and shifted in the seat to try and relieve the nagging throb between her thighs.

'Jack…'

The moment she sobbed his name he lifted his head, his breathing unsteady as he stared down at her. Then he released her abruptly and ran a hand over his face, obviously as shaken as she was.

Her whole body screamed in protest that he'd stopped and she looked at him in dazed confusion.

'Jack?'

She saw him tense and then he turned to face her, his handsome face totally blank of expression. 'Now do you see?'

She swallowed, finding it terribly hard to concentrate, still suffering from the aftershocks of his kiss. 'Now do I see what?'

'That kisses can get out of control.' His eyes dropped to her parted lips, still swollen and damp from the ruthless demands of his mouth and then dropped further still to the outline of her breasts which pushed boldly against her dress. He dragged his gaze away and stared into the darkness. 'That's what would have happened if you'd invited David Armstrong back for coffee.'

Bryony stared at him in silence.

She felt as though the world had changed shape. As if everything should look different. It certainly felt different.

For her, their entire relationship had changed in an instant. The moment his mouth had touched hers, everything had become different.

But evidently he didn't feel the same way.

Chewing her lip, she reminded herself that this was Jack. Jack, whose parents had divorced when he was eight and who had vowed never to get married himself when he grew up. And then he'd grown up and had shown no intention of changing his mind about that one fact. Jack didn't do relationships. Judging from the few conversations she'd overheard between her brothers, Jack did sex and not much else.

But even knowing that, her whole body flooded with disappointment as she realised that obviously the kiss hadn't meant anything at all to him. He'd actually been proving a point and in doing so he'd proved something to her, too.

That she'd been right all along about Jack.

He was an amazing kisser.

And she knew that the same thing would never have happened had she invited David Armstrong back for coffee. David might have kissed her, that was true, but she knew that there wasn't another man on the planet who would make her feel what Jack had just made her feel.

But it was totally hopeless.

And the raw, sexual attraction she felt for Jack shouldn't interfere with her determination to find a father for Lizzie, she told herself firmly.

That was just lust and lust always faded anyway.

She needed a man who would be kind, good company and a caring father to Lizzie. She didn't need raw sexual attraction. In fact, raw sexual attraction was starting to turn her into a nervous wreck.

So she lifted her chin and smiled at Jack, proud of how natural it seemed. 'Well, thanks for the practice,' she said lightly, leaning forward and kissing him on the cheek, resisting the almost overwhelming temptation to trace a route to his mouth with the tip of her tongue. 'I'd forgotten how to do it, but you reminded me. Now I know I'll get it right next time I go out with David.'

And with that she opened the door, climbed out of the car and walked to her cottage without looking back.

CHAPTER SIX

DAMN. Damn. Damn.

What the hell had he done?

He'd kissed his best friend.

Jack stared after Bryony, trying to decide what shocked him most. The fact that he'd kissed her, or the fact that he hadn't wanted to stop.

He sat in the car with the engine switched off, staring into the frozen darkness feeling as though something fundamental to his existence had changed.

Where had it come from? That sudden impulse to kiss her...

Blondie was family.

As much a baby sister to him as she was to Tom and Oliver.

And until tonight he'd never thought of her in any other way.

Or had he?

Had he really never thought of her like that or was it just that he'd trained himself not to?

He sat still, watching the house, and then suddenly the lights went on. He saw her walk into her cosy sitting room and shrug off her coat, revealing that amazing red dress and an avalanche of blonde hair.

For years he hadn't seen her in a dress and suddenly she seemed to be wearing a different one every week.

He closed his eyes and breathed deeply, still able

to detect the tantalising scent of her hair and skin. The instantaneous reaction of his body was so powerful that he gritted his teeth and shifted slightly in his seat, trying to find a more comfortable position.

There wasn't one.

Suddenly, somehow, she'd invaded every part of him.

He'd made an unconscious decision never to cross that boundary but now he'd crossed it there was no going back.

Whichever way he looked at her, he didn't see a surrogate sister any more. And he didn't see his best friend. He saw a woman. A living, breathing, stunningly beautiful woman.

But he couldn't do anything about it.

Lizzie was looking for a father. Someone strong who could swing her in the garden. Someone funny who'd let her watch television before school and who wouldn't make her eat sprouts.

Well, he could do that bit with no problem. He wasn't that keen on sprouts himself so he was more than happy to collude over their exclusion from their diet. And he had no trouble swinging her in the garden, hugging her and making her laugh. In fact, he was great at all those things.

The problem came with the last bit of her letter.

I want a daddy who will hug my mummy and stay with us for ever.

Jack leaned his head back against the seat and let out a long breath. He didn't do for ever. He had trouble doing next month. The whole concept of 'for ever' frightened the life out of him.

And Bryony knew that.

She knew him better than anyone.

Which was probably why she'd looked so shocked when he'd kissed her. Hell, *he'd* been shocked! And now he was confused, too, which was a totally new experience for him. He was *never* confused about women. He knew *exactly* what he wanted from them.

Everything, as long as it wasn't permanent.

Which meant that he had absolutely nothing to offer Bryony.

He started the engine and clenched his hands on the wheel. *He had to stop noticing her as a woman.* Surely it couldn't be that hard? After all, he'd only just started noticing her that way. It couldn't be that hard to go back to seeing her as his best friend.

He'd just carry on as they always had. Dropping round to see her. Chatting in her kitchen. And seeing other women.

It would be fine.

If working with Jack had been hard before the kiss, for Bryony it became even harder afterwards.

When he walked into a room she knew instantly, even when she had her back to him.

She didn't need to see him. She *felt* him. Felt his presence with every feminine bone in her body.

And she noticed everything about him. The way the solid muscle of his shoulders moved when he reached up to yank an X-ray out of the lightbox, the way his head tilted slightly when he was concentrating on something and the way everyone always asked his opinion on everything. She noticed how good he was with anxious relatives, how strong and capable he was with terrified patients and how well he dealt with inexperienced staff. He was the cleverest doctor she'd ever worked with and he had an instinctive feel for what was wrong with a patient before he'd even examined them.

If she'd had butterflies before he'd kissed her, they seemed to have multiplied since the kiss.

Which was utterly ridiculous because obviously, for him, nothing had changed.

Their relationship followed the same pattern of blonde jokes, man jokes and evenings when he sat with his feet on her table in the kitchen, watching while she cooked, a bottle of beer snuggled in his lap.

And now they were into December and there was no sign of a man who was even remotely close to fulfilling Lizzie's criteria for a daddy.

David hadn't asked her out again and she'd resigned herself to the fact that he was probably now dating Nina.

'Are you upset about that?' she asked Jack one evening, when they were curled up in front of the fire. She was writing Christmas cards and he was staring into the flames with a distant look in his eyes.

'Upset about what?'

'Nina.' She said the other woman's name as lightly as possible. 'Someone told me that she's seeing David Armstrong.'

'Is she?' Jack suppressed a yawn and stretched long legs out in front of him. 'Well, good for him.'

'You never should have sent them home together. I'm amazed you're not upset.'

He gave her a mocking smile. 'Come on, Blondie. How long have you known me?'

She stared at him. 'You engineered it, didn't you?'

Her pen fell to the floor as she suddenly realised what had happened. 'You got rid of her.'

His gaze didn't flicker. 'I encouraged her to find someone else, yes.'

'Why?' Bryony shook her head, puzzled. 'She was nice. And she seemed crazy about you.'

Jack looked at her steadily. 'She was.'

Which was why he'd ended it.

It was Jack's usual pattern.

Bryony sighed. 'Jack, you're thirty-four,' she said softly. 'You can't run for ever.'

He gave a funny lopsided grin that made her heart turn over. 'Watch me.'

'Listen…' She put her pen down and gave up on her Christmas cards. They could wait. 'I know your parents' divorce was really difficult for you, but you can't—'

'Drop it, Blondie. I don't want to talk about it.' His eyes glittered ominously and she saw the warning in the blue depths. Taboo subject.

She sighed. 'But, Jack, you can't—'

'Why did the blonde tiptoe past the medicine cabinet?' he drawled lazily, and she rolled her eyes, exasperated by his refusal to talk about his emotions.

'I don't know.'

'Because she didn't want to wake the sleeping pills.' Jack gave a wicked smile that made her heart jump in her chest.

He was so shockingly handsome it was totally unfair, and when he smiled like that she just melted.

'How many men does it take to change a toilet roll?' She smiled sweetly. 'No one knows. It's never been done. So what did Nina do wrong?'

Jack gave a sardonic smile. 'Frankly? She said, ''I love you'',' he said dryly, and gave a mock shudder. 'Which is the same as ''goodbye'' in my language.'

Bryony rolled her eyes. 'They always say that if you want to get rid of a man, you should say ''I love you, I want to marry you and most of all I want to have your children.'' It's guaranteed to leave skid marks.'

Jack laughed. 'That's just about the size of it. Why do you think I bought a Ferrari?'

Bryony sighed. 'Poor Nina.'

'She knew the score.'

But Bryony was willing to bet that knowing the score hadn't made it any easier. On the other hand, Nina seemed to have moved on quite happily to David so she couldn't have been that broken-hearted.

'One day you'll settle down, Jack,' Bryony predicted, licking another envelope. 'You'll be such a great father.'

'That's nonsense.'

'Look how great you are with Lizzie.'

'That's because I have all the fun and none of the responsibility,' he said shortly, frowning slightly as he looked at her.

'I don't think that's true. Lizzie expects a lot from you and you always deliver. How many netball matches have you been to this year?'

Jack grinned. 'Lots. You know me. Rugby, rock-climbing, netball—my three favourite sports.'

She laughed. 'Precisely. The sight of you standing on the side of a netball court would be funny if it wasn't so touching.' She added the envelope to the ever-growing pile. 'And it is touching, Jack. You're fantastic with Lizzie.'

A muscle worked in his jaw. 'But what she really wants is a father.'

Bryony shrugged. 'And who can blame her for that?'

'She doesn't realise that fathers aren't perfect.'

'I think she probably does, actually. But she still wants someone.'

'So how is the quest going? Any suitable candidates lined up? Obviously David is now off the scene…'

Something in his tone made her glance up at him but his expression was neutral.

'Well, it's not going that well,' Bryony muttered, licking another envelope and adding it to the pile. 'Christmas is three weeks away and I don't have another date until Saturday.'

His expression was suddenly hostile. 'You have a date on Saturday? Who with?'

Bryony blushed slightly. 'Toby.'

'Toby who?' Jack was frowning and she laughed.

'You know—our Toby. Toby from the mountain rescue team.'

'You're kidding!' He glared at her. 'Toby? He's totally unsuitable.'

'Calm down, Jack,' Bryony said mildly, gathering up all the envelopes and putting them on the table. 'Toby is nice. And he's always been kind to Lizzie.'

'Toby has a terrible reputation with women,' Jack said frostily, and she shrugged.

'So do you, Jack.'

'But I'm not dating you.'

And how she wished he was. Her gaze met his and held and then he sucked in a breath and rose to his feet, powerful and athletic.

'You can't date Toby.'

'Why not?'

There was a long silence and a muscle twitched in his jaw. 'Because he isn't right for you.'

She sighed. 'Jack, you're so jaded about relationships that you're never going to think anyone is right, but trust me when I say I'm not going to choose anyone who would hurt Lizzie.'

He took several deep breaths. 'I don't want anyone to hurt you either.'

'I know that.' She smiled at him, touched that he cared at least that much. 'You don't need to be so protective. It's nice, but I can look after myself.'

'Where are you going on Saturday?'

She wondered why he was asking and then decided that it was idle curiosity. 'Actually, I don't know. Toby is keeping it a secret.' She smiled. 'Isn't it romantic?'

'Suspicious is the word I would use,' Jack muttered, grabbing his coat and car keys and making for the door. 'I'll talk to him.'

Bryony gave an exasperated sigh. 'Jack, you are not my minder.'

'Toby is definitely not to be trusted when it comes to women,' Jack growled. 'I want him to know that I'm looking out for you.'

'I should think he knows that, seeing as you spend half your life in my house,' Bryony pointed out mildly, and he nodded.

'Well, let's hope so. I won't have him messing either of my girls around.'

His girls.

Bryony swallowed and her eyes clashed with his. Something flickered in those blue depths and she knew that he was remembering their kiss. 'We're not "your girls", Jack.'

He hesitated and a strange expression crossed his handsome face as he stared down at her. Then he muttered something under his breath, jerked open the front door and left the house.

The next day the temperature dropped further still and it started to snow. Wrapped up in her MRT gear, Bryony was posting her Christmas cards when her pager went off.

Relieved that Lizzie was spending the day with her mother, she drove herself to the rescue base, which was less than five minutes' drive from her house.

'Two women out walking,' Jack told her, zipping up his jacket. 'One has cut herself and one has an ankle injury.' He exchanged looks with Bryony. 'What is it with women and ankles?'

'I don't know but at least it gives you and me an excuse to climb mountains in filthy weather,' she said happily, and he smiled.

'I suppose there is that.'

The rest of the team gathered, picking up equipment and listening while they were given a brief.

'We're not sure where they are—' Sean, leader of the MRT, tapped a point on the map '—but this was where they were aiming for when it started to snow. The path is covered now and they're totally lost.'

Bryony looked at the map. 'It's really easy to lose that path in bad weather,' she said. 'I know because I've done it myself.'

Jack rolled his eyes. 'Never let a blonde loose on a mountain,' he drawled, but his eyes gleamed wickedly and she smiled back at him.

'At least a girl will ask for directions if she's lost. Men never ask for directions.'

'That's because they don't need to. Men don't get lost,' Jack returned blithely, and Sean sighed.

'Maybe you two could argue on the way,' he suggested mildly, pointing at the map. 'Ben, you go with Toby up this path and hopefully we'll come across them. Stay in touch. And watch yourselves. The weather is awful. I'll deploy the rest of the team as they arrive.'

Toby glanced at Bryony. 'I could go with Bryony…'

'No, you couldn't.' Jack's response was instantaneous, his blue gaze hard and uncompromising. 'I go with Bryony.'

Toby's eyes narrowed slightly and then he shrugged. 'Whatever.'

Bryony followed Jack out of the rescue base and they drove a short distance and parked the four-wheel-drive in a farm near the path.

Jack hoisted the rucksack onto his back and waited while she did the same thing. 'Come on. We need to get going before we freeze to death.'

They set off at a brisk pace and she glanced at the sky. 'It's going to snow again in a minute.'

'It's Christmas,' Jack pointed out. 'It's supposed to snow.'

Bryony gave a shiver and pulled her fleece up to her chin. 'Well, it looks nice on the Christmas cards but it's not so great when you're out on the mountains. Why didn't you let me go with Toby?'

'Because he'd be so busy staring at your legs he'd let you fall down a crevice.'

Bryony gaped at him. 'Jack, I'm wearing fleece trousers. They're hardly revealing!'

'Your legs would look sexy in a bin bag.'

She stopped dead. He thought her legs were sexy? He'd never said anything like that to her before. She was staring after him in confusion, wondering why he'd said that, when he glanced back at her.

'Why have you stopped? You needed to admire me from a distance?'

She grinned, suddenly feeling light-hearted. 'Why are men like placemats?' Shifting her rucksack slightly to make it more comfortable, she caught up with him. 'Because they only show up when there's food on the table.'

He smiled and as they continued up the path it started to snow again. 'I hope they've got some form of shelter,' Jack muttered, and Bryony nodded, her expression concerned.

'I hope we find them soon. It'll be dark in a couple of hours.'

They trudged on and the snow suddenly grew thicker underfoot.

'Crampons and ice axes, I think, Blondie,' Jack muttered, pausing by a snow-covered rock and swinging his rucksack off his back.

They stopped just long enough to equip themselves

safely for the next part of the rescue and then they were off again.

Bryony stayed behind Jack, watching him place his feet firmly and confidently in the snow, the sharp points of his crampons biting into the snow.

They walked for what felt like ages and then suddenly heard shouts from above them.

'Sounds hopeful,' Jack said, increasing his pace and altering his direction slightly. 'We'll check it out and then I'll radio in to base.'

Bryony breathed a sigh of relief when they rounded the next corner and saw two women huddled together.

'Watch your footing here,' Jack said, frowning slightly as he glanced to his right. 'There's a slope there and a sheer drop at the end of it. I know because I climbed up that rockface last summer with your brothers. This snow doesn't feel very stable to me.'

'Shall we rope up?'

He shook his head. 'We're all right for now, but we'll rope up before we go down.'

They reached the two women and one of them immediately burst into tears.

'Oh, thank goodness...'

Bryony dropped onto her knees beside her, aware that Jack was already on the radio, giving their exact location to the rest of the team.

'You're going to be fine,' she said gently, slipping her arm around the woman's shoulders and giving her a hug. 'Where are you hurt?'

'I'm not hurt,' the woman said, but her teeth were chattering and she was obviously very cold. 'But my sister slipped on the snow and hurt her ankle and cut her wrist. I think she must have hit a rock when she landed. It was bleeding very badly so I pressed on it hard with a spare jumper that we had in our bag and it seemed to stop.'

'Good—you did just the right thing.' Bryony shrugged her rucksack off her back. 'I'm Bryony and I'm a doctor and a member of the local mountain rescue team. What's your name?'

'Alison Gayle.' The woman was shivering. 'And my sister's name is Pamela. I feel so guilty dragging you out in this weather. We've put everyone in danger.'

'Don't feel guilty,' Bryony said immediately, 'and you haven't put us in danger. It's our job and we love it. And we have all the right equipment for this weather.'

Which was just as well, she reflected ruefully, because the weather was getting worse by the second.

The snow started to fall heavily and Bryony brushed the soft flakes away from her face with a gloved hand and looked at the sky with a frown. The visibility was reducing rapidly. She moved over to check on Pamela and Jack joined her.

'All right, the rest of the team is on their way up.' He dropped down next to her and smiled at Alison. 'Lovely day for a stroll in the hills.'

Bryony moved over to Pamela and noticed that the woman looked extremely pale and shocked.

'You're going to be fine now, Pamela,' she said firmly. 'I'm just going to check your injuries and then we're going to get you off this mountain.'

She pulled off her gloves and carefully unwrapped the blood-soaked jumper so that she could examine the wrist injury more carefully. As soon as she released the pressure and exposed the wound, blood spurted into the air and Bryony quickly grabbed the jumper and pressed down again.

'It's an artery, Jack,' she muttered and he was by her side in an instant, the bulk of his shoulders providing a barrier between her and the elements.

He was strong and confident and, as usual, she found his presence hugely reassuring.

'I've put Alison into a casualty bag so she'll be fine for the time being.' He unwrapped the wrist himself, quickly assessed the extent of the injury and then pressed a sterile pad over the laceration and smiled at Pamela.

'That's going to be fine,' he said smoothly, elevating her arm and handing a bandage to Bryony with his free hand. 'We're going to bandage it tightly and keep it up just until we can get you off this mountain.'

The woman looked at him with frightened eyes. 'I can't walk down—my ankle hurts.'

'Don't you worry about that. That's why we bring my blonde friend here,' Jack said cheerfully, winking at Bryony. 'She's the muscles of the operation.'

While he chatted and teased, Bryony tightened the bandage and gave him a nod. 'All done.'

'Good. So now let's check the ankle. How painful is it, Pamela?'

The woman looked at him, her lips turning blue with the cold. 'Agony.'

'So we'll give you some gas and air to breathe while we check it out,' Jack said immediately, reaching into his rucksack. 'I want you to take some slow breaths. Great—perfect.' He looked at Bryony. 'Right, can you cut that boot off and let's see what we're dealing with here? And make it quick. She's cold and we need to get her into a casualty bag.'

Bryony sliced through the laces and gently removed the boot and then the sock. 'The ankle is very swollen,' she murmured, and Pamela gave a little groan and took several more breaths of the gas and air. 'Could you put any weight on it after you fell, Pamela?'

The woman shook her head. 'It was agony. I fell straight away, that's how I cut my wrist.'

'What do you reckon, Blondie?' Jack asked, his arm around Pamela as he supported her.

'She's tender over the distal fibula and the lateral malleolus,' Bryony said quickly. 'I think it's probably a fracture. She's going to need X-rays when we get her down.'

'So we splint it now, give her some more analgesia and then get her into a casualty bag until the rest of the team gets here with the Bell,' Jack said decisively, his arm still round Pamela. 'You're going to be fine, Pamela.'

Pamela groaned. 'Have I broken it? And why do you need a bell?'

'A Bell is a type of stretcher that we use, and it looks as though you might have broken your ankle,' Jack said, watching as Bryony pulled out the rest of the equipment. 'Don't you worry. We're going to make you comfortable. We have these amazing fleecy bags that are very snug. In a moment you're going to feel like toast. Did you hear about the blonde who ordered a take-away pizza? The waiter asked her if she wanted it cut into six slices or twelve—' swiftly he helped Bryony apply the splint '—and she said, "Six, please. I could never eat twelve."'

'Just ignore him, Pamela,' Bryony advised with a smile. 'He doesn't know the meaning of politically correct and frankly it's amazing he hasn't been arrested before now. If I didn't need him to carry you down this mountain, I'd push him off the cliff myself.'

But despite the pain she was obviously suffering, Pamela was smiling. 'He's making me laugh, actually.'

Bryony groaned. 'Don't tell him that or he'll tell you blonde jokes all the way down the mountain. Trust me, you'd rather be left on your own in the snow than have to listen to Jack in full flow.'

She and Jack kept up their banter, taking Pamela's mind off the situation she was in, working together with swift efficiency. They'd just got Pamela into a casualty bag when the rest of the team approached out of the snow. Bryony's brother was among them.

Jack rolled his eyes. 'The last thing we need up here is an obstetrician,' he drawled. 'Who's delivering all those babies while you're wasting your time on the mountain?'

Tom adjusted the pack on his back. 'They're all queuing up, waiting for me to come back.'

'Well, you took so long you needn't have bothered coming.' Jack stood up, tall and broad-shouldered. 'You've missed all the action. Blondie and I have sorted it out as usual. Don't know why we need such a big team really.'

'If we weren't here you wouldn't have anyone to boss around,' Tom said dryly, working with the rest of the team to get a stretcher ready. 'We rang the RAF to see if there was any chance of an airlift but the weather is closing in so it looks like we're going to have to carry them down.'

Jack walked over and conferred with Sean, the other A and E consultant and the MRT leader, and discussed the best way to get the two women off the mountain while Bryony kept an eye on Pamela. Fortunately the casualty bag had zip access, which meant she was able to check on her patient without exposing her to the freezing air.

Finally Pamela was safely strapped onto a stretcher. Her sister had revived sufficiently to be able to walk down the mountain with some assistance from two bulky MRT members who roped her between them.

Bryony reattached her crampons and picked up her ice axe. The snow was thick now and she knew that one false step could have her sliding halfway down the mountain.

The snow was falling so thickly she could barely see and she scrubbed her face with her hand to clear her vision.

'Rope up, Blondie,' Jack's voice said, and as she opened her mouth to answer, the ground beneath her suddenly shifted and she was falling.

She didn't even have time to cry out, sliding fast down the slope towards the edge of the cliff that Jack had described so graphically.

Immediately she braced the axe shaft across her body, digging the pick into the snow slope and raising her feet so that they didn't catch in the snow. She jerked to a halt and hung there for a moment, suspended, her heart hammering against her chest, her hands tightly locked on her ice axe, which was the only thing holding her on the slope.

She heard Jack calling her name and heard something in his tone that she hadn't heard before. Panic.

She closed her eyes briefly and took a deep breath. She didn't want Jack to panic. Jack never panicked. Ever. Jack panicking was a bad sign. Realising just how close she was to the edge of the cliff, she kept a tight hold on her ice axe and gingerly moved her feet, trying to get some traction with her crampons.

'Hang on, Bry,' Tom called cheerfully. 'Jack's just coming to get you. You won't live this one down in a hurry.'

But despite his light-hearted tone, Bryony heard the anxiety in his voice. And it was hardly surprising, she thought ruefully, risking another glance below her. Another couple of metres and she would have vanished over the edge of a sheer cliff.

And it could still happen.

'Hang on, Blondie,' Jack called, and she glanced up to see him climbing down towards her, a rope attached to his middle.

'You think I'm going to let go?' Her voice shook slightly. 'You think I'm that stupid?'

As he drew closer she could see his grin. 'Of course you're stupid. You fell, didn't you? And you have blonde hair. You must be stupid. It says so in all the books.'

Bryony tried to smile but then she felt the snow give under her ice axe and she gave a gasp of fright and jabbed her feet into the slope. *'Jack!'*

'I've got you, angel.' His voice came from right beside her and he slid an arm and leg over her, holding her against the slope while he attached a rope to her waist. 'God, you almost gave us all a heart attack.'

She turned her head to look at him and his face was so close that she could feel the warmth of his breath against her cheek and see the dark stubble shadowing his hard jaw. He looked sexy and strong and she'd never been so pleased to see anyone in her life.

Then she glanced down at the drop beneath her and thought of Lizzie. 'Oh, God, Jack,' she whispered, and she felt his grip on her tighten.

'Don't even say it,' he said harshly. 'I've got you and there's no way I'm letting you go.' He glanced up the slope and shouted something to Sean, who was holding the other end of the rope. 'They're going to take you up now, sweetheart. Try not to do anything blonde on the way up.'

She gave a weak smile and he smiled back. 'Go for it.'

And gradually, with the aid of the rope and her ice axe and crampons, she managed to climb back up the slope, aware that Jack was behind her.

Finally she reached the top and Tom rolled his eyes. 'Thanks for the adrenaline rush.'

'Any time,' Bryony said lightly, but she was shaking badly now that the danger had passed, and Jack must have known that because he pulled her into his arms and held her until his warmth and strength gradually calmed her.

He didn't speak. He just held her tightly, talking all the time to Sean and Tom as they reassessed the best way to get safely down the increasingly treacherous slope.

Bryony stood in the circle of his arms, wishing that she could stay there for ever. There was no better place in the world, she decided, closing her eyes and breathing in his tantalising male scent.

And when he finally released her she felt bereft.

She looked at him, trying to keep it light as he checked the rope at her waist. 'I didn't know you were into bondage.'

He smiled down at her as he pulled on the rope. 'There's a lot you don't know about me, Blondie,' he drawled, his blue eyes teasing her wickedly. 'There's no point in learning to do all these fancy knots if you don't put them to good use.'

She smiled and then her smile faltered. 'Thanks, Jack.' Ridiculously she felt close to tears. 'I would have done the same for you.'

He winked at her, maddeningly self-confident. 'I wouldn't have fallen, babe.'

She gasped in outrage. 'You arrogant…!' Words failed her and he smiled and flicked her cheek with a gloved finger.

'That's better. At least you've got your colour back. Let's get moving.'

He turned to Sean and she realised that his inflammatory statement had been a ploy to rouse her to anger. Which meant he must have guessed how close she'd been to tears.

She gave a reluctant laugh, acknowledging once more just how clever he was.

It was much easier to get down the mountain feeling annoyed and irritated than it was feeling scared and tearful.

In the end it took several hours to get down safely

and the two women were immediately transferred to A and E in the MRT ambulance.

Jack drove Bryony home, the swirling snow falling thickly on the windscreen. 'If this carries on we're going to be busy in A and E,' he said, his eyes searching as he glanced at her.

'I'm OK.'

He nodded. 'Thanks to your ice axe technique. You did well. That's if you overlook the fact that you fell in the first place.'

She gaped at him. 'I did not fall,' she protested. 'The mountain slipped out from beneath me.'

'It wasn't my fault I crashed the car, Officer,' Jack said, mimicking her tone. 'The road suddenly moved.'

Bryony pulled a face. 'What's it like being so damn perfect, Jack?'

'I've learned to live with it,' he said solemnly, 'but I realise it's tough on those who struggle around me.'

'You can say that again,' she muttered darkly, dragging off her hat and scraping her hair back from her face. 'One of these days I'm probably going to shoot you.'

'Is that before or after I save you from falling over a cliff?'

She groaned. 'You're never going to let me forget that, are you?'

'Probably not.' He pulled up outside her house and switched the engine off. 'So are you going to invite me to supper tomorrow night?'

There was a gleam in his eyes and she felt butterflies flicker inside her stomach. 'I have a date with Toby,' she croaked, and his eyes narrowed slightly.

'Of course you have.' He was silent for a moment and then he smiled. 'Another time, then.'

He leaned across to open the car door for her and she fought against the temptation to lean forward and hug him. He was so close—and so male…

Suddenly she wished she didn't have the date with Toby. She would rather have spent an evening with Jack.

But then she remembered Lizzie's Christmas list. She shouldn't be spending her evenings with Jack. It was a waste of time.

'Lizzie and I are going to choose our Christmas tree tomorrow,' she said, telling herself that spending time with Jack during the day didn't count. 'Do you want to come? She'd love you to join us, I know she would.'

Jack grinned. 'Will I have to play Weddings?'

'Probably, but you're getting very good at it now so I don't see the problem.'

'All right, I'd like to come.'

'Goodnight, then, Jack,' she said softly, undoing her seat belt and gathering up her stuff. 'I'll see you tomorrow.'

And she scrambled out of the car without looking back.

CHAPTER SEVEN

'I WANT the biggest tree in the forest.' Lizzie clapped her hands together and beamed at Jack, her breath clouding the freezing air. She was wearing pink fleecy trousers tucked into pink fleecy boots, a bright, stripy scarf wrapped round her neck, and she was bursting with excitement. 'The tree has to be big if Santa is going to fit my present under it.'

Bryony chewed her lip and exchanged glances with Jack. 'You know, sweetheart,' she said anxiously, 'I'm not sure we gave Santa enough notice to find a daddy. That's a pretty big present.'

'He'll manage it,' Lizzie said happily, stamping her feet to keep warm, 'because I've been extra good. Sally stole my gloves in the playground and I didn't even tell.'

Jack frowned. 'Someone stole your gloves?'

'They were new and she liked them.'

Jack looked at Bryony. 'Another child stole her gloves?'

'It's fine, Jack,' Bryony said hastily, knowing just how protective Jack could be of Lizzie. 'She'll sort it out.'

'You should speak to her teacher.'

'*It's fine, Jack!*' Bryony shot him a warning look. 'Now, let's go and choose this tree, shall we?'

Jack sucked in a breath and smiled. 'Good idea.' He took Lizzie's hand in his. 'We'll get you some new gloves, peanut. Any pair you want. We'll choose them together.'

They walked amongst the trees and Lizzie sprinted up to one and tilted her head back, gazing up in awe.

'I like *this* one.'

Bryony looked at it in dismay. 'Lizzie, it's the tallest tree here!'

'I know.' Lizzie stroked the branches lovingly, watching as the needles sprang back. 'I love it. It's big. Like having the whole forest in your house. And I like the way it smells.' She leaned forward and breathed in and Bryony sighed.

'It won't fit into our living room, sweetheart. How about that one over there—it's a lovely shape.'

Lizzie shook her head, her hand still locked around one branch of the tree she'd chosen as if she couldn't quite let it go. 'I love this one. I want this to be our tree.'

Bryony closed her eyes briefly. 'Lizzie—'

'It's a great tree and we can always trim the top,' Jack said firmly, and Bryony lifted an eyebrow.

'You're planning to lop six feet off the top?'

He grinned. 'If need be.' He squatted down next to Lizzie, his hair shining glossily black next to the little girl's blonde curls. 'The lady likes this one. So the lady gets this one.'

'You need to learn to say no to her, Jack.'

'Why would I want to say no?' He scooped Lizzie into his arms and grinned at her. 'So you want this tree?'

Lizzie nodded and slipped her arm round his neck. 'Can I have it?'

'Of course.' Still holding the child, Jack slipped a

hand into his pocket and removed his wallet. 'Here we are, Blondie. Merry Christmas.'

Bryony shook her head. 'I'll pay, Jack.'

'My treat.' His eyes locked on hers, his expression warm. 'Please.'

She hesitated and then smiled. 'All right. Thanks.'

Lizzie tightened her arms round Jack's neck. 'Why do you call Mummy Blondie?'

'Because she has blonde hair, of course.'

'But I have blonde hair, too.'

Jack gave a start. 'So you do! Goodness—I never noticed.'

Lizzie gave a delicious chuckle. 'Yes, you did. I know you're joking.' She hugged him tight and then looked at him thoughtfully. 'Jack…'

His eyes narrowed. 'Don't tell me, you want to go home and play Weddings?'

'No.' She lifted a small hand and touched his cheek. 'I asked Santa for a daddy for Christmas.'

Jack went still. 'I know you did.'

'Well, now I wish I'd asked him to make you my daddy,' Lizzie said wistfully. 'I love you, Jack. No one plays Weddings like you do.'

Bryony swallowed hard, the lump in her throat so big it threatened to choke her.

'Lizzie…' Jack's voice sounded strangely thick and his hard jaw was tense as he struggled to find the right words. 'I can't be your daddy, sweetheart. But I'll always be here for you.'

'Why can't you be my daddy? I know Mummy loves you.'

Bryony closed her eyes, fire in her cheeks, but Jack just gave a strange-sounding laugh.

'And I love your mummy. But not in the way that mummies and daddies are supposed to love each other.'

Bryony rubbed her booted foot in the snow and wished an avalanche would consume her. But there wasn't much chance of that in the forest. So instead she looked up and gave a bright smile.

'But Santa is going to choose you a great present,' she said brightly. 'I know he is, and in the meantime we'd better buy this super-special tree before anyone else does. It's the best one in the forest and I can see other people looking at it.'

Lizzie's eyes widened in panic. 'Hurry up, then!'

Bryony took Jack's wallet and went to pay while he opened the boot of the four-wheel-drive and manoeuvred the huge tree inside, with Lizzie jumping up and down next to him.

'Most of the needles have just landed on the inside of the vehicle,' he muttered to Bryony as they climbed into the front and strapped Lizzie in. 'I think we might be decorating twigs when we get it home.'

Bryony glanced at him, wondering if he realised that he'd called her house 'home'.

'Are you getting a tree yourself, Jack?' she asked, and he shook his head, holding the wheel firmly as he negotiated the rutted track that led out of the forest onto the main road.

'What's the point? I'm going to be working for most of it.' He glanced at Lizzie who was listening to a tape through her headphones and not paying any attention. 'And, anyway, Christmas is for children.'

Bryony gave him a searching look. 'Are you coming to Mum's this year?'

Jack concentrated on the road. 'I don't know. Sean wants to be with Ally and the kids so I've said I'll work.'

'You come every year, Jack.' Bryony frowned. 'Lizzie would be so disappointed if you weren't there. All of us would. You're part of our family. At least come for part of it.'

'Maybe.' His shrug was noncommittal and she sighed.

'I know Christmas isn't your favourite time of year.'

There was a long silence and then he sucked in a breath, his eyes still on the road. 'Christmas is for families, Blondie. I don't have one.'

Bryony bit her lip. 'Have you heard from your mother lately?'

'A postcard six months ago.' He turned the wheel to avoid a hole in the road. 'She's with her latest lover in Brazil.'

Bryony was silent and he turned to look at her, a mocking look in his eyes. 'Don't feel sorry for me. I'm thirty-four. I certainly don't expect my mother to come home and play happy families after all this time. I think that's one game we never mastered in our house. When everyone else was unwrapping presents around the tree, my parents were at different ends of the house nurturing grievances.'

'Jack—'

'And that was a good thing.' He gave a grim smile. 'If they ever met the rows were so bad I used to run and hide in the garden. Once I was out there all night and they didn't even notice. I always used to think that was why we had such a big house with so much

land. Because no one wanted to live next door to anyone who argued as much as my parents.'

His experience was such a contrast to her own
happy childhood that Bryony felt suddenly choked.

'You used to come to us.'

'Yeah.' He gave a funny smile. 'You were the perfect family.'

Bryony looked at him, suddenly wondering for the
first time whether that had made it worse for him.
'Was it hard for you, being with us?'

He shook his head. 'It wasn't hard, Blondie. You
always made me feel as though I was Santa himself
from the moment I walked through the door. How
could that be hard?'

Bryony smiled. She used to stand with her nose
pressed against the window, waiting for Jack to arrive. Longing to show him her presents.

'You were just like Lizzie.' His voice softened at
the memory. 'I remember the year you had your ballet
dress from Santa. You wore it with your Wellington
boots because you were dying to play outside in the
snow but no one could persuade you to take it off.
You were in the garden building a snowman in pink
satin and tulle. Do you remember?'

'I remember tearing it climbing a tree.' Bryony
laughed. 'I just wanted to keep up with my brothers.'

On impulse she reached out and touched his leg,
feeling the rock-hard muscle under her fingers. 'Come
for Christmas, Jack. Please?'

He gave her a funny, lopsided smile that was so
sexy she suddenly found it hard to breathe. 'Better
see what Santa produces for Lizzie first,' he said

softly, turning into the road that led to her cottage. 'I might not be welcome.'

Bryony slumped back in her seat, the reminder that she'd so far failed to solve the problem of Lizzie's Christmas present bursting her bubble of happiness.

What was she going to do about Lizzie's present?

At some point soon she was going to have to sit her little girl down and tell her that Santa couldn't deliver a daddy. Otherwise Christmas morning was going to be a disappointment.

Trying to console herself with the thought that there must be something else that Lizzie would like for Christmas, Bryony realised that Jack had stopped the car.

'Ready to unload this tree?' He glanced behind him and winced. 'I can't believe you chose a tree that big.'

Lizzie pulled the headphones off her ears and giggled. 'It wasn't Mummy, it was you, Jack.'

'Me?' He looked horrified as he jumped out of the car with athletic grace and turned to lift the little girl out. 'I chose that?'

Lizzie was laughing. 'You know you did.'

'Well, we'd better get it in your house, then.'

Laughing and grumbling, Jack dragged the tree inside the house and proceeded to secure it in a bucket with his usual calm efficiency.

Bryony gazed upwards and shook her head in disbelief. 'It's bent at the top.'

'It's perfect,' Lizzie sighed, and Jack nodded solemnly.

'Perfect.'

Bryony rolled her eyes, forced to accept that she

was outnumbered. 'OK. Well, we've got it now, so let's decorate it.'

They spent the rest of the afternoon draping the tree with lights and baubles until it sparkled festively. Lizzie produced a pink fairy to go on top of the tree and Jack lifted her so that she could position it herself.

Then Jack went into the garden and cut boughs of holly from the tree and they decorated the fireplace.

Bryony produced mince pies and they sat on the carpet, admiring their decorations and enjoying the atmosphere.

Bryony smiled as she looked around her. 'I feel Christmassy.'

'That's because of the size of the tree,' Jack told her, his handsome face serious as he bit into a mince pie. 'Any smaller and you wouldn't be feeling the way you're feeling now.'

But watching him and Lizzie fighting over the last mince pie, Bryony realised that the warm Christmassy feeling that she had in the pit of her stomach had nothing to do with the tree and everything to do with the three of them being together. They felt like a family.

But they weren't a family.

Jack didn't want to be part of a family.

Watching Lizzie climbing all over him, dropping crumbs over his trousers and the carpet, Bryony wondered if he realised that he actually *was* part of a family.

Whether he liked it or not, he was a huge part of her life. And she couldn't imagine it any other way, even if ultimately she found a daddy for Lizzie. And just thinking of how she was going to tell Lizzie that Santa hadn't managed to produce a daddy on Christmas Day filled her with overwhelming depression.

Suddenly needing to be on her own, Bryony stood up. 'I need to get ready. Toby's picking me up at seven,' she said brightly, 'and I don't want to smell like a Christmas tree.'

She half expected Jack to say something about her going out with Toby. After all, he'd been less than enthusiastic about her other attempts to date men. But he just smiled at her and carried on playing with Lizzie.

Feeling deflated and not really understanding why, Bryony ran herself a deep bath and lay in a nest of scented bubbles for half an hour, telling herself that she was going to have a really great evening with Toby.

She was going to wear the black dress again.

And it was nothing to do with Jack's comments about her having good legs, she told herself firmly as she dried herself and dressed carefully. It was just that the dress suited her and she knew that Toby was planning to take her somewhere special.

She spent time on her make-up and pinned her hair on top of her head in a style that she felt suited the dress.

Finally satisfied, she walked out of her bedroom and into the kitchen, where Jack was making Lizzie tea and playing a game of 'guess the animal'.

'You're a tiger, Jack.' Lizzie giggled, watching with delight as he prowled around the kitchen, growling. 'Do I have to eat sprouts? I hate sprouts. Can I have peas instead?'

'Never argue with a tiger,' Jack said sternly, putting two sprouts on the side of her plate. 'Eat up. They're good for you.'

Lizzie stared at them gloomily. 'I hate things that are good for me.'

'He's only given you two,' Bryony said mildly, turning to lift two mugs out of the cupboard. When she looked back the sprouts had gone. Lizzie and Jack were both concentrating hard on the plate, neither of them looking at her.

'All right.' Bryony put her hands on her hips, her eyes twinkling. 'What happened to the sprouts?'

Lizzie covered her mouth and gave a snort of laughter and Jack tried to look innocent.

'Did you know that tigers love sprouts?'

Lizzie smiled happily. 'If Jack was my daddy I'd *never* have to eat sprouts.'

Jack shot Bryony a rueful look and ran a hand over the back of his neck. 'Lizzie, angel, we've got to talk about this.'

But before he could say any more, the phone rang. Bryony picked it up, expecting it to be her mother ringing about the babysitting arrangements for that evening.

It was Toby and when she finally replaced the receiver she was silent.

'What's the matter?' Jack was feeding Lizzie the last of her fish fingers. 'Is he going to be late?'

'He isn't coming.' Bryony looked at him, thinking that Jack didn't look that surprised. He just carried on feeding Lizzie. She frowned. 'She can feed herself, Jack.'

'I know she can, but we're playing zoos,' he said

calmly, 'and at the moment I'm feeding the tigers. So why is your date off?'

'Because Sean sent him over to Penrith to pick up some equipment for the team and it's taken him ages to sort it out and he's still there.' She frowned. 'Why didn't he tell Sean that he had a date?'

Jack stabbed the last of the fish fingers, not looking at her. 'Well, I suppose it was important.'

'It sounded pretty routine to me,' Bryony muttered, facing the fact that yet another date had turned into a disaster, this time before the guy had even turned up on her doorstep. She was jinxed. Or was she?

Suddenly she looked at Jack suspiciously, remembering his attitude to Toby when they'd gone on the rescue. Had he somehow engineered this so that they couldn't go out? She knew he wasn't comfortable with the idea of her finding a daddy for Lizzie. And if she found someone, obviously that would affect his relationship because he couldn't just come and go the way he did at the moment.

Was he the reason Toby hadn't turned up?

She glanced down at herself with a sigh. 'All dressed up and nowhere to go,' she said lightly, giving a shrug. 'I suppose I may as well go and get changed.'

'Why?'

Jack stood up and suddenly all she was breathlessly aware of were those sexy blue eyes watching her.

'Well, there's no point in wearing *this*—' she gestured down to herself '—to eat baked beans.'

'Who said anything about baked beans?' he drawled softly, walking towards her with a distinct air of purpose. 'Ring your mum and cancel.'

'Cancel?'

He was so close now she could hardly breathe, and he gave her that smile that always made her insides tumble.

'Yes, cancel.' He put a hand under her chin and lifted her face to his. 'I'll cook dinner and you can wear the dress. You don't need a babysitter.'

Her heart was pumping in her chest and her whole body throbbed with a sexual awareness that was totally unfamiliar. 'You hate this dress.'

'I never said I hated the dress.'

Their eyes locked and suddenly all she could think about was that kiss. The way it had felt when his mouth had claimed hers.

She wanted him to kiss her again.

'You two are looking all funny.' Lizzie was staring at them curiously. 'Are you going to kiss?'

Bryony gasped and pulled away from Jack, her face flaming. She'd forgotten that Lizzie was still sitting at the table. *'No!'* She was suddenly flustered. 'We're not going to kiss.'

'I don't mind if you do,' Lizzie said generously, sliding off her chair and carrying her plate to the dishwasher. 'Sally says it's yucky when her parents do it, but I think it would be nice.'

'Lizzie, we're not going to kiss,' Bryony muttered, not daring to look at Jack but feeling his gaze on her. She always knew when he was looking at her and he was looking at her now.

'You blush easily, Blondie, do you know that?' His voice was a soft, teasing drawl and Lizzie clapped her hands.

'Mummy only ever goes that colour when you're here, Jack.'

Deciding that the conversation had gone far enough, Bryony glanced at her watch. 'And you should be getting ready for bed, Lizzie,' she said quickly. 'Do you want Jack to read you a story?'

'Only if he doesn't skip bits.'

Bryony risked a look at Jack. 'Is that OK with you, or do you need to get going?'

'That depends…'

'On what?'

He winked at her. 'What you're cooking me for dinner—'

She rolled her eyes. 'Don't you ever go home and cook for yourself, Jack?'

'Why would I want to when I've got you to cook for me?' He smiled and held up a hand. 'Only joking. As it happens, I'm cooking for you tonight.'

'You're cooking for *me*?'

Jack never cooked. He lounged at her table, watching while she cooked. And actually she liked it that way. She found cooking relaxing and there was nothing she enjoyed more than an evening chatting with Jack.

'I'm cooking for you. A gourmet creation right under your very nose. It's your turn to be impressed, Blondie.'

'But I was going out. How can you have the ingredients for a gourmet creation?'

He stooped to pick up Lizzie. 'I just picked up a few things on my way home, in case I was hungry later.'

'But you don't even know where the supermarket

is.' Her eyes teased him. 'Or are you telling me you finally *asked for directions*?'

'No need.' He displayed his muscles, flexing his shoulders and his biceps. 'Man is a natural hunter.'

She lifted an eyebrow. 'You went to the supermarket in your *loin cloth*?'

'Of course. But I left my spear outside.' His eyes gleamed wickedly and she felt herself blush.

It was only as he walked out of the room with Lizzie that she realised that he hadn't actually answered her question about the food. How did he come to have the ingredients for a gourmet meal in his boot?

And why did he want her to keep the dress on when the last time she'd worn it he'd covered her up?

But the last time she'd worn it she'd been going out with another man.

Bryony plopped down on the nearest kitchen chair and wondered if Jack realised that he was displaying all the signs of a jealous male.

Probably not.

She hadn't realised it herself until two seconds ago.

But to be jealous you had to care, and Jack didn't care about her. Not like that.

Or did he?

She sat in silence, her mind running over everything that had happened since the night she'd walked into the pub and announced that she was going to start dating men again.

Jack had sabotaged every date.

Had he done that because of Lizzie? Because he didn't want Lizzie to have a daddy?

Or had he done it because he hadn't been able to see her with another man?

CHAPTER EIGHT

THE week before Christmas Jack, Bryony and Sean were in the staffroom discussing the mountain rescue team Christmas party, when Nicky rushed in, looking stressed.

'I just had a call from Ambulance Control,' she said breathlessly. 'Ellie has driven her car into a ditch.'

'Our Ellie?' Jack was on his feet immediately, his expression concerned. 'She's nearly eight months pregnant. Is she OK?'

Nicky shook her head. 'I haven't got many details but they had to cut her out of the car.'

Bryony was already hurrying to the door.

'She's been poorly right the way through this pregnancy,' Sean muttered, and Bryony remembered that he was very friendly with the couple outside work. 'That's why she gave up work early. Has anyone called Ben? This is his wife we're talking about.'

Ben MacAllister was another of the A and E consultants, and Ellie had worked as a nurse in A and E before she'd become pregnant.

'He's away on that immediate care course,' Jack reminded him, and Sean swore softly.

'Well, someone get on the phone.'

They heard the ambulance siren and Jack turned to Bryony. 'Call Tom,' he said urgently. 'I don't know whether there's a problem with the baby, but we're not taking any chances and I want your brother here.'

Without questioning his decision, Bryony hurried to the phone and called her brother and then hurried to Resus where the paramedics had taken Ellie.

Jack and Sean were already examining her thoroughly.

'Is Tom coming?' Jack was giving Ellie oxygen, clearly concerned about the baby.

'He's in Theatre, doing an emergency section,' Bryony told him, trying to hide her shock at seeing Ellie on the trolley. Her face was paper white and her blonde hair was matted with blood. 'He'll be down as soon as he can.'

Jack nodded and touched Ellie on the shoulder, lifting the mask away from her face for a moment. 'You're going to be fine, Ellie,' he said softly. 'The scalp wound is quite superficial. How are you feeling?'

'Worried about the baby,' Ellie said weakly, her normal exuberance extinguished by the shock of the accident and the pain she was in. 'Has someone called Ben?'

'He's on his way,' Nicky told her quickly, and Ellie gave a groan and closed her eyes.

'He'll be so worried—I wasn't sure whether we should have called him really...'

'He'd want to know,' Sean said, his face unusually white and strained as he looked at his friend lying on the trolley. 'What the hell were you doing, driving your car into a ditch anyway?'

Bryony saw Ellie smile and she lifted the oxygen mask from her face so that she could answer.

'I swerved to avoid a sheep,' she croaked, and Sean rolled his eyes.

'Well, of course you did,' he said gruffly, and looked at Jack. 'This is your show.'

Jack nodded and Bryony knew that Sean was handing over responsibility to someone who wasn't so close to Ellie. He was obviously finding it hard to be objective.

'Nicky, I need a pad for that scalp wound. We can glue it later.' Jack smiled down at Ellie. 'You're going to be fine, but I'm going to put a couple of lines in and check the baby.'

His voice was smooth and confident and he held out a hand to Nicky who'd already anticipated everything they were going to need.

Ellie shifted slightly on the trolley. 'I'm bleeding, Jack,' she murmured, her eyes drifting shut. 'I can feel it. Oh, God, I can't believe this is happening again. I'm going to lose it, I know I'm going to lose it.'

'You're not going to lose this baby,' Jack said firmly, his swift glance towards Bryony communicating clearly that she should call her brother again.

Bryony called Theatre again, and explained the situation. In the meantime Sean had put two lines in, and Ellie was connected to various monitors and had an IV running.

'Blondie, I want BMG, coagulation screen, rhesus/antibody status and a Kleihauer test. The foetal heart rate is good,' Jack said softly, his eyes on the monitor. 'Ellie, I'm just going to feel your uterus—I want you to keep that oxygen mask on now, please. No more talking, sweetheart.'

But Ellie clutched his arm. 'If Tom can't get here, I want you to section me,' she croaked, her eyes suddenly swimming with tears. 'Don't let me lose this baby, Jack. Please, don't let me lose this baby.'

Jack's eyes locked on hers, his gaze wonderfully confident and reassuring. 'If I have to section you here, I can and I will,' he promised, 'and you are not going to lose this baby, Ellie. I swear it. Trust me, angel.' He looked at Nicky. 'Get me a pack ready just in case. And someone tell Tom Hunter that if he doesn't get himself down here in the next two minutes, he's buying the drinks for the whole of next year.'

Swallowing back a lump in her throat, Bryony took blood and arranged for it to be sent to the lab, someone delivered the portable ultrasound machine and Jack carefully scanned Ellie's abdomen, staring at the screen with total concentration as he looked for problems. He squinted closer at one area and exchanged glances with Sean who gave a discreet nod.

'The foetal heart is still 140,' Jack said, carrying on with the ultrasound until he was satisfied with what he'd seen.

Ellie tried to move the mask and Jack put a hand on hers to prevent her, anticipating her question.

'The baby is fine,' he said softly. 'I can see the heart beating and he just kicked me really hard. He's better in than out at the moment.'

Ellie gave a weak smile and closed her eyes again just as Tom strode into the room.

'Sorry, folks—tricky section upstairs. How are you doing here?'

Jack briefed him quickly and Tom listened carefully, asking the occasional question, his eyes flickering to Ellie who had her eyes closed. For once he and Jack were serious, no trace of their usual banter or humour as they conferred. Tom washed his hands and approached the trolley.

'Hi, Ellie,' he said gently, 'it's Tom. I just want to check on that baby of yours.'

Ellie's eyes opened and she looked frightened as she pulled the mask away from her face. 'I want you to deliver it, Tom,' she croaked. 'Deliver it now. Please. I've got one of my feelings. A very bad feeling...'

Tom squeezed her shoulder briefly and then slid the blanket down so that he could look at her abdomen. 'Trust me, Ellie,' he said gently. 'I'm not going to let you lose this baby.'

'I marked the top of the fundus,' Jack told him and Tom nodded as he examined Ellie thoroughly.

Five minutes later he glanced at Jack. 'She's bleeding quite a bit. I'm going to section her. Is there anything I need to know? Has she had a head injury?'

'She has a minor scalp laceration but she wasn't knocked out and her cervical spine is fine,' Jack told him. 'She's all yours.'

Tom ran a hand over the back of his neck. 'Is Ben coming?'

Ellie looked at him, her face pale. 'Just do it, Tom,' she whispered. 'Don't wait for Ben. Sean, will you stay with me?'

Sean stepped forward. 'Try getting rid of me,' he said gruffly, taking Ellie's hand in his. 'Let's get her up to the labour ward and get this baby out.'

Everything happened swiftly after that.

Sean and Jack transferred Ellie up to the labour ward while Tom phoned around and called in the assistance of the top anaesthetist and two paediatricians, and then he sprinted up to Theatre after them.

Bryony and Nicky cleared up Resus, both of them quiet and worried about Ellie. They were still talking quietly, enjoying a brief lull in the usual run of patients, when Ben strode into Resus, his face drawn with worry.

'Where is she?'

'In Theatre on the labour ward,' Bryony said immediately. 'Tom is sectioning her.'

Ben sprinted back out of the room and Nicky sighed.

'There goes a man in love. I remember when those two met. Ellie just wouldn't let the man say no. Now he can barely let her out of his sight.'

'Ellie will be fine,' Bryony said firmly. 'Tom is a brilliant obstetrician.'

She had every faith in her brother, and every faith in Jack. Surely there was no way that anything could happen to Ellie or her baby?

'To baby MacAllister, as yet unnamed, and to Jack and Tom—' Sean raised his glass '—and a job well done.'

The whole mountain rescue team was gathered in the Drunken Fox to celebrate the safe arrival of Ben and Ellie's little boy.

Despite being just over four weeks early, he was doing well and was with Ellie on the ward.

Tom slung an arm round Jack's shoulders, his expression solemn. 'Just a question of knowing how, wouldn't you agree?'

'Absolutely.' Jack nodded sagely. 'That and natural brilliance.'

Tom reached for his beer. 'And years of training.'

'And finely honed instincts.'

Bryony rolled her eyes. 'And massive egos.' She looked at Sean. 'Better book two extra places at the Christmas party just to make room.'

There was general laughter and the conversation switched to the annual Christmas bash.

Bryony slid onto a barstool. 'So it's tomorrow night?'

'The venue has changed,' Sean told everyone, and Bryony frowned when she heard where it was.

'But that's miles away.'

'Over the other side of the valley,' Sean agreed, 'and if the weather carries on like this we'll have to all go in the four-wheel-drives or we'll be stuck in snowdrifts.'

'That would make a good newspaper headline,' Tom said mildly. 'ENTIRE MOUNTAIN RESCUE TEAM RESCUED FROM SNOWDRIFT.'

'It would be too embarrassing for words,' Jack agreed with a mock shudder, 'and it isn't going to happen.'

'Think of his ego,' Bryony said seriously, her blue eyes wide. 'It might never recover from the shock of such a public humiliation. It might shrivel to nothing.'

Sean finished his drink. 'We'll meet at the rescue centre at seven and go from there.'

'Bryony and I don't finish work until seven.' Jack

reached for his jacket. 'I'll drive her there in the Ferrari.'

Sean gaped at him. 'You're taking your Ferrari out on these roads? You'll land it in a ditch.'

'I will not.' Jack looked affronted. 'I am invincible.'

'And so modest,' Bryony said mildly.

In the end they were late leaving A and E and Bryony struggled into her dress in the staff toilet, thinking longingly of scented bubble baths and hairdressers. Most people spent hours getting ready for a Christmas party. She had less than five minutes and she could already hear Jack leaning on the horn of the Ferrari.

'All right, all right, I'm here.' She fell into the seat next to him, her work clothes stuffed haphazardly into a bag, her blonde hair tumbling over her shoulders. 'I haven't even had a chance to do my hair.'

'You can do it on the way. We're already late.' Jack reversed the car out of his space and drove off in the direction of the next valley.

Bryony rummaged in her bag for her hairclips and gave a groan of frustration. 'I think I left them at work.'

'Left what at work?'

'My new hair slide.'

Jack glanced towards her and frowned. 'You look great. Leave it down.'

Bryony lifted a hand and touched her hair self-consciously. 'I look as though I've just woken up.'

'Precisely.' Jack gave her a wicked smile, his voice a lazy, masculine drawl. 'As I said—you look great.'

Was he flirting with her?

Bryony felt her stomach turn over and she looked at him, trying to read his mind, but he was concentrating on the road again. She stared at his strong profile, her gaze lingering on his mouth.

Something felt different about their relationship, but she wasn't sure what. He hadn't laid a finger on her since that one incredible kiss, but something was different. He looked at her differently.

'I can't think why Sean booked it all the way out here,' Jack grumbled as he turned the car up a narrow road and put his foot down. 'There must have been somewhere closer.'

'He wanted to just give us a grid reference and see where we all ended up,' Bryony told him, removing her gaze from his mouth with a huge effort. 'At least we managed to talk him out of that one. Do you want me to look at a map?'

'I know where I'm going.'

Bryony looked at him in surprise. 'You've been here before?'

'No.' Jack glanced across and gave her a sexy wink. 'But men have an instinctive sense of direction.'

Bryony rolled her eyes. 'Which means we're about to get lost.'

But they didn't get lost and less than twenty minutes later Jack pulled into the restaurant car park with a smug smile.

'I am invincible.'

'Unbearable, more like,' Bryony muttered, shivering as she opened the door and the cold hit her. 'It's going to snow again. It's freezing.'

'Men don't notice the cold.' Jack locked the car

and held out a hand. 'Don't want you to slip, Blondie.'

'Believe it or not, I can put one foot in front of the other quite effectively,' she said tartly. 'I've been practising hard lately and I've finally got the hang of it.'

Ignoring his outstretched hand, she stalked towards the restaurant with as much dignity as she could given the amount of ice and snow on the path. She didn't dare take his hand. She was afraid she might never want to let go.

The rest of the team was already there and they had a fantastic evening, laughing and eating and drinking. Halfway through Jack looked at Bryony.

'You seem to be on water. How do you fancy driving the Ferrari home tonight?'

Her eyes gleamed. 'You trust me to drive your Ferrari on ice?'

'I'll be beside you. What can go wrong?'

But when they finally left the restaurant, several inches of snow had fallen and Bryony looked at the road doubtfully.

'I'm not sure about driving—we could cadge a lift in one of the four-wheel-drives.'

'They're full,' Jack told her, pushing her gently towards the car. 'You'll be fine.'

Bryony drove slowly but gradually she got the feel of the car and her confidence increased. Surprised by the lack of teasing from the passenger seat, she glanced sideways at Jack and realised that he'd fallen asleep.

Turning her attention back to the road, she turned

right and followed the road for a while then gradually realised that it didn't look at all familiar.

She carried on for a while, hoping to see a sign of some sort, but there was nothing. The snow was falling heavily now and she could barely see the road in front of her so it was a relief when she saw the lights of a pub ahead. At least they'd be able to find out where they were.

She stopped the car and Jack gave a yawn.

'Are we home?'

Bryony slumped back in her seat and braced herself for some serious teasing. 'I haven't got a clue where we are.'

There was a moment's silence while Jack squinted at the pub. 'Well, if you had to get us lost, Blondie, at least you did it by a pub,' he said mildly, undoing his seat belt and opening the car door.

'Where are you going?' She stared at him. 'Are you asking for directions?'

He grinned. 'Of course I'm not asking for directions. I'm a man. But I'm going to check whether the road is open further on. My ego doesn't want to spend the night stuck in a snowdrift. It isn't well enough insulated.'

He vanished into the pub and reappeared moments later, his expression serious. 'As I thought, the road is blocked ahead and they won't be able to clear it until the morning. We can stay here for the night. Do you need to ring your mum?'

Bryony shook her head and unfastened her seat belt. 'She's got Lizzie until tomorrow night. They're going Christmas shopping together tomorrow.'

'Great. In which case, we'll stay here for the night

and they can clear the road while someone cooks me bacon, sausages and mushrooms for breakfast,' Jack said cheerfully, holding the door open and grabbing her arm so that she didn't slip.

'I haven't got anything to sleep in,' Bryony protested, and Jack shrugged, pushing open the door of the pub and hustling her into the warmth.

'You can sleep in your underwear,' he drawled, 'unless you'd rather sleep in mine.'

She shot him a withering look and the amusement in his blue eyes deepened.

'Just a suggestion.'

The landlady smiled at Jack and handed over a key. 'It's the last room. You're lucky. It's the honeymoon suite. We did it up specially because we have so many couples up here looking for somewhere to spend a romantic night.'

Bryony followed Jack up a flight of stairs, a frown on her face. 'The last room? There's only one room? And it's the honeymoon suite?'

'It'll be fine.' He unlocked the door. 'I'll sleep in the armchair.'

But there wasn't an armchair. Just an enormous bed draped in fur and satin, a small dressing room and a huge, marble bathroom.

They looked at each other and Bryony gave a snort of laughter as she saw Jack's face.

'It's the honeymoon suite, Jack,' she cooed, unable to resist teasing him and he shook his head, gazing round the room in disbelief.

'I knew there was a reason I never wanted to get married.' He peered at the bed in amazement. 'Hasn't Lizzie got a bed just like that for one of her dolls?'

'There's no chair,' Bryony said, glancing round for some alternative suggestion. 'You'll just have to sleep on the floor.'

'There's no way I'm sleeping on a fluffy carpet.' Jack ripped off his jacket and dropped it over the end of the bed. 'That's an emperor-size bed at least. There's plenty of room for two of us in that. And if we shut our eyes tightly we can probably forget about the satin and fur.'

Bryony stared at him. He was suggesting that they sleep in the same bed?

Jack took one look at her face and lifted an eyebrow in question. 'We've known each other for twenty-two years, for goodness' sake. Don't you trust me, Blondie?'

Bryony looked at the bed and swallowed. She trusted him. It was herself she didn't trust. But she could hardly protest without revealing what she felt for him.

So she'd climb into the bed, turn her back on him and try and forget it was Jack lying next to her. It wasn't as if the bed was small...

Throwing a casual smile in his direction, she walked into the enormous bathroom and closed the door firmly behind her. *Oh, help!*

She stared at herself in the mirror and wondered whether she should just sleep in her dress. It was either that or take it off, and if she took it off...

She was still standing there five minutes later when Jack banged on the door. 'Have you been sucked down the plughole or something? Hurry up!'

Bryony closed her eyes briefly and then decided that she may as well get on with it. He was obviously totally indifferent to the fact that they were about to spend a night in the same bed, so perhaps she could be, too.

She used the toiletries and then opened the bathroom door and gave him a bright smile.

'All yours. You're going to *love* the mermaid taps.'

She strolled past him, waited until she heard the door close and then wriggled out of her dress and leaped into the bed, still wearing her underwear. The bed was huge and absolutely freezing and she lay there, her whole body shivering, wondering how she was ever going to sleep.

She heard sounds of the shower running and then finally the door opened and Jack appeared, a towel wrapped around his hips.

Bryony's heart started to thud rhythmically in her chest and suddenly she didn't feel cold any more.

She'd seen his body before, of course. In the summer at the beach. In the swimming pool when they'd taken Lizzie together. But she'd never seen his body when she was lying half-naked in bed. Suddenly all she could think about was the fact that he was about to slide in between the sheets next to her.

And he wasn't wearing anything.

In the dim light of the bedroom he was breathtakingly sexy. Her eyes followed the line of his body hair, tracking down over his muscular chest, down his board-flat stomach and down further still until it disappeared under the towel.

Refusing to allow herself to even think about what was underneath the towel, Bryony forced herself to breathe before she passed out. 'Are you planning to wear a towel to bed?' she croaked, trying to keep it light but feeling anything but light. In fact, her whole body felt heavy.

Jack eyed the bed with amusement. 'This bed is huge. I'm going to need a grid reference to find you.'

'You don't have to find me,' Bryony said hastily. 'It's really late. Just go to sleep.'

And with that she rolled over and closed her eyes tightly. Not that it made any difference at all. Even with her eyes shut she could still see every inch of his incredible body. The image was embedded in her brain and when she felt the bed dip slightly and heard him switch the light off, she curled her fingers into the duvet to stop herself from reaching for him.

For a moment neither of them moved and then he cursed softly. 'I'm developing frostbite. This bed is freezing.'

'Just go to sleep, Jack.'

'I can't go to sleep, my teeth are chattering too much.'

She gave a sigh and turned towards him, telling herself that it was dark anyway so she couldn't see him and he couldn't see her.

'Well, go and put your shirt back on.'

'I'm not sleeping in my clothes.'

She chuckled. 'Put my clothes on, then.'

'Good idea. I could wear your dress as a T-shirt.' He gave a shiver. 'Alternatively, we could cuddle each other. Warm me up, woman, or I'll be found dead in the morning.'

Before she could anticipate his next move, he reached for her and pulled her firmly against him so that they were lying side by side and nose to nose.

'Jack!' She tensed and planted her hands firmly on

the centre of his chest and pushed against him, but he didn't budge.

'Just relax, will you?' His voice sounded very male in the darkness. 'You know as well as I do that bodily warmth is an important source of heat.'

A source of heat?

Being this close to him, her fingers tangled with the hairs on his chest, her palms feeling the steady thud of his heart. It wasn't heat she was producing, it was fire.

And she realised that he wasn't cold at all. His body was warm and hard and throbbing with vital masculinity and it was pressed against hers.

'Jack, I can't—'

'Shut up, Blondie.' He slid a hand round the back of her neck and found her mouth with his. His tongue traced the seam of her lips and her mouth opened under his, breathing in his groan of desire.

'Jack, this is a mistake.'

'Probably.' His mouth was warm against hers, his kiss maddeningly seductive. 'But I like making mistakes. It's the only thing that prevents me from being completely perfect.'

She chortled and thumped his shoulder. Or at least she meant to thump his shoulder, but somehow her fist uncurled itself and she slid a shaking hand over the smooth skin, feeling the powerful swell of muscle under her fingers.

'Jack…' This time her voice was a whisper and he rolled her onto her back and covered her body with his.

'Stop talking.' He brought his mouth down on hers and kissed her again and suddenly she was kissing him back. And it felt like all her dreams because darkness was where she always dreamed about Jack, and when she dreamed, this was always what he was doing.

Kissing her.

And in the darkness the rest of the world ceased to exist. There was only Jack and the seductive brush of his mouth against hers, the erotic slide of his tongue and the weight of his body holding her still.

She felt his hand slide down her body and then his fingers found her tight, aching nipple through the silky fabric of her bra. She arched into his hand and he deepened the kiss, seducing her with every stroke of his tongue and every brush of his fingers. He removed her bra with an expert flick of his fingers and then reached out and switched on the lamp by the bed.

Bryony gave a gasp and looked at him in confusion. 'What are you doing?'

'Looking at you.' The expression in his eyes was disturbingly intense. 'I'm looking at you.'

Colour seeped into her cheeks and she reached out a hand to switch off the light, but he caught her arm and pinned it above her head.

'Jack, please…'

'I want to look at you because you're beautiful, Blondie, do you know that?' His voice was hoarse and he dragged the covers back, his eyes sliding down her body with male appreciation. Then he lifted a hand and touched her hair, running his fingers through it and stroking it as if he was seeing it for the first time.

She lay beneath him, powerless to move, watching

in breathless anticipation as hunger flared in his eyes. It was the look she'd always dreamed of seeing and suddenly her breathing was shallow and every nerve ending in her body tingled.

She didn't know what had finally changed for him but she wasn't going to question it.

For a suspended moment they stared at each other, and then he brought his mouth down hard on hers.

Her hunger was every bit as intense as his and she kissed him back, sliding her arms around his neck, her heart beating frantically as she arched against him. He kissed her until she was crazy for something more and then he lifted his head fractionally, his breathing unsteady as he looked down at her. His eyes glittered strangely in the dim light and for once there was no trace of humour in his expression.

'Do you want me to stop?' His voice was husky with unfulfilled desire and her own breathing jerked in response to this blatant evidence of masculine arousal.

'No.' Her hand slid down the warm, smooth skin of his back. 'Don't stop.'

Something flared in his eyes and he slid down her body, his tongue finding a path down her sensitised skin. His mouth closed over the tip of one breast and she cried out, sensation stabbing the very heart of her. He teased her skilfully with slow flicks of his clever tongue and then, when she was writhing and sobbing beneath him, he sucked her into the heat of his mouth and she gasped and sank her fingers into his dark hair, holding him against her. She shifted restlessly, trying to relieve the throbbing ache between her thighs.

Immediately his hand slid downwards, ready to satisfy her unspoken request.

With a swift movement he removed her panties and then moved back up her body until he was staring down at her, his glittering blue eyes holding her captive as his hand rested on her most intimate place. He looked dark and dangerous and unbelievably sexy and she was burning with a sexual excitement so intense that she felt as though her whole body was on fire.

And then he bent his head and took her mouth in a slow, seductive kiss and she gasped as she felt his long fingers stroking her for the first time. He explored her with an expert touch, the maddening caress of his fingers driving her wild. And all the time his eyes held hers, stripping down all the barriers between them, his gaze every bit as intimate as his touch.

She lifted a hand and ran her fingers over his rough jaw, loving the male contrast to her own softness. And suddenly she wanted to touch him as he was touching her. Her hand trailed over his wide shoulders and down his powerful body until her fingers closed around the pulsing heat of his arousal. He felt hot and hard and excitingly male and she stroked him gently until he muttered something under his breath and reached down.

'Stop.' His voice was thickened as his hand closed over her wrist. 'You need to give me a minute.'

But she didn't want to give him a minute. She was *desperate*, her body driven to fever pitch by his skilled touch.

She curled her legs around him, consumed by a feminine need so powerful that she raked his back with her nails in desperation.

'Jack, *please…*'

Breathing heavily, he slid an arm beneath her and she felt the silken probe of his erection against her. She arched invitingly and he entered her with a hard, demanding thrust, filling her with a heat and passion that she'd only known in her dreams.

She cried out in ecstasy and he gave a groan and thrust deeper still, his eyes locking with hers, fierce with passion. And she was lost in that gaze, the connection between them so powerful that she felt part of him.

'Bryony—'

It was the first time she could ever remember him calling her by her name and she stared into his eyes, overwhelmed by emotion and sensation, every part of her body feeling every part of his. And then he started to move slowly and with every measured thrust he seemed to move deeper inside her, closer to her heart. She felt his strength and his power and was consumed by a rush of pleasure so agonisingly intense that she sobbed against the sleek muscle of his shoulder. She clung to him, fevered and breathless, totally out of control and not even caring. Every time her eyes drifted shut he muttered, 'Open your eyes.' And so she did, and finally she couldn't look away as he drove her higher and higher until finally she felt the world explode and her whole body convulse in an ecstasy so powerful that it pushed him over the edge and she felt the hot, hard pulse of his own climax.

It was so powerful that for several minutes neither of them spoke. They just held each other, breathing unsteadily, their gazes still locked, sharing a depth of emotion that neither of them had felt before.

And then finally he gave a small, disbelieving shake of his head and rolled onto his back, taking her with him.

Bryony lay against him and allowed her eyes to drift shut, so utterly swamped with happiness that she started to smile.

Jack loved her.

She'd seen it in his eyes when he'd stared down at her. And she'd felt it in the way he'd made love to her.

Jack *definitely* loved her.

CHAPTER NINE

SHE awoke feeling warm and safe, wrapped tightly in his arms.

Bryony's body ached in unfamiliar places and she smiled as she remembered every tiny detail of the night before. She snuggled closer to him and kissed him gently on the mouth, watching as he woke up.

'I love you, Jack.'

Finally she could say the words she'd been longing to say for almost all her life.

And she sensed his immediate withdrawal. Physically he didn't move, but she saw something flicker in his eyes and felt his lack of response with every fibre of her being. Her insides lurched.

'Listen, Blondie.' His voice cracked slightly and he cursed under his breath and released her, rolling onto his back and staring up at the ceiling. His eyes were shut and a tiny muscle worked in his rough jaw. 'About last night…'

'*Don't* call me Blondie,' she said, her voice shaking as she lifted herself on one elbow and looked at him. *She wasn't going to let him do this.* She wasn't going to let him pretend that what they'd shared hadn't been special. 'Do you realise that last night you called me Bryony for the first time in your life? That was when you were making love to me, Jack.'

His eyes stayed closed. 'I thought we agreed that last night was a mistake.'

'It wasn't a mistake for me.' She knew she was taking a huge risk but there was no turning back now. 'I love you, Jack.'

His eyes flew open and he stared at her for a moment. Then he sucked in a breath and sprang out of bed so quickly that she blinked in amazement.

'Blond— Sorry, *Bryony*,' he corrected himself quickly as he reached for his clothes. 'You do not love me, all right? You just *think* you love me because last night we had sex and women think soppy thoughts after sex.'

She watched, thinking that she'd never seen anyone dress so quickly in her whole life. Trousers, shirt, jumper—in seconds he was fully clothed, his expression desperate as he searched for his boots.

'Why are you panicking, Jack?'

'I'm not panicking.' He found his boots and dragged them on without untying the laces. 'I just think we need to get going.'

'You are panicking. You're panicking because I told you that I love you.'

He scowled at her and ran both hands through his already tousled dark hair. 'I'm not panicking about that, because I know it isn't true.'

'It *is* true.' She took a deep breath. 'And I know you love me, too.'

He went completely still, his eyes fixed on her as if she were a dangerous animal that could attack at any moment. Then he swore under his breath and gave a sigh.

'Bryony.' He said her name firmly. 'We spent the night together, sweetheart. We had good—' He broke off with a frown '—well, *amazing*, actually…' He cleared his throat. 'We had amazing sex. It doesn't mean we're in love.'

'Of course it doesn't.' She sat up in the bed, deriving considerable satisfaction from the way that his eyes lingered hungrily on her breasts before she tucked the duvet under her arms. 'But we were in love before we had sex. The sex was amazing *because* we're in love. You felt it, too, Jack. I know you did. I saw it in your eyes. I *felt* it, Jack.'

'What do you mean—we were in love before we had sex?' He licked dry lips and his eyes flicked towards the door. 'We've been friends for twenty-two years, Blondie. We love each other, of course we do, but not *like that*.'

'I love you *like that*,' Bryony said quietly, 'and I always have.'

There was a long, tense silence and then he shook his head. 'We both know that isn't true. There's Lizzie's father for a start.'

Bryony felt her heart thump heavily in her chest. She'd never talked about Lizzie's father to anyone before. Never.

'Lizzie's father was my one attempt to get you out of my system,' she said quietly, watching as his face drained of colour. 'I've loved you all my life, Jack, but I resigned myself to the fact that you were never going to marry anyone. I decided that I needed to stop dreaming about you and get on with my life.'

He was staring at her. 'That isn't true.'

'It's true. I met Lizzie's father at a party. He was good-looking and fun to be with—'

Jack's mouth tightened. 'Spare me the details.'

'I thought you wanted the details.'

'I *don't* want to know that you found him attractive,' he grated, and Bryony stared at him in exasperation, wondering if he realised just how contradictory he was being. One minute he was saying that he didn't love her and the next he was showing all the signs of extreme jealousy.

'We spent the night together,' she said finally. 'I was determined to forget about you.'

'And it worked, yes?' His eyes glittered strangely. 'I mean, you've never given even the slightest hint that you cared about me, so it must have worked.'

She sighed. 'I didn't give the slightest hint that I cared about you because you would have done what you're doing now. Panic. And, no, it didn't work. At least, not in the sense that you mean. It taught me that I'm a one-man woman, and that man is you, Jack.'

'But you slept with him.'

She blushed and gave a wry smile. 'Just the once.'

'And then you slept with other men—yes?'

She shook her head. 'No other men. There didn't seem any point when none of them were you.'

He ran a hand over the back of his neck, visibly shaken by her admission. 'You're saying that last night was only the second time you've had sex in your life?'

She nodded. 'That's right, Jack. Why? Did I disappoint?'

There was a faint sheen of sweat on his brow. 'You know you didn't disappoint.' He let out a long breath and closed his eyes briefly. 'Blond—Bryony, I don't know what to say.'

'Say that you love me, too,' she croaked, 'because I know you do, Jack. I saw it in your eyes last night.'

He shook his head, his expression bleak as he looked at her. 'I can't say that.' His voice was hoarse. 'I wish I could, but I can't. You know I don't do commitment, Bryony.'

'Yes, you do.' She tipped her head on one side and watched him. 'You have been there for me for every second of the last twenty-two years, Jack, and since Lizzie was born you've been there for her, too. If that isn't commitment, then I don't know what is. I *know* you love me, Jack.'

She knew she was pushing him and her heart was thudding in her chest as she anticipated his reaction. Maybe it was the wrong thing to do, but what did she have to lose?

He shook his head. 'I can't be what you want me to be. I'd let you down. I'd let Lizzie down.'

'I don't believe that,' she said softly. 'I know that you had a terrible childhood. I know that your parents had a terrible marriage, but they never loved each other. That was so obvious. We do. We *really* love each other. We were always meant to be together.'

'Is that why you slept with me last night?' His eyes burned into hers. 'Because you thought I'd say—I'd say those three words?'

Which he couldn't even bring himself to say as part of a conversation, Bryony observed sadly.

'I slept with you because it felt right and because I love you,' she said quietly. 'I'm not trying to trap you, Jack. You're my best friend. It's just that I know you love me, too.'

'That's not true.'

'Jack.' Her tone was patient. 'Since November I've been dating other men. Or, at least, I've been trying to. It hasn't been going that well and lately I've been asking myself why.'

He looked at her warily. 'And what has that got to do with me?'

'Everything.' She stared at him and sighed. 'Jack, that first night I went out with David. You hated my dress. You said it was indecent.'

'It was indecent.'

'But the other night you wanted me to wear it for you. You didn't find it indecent then.'

Hot colour touched his cheekbones and he breathed in sharply. 'That's different.'

'You wouldn't let me invite him in for coffee, you wouldn't let him drive me home...' She listed the various incidents and he grew steadily more tense.

'I never said I didn't care about you,' he said stiffly, 'but just because I don't want you to marry the wrong man doesn't mean I love you. You're reading too much into it, which is a typically female pastime.'

'Is it?' She looked at him calmly. 'Where do you spend most of your free time, Jack? Do you go home?'

'I have an active social life.'

'Which basically means that you have sex with different women,' she said gently, 'but you don't spend time with those women, do you, Jack? You have a massive house but you never go there. You spend time with me. In *my* house. Sitting in my kitchen. Chatting about everything. Being part of my life. And Lizzie's life.'

'You're my friend.'

She nodded. 'And that's the best thing about a good marriage. I know because I saw it in my parents' marriage. In a good marriage you are friends as well as lovers.'

He backed away and stared at her incredulously. 'You're proposing to me?'

'No.' She held her breath. 'I'm waiting for you to propose to me, Jack. And then we can spend the rest of our lives having fantastic sex and enjoying the special friendship we've always had. And Lizzie gets the daddy she's always dreamed of.'

He stared at her for a suspended moment and then he grabbed his jacket. 'No.' He thrust his arms into the jacket and zipped it up firmly, his jaw set in a hard line. 'I think you've gone mad. For me it was just sex, Blondie—great sex, but just sex.'

'Jack—'

His eyes blazed into hers. 'We won't talk about it again.'

'*Jack!*'

'I'll go and warm the engine up.'

'Why are men like mascara?' Bryony murmured to herself, watching him go with tears in her eyes. 'Because they run at the first sign of emotion.'

'I bet Lizzie is excited about Christmas.' Nicky handed Bryony a syringe and she slowly injected the antibiotic into the patient's vein.

'Of course.' Bryony didn't look at her. 'It's Christmas Eve tomorrow.'

'What have you bought her?'

'Oh, you know, all the usual girly things. Stuff for

her hair, lots of stuff for her dolls, a new doll that she likes.'

Everything under the sun except the one thing she wanted.

A daddy.

And she still hadn't confessed to Lizzie that Santa wasn't going to manage to deliver her the present she wanted this year.

'Are you all right?' As they moved away from the patient, Nicky touched her arm. 'You're so quiet and you look really pale.'

'I'm fine, really.' Bryony gave her a wan smile. 'Just tired and looking forward to the Christmas break.'

Nicky was frowning. 'Well, you've certainly been working long hours for the past few days, thanks to Jack doing a vanishing act. Do you know where he's gone?'

Bryony shook her head. After their night in the honeymoon suite, he'd driven her home in brooding silence, dropped her off without saying a word and then disappeared from her life. Even Sean didn't know where he was, although he did confess that Jack had called him and told him that he needed time off.

Bryony sighed. So not only had she frightened Jack off a relationship, she'd frightened him out of her life altogether.

She'd thrown herself into her work and had seen a steady stream of fractures and bruises as people had slipped on the ice, and she'd dealt with quite a few road accidents as people stupidly decided to drive home after Christmas parties.

And that night when she tucked Lizzie in she felt a huge lump in her throat.

'Lizzie…' She settled herself on the edge of the bed and took a deep breath. 'We need to talk, sweetheart.'

'Mmm?' Lizzie snuggled down, her beautiful round cheeks pink from excitement.

Bryony couldn't bear the thought that she was about to dim that excitement, but she knew that she had to say something. She couldn't let Lizzie carry on believing that Santa was going to deliver a daddy for Christmas.

'Sweetheart, you remember your letter to Santa?'

Lizzie nodded. 'I wrote it ages ago.'

'I know you did.' Bryony swallowed. 'But you also said you did it in November because you wanted to give Santa time, because you knew it was a pretty hard present for him to find.'

'That's right.' Lizzie smiled. 'And he's had *ages*.'

'It isn't a time thing, Lizzie,' Bryony said softly, reached out and brushing her daughter's face with her finger. 'And a daddy isn't really something that Santa can bring you.' Tears spilled down her cheeks and she scrubbed them away quickly, not wanting her daughter to see her cry. 'It's up to me to find you a daddy, and so far I haven't managed it.' She broke off, totally choked by emotion and afraid to say anything else in case she started to sob.

Lizzie sat up and curled her little arms round her neck. 'Don't be sad. You don't have to find a daddy for me. That's why I asked Santa. So that you don't have to worry about it.'

Bryony shook her head, tears clogging her lashes. 'Lizzie, no, he can't—'

'I've been good,' Lizzie said firmly, climbing onto Bryony's lap. 'I've been so good sometimes I've almost burst. And once I've got my daddy I'm never speaking to Sally again because she's just *horrid*.'

Bryony smiled through her tears and stroked her daughter's hair. 'I know you've been good, angel, but it doesn't make any difference. Santa can't get you a daddy. I should have told you that before. He can get you toys and things like that, but not a daddy.'

'Just wait and see.' Lizzie gave her a smug smile and nestled down in her bed. 'Night-night.'

Bryony closed her eyes. 'Night-night.'

What was she supposed to do? She'd just have to wait until Christmas morning and hope that all the other presents that she'd chosen would compensate in some small way for not being able to produce a daddy.

But she knew that her daughter was heading for a crushing disappointment.

Bryony worked the morning of Christmas Eve and there was still no sign of Jack.

'I think he's at home,' Sean said when she tentatively asked if he knew where Jack was.

Bryony frowned, knowing that it was very unlikely that Jack would be at home. He hardly spent any time at home, especially not at Christmas. He either stayed at her house or camped out with Tom or Oliver or stayed in his room at the hospital.

'Are you spending Christmas with your mother?'

Sean pulled on his coat and reached for his mobile phone.

'Lizzie and I are staying in our house tonight,' Bryony told him, 'and then we're all going to Mum's for lunch tomorrow. Tom and Oliver will be there, too, patients permitting.'

Sean lifted an eyebrow. 'And Jack?'

She shrugged. 'I don't know. He usually comes but this year…' She broke off and flashed a smile at Sean, suddenly needing to get away. 'Are you off to see Ellie and the baby?'

Sean nodded. 'They're being discharged this afternoon, all being well.'

'Give her my love.'

They went in different directions and Bryony drove to her mother's, picked up Lizzie and headed for home.

Lizzie was so excited she was bouncing in her seat like a kangaroo and Bryony felt something tug at her heart.

'It would be great if Santa brought you that nice new doll you saw,' she said, but Lizzie shook her head.

'I don't want to be greedy. A daddy is enough.'

And after that Bryony fell silent, totally unable to find a way of persuading her daughter that her dream might not come true.

She cooked tea with a cheerful smile, hung the stocking on the end of Lizzie's bed and left a mince pie and a glass of whisky by the fire for Santa.

'Do you think he'd like more than one mince pie?' Lizzie asked, and Bryony shook her head.

'He's going to eat a mince pie in every house. That's rather a lot, don't you think?'

'Can we leave carrots for the reindeer?'

'Sure.' Bryony smiled and fished in the vegetable basket, hoping that Santa's reindeer weren't too fussy. Her carrots had definitely seen better days.

Lizzie bounced and fussed and squashed some of her other presents but finally she was bathed and in her pyjamas.

'This is going to be the best Christmas ever.' She hugged Bryony and snuggled down, her eyes squeezed tightly shut. 'Santa won't come while I'm awake so I'm going straight to sleep.'

Bryony bit her lip and then bent to kiss her daughter. 'Goodnight, sweetheart. Sleep tight.'

And with a last wistful look at the blonde curls spread over the pink pillow she switched on the tiny lamp and left the room.

CHAPTER TEN

'MUMMY, Mummy, *he's been.*'

Bryony struggled upright in bed, watching as Lizzie dragged her stocking into the bedroom.

She looked for signs of disappointment but Lizzie's eyes were shining with excitement.

'This stocking is *so* lumpy. Can I eat chocolate for breakfast?' She giggled deliciously as she poked and prodded and Bryony smiled.

'I suppose so. Come into bed and we'll open it together.'

'In a minute.' Lizzie dropped the stocking and sprinted out of the room. 'I've got to find my daddy first.'

Bryony sank back against the pillows and gave a groan. 'Lizzie, I've already tried to tell you, there won't be a daddy.'

'Well, not in my stocking,' Lizzie called back, 'because no daddy would fit in there, silly. I'm going to look under the tree.'

Bryony closed her eyes, listening to the patter of feet as her child raced downstairs, and she braced herself for Lizzie's disappointment. It was perfectly obvious that all the dolls in the world weren't going to make up for not having a daddy on Christmas day.

She should have tried harder.

She should have used a dating agency or gone speed-dating.

She should have tried *anything*.

Deciding that she'd better go downstairs and comfort Lizzie, she swung her legs out of bed and then heard a delighted squeal from the sitting room.

Bryony froze. What could Lizzie have possibly found underneath the tree that excited her so much?

Maybe the doll was a hit after all.

And then she heard a laugh. A deep, male laugh that she would have recognised anywhere.

Jack?

Hardly able to breathe, she tiptoed to the top of the stairs and peeped down, a frown touching her brows as she saw Jack sprawled on the carpet under her Christmas tree, talking softly to Lizzie who was sitting on him, giggling with excitement.

'Jack?' Bryony walked down the stairs, holding the bannister tightly. 'What are you doing here? Why are you lying under my Christmas tree?'

He sat up, his blue gaze curiously intent as he looked at her.

'Because that's where Christmas presents are supposed to be.' His voice was husky and he gave her a lopsided smile. 'And I'm Lizzie's Christmas present.'

Bryony felt a thrill of hope deep inside her and then she buried it quickly. Lizzie's Christmas present. Of course. He was doing this because he couldn't bear to see Lizzie disappointed. But that wasn't going to work, was it? Sooner or later he'd have to confess to Lizzie that it wasn't real.

'Jack.' Her tone was urgent but he simply smiled at her and then sat up, still holding Lizzie on his lap. He reached under the tree and handed the little girl a beautifully wrapped box.

'And because I couldn't exactly wrap myself up, I wrapped this up instead.'

Lizzie fell on it with a squeal of delight. 'It's for me?'

'Certainly it's for you.' His gaze slid back to Bryony, who was standing on the bottom step, unable to move. She wanted to know what was going on.

Lizzie tore the paper off the present and then gave a gasp of delight, holding up a silk dress in a beautiful shade of pink. 'Oh, and matching shoes. And a new tiara.'

Jack's eyes were on Bryony. 'Someone once told me that a little girl could never have too many tiaras,' he said softly, a strange light in his eyes. 'And that's the sort of thing you need to know if you're going to be a decent daddy.'

Bryony gave a faltering smile and looked at the dress her daughter was holding.

It looked like...

'It's a lovely dress, Jack,' Lizzie said wistfully, stroking it with her hand. 'Can I wear it now?'

Jack shook his head. 'But you can wear it soon. Or at least I hope you can. Do you know what sort of dress this is, Lizzie?'

Lizzie shook her head but Bryony's heart was thumping like a drum and she sat down hard on the bottom stair as her knees gave way.

'It's a bridesmaid's dress,' Jack said quietly, his eyes still fixed on Bryony. 'And I want you to wear it when I marry your mummy.'

'You're going to marry Mummy?' Lizzie gave a gasp of delight. 'You're going to play Weddings?'

Jack gently tipped Lizzie onto the floor and rose to

his feet. 'I'm not playing Weddings,' he said quietly, walking across the room towards Bryony, his eyes locked on hers. 'I'm doing it for real.'

He reached into his pocket and pulled out a tiny box beautifully wrapped in silver paper. It caught the light and glittered like the decorations on the tree, and Lizzie gasped.

'It's so pretty.'

Bryony was looking at Jack and he smiled.

'Are you going to stand up?'

She took his hand and allowed him to pull her to her feet. 'Jack—'

'Bryony Hunter.' His voice was sexy and seductive and a tiny smile played around his firm mouth. 'Will you marry me?'

Her stomach turned over and she stared at him, not daring to believe that this was real. Then she looked at her daughter who was leaping up and down in undisguised delight.

Bryony took a deep breath and looked at the box. 'Jack—you don't want to get married. You were never going to get married,' she began, and he pressed the box into her hand.

'Sometimes I make mistakes, remember?' He winked at her and she rolled her eyes.

'I know, I know. Mistakes stop you from being perfect.'

'Precisely.' His voice was a velvet drawl. 'Open it, Blondie.'

'Yes, open it, Mummy!' Lizzie danced next to them and Bryony pulled the paper off with shaking fingers and stared down at the blue velvet box.

'It *can't* be a tiara,' Lizzie breathed and Bryony smiled.

'You think not?' Her eyes slid to Jack's and then back to the box again and she took a deep breath and flipped it open.

'Oh, Mummy!' Lizzie gasped in awe as the enormous diamond twinkled, reflecting the lights from the Christmas tree. 'That's *beautiful*.'

'It is beautiful.' She swallowed hard and looked at Jack. 'How—? Why—?'

Jack's gaze lingered on hers for her moment and then he turned to Lizzie. 'On second thought, why don't you go up to your bedroom and try the dress on?' he suggested. 'Then we can check if it fits.'

Without questioning him, Lizzie darted up the stairs and Bryony was left alone with Jack.

Her heart was racing and she felt strange inside but she still didn't dare believe that this was real.

'You've made her Christmas, Jack.' She looked after her daughter, her heart in her mouth, not knowing what to make of the situation. 'But you can't get married just for a child.'

'I didn't do it for Lizzie, Bryony,' he said softly, taking her face in his hands and forcing her to look at him. 'I did it for me. And for you.'

She tried not to look at his incredibly sexy mouth. 'You don't want commitment,' she croaked. 'You don't do for ever.'

'I didn't think I did, but I was wrong.'

She shook her head, forcing herself to say what needed to be said, despite the temptation just to take what she'd been given without question. 'There's only one reason to get married, Jack, and it isn't to please a child.'

'I know there's only one reason to get married,' he said hoarsely, stroking her blonde hair back from her face with a gentle hand. 'In fact, I know that better than anyone because I saw my parents together for all the wrong reasons.'

She looked at him, her mouth dry. 'So what's the reason, Jack?'

He bent his head and his mouth hovered close to hers. 'I'm marrying you because I love you,' he said softly. 'And why it's taken me so long to work that out I really don't know.'

She stood still, unable to believe that he'd actually said those words. And then a warm glow began inside her. 'You love me.'

He gave her that lopsided smile that always made her insides go funny. 'You know I love you. You were the one who told me that I love you.'

'And I seem to remember that you ran away from me so fast you left skid marks in the snow.'

He grinned. 'I know. And I'm sorry about that.'

'Where did you go?'

'I went back to my house.'

She looked at him in surprise. 'Your house? But you hardly ever go there.'

'I know that.' He pulled a face. 'Which is ridiculous really because it's a beautiful house with lots of land and a great view.'

'But it's never been a home for you, has it?' she said quietly, and he shook his head.

'No, it hasn't. And you're one of the few people that understand that.' He looked deep into her eyes. 'I went home and I sat in that house and I thought about all the years that I'd been miserable there. And

I suddenly realised that home for me is nothing to do with beautiful houses and land. It's to do with people. Home for me is where you are, Bryony, and it always has been.'

She swallowed hard. 'Jack—'

'I was scared of commitment, of having a marriage that was like my parents', but we are nothing like my parents.' He pulled her into his arms. 'The other night, when you said you'd loved me for ever, was it true?'

She nodded. 'Completely true.'

He let out a breath. 'And I've loved you for ever, too. But I associated marriage with disaster so I didn't want to take that risk with our relationship.'

'There's no risk, Jack.' She smiled up at him. 'Lizzie and I will always be here for you.'

'And I for you.' He released her and took the box out of her hand. 'This says that you're mine. For ever. No more dating. No more looking for a man to take your mind off me. From now on I want your mind well and truly *on* me. All the time.'

She gave a shaky smile, watching as he slid the beautiful ring onto her finger. 'It's huge. I've just put on half a stone and I haven't eaten any turkey yet.'

His eyes dropped to her mouth. 'I love you, sweetheart.'

There was a noise from the stairs. 'This time Jack is *really* going to kiss you, Mummy, I can tell by the way he's looking at you. Sort of funny.'

Bryony rolled her eyes and pulled a face. 'Nothing is ever private,' she muttered, and Jack grinned.

'Oh, believe me, later on we're going to be very private.' He pulled her against him and kissed her gently, but it was a fairly chaste kiss, given that Lizzie was watching avidly, and Bryony was touched by that. He always did the right thing around her daughter.

She reached out a hand to Lizzie.

'So, angel, did Santa do well?'

Lizzie smiled, her whole face alight with happiness. 'I knew he'd do it if I gave him enough time. And just to make sure that I get what I want next year, I've just written my letter for next Christmas.'

Bryony looked at her in disbelief. 'Sweetheart, you haven't even eaten your turkey yet! You can't already be thinking about next Christmas.'

'I can.' Lizzie looked at them stubbornly and waved the letter under their noses. 'I know exactly what I want. And I know that if I'm *really* good Santa will give it to me. But he's going to need a lot of time to get ready for this one because it's *very* special.'

Bryony exchanged looks with Jack who swept Lizzie into his arms and gave her a hug, laughter in his eyes.

'Go on, then. What is it that you want from Santa next year?'

Lizzie smiled. 'Well…' she said, smiling into Jack's face and wrapping her little arms round his neck. 'For Christmas next year, I really *really* want a baby sister. And I *know* that Santa is going to bring me one.'

SNOWBOUND
REUNION

BY
BARBARA McMAHON

Barbara McMahon was born and raised in the South but settled in California after spending a year flying around the world for an international airline. After settling down to raise a family and work for a computer firm, she began writing when her children started school. Now, feeling fortunate in being able to realise a long-held dream of quitting her 'day job' and writing full-time, she and her husband have moved to the Sierra Nevada mountains of California, where she finds her desire to write is stronger than ever. With the beauty of the mountains visible from her windows, and the pace of life slower than the San Francisco Bay Area where they previously resided, she finds more time than ever to think up stories and characters and share them with others through writing. Barbara loves to hear from readers. You can reach her at PO Box 977, Pioneer, CA 95666-0977, USA. Readers can also contact Barbara at her website: www.barbaramcmahon.com

Don't miss Barbara McMahon's exciting new novel,
The Daredevil Tycoon,
available January 2010 from Mills & Boon® Romance.

CHAPTER ONE

CATH MORGAN drove through the Virginia countryside anxious to reach her destination. She ignored the stand of trees lining the road, raising their barren branches to the winter sky. It was a beautiful day, cold and sunny. She should have been enjoying the scenery, but heartache was her companion and she never gave a thought to anything but reaching the house at the end of the journey. Sanctuary. The place she had loved as a child, and wanted to escape to now that things were unraveling.

She'd left Washington, D.C., that morning, after months of soul searching. It wasn't easy walking out on a marriage. But for a woman married six years, it had not been as hard as she had expected. Out of all that time, her husband had only been home a total of one year, seven months, two weeks and three days. She'd counted it up.

She'd spent two summers in Europe, to be closer to where Jake was. But even then, he'd rarely been able to spend more than a few days with her.

What kind of marriage was that? For all intents and purposes she was a single person unable to have a normal social life because of a legal tie to a man half a world away.

Time to change all that.

She felt as if she were cutting a part of herself out with a dull knife.

Cath noted on the highway sign flashing by that she was drawing closer to her turnoff. The exit that would take her to the house her aunt Sally had left to her when she died last summer.

Jake had come home for the funeral. That had added the three days to the tally. But then he'd left. She hadn't wanted him to go, had begged him to stay, but some skirmish captured the world's attention, and he went to report it.

Aunt Sally's death had been the catalyst for this change. She had been Cath's last living relative. There was no one else. If Cath wanted children to live on after her, she had to do something about it.

She'd talked to Jake several times on the phone, e-mailed him almost daily—at least at first. But he didn't want to discuss things long distance. And would not return home.

Cath gripped the wheel tighter. She wasn't going to think about the past. For far too long she'd put her life on hold for Jake Morgan. Now she was taking it back.

She'd known when she married him that he was a reporter with a travel lust that took him all over the globe. From armed skirmishes to natural disasters, Jake Morgan always sought to be in the middle of the next late breaking news. It had been exciting in those first months to be a part of his life, to tell friends and co-workers that her husband was Jake Morgan.

E-mail and phone calls had kept them connected. And she'd been thrilled each time he came home, hoping that this was the time he'd stay. Her summer in Athens and the one in Rome had seemed romantic at first. But she was as lonely there as at home, and didn't speak either language.

After six years, she was tired of their electronic relationship. She was tired of constant disappointments. She wanted a husband at home every night, someone to eat dinner with and discuss their respective days. Someone to share child raising with. Someone to give her the baby she longed for. Someone to grow old with.

Jake was not that man. The realization had come slow and hard. But she'd admitted it finally. And taken steps to change the status quo.

She recognized her exit approaching and slowed to turn off the highway onto a quiet country road. It soon narrowed and twisted as it meandered through the wooded area. Historic Williamsburg was not too far from the house on the James River that had once been her aunt's. Cath's parents had died of influenza when a particular virulent strain had swept through the country the winter of her senior year in college. Her mother's parents had been dead before she was born, her father's dying within months of each other when she was still a young child. Her birth had been a surprise to everyone, occurring when her parents were in their forties and had long given up any hope for a baby.

Cath began to recognize familiar landmarks. She smiled sadly as she rounded the last bend and saw the old house in solitary splendor on the banks of the historic river. She'd spent many summers here with her aunt. Even knowing Aunt Sally had died last summer,

Cath halfway expected to find her peering through the windows, watching for her arrival.

She turned onto the dirt driveway, heading past the house toward the old carriage house in back. For a moment her imagination flickered to the past. The house had been built in the 1770s, had withstood the war for American independence, and then the bloody Civil War that almost tore the country asunder ninety years later. The clapboard structure had been renovated a time or two. The plumbing wasn't the best in the world, but sufficed. Electricity had been added long ago and probably needed to be updated to accommodate all the modern electric devices.

Cath wasn't sure if she'd be the one to handle that. One of the reasons for her visit was to decide what to do about the place.

She stopped near the back door and shut off the engine, looking around her. The grass lay dying in the winter sun, long and shaggy. She'd tried to get a caretaker for the grounds, but dealing with a firm long distance wasn't the easiest way to handle things, and it looked as if they had neglected the job.

Cath thought she'd best sell it and get from under the responsibility. Yet every once in a while, she daydreamed about moving to Williamsburg and living in the old house.

She hadn't voiced that option to anyone, but it rose higher on her list of things to think about. She was a great teacher and would have no trouble finding a job wherever she went. Maybe a clean break from everything would be best. If she moved here, she'd have a place to live in that wouldn't have a single memory of Jake.

She planned to spend her entire school break

working on the house—and considering her options. Sadly she was doing it alone.

Her aunt had been a spinster, never married. She'd loved Cath's visits and always made sure they toured Historic Williamsburg each summer and went many times to the beach. Cath remembered most fondly the lazy days lying in the grass in the backyard beneath the weeping willow tree, on the banks of the river, watching the water drift by. The trees had been in full leaf every summer, providing plenty of dapple shade in the hot Virginia summer. They looked bare and bleak without their leafy canopy.

Everything looked a little bleak in winter, reflecting the way she felt.

She and Jake had only managed one Christmas together, their second. Other years she had spent part of the day with her friend Abby and Abby's family. She'd been invited again this year, but Cath had wanted to spend it in the old house. She needed to get used to doing things by herself if she was serious about ending her marriage.

She climbed out of the car, studying the old, two-story clapboard house. It had been around for a couple of hundred years and Cath expected it would survive another couple of hundred.

She'd tried to keep up her spirits the last weeks of the school term. There was no sense letting anyone else know how difficult the last few months had been. Once her decision had been made, Cath thought it would become easier. It was not proving so. Her heart ached in longing and wishful thinking. But she was determined to see the change through, and make a different kind of life for herself in the future.

Cath had wished she could be a part of a large family when she'd been a child. But she'd been the only child of older parents. Her desire for siblings had faded as she grew up. And she found lots of joy in teaching her third-grade class every year.

But this year, with the death of Aunt Sally, the desire for children of her own had escalated. She'd tried to talk to Jake about it, but he'd pooh-poohed the idea, saying their lives were full the way they were.

His maybe, not so hers.

Others spent weeks shopping for Christmas, making cookies and pies and decorating their homes. She had finished her short list before Thanksgiving. And there wasn't much reason to decorate their condo when she was the only one there.

She needed to get this place sorted out and packed up. If not now, then it would have to wait until summer. That was a long time for the house to remain empty. She wondered what it would be like filled with childish laughter, the sound of running feet and shrieks of delight.

She drew a deep breath. She wasn't out of love with Jake, but she couldn't stay in a marriage that existed more on paper than in reality. One day she hoped to make a happy life with someone else. Once she got over Jake. If she ever did.

Opening the car door, she caught her breath at the cold air. Time to get inside and see about warming up the big old house before bedtime. There was plenty to do and not as much time as she wished to do it all. Could she have the place ready for sale by January first?

The project gave her something to focus on. She would hardly notice another holiday was passing without her husband.

Her e-mails over the last several weeks had urged him to return home. Jake had always said things were too hot to leave. She tried to explain her unhappiness and the decision she was making, but couldn't come right out and tell him via e-mail. She wanted to tell him in person.

If he didn't return home, soon, however, she wasn't sure what she'd do. She'd have to write him, not let him find out from an attorney. She'd even written a practice note and left it at home. Not that she expected him to show up. It was more important to Jake to report the news from some hot spot than spend the holidays with his wife. She'd have to write him in January, when she returned home.

She had to tell him their marriage was over.

Tears filled her eyes. She dashed them away, blaming them on the cold wind. Time to get inside and warm up.

Jake Morgan let himself into the town house. He was exhausted. The flight home had been one delay and mishap after another. He should be thankful the plane hadn't crashed, but that was about the only holdup he hadn't experienced.

Maybe it had been a sign he wasn't supposed to come home for Christmas. But Cath's e-mails lately had been disturbing. She'd almost demanded he come home. She rarely even asked. Plus, he wanted to see her. His flying visit in August had been solely to attend her aunt's funeral. Not enough time to spend together beyond the duties of that sad event.

"Cath?" he called.

The place was silent. Jake headed for the bedroom.

A quick shower, a nap and he'd be good to go. She must be out shopping. He knew school was out for the Christmas holidays, so she wasn't at work.

Maybe she was visiting her friend Abby. They could be baking Christmas cookies with Abby's kids. Cath always liked the season. Her notes were usually full of decorating at the school she'd done, or the treats she baked for colleagues.

The house felt cold and lonely with her absence.

He glanced into the living room as he passed, stopped by the envelope propped on the mantel, his name in large print.

A sickening dread took hold. His instincts had been honed by years of dangerous assignments. He knew better than to ignore them.

Dropping his duffel bag, he crossed the expansive living room and picked up the envelope. He ripped it open and stared at the words for endless moments. He crushed the letter, the words almost unfathomable—she wanted to end their marriage.

Cath had left him. She was gone. The house was empty and lifeless for a reason—the heart of it had gone.

Jake reread the words, as if doing so could change them. They remained the same, indelibly engraved in his mind. He felt sick. Disbelief warred with the words dancing before his eyes.

The woman he loved beyond all else had not loved him enough to stay.

Crushing the paper in his hand he turned, as if seeking her.

It was his fault, and he knew it. He'd deliberately

stayed away this fall as if sensing the change in her, fearing this very thing. Why had he thought she wouldn't take such a step unless consulting him first? So they could *talk*. She always wanted to talk about things, nitpick them to death. She'd given enough hints all fall that he should have picked up on them. Subconsciously maybe he had. Why else change his plans at the last moment and return home for Christmas?

But he was home now, dammit. Where was Cath?

He ran up the stairs to their bedroom. Throwing open the closet door, he breathed a sigh of relief when he saw most of her clothes. She hadn't moved out. Not yet, at least.

Her suitcase was gone.

He went into the bathroom, assessing what was there and what was not. She'd gone somewhere for Christmas, she was coming back. He could wait.

Jake shook his head and turned. He was not going to sit around while Cath ended their marriage. He wanted to set her straight on that. Only he had to find her first.

Walking slowly downstairs, he tried to think. He was known for his coolness under fire, why couldn't he think now?

Abby would know. She was Cath's best friend.

It took a few moments to locate Cath's address book. Jake looked around the condo with impatience. It was his home, too. Just because he wasn't often here didn't mean he should feel like a stranger in his own home. He dialed Abby's number.

"Hello?"

"Abby?"

"Yes?"

"Jake Morgan here. Do you know where Cath is?"

"Where are you?"

"Home."

"She said you weren't coming home for the holidays."

"I planned to surprise her. Only she got the first surprise in."

"What do you mean?" Abby's voice was cautious.

"A letter."

There was silence on the other end.

"Where is she, Abby?"

"She says it's over, Jake. She's been agonizing over this all fall. Let her go."

"Like hell, I will. Where is she?"

"If she wanted you to know, she'd have left word. I can't help you, Jake."

She hung up.

Jake swore and slammed down the phone.

If she had not expected him home, Cath wouldn't have gone to stay at Abby's. They could drive over to each other's place in less than ten minutes. It meant she went somewhere else. But where?

Aunt Sally's house.

Her refuge, she'd once said.

He scooped up his duffel and headed out. A bath and sleep would have to wait. He needed to find his wife and talk her out of her plans to leave.

Cath finished the makeshift meal and cleared the kitchen. She still wore her jacket, the house was too cold to take it off. The old furnace had been difficult to start, but she'd finally managed. Now it was just a question of time before the coldness was dispelled.

She'd made up the bed in the room she'd always used. Aunt Sally's room was larger, but Cath wasn't ready to make that step yet. She wished her aunt had electric blankets. Something was needed to warm the bed if she wanted to sleep in it tonight. Maybe she could use the old-fashioned bed warming pan that had hung in the cellar for as long as Cath could remember. Her aunt had told her how generations of Williamsons had used it to warm their beds before retiring. Long before central heating kept the house a comfortable temperature.

Tonight Cath knew how the early settlers felt. She didn't think she could take off her clothes to get into her nightgown without freezing. But she hesitated before going down in the dark old cellar. She didn't like going there in daylight, she really didn't want to go now, warming pan or not. Plus, she wasn't sure she knew how to use one

The warm water felt good on her hands as she washed the few dishes. She'd found the pilot light had remained on for the hot water heater, so she had instant hot water. Maybe she should take a bath. Wasn't there a small space heater in the bathroom? Aunt Sally hated to turn on the big furnace before it was needed, as she put it. She'd delayed the lighting of the furnace until way down in the fall, using the space heater in the bathroom, and letting the sunshine streaming in through tall windows warm the ambient temperature through the house during the day.

Cath wasn't as stouthearted. She liked comforts—at least heat and lights.

She'd brought some books to read, and considered heading for bed now just to get beneath the covers. But it was only seven-thirty—too early to go to bed.

Cath had dusted and vacuumed the main rooms downstairs, and cleaned the one bathroom and her bedroom since her arrival. Giving all a lick and a promise, as her aunt used to say. Too much to do in one day, but she had two weeks ahead of her. She was tired, still cold and lonely. She wished… No, don't go there. A good night's sleep would be just the thing. In the morning she'd start cleaning and clearing in the back bedroom and work her way through the second story and then the first to clear clutter and decide what to do with Aunt Sally's furnishings and mementos. Her clothing had been donated last summer. But there were still generations of things in the house to sort, if she included everything stored in the cellar.

She'd leave the cellar for last. No telling what was down there. It was dark, with faint illumination, and piles of boxes, trunks and old furniture. As a child, she'd found it spooky. The door often slammed shut, apparently for no reason. Aunt Sally said it contained the remnants of all the families who had lived in the house.

Cath had asked about ghosts when she'd been little. Nothing to be afraid of, her aunt assured her, just gentle reminders of ancestors long gone. Cath was not looking forward to that clearing job.

She checked the locks on the front door before going up to her bedroom. A sweep of headlights came in through the beveled glass. She stared at the driveway. Was someone lost and asking directions? Or was it a neighbor who had seen the lights and wanted to know who was in Sally Williamson's house?

The beveled glass distorted the man who got out of the car. He reached in for a bag and slammed the door.

The night wasn't completely black. She could still make him out from the faint starlight, striding toward the house. He might not be clearly visible in the darkness, but she'd recognize that stride anywhere. It was Jake.

Her heart skipped a beat, then raced. For a split second, gladness filled her—then dismay. What was he doing here? Why hadn't he told her he was coming home for the holidays? How had he found her?

She stepped back from the door, to one side, out of sight, wanting to run to her bedroom and hide beneath the covers. Instead, like a deer caught in headlights, she watched as he approached the door. She hadn't seen him since last August. He e-mailed as regularly as he could, complaining if she didn't write to him often. But there wasn't as much to share as there used to be. And once she began thinking about leaving, she had found it difficult to communicate as if everything was fine.

He knocked on the door.

Do or die time, Cath thought. Why had Jake come? Surely he'd seen the letter she'd left just in case he arrived at home.

She opened the door a crack, standing slightly behind it. The cold air swept in.

"Hi, Jake. I didn't expect you."

He pushed gently and stepped inside, dumping the bag and glaring at her.

"What the hell kind of letter was that you left?"

"An explanatory one," she said. "I thought if you showed up and I wasn't there, you might worry."

"But not worry about your leaving me?"

"I'm safe."

"That's not the point and you know it," he said. "I

busted my butt to get home for the holidays and you weren't even there. Instead I get some damn-fool letter saying you're calling it quits."

"That's right," she said evenly. She could do this. She just had to ignore the spark of feelings that flared at the sight of him. All the pain of her decision, the regrets and might-have-beens sprung up. She pushed the thoughts away.

He looked drawn and tired. There was a two-day's growth of beard on his cheeks and chin, and his eyes were bloodshot and weary-looking. His clothes were rumpled. Despite it all, her heart called out, unhappy with her choice.

"I didn't come all this way, through the worst connection of flights I think I've ever taken, to be dumped. I've come home to my wife," Jake said, reaching out, pulling her into his arms and kissing her.

CHAPTER TWO

CATH resisted as long as she could, but his kisses always drove her wild. Despite her best intentions, she returned the kiss, reveling in the feel of the man holding her. It had been too long. She had missed him so much! She loved being held by him, being kissed. She felt alive, whole, complete. Why couldn't it always be like this?

Then reality returned. Common sense took over and slowly she pushed against his embrace. They'd always been terrific together in a physical sense. But it wasn't enough. No longer.

She couldn't stay married to Jake Morgan. She wanted more than to be a part-time wife. She deserved more!

She pushed harder and he released her. Breathing fast, he looked at her, his gaze intense and assessing.

"Nice of you to stop by," Cath said, opening the door. "Have a nice holiday."

He reached around her and slammed it shut. "I'm staying, get used to the idea."

"You can't stay here. I'm leaving you."

"So leave."

"This is my house. You leave."

Cath realized they were starting to sound like four-year-olds. She didn't need this.

"Not tonight. I've been up for more than twenty-four hours. I had planned to get some sleep this afternoon, but instead had to drive down here," he said, looking around.

"No one invited you," she said, glaring at him.

"I invited myself. It's cold in here."

"The heater's on, it was freezing before. It'll take a while to warm the entire house. You could have told me you were coming home. I asked you often enough in the past weeks."

"I didn't know for sure if I could make it and I didn't want to get your hopes up. No worries there, I guess," he said.

"We could have had this discussion in Washington if I'd known you were coming. I could have come down after talking with you," Cath said. She didn't want him to stay. She was too afraid her carefully constructed rationale would crumble around him. But it was late and he looked exhausted. Could he find a motel room in town? Williamsburg was bursting at the seams with all the tourists who came for the holidays. Most places had been booked solid months ago.

"We definitely need to discuss things, but not tonight. Where are we sleeping?" he asked.

"*I'm* sleeping in my old room. If you insist on staying, you can have Aunt Sally's room. I'm not sleeping with you. You read the letter, I'm calling it quits, Jake." For a moment, she hoped he'd sweep away all the points leading to her decision. But he picked up his duffel and started for the stairs.

"We'll talk in the morning. Isn't that what you like to do, talk things to death?" he asked

"Not this time," Cath said quietly. She had no words left. No hope.

Jake paused at the bottom of the stairs and looked back at her. In two strides he crossed the short distance, leaning over to kiss her. She clenched her hands into tight fists, resisting with all she was worth.

"We're not over, Cath," he said.

She watched as he climbed the stairs, her heart pounding. The wooden floors echoed his steps. She could trace his location by the sounds. He paused at her room then moved on down the hall to the next one. A breath escaped, she hadn't known she was holding. None of the other beds were made, he'd have to fend for himself. And leave in the morning. Tears threatened. His being here would make everything that much harder.

Cath couldn't believe Jake had shown up out of the blue. Nothing in his recent e-mails had even hinted he was thinking of coming home. The last she'd heard, he was someplace in the Middle East.

She hugged herself against the chill, and not just the temperature in the room. She couldn't go to bed now, her thoughts were a total mishmash, spinning and jangled.

His kiss had been all she could have ever hoped for. He could always make her feel like the queen of the world with one kiss.

But the important things—discussions of their future together, planning their family—he always sidestepped, only saying they'd deal with whatever fate decreed. She wasn't going to go along with that anymore. She wanted her freedom from this marriage, wanted to be able to forge new ties eventually, and even try for a baby. And she didn't plan to wait until she was in her forties as her parents had been!

It was late when Cath finally went upstairs. She had paced the living room until she couldn't stand it, exquisitely aware that Jake was asleep upstairs. She was halfway tempted to wake him up and have that discussion now. She'd been a long, agonizing time coming to this decision. She just hoped Jake accepted it with some grace.

But she was not going to wake him up. She'd be civilized and wait until morning. The house had warmed enough she was willing to try changing into her nightgown, glad she'd brought the long flannel one with rosebuds and pink ribbons. She needed the high neck, long sleeves and long length to keep her warm. And to keep from thinking romantic thoughts about her husband.

Sleep was the farthest thing from her mind, however, when she did get into bed. All she could think about was Jake in a room down the hall. She hoped he wasn't going to be difficult about this. He ought to be glad she'd started the ball rolling. He was never home. This way, he never even had to fly back to the U.S. between assignments. He could flit off to whatever late-breaking news spot drew him without any cares in the world.

Somehow she knew he wasn't seeing it quite that way.

When Cath awoke the next morning, she immediately thought about Jake. His being here was a complication she didn't need or expect. Why had he returned? He hadn't made it home for the last four Christmases, why this one? Had her pleas in her e-mails finally made a dent? Or was he planning another brief stay like last August? She knew better than to get her hopes up. Six years of living on the periphery of Jake Morgan's life had taught her well.

Dressing rapidly in the large bathroom, she became convinced her aunt Sally had been of far sturdier stock than she. It was still cold enough to show her breath and Cath didn't like it one bit. She'd have to see about turning the heater higher. The small space heater wasn't up to the task of dispelling the chill.

Once dressed, she went downstairs without hearing any sound from Jake's room. He'd looked exhausted last night. If he'd been up for more than twenty-four hours, then maybe he'd sleep in late.

Or at least late enough to enable her to get her priorities straight and her ducks in a row. He'd want an explanation, she'd give him one—logically and calmly. He could rant and rave all he wanted, but her mind was made up. She just hoped she could keep from descending into a rant herself. She'd kept a lot of her disappointments and anger inside. Only lately had she allowed herself to admit to all the things wrong with their union. It wouldn't be fair to dump them on Jake all at once. She should have told him all along how she resented the time he spent away from her. How lonely she had been for years.

Looking into the empty refrigerator, Cath wondered what to do for breakfast. She'd originally planned to eat at one of the cafés in town and then go grocery shopping. Maybe she should follow through with her plan, no telling how long Jake would sleep. And if he did waken before she returned, it might show him she was serious about their ending their marriage. In the past she would have stayed to prepare him breakfast. Today he was on his own.

It was after eleven when Cath returned. The minute she opened the kitchen door, she knew Jake was up. The fragrance of fresh coffee filled the kitchen. Where had he unearthed that old percolator of her aunt's? And the coffee to go with it? She'd made do with instant yesterday when she'd arrived.

Cath placed two grocery bags on the counter and turned to get the rest.

"I'll help," Jake said, coming into the kitchen from the hall.

She shook her head. "No need, I can manage." She wasn't giving in an inch.

Jake ignored her, however, and followed her to the car, reaching in the trunk to withdraw two more bags. Cath took the last one and closed the trunk.

"I said I could manage," she said, following his longer stride to the house.

"I'm sure you can, but why not take help when it's offered?" he asked reasonably.

She placed her bag on the table and shrugged out of her coat. Did he realize how much she didn't want him there? Jake had always had a stubborn streak. Now was not the time for it to take hold.

Putting the things away, Cath geared herself up for the coming confrontation. She had to stay calm, she told

herself over and over. Not let Jake rile her or make her
angry or talk her out of her decision. She'd tried not to
look at him, not wanting to worry that he looked almost
gaunt and tired beyond belief.

She'd thought everything through all fall long. She
would be rational and certain.

She looked across the room. Jake leaned against the
counter, legs crossed at the ankles, arms crossed over
his chest, his gaze steady-focused on her.

"Want to tell me what this is all about?" he asked.

She put the cans of corn and beans in the cupboard.
"I thought the letter said it all. I'm ending our marriage." She almost smiled in relief at how calm she
sounded, but she didn't feel like smiling. She felt like
crying.

"Why?"

No outburst, no denial, just one quiet word.

Cath turned to him, taking a deep breath. Do or die
time. "Our marriage is not working for me. I want more
than what we have. This is nothing new. We've argued
about the entire setup more than once. I say what I
want, you say things that sound placating, then take off
for another five months to someplace I've never heard
of until it's so common on the nightly news it becomes
part of everyday life. I worry about you, but you don't
seem to worry about me. I want a family, you don't.
Jake, there are dozens of reasons to end this. I can't
think of one to keep on the way we've been."

"How about love?"

"What about it? Do you love me? You have a funny
way of showing it. I think you're comfortable with me.
You like having me in D.C. to keep a place for you to

return to when you get stateside. But how much of a relationship do we really have? Do I know any of your co-workers? Do you know any of mine? What was I most worried about this fall? What was your happiest moment last month? We don't know any of that, because we aren't really a couple. We're two people bound by a marriage license, who don't even live in the same country most of the time."

Jake didn't say a word. Cath had thought about this long and hard and she wasn't going to make it easier for him. Her nerves shook, but she continued to put up the groceries. Sooner or later he'd say something. She was not going to be the first to break the silence. Not this time.

"You knew what my job was like before we were married," he said at last.

"Yes and no," she replied. She knew this would be one argument. "I knew you worked for an international news bureau. But I had no idea of the reality of that. I didn't know until we lived it that you would be gone more than you're home. That I'd be so lonely and yet unable to do much about it. I certainly didn't know that when I was ready to think about a family, you wouldn't be as excited to start as I was."

"We never talked about having kids."

"Aunt Sally's death shook me up, more than I suspected at first. I want to have a family, be connected to others on the planet. We're not getting any younger. I don't want to be old like my parents were."

"I thought we wanted the same thing—living in the capital, having friends, doing things—"

"That's just it, Jake, we don't. Not together. We went to a concert at the Kennedy Center five years ago. Five years. Other than that, if I want to see a play or concert, I have to get Abby or another friend to go with me. What kind of marriage is that?"

His jaw clenched. Cath could tell he was keeping a tight leash on his emotions. Maybe, once, she'd like to see that leash slip. To really know what he was feeling. But Jake was too good a reporter to insert his feelings into things. Maybe that was part of the problem; she never felt he was totally involved, but was always observing. Or getting ready to make a commentary.

"Maybe there's room for improvement, but you don't just throw away six years of marriage without trying to save it," he countered.

"If you wanted this to work, you needed to do something before now. I haven't gone anywhere. What do you suggest, quitting your job? I don't see that. And if you don't, you won't be home nights, so we're in the same loop as always."

She folded the grocery bags, stuffed them in a cupboard and turned to leave, her knees feeling weak, her heart racing, tears on the verge. But she'd done it. She'd maintained a cool facade. He'd never know how sick she felt inside, how her heart was truly breaking.

It was pointless to argue. Nothing was going to change. Her mind was made up. One day he'd admit she'd been right. She hoped she herself felt that way!

"Wait, Cath. I'll admit maybe things have been in a rut lately. But this is my career we're talking about. It takes me where the news is. I can't say I'll stay in D.C. and only report on what's happening in Washington."

She paused at the doorway and looked back at him. "It's more than a job, or even a career, it's your life,

Jake. Face it. You love the adrenaline rush of plunging into a war zone, or daring mother nature when faced with catastrophes. A job is something you go to for a few hours a day and then go home and have a real life."

"Someone has to report the news, Cath."

"I'm not arguing that, I'm just saying I don't want to be the person contributing to it by giving up my husband. I want a man I can rely on to be there for me."

"I'm only a phone call away."

"How long did it take you to get back this trip? You said you'd been up more than twenty-four hours. You may be a phone call away, but it took you a long time to physically get back. What if there'd been an emergency? What if I really needed you?"

"What if you do in the future? I won't be there if we get divorced."

Cath stared at him for a moment. "I want to get married again."

Jake looked dumbfounded. Then anger flared. "Your letter said there wasn't another man."

"There's not, where would I meet someone? There's no one now, that's the truth. But I hope to find someone, a man who wants the same things I do—especially children. I feel I've wasted six years of my life hoping you'd want what I want and we could start a family. It's never going to happen, is it, Jake? You'll always have a dozen excuses and then be off to Beirut or Singapore."

"You and I need to work on things a bit more, maybe. No, wait." He held up a hand when she started to speak. "No maybe about it. I see where you're coming from. I can try to meet you partway, Cath, but to just chuck everything after all these years doesn't make sense."

"Only because you're just hearing about it now. I've been thinking about this since you left last August. I wasn't ready to be alone after Aunt Sally died. She was my last relative."

"I'm a relative. I'm your husband."

"I'm talking blood kin and you know it. I felt absolutely alone in the world. I needed you and you took off."

"I didn't realize that," he said slowly.

"I came to that conclusion several weeks later," she said, smiling sadly. "It's because you don't really know me anymore. I'm not the twenty-two-year-old, excited to be falling in love with a man of the world. I'm a responsible adult who has really been living on her own for most of the six years of our marriage. I've grown up. My goals and dreams have changed. I've changed."

Jake studied her a long moment. "Maybe I have as well."

"Maybe, but I wouldn't know, would I?"

"I don't want a divorce."

"It's not all about you anymore, Jake."

He looked startled at that. "It was never just about me," he said.

"Yes, it has been, but no more. I've made up my mind to take back my life and make it like I want."

Cath turned and walked down the hall to the stairs. She'd planned to start cleaning the upstairs bedrooms today. She only had four days until Christmas, and then a week after that before she had to return to Washington. If she did one room a day, she'd be finished on time. She had to focus on that and not what might have been.

Jake followed her. "Cath, that kiss last night should have told you something," he said.

She paused midway up the steps, holding on to the banister as she turned to look at him. "Sure, sex between us has always been great. But there's more to marriage than sex a few times a year. Don't you get it, Jake, it's over. I'm moving on. You can do what you want. Preferably from Washington. I think you should leave."

"We're not divorced yet, Cath. I'm staying."

Cath wanted to yell at him that she didn't want him around, that his mere proximity was disturbing, giving her ideas she had no business entertaining. She'd loved him so much, why couldn't he have seen that and offered more than what they'd shared? She needed to keep her goal firm and not be swayed by the dynamic presence of the man or her lost dreams.

"I don't want you to stay," she said.

"I don't want to leave. I don't think you can physically remove me."

Cath shook her head in frustration. "Of course not. Stay if you wish. Just keep out of my way."

"What are you doing here anyway? Running from Washington?" he asked, ignoring her last comment.

"I'm planning to sort through things. See what the house needs to fix it up. I'm not sure what I want to do with it." She started to turn back up the stairs, but continued to look at him over her shoulder. "I may move here and get a job locally." How would he like that bit of news?

Jake scowled and began to climb the stairs. Cath didn't exactly run the rest of the way up, but she wanted to make sure she was firmly on the second floor before he could crowd her on the steps, or touch her. Or kiss her again. She needed to make sure there was none of that to muddle her thinking, or give her ideas that would fizzle to nothing as soon as the call of adventure summoned him back.

For a moment Cath felt a pain that almost doubled her over. She had loved Jake so much, had such high plans for their lives together. And it had come to this. Trying to be civil a week before Christmas. Tears threatened again.

"Can I help?" he asked.

"You should get started if you want to get to Washington before dark," she said.

"I'm staying, Cath. If you're serious about going through with a divorce, this will be our last Christmas together."

"Or second one, depending on how you look at it."

Jake sighed. "You're right and I'm sorry. I should have been home for Christmas every year."

"That surprises me to hear. You've never been sentimental. Why the change of heart?"

"Getting older, I guess. Doesn't everyone make decisions they later regret? I regret not spending more time with you. Especially in light of what you've just said. Don't you know the thought of you at home kept me going when times got rough?"

Cath had a boatload of regrets—that things had turned out the way they had, that she had spent so many lonely years wishing Jake had been with her watching TV together instead of her watching alone for glimpses of him. Wishing she'd shared more of her dreams with him. The biggest regret was that they'd not had any children. She could have stood the empty nights better if she'd had someone to lavish her love upon.

She stepped into the back bedroom. The curtains were

dusty and closed. She pulled them open, dislodging a cascade of dust while letting in the cold winter light.

"I wish I could open the window to clear the air, but I had enough cold yesterday," she said, surveying the furnishing.

"Do you know anything about antiques?" Jake asked, stepping close enough beside her she could feel the radiant heat from his body.

"Not much. But I can recognize good quality furnishings. I'm only keeping things I like. I thought I'd ask a couple of antique dealers to come and give me an estimate on what things are worth." Hoping he wouldn't notice, she stepped to the side, putting a bit more distance between them.

"Tell them you're doing it for insurance purposes, you'll get a better reading," he suggested, stepping farther into the room and trailing a finger across a dusty table.

"Good idea. Good grief, where do I start?"

"With a vacuum and dust cloth. I'll help."

Cath tilted her head slightly. "You'll be late getting off for Washington."

He looked at her and grinned, the expression causing her heart to skip a beat. "I'm not going back to Washington without you. You might as well make up your mind to that. So I guess I'm here until the new year. Where are the dust cloths?"

Cath gave in. If the news bureau called, he'd be gone in a heartbeat. And she could use some help if other rooms looked like this one.

"Just as long as there's no misunderstanding," she cautioned.

"I'm clear on everything you've said," he replied, amusement lurking in his gaze. "But that doesn't mean I won't try to change your mind."

Cath smiled sweetly, though it took effort. "You can try. But I think you'll find I'm not the easily impressed young girl you married."

She didn't want him to try. She wanted him to make things easy for her for once. But he looked as if it would take a tank to budge him, so she gave up. She would remain strong. He'd give up soon, she'd bet on it.

"I'll get the dust cloths and vacuum," she said, turning to escape. There was enough work to keep them both too busy all day long to talk or think. He'd get tired of housework and yearn for the excitement of a natural catastrophe or some war skirmish.

Hell of a way to spend his homecoming, Jake thought as Cath left to get the cleaning supplies. He pushed the curtains wider apart, and was showered in dust. He thought about the fantasies he'd daydreamed on the flight across the Atlantic, him and Cath in bed, only getting up for food from time to time. It didn't look good for that scenario coming true anytime soon. He'd have to convince her what they had was worth saving. Even if it meant making changes on his end. God, he didn't know what he'd do if she really went through with a divorce. He'd been crazy about her from the first day they met.

He loved his job, but he loved his wife more. Didn't she know he'd love to come home every night to be with her? But unless she lived in the troubled spots of the world, that wasn't going to happen.

How many nights had he lain awake in bed, wishing

she was there with him, just to hold, to talk to, to kiss? How many days had he taken a break from the grueling schedule and wished she'd shared the quiet afternoon, kicked back and doing nothing but being together?

Did she really think she didn't mean everything to him?

Maybe it was selfish on his part, but he wanted her to want him, be there for him. Want to share what they could together. And for him to be enough for her without having to have others to make a family.

Cath returned, lugging a vacuum and two dust clothes.

"I think you need more than a vacuum to clean these curtains," he said, slapping one. The cloud of dust almost enveloped him.

"I guess you're right," she said, frowning. "Can they be washed do you think?"

He looked at the material. There were spots burned by the sun. The hem looked frayed.

"I'd chuck them and get new ones."

"Another thing to do. If you'll take them down, I'll go hunt up some trash bags."

"Let's pile everything in the yard for the time being. We'll see how much accumulates and then decide if we want to make a run to the dump or if the local trash company can come and pick it up," Jake suggested.

"You're saying you think there'll be a lot of trash?"

"Don't you?"

Cath looked around the room and shrugged. "Maybe. We'll know better after I assess each room."

"You're going through every room in this place?"

"Yes."

"Over this one holiday?"

"You have a problem with that?" she asked, giving him a look.

"It's Christmas, Cath, don't you want to celebrate?"

"Sure, I'll take Christmas Day off."

The last several years she'd spent the day with Abby and her family. Wouldn't she want to decorate and all this year?

"You'll need decorations," he said.

"Give me a break, Jake. When did you ever care about decorating for Christmas?"

"The year we shared it in Washington."

He could tell she remembered. She looked away with sadness. He should have come home for that holiday each year. He could have found a way. Regret began to eat at him for the lost opportunities. All the more reason to make this one special. To find a way to change her mind.

For a moment a touch of panic swept through him. What if he was unable to change her mind?

"Whatever. If we get through this room today, I'll look for Aunt Sally's decorations. Funny, I never spent a Christmas with her. I only came in the summers. I wonder if she was lonely on Christmas. She didn't come to visit us. What did she do all those holidays?"

"What will you do over the holidays if we're not married?" he asked. Maybe thinking like a single person would give her a better picture of what life would be. He hoped she hated it.

"Visit with Abby like the last four, I guess," she replied. "Until I meet someone else to marry. Then we'll establish our own Christmas traditions."

He frowned and yanked on the curtains. They ripped

at the top and came tumbling down. The dust made him cough. Served him right for letting his temper take control. He was usually cool under trying circumstances. The thought of Cath with someone else, however, made him see red. She was *his wife*. She loved him, he knew she did. He just had to get her to see that she wouldn't be happy with anyone else. He wasn't giving up on their marriage!

She began opening drawers in the dresser as he bundled the curtains up. Heading for the door, he hoped being outside for a few minutes would cool his temper and give him some insight in how to get Cath off the idea of divorce and back into his arms.

Two hours later they were almost finished. Jake was working on the windows, the outside could stand cleaning as well, but he'd need a ladder for that. The room sparkled. The dresser had held little. The closet was empty. The room had obviously been a little-used guest room.

He glanced at Cath, remembering the slinky nightie he'd picked up in Paris. He had planned to give it to her on Christmas Day, and then have her model it for him. That dream popped like a bubble. She was wearing sweats, on her hands and knees, washing down the dirty floor molding. Her blond hair was pulled back in a ponytail to keep it out of her eyes as she worked. There was nothing romantic or sexy about it, but just looking at her sparked a flare of desire. The thought that she no longer cared enough about him to fight for their marriage hurt. He had to find a way to ignite the flame that once blazed between them.

CHAPTER THREE

JAKE was driving her crazy, Cath thought as she surveyed the clean bedroom, glad to see how nice it looked. Even with the windows bare, it looked much better than when they'd started. Jake had worked as hard as she had. Which was causing problems. She'd believed by now he'd give up and wander away to do something else. But he'd surprised her. He hadn't complained once. Hadn't tried to get out of anything, from carrying the dirty curtains outside, to washing each tiny pane of glass in the tall windows.

Every so often she'd feel his gaze on her. It took all her self-control to keep from looking back. She swallowed hard. She didn't want that tingling awareness when he was near. She certainly didn't need the memories of them together in happier times crowding her mind, of the love that had flowed, the laughter shared. How long ago that seemed.

This was now. Nothing had changed with his arrival, except to throw her into confusion. She dare not believe in happy endings again. She would only be disappointed.

"That's that," he said. "Anything else left here?"

She looked around, loath to leave the task. What would they talk about without the room's work between them? She was too tired to start another room today, yet dreaded having to make conversation. Why couldn't he just leave?

"It looks nice," she said. "Thank you for helping."

"It's what husbands do," he said.

"Stop it, Jake. That's not going to change my mind. You're here for how long before being gone another six months? If you really wanted to change things, you'd start with your job."

"Or you could quit your job and come with me," he said.

She looked at him in disbelief. "I have no desire to go to war zones or spend my life traveling around after you. I did that twice. You were rarely there, and I was far from home and friends. I want a home to be a refuge each night to return to. I like the furnishings and the artwork I chose. I'm not a nomad and have no intentions of becoming one."

"I'm not a nomad. I have a home."

"No, Jake, you have a place to stay when you're in Washington." Cath gathered up the dirty dust rags and reached for the vacuum. She'd put it in the next room for tomorrow's work. Then she wanted to take a quick shower and get rid of the sixteen layers of dust that she'd accumulated during the cleaning.

Looking at Jake, she was surprised to find his expression thoughtful. She'd thought he'd come back with an instant reply, but for once he seemed to be thinking about what she said. And if he followed it through, he'd know she was right.

"I'm going to take a quick shower and then make something for dinner," she said.

"Early for dinner."

"We didn't have lunch and I'm starving."

"Go take a shower. I'll clean up after you're fin-ished," Jake said. "Unless you wish to share the shower?"

The devilish gleam in his eyes caused Cath's heart rate to kick into high. She was not going to give into temp-tation. She couldn't foresee a future where as former lovers they got together from time to time for old times' sake. The break had to be clean and sharp. And final.

"I'll hurry and try not to use all the water," she said and turned and fled.

Cath put together sandwiches and heated some soup for dinner. It wasn't fancy, but was plenty for the two of them, and would have to do. She wasn't trying to impress anyone with her culinary skills. She was used to making do with abbreviated meals because she didn't feel like cooking at the end of the day when it was for herself alone.

They ate at the kitchen table. Cath was careful to set their places as far apart as practical. Jake said little, digging into the food like a starving man. She realized that except for the coffee he'd made that morning, he'd had nothing to eat all day. She felt guilty and tried to squelch the feeling. Let him fend for himself. But saying it to herself didn't work. She should have offered him something earlier.

"We can look for the Christmas decorations when we finish," he said a few moments later.

"You're serious about decorating?"

"Don't you want to?" he asked.

Cath thought about it for a minute. The house would seem more welcoming if decked out for the holiday. "I guess. I don't know what Aunt Sally might have. And I didn't bring any of our ornaments."

"Is there an attic?"

"Just a small one. My guess is the decorations would be stored in the cellar with everything else from the last two hundred years."

"That's some cellar."

"I remember going down there when I was a kid and being scared silly. There are cubicles and narrow passageways making it like a maze. Furniture and boxes and old trunks are everywhere, and cobwebs. Aunt Sally once said the family never threw anything away. I believe her. I guess if she had decorations that's where they'd be, but exactly where is anyone's guess."

"So we go exploring."

Cath wasn't thrilled with the idea, but her curiosity was roused. Aunt Sally must have decorated at the holidays, yet Cath would never know the significance of any of the ornaments. She wondered if her aunt's collection contained any very old baubles or if any had had special meaning to her. She regretted not spending any Christmases with the elderly woman. She should have insisted Aunt Sally spend the last several Christmases with her. Each time she'd invited her, Aunt Sally had given an excuse. Hadn't she been lonely spending the holiday alone?

The dim bulb over the bottom of the cellar steps did not provide much illumination when they started downstairs sometime later. Cath had propped the door open and let Jake lead the way. When they reached the cement floor, he looked around.

"We should have brought a flashlight," he said.

"There's lighting throughout, just not very bright. I don't know if the wiring can stand it, but I'd like to replace every bulb with a brighter one." She found the old light switch and flipped it up. Throughout the cellar lights went on, throwing deep shadows among the items stored there.

"Spooky," she said with a shiver.

He laughed, and reached out to take her hand. "I'll protect you from the bogeyman."

She snatched her hand back. "I can take care of myself." As if to prove that, she stepped to the right and started down one aisle. There were boxes and boxes stacked shoulder high. None were labeled. If they had to look through each one, they could be here all week.

The thought of clearing the cellar was mind-boggling. Cath studied the items as she walked along. There was no way she could clear this area during the holiday break. It would take days to go through things. The furniture alone would be enough to furnish another house. She wandered down one aisle and over to another. The light cast odd shadows. She ran her fingertips over some of the tables, coming away dusty. There were old chests and armoires, chairs and tables. A cradle. She stopped at that and rocked it gently, imagining a baby of her own nestled snugly asleep beside her own bed. The cradle looked old, with hand carvings on the headboard and footboard. The wood was burnished from years of use.

She moved on, opening a drawer here and there, lifting the lids of some of the boxes—clothing from an earlier era, books long forgotten, mementos from ancestors long gone.

She lifted one lid of a very old trunk and saw lace and silk. To one side a small leather-bound book. She took it out and opened it. It looked like a journal of some kind.

"I found them," Jake's voice sounded from a distance.

"I'll be right there." She tucked the book under her arm and closed the trunk. She'd read through it later. Maybe it belonged to one of her ancestors.

"Call again so I can find you," she said.

"I went left from the stairs. You went right, so I'm probably directly across the cellar from you," he said.

She followed the sound of his voice and rounding a corner found him standing in an open area, two boxes of Christmas decorations opened at his feet.

"There're more," he said, pointing to the stack at his right.

"Let's take them upstairs and see what we can use." She reached for the closest box and the journal dropped to the floor.

"What's that?" Jake asked, reaching for it.

Cath scooped it up. "A book I found. It looks like a journal or something and I thought I'd read it."

His hand dropped. "Family history?"

"Maybe." She put it on top of the box, and lifted both. "I'll take these upstairs."

Jake stacked another two boxes on top of each other and followed.

Two more trips and all the boxes of decorations had been brought up to the dining room and put on the large table. Cath placed the journal away from the boxes, for some reason not wanting to share with Jake. Time they broke ties, not made them.

"We need a tree," he said, pulling out a string of lights. "Your aunt must have had a tree each year, and a large one to boot if the number of strings of lights is any indication."

"We don't need a tree."

"Sure we do. I know just the spot in the living room where it should go, in front of the two windows on the front wall," he said.

Cath knew where he meant. Shifting the furniture would center the tree as the focal point of the room.

It would be festive, and more like Christmas, with decorations and a tree. She loved Christmas. But to share it with Jake felt awkward. She wouldn't have bothered on her own. Why should she just because he came home unexpectedly?

"Maybe I'll see about getting one tomorrow," she said reluctantly.

"We'll go together. Let's cut one at a tree farm," he suggested.

Cath looked at Jake with surprise. The one Christmas they'd spent together, they'd picked up a tree at the Boy Scout lot. As she recalled, she'd done most of the decorating, he'd been on the phone with the news bureau.

"I don't know if they have any tree farms around," she said. Nor did she want to get the tree with Jake. It was bad enough having him here, but she didn't want to do things that would build memories. Even if he didn't agree at this moment, he would soon have to acknowledge their separating was the best thing.

"I'll check." He headed to the kitchen and the phone book beneath the telephone.

"Where's Windsor Drive?" he called.

"I have no idea."

"The exchange is the same as this one, so it can't be too far away. We'll call in the morning and find out," Jake said, returning to the dining room, phone book in hand.

"It says it's open seasonally, which has to mean now. And they open at ten. Shall we go there before tackling the next bedroom?" he asked.

Cath felt a shiver of awareness go through her at his tone. She wanted to turn and run away from the powerful attraction the man held for her. If she gave in, he'd only leave in a few days. Leave her with more regrets.

Could they have done things differently at some stage of their marriage?

She looked back at the decorations, many wrapped in tissue to protect them. A premonition shook her. She should not be going on any Christmas tree search with Jake. Either she wanted to end the marriage or not, and doing things together wasn't ending their relationship.

"I don't think so," she said.

"Why not?" he asked, closing the telephone book and putting it on the table.

He crossed to her and turned her slowly to face him. "It's only getting a tree, Cath, what can that hurt? It's not like it's going to change anything, is it?"

It would, but how to explain? He made it seem so innocuous, but she knew it could hold danger. To her recent decision. She remembered so many of the happy times together. There had not been enough of them. But in the end, Jake always left. And her heart broke a little with each departure. She needed to make this break clean, not linger, have second thoughts, or—

"Cath?"

She looked up, into once dear, familiar dark eyes. Eyes that seemed to see right down to the heart of her. Slowly Jake came closer. He leaned over her until his mouth touched hers, his lips warm and firm, pressing against hers.

For a heartbeat she was where she always longed to be. Then she remembered and pushed against him.

"No, Jake. Leave me alone." She broke away and stepped across the room.

"I don't want you staying here, you know that. But I can't force you to leave. I can insist on your keeping your distance from me, however. If you won't, then I will leave."

"And go where?"

"To Abby's. She invited me for Christmas, I'm sure she would be happy to have me visit."

And not Jake. The unspoken message was clear.

He held up his hands in surrender. "Fine. I'll keep my distance. You keep yours."

"What?" She blinked. She had done nothing.

"Just in case you get a case of the hots for me you can't control," he said audaciously.

Cath wished she were closer, she'd slug him one. He could be so annoying on occasion.

"I'm sure I can control myself," she said primly. Reaching for the diary, she turned and headed for her room. At least she could be alone there. She had a feeling delving into the past would be safer than dealing with the present.

"Wait," he called.

She paused, looking at him over her shoulder.

"What about tomorrow?"

"Get the tree yourself," she said.

She shut the door to her bedroom and went to climb into the bed. It was too early to go to sleep, but she could begin reading the old book. She was tired enough to relish lying down while she did it. Bending and reaching while cleaning had strained muscles beyond their normal use.

Cath covered herself with the top quilt, trying to ignore the fact Jake was downstairs going through Christmas decorations. This wasn't a real Christmas for them, just the last one they'd share together. How sad. Maybe she should spend it with him. He was alone, so was she.

But that would give him false hope. And she was firm in her decision to wrest back her life and put it on a different path.

She lifted the journal, snuggled down beneath the covers and opened the cover. The first words sent a chill through her.

Four days until Christmas. The handwriting was tiny, but legible. Who had written it? Cath looked at the inside cover, but there was no name, no indication what year it was written. The person who wrote it knew who he or she was. The book probably had never been intended for anyone else to see.

Cath couldn't believe she was reading it four days before Christmas. How spooky was that?

I hate this war. At last I heard Jonathan is in North Carolina. Can he return home for Christmas? I

pray so. He was at the battle at Kings Mountain,
clear across the state. A great distance in the
snow. I haven't heard from him since. I wish he'd
send word. Or come home. Maybe he is on his
way even as I write. I'd give anything for him to
stride into our kitchen and say, come here Tansy
darlin' and give your husband a kiss.

Was she talking about the Civil War? Cath tried to
remember the battles of that war, but Gettysburg kept
popping into mind. She'd have to look up Kings
Mountain. She wished her memory of history was
better.

Mrs. Talaiferro had her boy Ben bring me some
butter this morning. He repaired that loose hinge
on the hen house for me. I send back some of the
ham slaughtered from the hog a few weeks ago.
Without neighbors helping out, I don't see how I
could manage. Farming is really a man's job.
Jonathan is so good at it. I hope he's home for the
spring planting.

The nights are lonely. The days are so short
and cold. I can scarcely go outside to gather eggs.
My fingers were half frozen by the time I fed the
hens and hogs. I hope Jonathan is warm. I sent
him a new muffler I knitted, but haven't heard
from him in so long, I don't know if he got it or
not.

I miss my husband. Please God, let this war
end soon. Let the British be driven to the sea!

The British! Cath sat up at that. Was this diary from the time of the Revolutionary War? Who were Tansy and Jonathan? Early relatives of hers? They must be if her journal was in the cellar. As Aunt Sally had always said no one in the family seemed to throw anything away.

Eagerly Cath read more. The pages that followed related the loneliness Tansy felt with her husband absent. Cath wondered how old the writer had been, how long they'd been married. Why was there no other family mentioned? It appeared that Tansy lived alone. Would later pages reveal more? This was obviously not the first journal the woman had kept. Could she find the others? Coming to the end of the entry several pages later, Cath noted the next one started: *Three days until Christmas.*

Closing the book, Cath decided to read each day's entry as it matched her own countdown until Christmas. How odd to find the journal today—on the exact same day it was written. How could she find out about the Battle of Kings Mountain? That would give her an idea of what Christmas Tansy was writing about. Did Jonathan make it home in time for the holiday? She wanted to skip ahead, but refrained. It was tantalizing to have to wait until tomorrow to find out what happened next. But gave her something to look forward to.

She quickly got ready for bed and climbed back in. Drifting off to sleep a short time later, Cath was anxious to return to the cellar for the first time. She'd love to find out more about Tansy. To see if there were more journals, or a portrait or something. She bet her

Aunt Sally could have told her about Tansy. If only she'd known about her earlier.

It was pitch-dark when Cath awoke. A nightmare frightened her awake. She lay in bed searching the blackness, feeling the tendrils of the horror reluctantly let her go.

She rolled to her side, eyes wide, straining to see something. The images of men on the battlefield wouldn't go completely away. Blown apart by guns and cannons, everyone had Jake's face.

She shuddered and pushed back the covers. She wanted to shake the fear that coursed through her at the nightmare. Jake was fine, sleeping down the hall. The old diary had sparked the dream—she knew that from the images of the men that had populated it—dressed as farmers and soldiers had so long ago. It was just a bad dream.

She pulled on a thick robe, found her slippers and headed for the kitchen. Some light, warm milk and semblance of normalcy were what she needed. Turning on the hall light, she descended the stairs and padded softly into the kitchen.

Flipping on that light, she was startled to discover Jake, sitting near the window, gazing out at the darkness. Beside him on the table was a bottle of scotch whiskey and a half empty glass.

He turned and looked at her, squinting slightly in the light.

"What are you doing up?" Cath asked. Glancing at the bottle, she raised her eyebrows in surprise. "Where did you get that?"

"Your aunt Sally had a stash." He raised the glass.

"To Aunt Sally." Taking a hefty swallow, he carefully placed the glass beside the bottle.

"What time is it?" she asked, glancing at the kitchen clock. It was almost three o'clock in the morning!

"Why aren't you in bed?" she asked.

"Couldn't sleep. This homecoming isn't exactly what I was looking forward to, you know? Hell of a way to spend Christmas, get slapped in the face with a divorce demand." He turned away.

Cath stared at him. He stared out the window. What could he see in the dark?

"What are you doing up?" he asked a minute later.

"I had a nightmare. I thought some warm milk would help me go back to sleep. Want some?"

He laughed, but the sound held no humor. "No, this'll do me," he said, reaching for the glass again.

"I never knew you to be much of a drinker," Cath said, moving to the refrigerator to get the milk.

"Never had a need before. Trying to forget my sorrows," he mocked.

"Come on, Jake, don't be dramatic."

He slammed his hand down on the table and rose, turning to glare at her.

"Dramatic? Hell of a homecoming, Cath, to an empty condo and a cold note on the mantel. I drive like a maniac to get here and for what? An icy reception. This is not how I wanted to spend Christmas. I busted my butt getting here. You're talking about leaving me, giving me no chance to change things and blabbering on about finding another man when you're my wife! What do you expect me to do, just sit back and say have at it? Dammit, I'm not going to do that! You won't even go shopping for a blasted Christmas tree with me. What—do I have the plague or something? Cath, I love you. I married you because of that and nothing has changed!"

Cath stared at him, taken aback at his vehemence. She'd never seen Jake so angry, not even when talking about injustice in the world, which really riled him.

She looked at the whiskey bottle. Was that loosening his tongue? She'd wanted to understand how he felt about things. Maybe liquor was the way to go.

He followed her glance and picked up the bottle, holding it out for a moment, then took a healthy swig from it. "It's the only warm thing in the house right now," he said, setting the bottle back on the table.

Taken aback, Cath opened her mouth to defend herself. Then thought better of it. She tried to see things from his point of view. She'd been thinking of this separation all fall, had discussed it endlessly with Abby. But she'd only given him a vague clue in all her e-mails. Essentially he'd walked into the situation cold.

He'd expected Christmas at home, and she'd been gone.

Had he been as lonely as she during the months apart? Did he sometimes wish things would be different?

Guilt played on her. She should have told him in her letters which way she was thinking. Should have given him a chance to open a discussion before now. Cath tried to be fair, and if she were fair to Jake, she would ease up some. They were only together for another few days. She could be cordial during that time. They'd married thinking they'd be together forever. She'd known when she married him what his job was. Just because she couldn't cope wasn't a reason to condemn the man. The fault lay with her.

"Okay, I'll go get the tree with you," she said before she thought.

He looked at her, then at the bottle. "Gee, thanks a bunch for the mighty concession." He picked up the bottle and walked out of the room.

Cath stared at the place he'd stood, hearing the echo of his anger. Tears filled her eyes. She never thought he'd care. She thought she'd be the only one to mourn the ending of their marriage. But maybe she'd been wrong about Jake.

Turning to the stove, she blinked, trying to clear her vision. Once the milk heated, she added cinnamon and poured it into a mug. She left the pan soaking in the sink. Carefully carrying the mug of warmed milk, she turned off the lights behind her. She didn't hear anything from Jake's room. Her heart ached that he'd drink himself stupid because of her. It was so unlike the man. Or at least the man she thought she knew.

Going into her bedroom, she wondered what else she could have done. Written him sooner? But if he thought the letter on the mantel was cold, what would he have thought of an e-mail telling him they were through?

She could have discussed it with him—if he'd ever come home. Even today, when he'd tried to talk about it, she'd been stubbornly reticent—saying only she wanted it to end.

She slipped into bed and sipped her milk. She was feeling as melancholy as Tansy had sounded in her diary. She could relate to the loneliness Tansy wrote about. How many nights had she lain in bed wishing so hard that Jake was with her? How many days had she gone through the motions of living, always feeling a part of her was missing? Did Jonathan come back to Tansy? Did they have a long and happy life together? They were probably her great-great-great or more grandparents. She should find out about them before the end of the holiday.

As to what to do with the house, Cath was growing attached to it. She liked the location on the banks of the wide James River. She was in the country, yet only a short distance from Williamsburg, and not too far from the bigger cities of Norfolk and Richmond. It was a lovely, ideal setting in which to raise children.

A pang struck her. She'd so love to have a child with Jake, a little boy with his daddy's dark hair and eyes, or a small girl with Jake's determination and observation traits. But she didn't want to raise a child alone. She wanted its father actively involved. Home for school events, and soccer meets, to have the house filled with love and laughter. But it wasn't going to happen and she had to let go those dreams and forge new ones.

She'd find a man to love. A man who wanted what she wanted, a home, a close-knit family that shared every aspect of living. And together they'd have a perfect future.

She just had to get through this holiday with Jake.

CHAPTER FOUR

THE next morning was blustery. The wind blew the bare trees, snapping them back and forth at its whim. The sky was a steel-gray, clouds roiling along the path of the wind.

Cath gazed out the kitchen window. There were whitecaps on the river. It looked cold and miserable. She didn't want to go out at all, much less to search for a tree. She set the coffee to brew and pulled down a box of her favorite cereal. She wasn't cooking breakfast this morning.

She filled her bowl and got the milk. A movement outside caught her eye and she leaned over the sink to see better. Jake was walking along the bank of the river, hands in his pockets, head bent against the wind. He stopped opposite the window and gazed out across the river for a long moment. She wondered what he was doing out there. Then she wondered if he were freezing. His jacket didn't seem heavy enough for the wind that was gusting.

For a long moment Cath watched Jake. He seemed frozen in place. What was he thinking? Any regrets about their marriage? Or was he miles away at some newsworthy site, wondering how long before he'd be back in the field again?

When he turned and began walking toward the house, she darted away from the window. Pouring the milk on her cereal, she sat down just as he came in the back door. It would weaken her stance if he knew how much she longed to be with him. If he'd only agree to stay home, they could make the best future in the world. But that would mean changing almost everything about him, and Cath didn't see that happening.

"Morning," he said, closing the door behind him. It slammed when the wind snapped it from his hand.

"Good morning," Cath replied. "Coffee's ready and there's cereal for breakfast. What were you doing outside so early?" Especially after your late night, she wanted to add, but prudently didn't voice the thought.

"I wanted to see some of the river. Could you have a dock here? Maybe a small boat to take out on the water?"

"I guess. I never asked Aunt Sally. She was in her sixties when I first started coming during the summers. She had a neighbor a few doors down who had a boat, which they tied to a small dock. I used to go out in it a lot. We'd even swim from the dock in the hot weather. The river current isn't that strong."

"Nice house and yard. You have a lot of land around it."

"An acre, I think it is."

He poured himself a cup of coffee. Cath watched him as she ate. He didn't seem any the worse for wear after last night.

She was still a bit shaken from her nightmare, and from the poignant words from Tansy. Which reminded her.

"What do you know about a battle at Kings Mountain?" she asked.

"We won it," he said, getting a bowl and spoon. He snagged the box of cereal and filled his bowl. Sitting near Cath, he reached for the milk.

"When was it?"

He looked at her in puzzlement. "It was during the Revolutionary War. One of the battles that began changing the tide for the colonists. Can't remember exactly when it was, but I think it wasn't too long afterward that Washington met Cornwallis at Yorktown, maybe a year or so. So maybe 1780, around there."

"Imagine that," Cath said softly, amazed she had a journal from the 1700s.

"Why do you want to know about Kings Mountain?" he asked.

"It's mentioned in that diary I found yesterday. I want to see if I can find others. I didn't realize it was so old. The leather is still in good condition, the writing a bit faded, but it's not deteriorating like I'd think a book that old would."

"Probably not made like paper was later. If it's from the 1700s rags were the primary component, lasted much longer than the later wood pulp paper. Are you still going with me to get that tree?"

"I don't know. It looks cold outside." She was having second thoughts, and thirds. Being with him and not hoping for a future was almost more than she could bear. She wanted him to storm in and say he loved her more than anything—even his job—and would never leave.

"It's cold and blustery and threatening to storm. We might have snow before night. But it feels good after the heat of the Middle East. Bundle up, you won't freeze," he said.

So much for a promise never to leave.

They ate in silence. Cath was afraid to disturb the quiet. She hadn't a clue what Jake was thinking. At the end of the holiday, would he quietly go back to work and let her get the divorce uncontested? Or would he argue against it for whatever reason, and then take off? The only thing she knew for certain, he would not be remaining long in Washington.

Glancing at the kitchen clock, she saw it was too early to go for the tree, yet she didn't want to get started on another room until after they got back. She knew how dirty she'd get.

"I sorted through some of the decorations last night," Jake said, rising to take his bowl to the sink. "I even tested the lights. Most work. We can get replacements at a store. You'll like the ornaments…your aunt had some unusual ones."

Cath looked out the window at the signs of the wind. She wasn't sure she wanted to go tree hunting in the best of times, and today's weather didn't qualify for best. Why had she agreed to go?

Promptly at ten they arrived at the tree farm. Despite it being so close to Christmas, they were not the only ones there, but the other two families had a half dozen children between them running around, exclaiming which tree was the biggest and begging their parents to buy it quick before someone else got it.

"Cut it yourself or we'll do it," the man by the gate said. He gestured to saws and small hatchets.

Jake looked at them and then at Cath.

"At the risk of proving totally inept, I say we try cutting it ourselves," he said.

"Don't look at me, I know nothing about being a lumberjack."

The man on the stool laughed. "Nothing to it, ma'am. Just cut near the ground, level so it'll set right in your stand. No need to be a lumberjack."

Jake laughed and took a small saw. He started down one row.

Cath followed slowly, watching the children. If they had had children earlier, their kids would be running around now, excited about getting a tree. What an exciting time holidays were with children. The boys and girls were having such fun running up and down the rows. She could just imagine that fun continuing after they chose their tree. They'd go home and each mother and father would encourage them to decorate it. Ornaments that were family heirlooms would be lovingly placed on the branches. Maybe each child would get a special ornament commemorating this Christmas. Tinsel would be hung— carefully by the mother, and thrown on by children. Laughter, hot chocolate, dreams would be shared. She wanted those happy days for herself. She wanted a family.

Jake was way ahead of her when she looked for him. She hurried down the aisle, thinking how bland the outing was with just the two of them.

When she caught up with him, she was startled by the happiness in his eyes.

"I measured the space in the living room and we can have a seven foot tree. This starts the seven footers," he said, pointing to a tree a few inches taller than he was.

Cath hadn't even thought about that aspect.

"Did you see those kids?" she asked, looking back down where they were.

"Yeah, noisy, weren't they?"

"Jake! They're so excited about getting a tree. I can't wait until I have children to share days like this with them."

He looked away. When she glanced at him, the happiness had faded. Was that sadness she saw in his gaze? A reminder that if she had children, it would be with another man. She'd start a family without Jake.

The thought pierced like a knife. She couldn't imagine another man filling her heart like Jake had. Would there be anyone else for her? Or was she risking a long and lonely future by saying goodbye?

He didn't like the idea of her with someone else, yet he refused to do anything about them. He had his job, she wished him joy in it. Surely he could see there was no future for the two of them.

"This is a nice tree," she said, trying to get the expedition over with. It was safer back at the house. She wasn't trying to make things any more difficult than they were. But if he thought taking her to buy a tree would repair six years of neglect, he had to have rocks in his head.

"If that's the one you like, I'll cut it down."

She could be imagining the disappointment in his tone, but she wasn't sure. It wouldn't hurt to extend the expedition a little longer. "Oh, wait. Let's look at a couple more. Just to be sure."

They spent more than a few minutes looking at different trees. While the conifers had been trimmed to conform to a perfect shape, there were slight imperfections in each one.

Jake commented on some, Cath on others until they had been there almost an hour, and not settled on a tree.

"I'm freezing," she said. The earlier families had left. Another group had shown up. The tree farm seemed to be doing a good business for three days prior to Christmas.

"I wanted that last tree. Agree with me so we can cut it down and head for home," she said. "My fingers may have frostbite."

"It's not that cold. If that's the one you want, I'll settle for it."

"Settle? It's a gorgeous tree!"

"It has a gap near the bottom."

"Put that side next to the wall. I want that tree!"

"Fine, we'll take that one. We also need to stop at the store on the way home, to get the bulbs for the burned out lights. Do we need tinsel?" he reminded her.

Cath walked around her chosen tree slowly, examining it from top to bottom. There was one bare spot, but not a large one, it could be right next to the wall where no one would see it. The fragrance filled the air. It would be wonderful in Aunt Sally's old house.

Not that anyone would see the tree except Jake and her. They had no friends here, had not invited anyone to share the day with them. Still, she wanted it to look nice—in honor of using Aunt Sally's ornaments, she told herself. But mostly she wanted to get out of the cold.

"Glad that's settled," she said in mock frustration. She laughed, feeling joy rising at the thought of decorating it. Christmas had always been her favorite holiday. "Can you cut it?" she asked.

"I can try. Hold it steady as I cut through the trunk."

Jake knelt down and applied the saw. When the tree began to wobble, Cath grabbed hold and held on, trying to keep it upright. With a final swipe of the saw, the tree tumbled onto her, engulfing her completely in fragrant branches.

"Ohhh, get it off me before we both fall," Cath called, giggling at the unexpected fun.

Jake pulled it away, and gently tipped it into the pathway. "Grab the top, I'll get the trunk and we'll carry it to the car."

"Will it fit on the car? It's huge!"

"We'll tie it on top. Hope it won't cover the windshield."

With the help of the lot owner, they tied the tree on the car. After paying him, Jake opened the passenger door for Cath.

"Next stop that store we passed when we turned on Winston, then home," he said.

"I'll stay in the car to make sure no one steals our tree. It's a pretty one, isn't it?" she asked.

"Lovely," he said, but his eyes weren't on the tree, they were on her.

Cath caught her breath, almost swept away by the light in Jake's eyes.

She looked ahead, motioning him to close the door. "I'm cold, shut the door." She was not getting caught up in some romantic notion that getting a tree together changed anything. It was another memory to cherish. But it also signified the end of a relationship. Her heart ached with the thought of no more Christmases with Jake.

As he rounded the car, she saw another family walking to their car, all four children struggling to hold on to the large tree. The mother and father exchanged loving smiles.

Cath caught her breath and looked away. She needed to hold on to her dream, and ignore the temptation that called to her. She wanted her own family, not a man who spent most of his life half way round the world!

It was early afternoon by the time they turned into the road that Aunt Sally's house was on. Jake was satisfied their outing had been a step in the right direction. Cath had been distant at the beginning, but warmed up to the fun of finding a tree as the morning went on. She'd been laughing at the end. He knew she'd mentioned clearing and cleaning another bedroom this afternoon, but he had a feeling she'd rather decorate their tree.

He'd bought some cider in the store and some Christmas cookies. They weren't homemade, but would do in a pinch.

As they pulled into the long driveway the cell phone in Cath's purse rang.

"Expecting someone?" he asked.

"No," she said, rummaging around in the purse and pulled out her phone.

"Hello?" Cath listened a moment, then gave him an odd look.

"I know, Abby. He's here now."

So her friend was calling to warn her. Interesting.

"The phone was in my purse which I left on the kitchen counter. Unless I was in that room when you called, I wouldn't have heard it ring."

She was silent another moment.

"It's okay," she said slowly.

Jake would bet Abby asked how things were going between them. Jake squelched the urge to reach for the phone and tell Abby to mind her own business. He and Cath would work things out. But Cath was acting more emotional than usual and he had to walk warily around her. Alienating her by being rude wouldn't help.

Jake slowly got out of the car. He could stay and listen to one half of the conversation, or get going on unloading the tree and enticing Cath to forget cleaning the old house and concentrate on decorating it instead.

Though if she insisted on cleaning this afternoon, he'd suggest the room he was using. She had done nothing to make him feel welcomed. His room wasn't dusted or aired. He'd just collapsed on the bed both last night and the first night and made do with the covers that were there. He'd slept in worse, so hadn't complained, but a bit of the welcome he had hoped to find upon returning home would have helped.

"Want to help me take the tree inside?" he asked, peering back into the car.

Cath turned, frowning when she saw him. "Oh. Sure. I'm going to have to go, Abby. I'll call you later." He could almost feel the dismay when she realized he was still there. Tough.

Angrily he turned and began to untie the tree. Cath had enjoyed the morning. He knew she had. Now the phone call brought back her intent with a vengeance. Time was fleeting. It was already three days until Christmas. If he didn't make some progress soon, she'd be returning to Washington before he knew it and to the divorce she wanted so passionately.

He had to find a way to turn that passion toward their marriage.

Dragging the tree off the car, he waited for her to get the light end and they carried it to the front of the house.

"Lean it against the railing. I'll get something to make a stand," he said.

"Try the carriage house. Aunt Sally had tools and other things there. Maybe some scrap wood," she said. "I'll get the things from the car." Gone was the excitement she'd displayed when finding the tree. Now it was back to the business of ending a marriage.

Jake headed for the carriage house in the rear, wishing Abby hadn't called. A man could only stand so much. He needed time to get his emotions under control. It wouldn't pay to make himself look like a fool by railing at Cath. He had time and a hope from the response she'd given when he kissed her. She wasn't immune to him, or out of love, despite what she was saying. She couldn't be.

The carriage house hadn't been used for horses in decades. It had served as Aunt Sally's garage and catch-all—what the cellar didn't hold looked like it was out here. There was a workbench of sorts along one wall. In the back was an old carriage, rotten wheels and all. The cleared space on the right had held Sally's car until she'd given up driving several years prior to her death.

Jake rummaged around the area and found some loose wooden boards. Taking the hammer and some nails from the workbench, he banged together a make-shift stand and headed back to the tree.

His optimism restored, Jake set to work. He liked

challenges. He had to get through to Cath. One way or another, he would do it or die trying.

Cath was feeling oddly flustered. She hadn't expected to enjoy getting the tree, but the outing had ended up being fun. And she loved the tree they'd selected. Her arms were full of the packages from the store, more lights, tinsel and a star for the top. The tree itself was thick and full, and smelled so divine it would keep the house fragrant for days.

They could use Aunt Sally's decorations and make it beautiful. But for a moment, she wanted to flee to a dirty bedroom and plunge into cleaning. It was safer than making Christmas memories with Jake.

She looked at the old house. How many Christmases had it known? Had Aunt Sally decorated it each year, or being alone, had only the minimum ornaments displayed to mark the occasion?

She couldn't believe she never inquired after her aunt's practices. She'd invited her to spend the holidays with them more than once, but Aunt Sally had always said she liked to be in her own home at Christmas.

For a moment, Cath wondered if she should decorate. She loved classroom decorations with all the children participating, chaotic, frenzied though it was. She looked forward to it every year. And to helping Abby decorate her home with her two children. Cath loved decorating their condo, too, though it was only seen by herself and a few friends. Always, every year, she hoped Jake would make it home for the holiday. If she moved here, she'd want all the trappings of family and home. Maybe she should make this year a practice run. Next Christmas she'd know what else to plan on. Maybe outlining the old house in outside lights.

Jake came around the side of the house, boards and hammer in hand.

"Do you know what you're doing?" she asked. She didn't believe she'd ever seen Jake with a hammer in hand.

"I did this as a kid," he said.

She was surprised. Jake rarely talked about his past. His father had died when he'd been nine and his mother had remarried to a man who hadn't liked Jake. She knew he'd been an unhappy teenager who had had to live in a family with new babies and happiness all around—except for him.

"I think this will hold," he said a few moments later. He righted the tree and stepped back. It remained standing, tall and straight.

He looked over at the front door. "Open that and we'll take the tree in that way. I need your help to keep the branches from dragging."

Cath went through the kitchen, dropping her packages, and continued on to the front door. She flung it wide and went to help Jake with the tree.

In only a few moments they had it situated between the two front windows. The fragrance of pine filled the room. Cath thought the place felt warmer just by having the tree. Maybe they could find some logs and have a fire. She'd love an old-fashioned Christmas. Maybe it would even snow as Jake had predicted.

She watched Jake as he turned the tree slightly, hiding the bare spot. What was she going to do with him for the next few days? Surely he'd get bored and head for more exciting places before Christmas. She fully expected him to leave at the first sign of any breaking news.

"I'm going to fix lunch," Cath said. She was torn with the desire to decorate and the need to put distance between herself and Jake.

As she walked down the hall, she heard Jake's cell phone ring. So it happened earlier than she thought.

She took her time making sandwiches. There was nothing she wanted to prepare for dinner. Maybe she'd go out. She could head for Williamsburg, find a place to eat and then wander around the shops that were decorated for the holidays.

Jake came in just as she began to eat. His plate with a sandwich and some chips was at his place.

"Thanks," he said, taking the chair. He ate two bites before looking at her.

"We can put on the lights and ornaments this afternoon."

She shrugged. "I need to get the rooms cleaned, if I want to stay on schedule."

"Hire a service," he said. "It's a holiday, take some time off."

"It's not just the cleaning, I'm trying to assess what to do with everything—the furniture and knickknacks."

He ate in silence for a few minutes.

"Was that your office that called?" she asked, unable to resist.

He nodded.

"A new assignment?"

"No."

If he thought she was going to play twenty questions, he didn't know her. But curiosity burned. Who had called?

"Tell you what," Jake said. "Let's clean Aunt Sally's old room, then after dinner, we'll build a fire in the fireplace and decorate the tree. Tomorrow we'll decorate the rest of the house if you like."

She looked at him suspiciously. How had he known she wanted a fire in the fireplace?

"Maybe."

"For heaven's sake, Cath. Stop blowing hot and cold. Let's agree to spend this Christmas together in harmony. We can make decisions about the future before the New Year, but let's take the next few days for ourselves."

She grudgingly admitted to herself she would have been shocked if Jake had just up and told her out of the clear blue that he wanted to end their marriage. Maybe she needed to give him time to get used to the idea without sniping at each other. It wasn't as if she no longer cared about the man. That was the problem. She was beginning to think she would never get over Jake Morgan.

"I'm not blowing hot and cold. I'll agree to spend the few days until Christmas in harmony. But no talking about the future, one way or the other. And no trying to get me to change my mind," she said, wondering what she'd do if she never did find someone else to love. She'd end up an old lady living in a big house all alone like her great-aunt.

"Fine. Tell me about your work," he said.

"What?"

"You pointed out I don't know a lot about where you work, or your co-workers except for Abby. So tell me."

Cath thought about it for a moment, then nodded and began to tell him about a typical day, mentioning her children—the sweet ones and the troublemakers. She talked about how excited she was each year to be encouraging a new group of students to do their best, to learn what they could and to establish good study habits.

He listened without interruption, watching her as she talked, his eyes narrowed as if assessing all she said.

She didn't care, she loved sharing that part of her life with him. She had all along but he had never seemed interested before. She loved working as a teacher, and was happy she got to see her students for another few years after her class before they went on to other schools.

"What about the other teachers?" he asked at one point. She had refilled their beverage glasses, the sandwiches long gone.

"Except for Abby, I don't interact all that much with the other teachers—not away from school. I do share yard duty with Brent Mulphy and Stella Hawkins. We keep an eye on the students when they take recess. Of course Abby and I have been friends for years."

"No trouble with parents?"

"One or two each term, but nothing I can't handle."

He shook his head. "A room full of eight-year-olds, sounds more intimidating than front line firing to me."

She smiled. "I love children. And that's the best age, in my opinion. They can read, they've started doing more complicated math than just addition and subtraction, and they aren't in their snotty stage of life."

"Ever think of moving into administration?"

She shook her head. "I love teaching. And I'm good at it. That's why I think I could get a job down here without too much trouble."

He pushed his plate away. "You're serious about moving here?"

"I'm seriously thinking about it," she said carefully.

His cell rang again. He fished it out of his jeans pocket, checked the caller and frowned. "I need to take this."

Cath rose and gathered their dishes as Jake headed for the front of the house. She rinsed, dried and put away the plates, and headed upstairs. She wanted to keep to her timetable on clearing the house, but when she stood in Aunt Sally's old bedroom, she paused. Jake's duffel was on the floor, opened, a few items of clothing spilling out. His laptop was closed, sitting on top of the dresser. She never understood how the thing stood up to the casual abuse he gave it. Stuffing it in a duffel, under his arm, or in a backpack didn't seem her idea of ways to handle a sensitive piece of equipment like that. But it seemed to work fine instead of being totally wrecked with his usage.

Looking at the old furnishings in the large room, including the tall secretary with books behind the glass doors, Cath thought about the journal she found. Would there be others in Aunt Sally's bookcase? Or in other boxes in the cellar? She hadn't read but one entry and was anxious to know more about Tansy and Jonathan. Maybe Jake would let her use his laptop to research historical sites so she could see what she could find out about the battle at Kings Mountain.

"Ready to work?" he asked, joining her before she knew it. She had been woolgathering if she missed hearing him climb the stairs.

"This is the largest of the bedrooms. Maybe I should wait and do it last," she said, feeling daunted by the task.

"I wouldn't mind a clean room to sleep in."

Another pang of guilt with the cavalier way she'd treated him. He deserved better.

"You're right. There are clean sheets in the cupboard. They might be a bit musty, but that's all there is. Let's get going."

The afternoon went fast as they developed a working relationship that melded their different abilities. Jake brought down the old curtains and hauled them away. He moved the furniture for Cath to clean behind and beneath, then pushed them back.

Since she'd already donated all of Aunt Sally's clothing last summer, there was little in the room beyond the furnishings. All knickknacks were confined to the large secretary desk, along with several shelves of books.

"You'll need to check to see if any of these are worth anything," he said, opening the double glass doors and reaching for a couple of books, leafing through the volumes.

"The lawyers did an appraisal for inheritance taxes. No first editions or anything," she murmured, scanning the spines of the books. One looked like a journal. She pulled it from the second shelf and opened it. It was, but written by Aunt Sally herself, many years previously. Cath would like to read it, but right now her focus was on finding out more about the lonely woman whose writings she'd found yesterday.

It was dark outside by the time they finished the room. They made the bed, and Cath tried not to think about their large king-size bed at home. It had seemed too large for one person whenever Jake was gone from home. Cath had even thought about using their guest room, but she felt close to him in their bed, so never moved out of the room.

Jake put his duffel on a chair when she mopped the hardwood floor. A good coat of wax would go a long way to making the floor look good. She surveyed the room when finished. Almost all traces of Aunt Sally had disappeared. Jake's things now dominated. She turned, not liking the yearning that seemed to rise every time she looked at Jake.

Cath was tired, and not in the mood to get dressed enough to go out once she showered. Soup and sandwiches again, it looked like. Jake might count himself lucky to be getting out of a marriage if that's all she fed him.

"How about we order pizza?" Jake suggested as he prepared to haul the last of the rags and trash downstairs. "Saves us going out, or either of us cooking. Go take your shower and I'll call in the order. It'll probably be here by the time you're through and I grab a quick shower."

If she let herself think about it, it would seem just like being married. Which of course they were, but they had so little experience in acting like a married couple. They ate out a lot when Jake was home. He claimed he didn't want her to have to spend time in the kitchen when she could be with him. But he sometimes joined her in preparing meals. He had on several occasions, and she almost smiled at the memories. So much of their marriage had been spent apart. But there was nothing to complain about when they'd been together.

"That sounds good," she said, glad not to even have to heat soup.

Cath quickly showered and changed into comfortable slacks, a warm sweater and house slippers. She
passed Jake on the stairs when she headed down. He
held out his wallet.

"Pay the guy if he shows up before I get out."

She took it, still warm from his body. The leather was
soft and supple. It was stuffed with money, credit cards
and his driver's license. She flipped it open. Facing her
was an annual school photo teachers got each year. She'd
given him this one several years ago. She hadn't known
he kept it in his wallet. It made her feel funny. Hadn't he
said thinking of her kept him going sometimes? Did he
pull out the wallet and look at the photo often?

She felt sad at the thought of him thousands of miles
away and as lonely as she was. Where had they gone
wrong? Could anything be fixed?

CHAPTER FIVE

As soon as they finished the pizza, Cath pleaded tiredness and escaped to her room. She wasn't as tired as she said, just unable to face an evening with Jake, trying to keep her distance when half the time she yearned to feel his strong arms around her, wanted to hear the steady beat of his heart beneath her ear. She wasn't in the mood to decorate a tree. Being with him was an exercise in trying to ignore her rising awareness. She wished she knew more about what he'd been doing since she'd seen him last. How much danger he'd been in, did he get enough to eat? What did he do for recreation?

But to ask would give rise to his thinking she was mellowing and maybe even reconsidering her decision. She didn't plan to give any false or overly optimistic messages. Her decision had been hard fought, and she couldn't allow emotions to cloud the issue.

She took the journal and pulled the afghan from the bed, going to the chair near the window. It was a bit drafty, but the wool afghan would keep her warm. The light on the small table gave a softness to the room that enabled Cath to imagine how it had looked in the days before electricity, when candles and oil lamps had been the means of illumination.

The entry began:

Three days until Christmas. It began to snow today. I worry about Jonathan getting through the drifts. His horse is old, if still alive. He talked about fighting on foot in the last letter I received from him. If it snows, do they cease fighting? He made no mention of the warm muffler I sent in that hastily scribbled missive. Had he not received it? I sent it with Master Jerome who was riding to rejoin the regiment. I fear Jonathan will get a chill and pray he doesn't get sick. I wish he would come home for Christmas. He said he would try.

I'm so lonely with him gone. I miss him so. Maybe if I had babes to care for my mind would not dwell on my husband. But our marriage is young and I don't like the days slipping away without him here.

I worry about him. Would that I could go where he goes, keeping some kind of accommodation for him to make sure he eats properly and stays warm and dry. It is probably very shocking of me, but I miss lying in his arms at night. I felt so safe and cherished with him holding me close. It's this horrible war that is making things so difficult. When will it end?

Cath gazed off into space, feeling warm and safe in the room, despite the slight draft. She could empathize with the longing and worry of the long-ago Tansy.

Hadn't she lain in bed at night worrying about Jake, wondering if he were all right? How long after he was injured or killed would it have been before she heard anything? Unlike the Revolutionary War days, communications were much faster now. Still, in war zones, or disaster areas, difficulties cropped up making communications impossible. She'd been kept awake long into the night many times, worrying about hearing from him. Imagining him dying far from home, and far from her.

She shivered. He was safe. Maybe he was one of those individuals blessed through danger. He thrived on it. It scared her to death when she learned of some of the situations he'd come through unscathed. How long could his luck hold?

Maybe she should have thoughts like Tansy, going with Jake, to make sure he ate right. He was too thin, she'd noticed that on the first night. And she wasn't doing much to help him gain back that weight. Soup and sandwiches and pizza weren't a substitute for good nutrition.

Feeling restless, Cath laid down the journal and pushed aside the afghan. She rose and went to the stairs. The light was on in the living room. Slowly she descended and walked quietly to the door of the front room.

Jake was winding lights around the tree. The bottom third of the tree had been encircled, he was now working on the upper branches. He had all the lights on, and the sparkling spots of color shimmered in the tears that filled her eyes.

Alone. It seemed so sad to decorate a Christmas tree alone. She had not done it in recent years, preferring to spend the day with her friend Abby and her family. At the condo, she'd have lots of other decorations, but not a tree.

Watching Jake, her heart felt a tug of sadness. He'd come home expecting to celebrate the holidays with her and she'd been gone. According to him, he'd done extraordinary things to get this time and she had shoved it back in his face. He had nowhere else to go, except back to the dangerous places that made news. He and his family had been estranged for years. He'd never returned home after leaving for college.

She blamed his mother for her total switch of allegiance when she remarried. How sad for her son. She would never understand how the woman could ignore her firstborn child. Granted her other children needed her love as well, but to turn from her first was inconceivable to Cath.

Maybe their own marriage wasn't going to last. But she could be kind enough, generous enough to offer him one happy last holiday together.

"Jake?"

He looked over at her. "I thought you went to bed."

"No, I wanted to rest for a little while. I was reading. Why didn't you wait until tomorrow? We could have done this together."

"Really? I got the feeling you didn't want anything to do with me," he said, turning back to the tree. "If I wanted to see it decorated, I had to do it myself."

She stepped into the room.

"I haven't had a tree since the one we got together on our second Christmas," she said slowly. The ornaments they'd brought up from the cellar had been put on the coffee table, the lids of the boxes off so each one could easily be seen. There were globes and spirals, fancy ones and plain. Each held a memory for her great-aunt, lost now to the ages.

"I can help," she said lowly.

He glanced over and shook his head. "Not if it's a chore, Cath. I don't know a lot about holidays, usually working right through them as if they were any other day, but I do know they should be celebrated. Doing it as an obligation doesn't work."

"Christmas used to be my favorite holiday," she said, lifting a shiny ornament and studying it. She remembered the days her parents had made so special for her. Lots of presents, big ham dinner with biscuits, sweet potatoes and of course plum pudding. Her mouth watered for some of that dessert, usually made months before the holidays and brought out as a special treat.

"As I said, usually just another day for me," Jake said.

"What about when you were a child? It had to be special then."

She watched as his expression turned bleak. She wished she hadn't brought it up.

"Maybe when I was young. But it all changed after my dad died."

She knew some of the story, how his mother's new family became more important than her first child. How his stepfather and he had never gotten along, and his mother always sided with the man. Jake had earned a scholarship for college and left home, never to return.

Cath had wished for brothers and sisters as she'd grown up, but when she'd learned of Jake's family life, she'd been glad to be spared that. How awful not to feel loved and cherished as her family made her feel.

As Jake had made her feel in the early days of their marriage.

As he still could.

"What?" he said, catching her gaze.

"I was remembering," she said softly. "We started out so great, why did it go wrong?"

"I don't think anything went wrong," he said.

She snapped out of her mood. "Well it did." She turned and searched the box for a hook for the ornament. "When you get the lights on, I'll start with the ornaments," she said, looking for the box of hooks they'd bought earlier. She'd get the ornaments ready to hang. It would give her something to do, besides being melancholy about Tansy and her Jonathan being separated so long, or her and Jake's situation.

For several awkward moments they continued working. Cath's nerves stretched thin. She moved around the boxes until Jake was behind her and she couldn't see him, hoping it would calm the rampaging awareness that had her as antsy as a cat in a room full of rocking chairs. She could still hear him moving, hear the soft swish of the branches as he fastened the lights.

"We need Christmas carols," she said at last, almost about to explode. She looked around the room, but saw nothing that looked like a radio or CD player.

"I think there're some records in the room off the dining room," Jake said.

"Records?"

"I take it your aunt was a bit old-fashioned," he said. "Though I wouldn't have expected it."

Jake had met Aunt Sally at their wedding where she and he had hit it off. Cath and Jake had spent a long weekend with Aunt Sally that first year. He hadn't been able to come to visit after that—work.

She left the room, not wanting to think about the past. Or the present. What she should focus on was the future. The glorious future when she'd have lots of family around her at holidays and not feel sad and lonely.

She found the record player and a cabinet full of albums. Skimming through them quickly, she found several Christmas carol albums bunched together. In less than ten minutes, she had the record player hooked up in the living room and the sound of carols filled the room.

"I thought everyone had CDs now," she commented, resuming her task of putting hooks on ornaments. She had worked through two boxes and was starting on the third.

"What else goes on before the ornaments?" Jake asked, looking at the tree.

"The garland. That silvery thing."

"I know what a garland is," he said, lifting it from one box.

When the record player changed, the song "Silver Bells" began. Jake looked at her, and then stepped over, sweeping her into his arms.

"What are you doing?" she asked, startled.

"Dancing," he said, moving them around the large living room.

Cath laughed. "It's hardly dance music."

"Sure it is, we're dancing, aren't we?" He danced with an ease that belied his years in rough places. It was as if he did it all the time.

Cath started to protest, the words dying on her lips. This was fun. She loved to dance and had done so little over the length of their marriage. Giving herself up to the moment, she swayed with the music, following Jake's lead, imagining them at a huge Christmas ball. She'd be wearing a sexy red dress—for the season, and for sex appeal. Jake would be in a dark suit, or even a tux. She knew he looked fabulous in a tux; he'd worn one to their wedding.

They'd dance the night away.

When the song ended, the next one was definitely not one to dance to. Slowly they came to a halt.

She looked up into his face, still caught up by the magic of the moment. "Thank you," she said.

"Thank you," he replied, and kissed her.

Still held in his arms, Cath didn't have to move an inch. She let herself continue in the magic, kissing him back, reveling in the sensations so long missing from her life. His body was strong against hers, his muscles a complement to her softer curves. She'd always felt special with Jake—that hadn't changed. The old memories and affection swelled and she let the future fade for a moment. Capturing the present was as good as it got.

Jake ended the kiss slowly. He wanted to carry his wife up the stairs and make love to her all night long. But he hesitated. She'd been as much a participant in the kiss as he had been. Her breathing attested to the fact. He didn't want to spook her. He wasn't going to settle for one night. And if he pushed the issue, he knew she could kick him out and refuse to see him again.

She opened her eyes and looked at him. The temptation to sweep her up was almost more than he could resist. She looked beautiful.

"I bought cider and Christmas cookies today. Want some?" he asked, hoping she wouldn't comment on the fact they shouldn't be kissing if they were getting a divorce. He wasn't sure he could handle that discussion tonight.

"Sure. Want the cider warmed?"

"Of course."

They went into the kitchen, just like old married folks, he thought wryly. Which in a way they were. But this was only their second Christmas together. How had he let work keep him away?

He opened the package of cookies while Cath heated the cider. Sitting at the table, he watched her, wishing so many things had been different. Knowing the future wasn't going to go like he wanted and helpless to change anything. He should be used to it. Life had not gone the way he'd expected since his father died so long ago.

"Tomorrow I have to get back to my schedule," she said.

"Cleaning another room?"

"Yes. One way or another, I want this place ready for whatever I decide by the time I leave at New Year's."

"Are you serious about moving here?" he asked. Another drawback. He couldn't see living in this old house, surrounded by old families who'd lived here for generations, several miles from Williamsburg. It would take an hour or longer to get to Richmond or Norfolk, and neither city was exactly the hub of the world.

"I'm still thinking about it. It's a great place to live and would be wonderful for children."

He bit a savage bite from the cookie. "There's a lot more in life than children," he said.

She looked at him and shrugged. "Jake, let's not fight over anything. Let's enjoy this Christmas. For all the things that might have been, let's give ourselves a terrific memory to last all our lives."

"Why?"

"Why not?"

He studied her for a moment. "Why the change of heart? Yesterday you ordered me out."

She licked her lips. "I was thinking we don't have a lot of memories since we haven't spent a lot of time together. Don't you think one day you'll regret not having a family, not spending time with that family? Careers are fine but are not supposed to be so consuming people don't have time for other things."

He didn't look ahead that far. One day he'd be too old to investigate the news in foreign locales. Maybe too old to work at all. What would he do then? Thinking back to the past didn't figure in his plans. But if he was alone, wouldn't it be something to have one special memory of the girl he'd loved enough to marry six years ago? He'd failed her, he knew. But that was something else he couldn't change. Maybe Cath was right, take the gift of a perfect Christmas and treasure the memory all the rest of his life.

He wasn't willing to concede he'd be alone. There had to be some way he could reach her, show her they belonged together. Convince her to stay with him.

If they had the best Christmas ever, wouldn't that sway Cath they were good together? Make her see they shouldn't throw away what they had on a nebulous future which might not include that huge family she was always talking about.

"We can give it a try," he said, already coming up with ideas to change his wife's mind and keep their marriage intact. Wasn't Christmas the time of miracles? He'd need one to keep Cath, and he was way overdue to receive a miracle.

She poured the cider into mugs and went to sit at the table, handing Jake one.

"I forgot to ask you earlier if you'd check on the battle of Kings Mountain for me. I saw mention of it in the journal I'm reading."

"Know who wrote it?"

"Tansy. Her husband was Jonathan. I'm guessing Williamson, since Aunt Sally said that her family had owned the house since it was built. She never married. I guess it came down through the sons, but don't really know. You'd think I'd know more about my family history."

"Most people don't know much beyond the relatives they actually knew. We can look up on the Internet if you like. I brought my laptop."

"Naturally," she said dryly. Then wrinkled her nose. "That was tacky. Of course you'd have your laptop. Thanks for the offer. Aunt Sally didn't have a computer and I'd hate to wait until I return home. I want to know about the war. And if Jonathan came home."

"Doesn't the journal say?" he asked.

"I'm reading a day at a time. She wrote several pages each day." Cath toyed with her mug for a moment, darting another glance at Jake.

"In a way, I'm seeing some of myself in her journal. She's home alone—here I guess—and missing her husband. It must have been hard to be a woman back then with her husband gone. She mentions neighbors helping out with some of the farm chores. I think Jonathan had been gone for months."

"Some men were gone years. Some went to fight except when they had to return home for harvest. It was a rag-tag army at best."

"She was so lonely. I wish I knew how old she was. Sounds like she and Jonathan hadn't been married that long."

"Maybe there're other journals."

"I hope so. I wanted to look in the trunk again. Maybe I missed another one. It was mostly full of clothes, so another journal could have slid down."

"We can look tomorrow."

"What about cleaning?"

"How long will it take to look through a few boxes to see if there are other journals? You remember where the trunk was?"

She nodded. Right by that old cradle. Had it been Tansy and Jonathan's?

"Then look in nearby boxes, chances are stuff is stored by age. There sure doesn't seem to be any other method to the storage."

"Mmm." Cath sipped her cider, wondering about Tansy and the past and how closely she felt tied to the woman. Was history repeating itself with a slight twist? Jake wasn't going to war to fight, but he was away for long periods of time, and usually reporting on armed conflicts.

"I'm tired. I'm going up to bed for good now," she said, rising a little later.

He followed her to the foot of the stairs.

"I'm glad you came back down to decorate the tree," he said.

"Me, too. It's pretty, isn't it?" she asked, looking at it through the archway. It sparkled and shimmered with lights and ornaments.

"We didn't get any tinsel on it," she said.

"It doesn't need it. Good night, Cath."

He kissed her briefly and headed to the living room. He'd clean up the boxes and other clutter and then head for bed. Tomorrow he'd begin his campaign.

Cath awoke with a feeling of anticipation. She and Jake had reached a truce last night. They'd enjoy each other's company for the next couple of days, and then separate. It would be nice to have someone to share the holidays with. And with this new truce, there'd be no pushing to change her decision.

She frowned. At least she hoped so. The kisses he'd given her last night didn't seem as platonic as they could be. But he'd been away for a long time. What was a kiss or two between friends?

Could they be friends? She tried to picture them meeting for dinner or something each time he returned to the States. She could not picture them reminiscing together.

There was too much between them, including that flare of attraction and awareness that rose every time he came near her. Just lying in her bed she felt fluttery merely thinking about Jake. God she wished things were different and that he'd be home for her every night!

Pushing aside her confused thoughts, she rose and quickly dressed. Despite the heater, it was still cold in the bedrooms. One glance out the window showed a storm was brewing. The intermittent sunshine of yesterday was gone. Gray skies made the day seem dreary. There would probably be rain by afternoon, she thought.

Wearing old jeans and a sweatshirt, she went downstairs. The house was silent. The Christmas tree lights had been turned on, sparkling in the pale morning light. Jake was already up.

But when she went into the kitchen, he wasn't there. The coffee was warm on the stove. The box of Christmas cookies was on the table. Had that been his breakfast? She looked out the window to see if he was on one of his walks and spotted him near the river. He seemed to like walking along the bank. It must be so peaceful and serene after the places he'd visited.

Still, wasn't he cold? The branches on the trees swayed in the wind. She looked at the sky again, ominous in its grayness. Would it snow? She wished she had a radio to keep up with the weather forecasts. Aunt Sally hadn't had a radio, only an old television set that was on its last legs the last time Cath visited. She hadn't seen a new one since she'd been here. The old one was in Aunt Sally's bedroom—not a place she was going with Jake ensconced there.

Pouring herself a cup of coffee, she watched Jake. He stood near the edge of the bank, a short drop to the river. She almost called out to be careful. What if he slipped or tripped and fell into the icy river?

Then she almost laughed. How foolish. The man

practically lived in danger zones. What was a riverbank?

He turned and walked with his head bent, pausing and then stooping down. She could not see what he was doing, but watched until he stood. He glanced at the house. Could he see her at the window?

Cath turned quickly and went to the refrigerator to pull out some eggs. She'd prepare a big breakfast, mainly for him, and then get ready to plunge into the cleaning she had scheduled.

By midmorning, Jake has received two calls, each pulling him away from the tasks at hand. They'd started on the room across from the one he was using as soon as breakfast was finished. They worked well together and the task went quickly, despite the interruptions.

"Another room?" Jake asked as they left that one, cleaning supplies in hand.

"Not today. After I shower and fix lunch, I want to use the laptop to see what I can find out about the war. Maybe even find mention of Jonathan. I suppose his last name was Williamson. But it could have been a different one that many generations ago."

"I have a couple of calls to make this afternoon, so you can be searching for your long lost kin while I work."

She bit her lip. Was this when he'd get a new assignment and be off? Would he leave before Christmas? It was two days away. Even if something was happening that needed reporting, surely Jake could stay for two more days. Let someone else cover the news.

When had she gone from wishing him not there to hoping he'd stay another two days?

CHAPTER SIX

CATH settled in the living room with Jake's laptop. The lights still shone from the tree. Looking out the window, she was surprised to see light snowflakes drifting down. She'd known a storm was brewing, but hadn't expected snow. So it might be a white Christmas, she mused.

She spent the next couple of hours researching the War for Independence, noting major southern battles, searching for Jonathan Williamson. There was no record of a soldier by that name that she found, but she was fascinated about the accounts of the different skirmishes.

"Find anything?" Jake asked, standing in the doorway. He'd been on the phone the entire time. She'd heard the murmur of his voice coming from the kitchen.

"Lots of information, nothing on a Jonathan Williamson from Virginia. Are you finished your calls?"

"For the time being."

"No major story needing your reporting?" she asked, stretching out her legs. She was feeling a bit stiff from sitting for two hours in front of the computer after all the bending she'd done while cleaning.

"No." He walked over to one of the front windows

and looked out. "It's snowing heavier now than before," he said.

She put the computer on the table and rose to join him. Several inches of snow blanketed the yard and trees. She shivered, not really cold, but feeling the chill from the air near the glass.

"You have the only television in your room," she said. "Check the news to see what to expect."

"Or look it up on the Internet," he said.

She complied and found the forecast more severe than she'd expected. "It says we could have more than a foot of snow. And the cold weather is due to continue through the week, so it's not going to melt anytime soon."

"Do we need to go anywhere?"

Cath shook her head, staring at the five-day forecast on the computer. She'd bought enough food to last a week or longer. She had made sure she bought all she needed for a nice Christmas dinner. It wouldn't be a hardship to remain inside.

"I wish we had some wood for a fire," she said wistfully, shutting down the computer.

"There's some stacked beside the barn."

"Carriage house," she corrected absently. "Is there? Do you suppose it'll burn?"

"It's been there at least since last summer, probably longer. It'll be nice and dry. I'll bring some in."

"I'll help."

They bundled up and went out into the snow. Cath lifted her head to the falling flakes, delighting in the feel of them landing on her cheeks. She laughed and spun around.

"This is so much fun. Usually I hate having it snow,

because I have to go to work and know the streets are going to be treacherous. But this is different. No responsibilities until January. It can snow all week!"

He watched her with a brooding gaze. "If it snowed all week, we'd have ten feet of snow to plow through at the end."

"You know what I mean. Isn't this fun?"

"It beats the dry heat of the Middle East," he said. "Come on, the wood is on the far side."

They brought in several armfuls of split logs, stacking them near the large fireplace. Then Jake found a tarp in the carriage house and covered the rest of the pile so it wouldn't get wet with the snow.

"Isn't that a little late?" Cath asked, watching him. "There's already snow sticking."

"But it's not much and we may end up needing this for heat if something happens to the power. This will keep any more snow from accumulating directly on the wood."

"Want to walk along the river?" Cath asked, not ready to go back inside. She'd seen him several times along the bank of the river. What was the appeal? In the muted light, the water looked gray and cold as it silently flowed on its way to the sea.

"Until our feet get cold," he said.

"We should have brought boots."

"I wasn't expecting to come at all," he reminded her. Taking her hand in his, he gestured upstream. "Let's go this way, I haven't explored this direction."

The snow made walking treacherous. They stayed well away from the riverbank, slipping and skidding from time to time as they trudged along in the quiet of the afternoon.

Soon they passed another house, lights blazing from the downstairs windows, necessary with the storm darkening the sky.

"Do you know who lives there?" Jake asked.

"Mrs. Watson. She was one of Aunt Sally's favorite friends, though she was younger by a decade or more. When I visited, she'd often have us over for dinner. Other than Mrs. Watson and the McDonalds, Aunt Sally devoted herself to me and didn't visit with her friends or neighbors while I was staying with her. The McDonalds were the family on the other side who had the boat I used."

The next house they walked behind was dark. No one home, obviously. "The Carstairs live here. Wonder if they've gone off for the holidays."

Some time later Cath stopped. "My feet are freezing." She was getting cold all over, except for her hand held by Jake. Her hair was covered with snow, as was Jake's. She shook her head, dislodging a shower of flakes. Shivering in the cold air, she noticed the wind seemed to have picked up.

"Time to return anyway," Jake said. "Can you feel the wind?"

She nodded.

They hurried back to the house. Entering the kitchen, Cath toed off her shoes, wiggling her toes against the linoleum floor. "It feels so much warmer in here."

"Want to get that fire going now, or later?" Jake asked, shrugging out of his jacket.

Once again Cath wondered if it were warm enough for him. She should have thought of that before suggesting the walk.

"Now's fine, I guess. What are we going to do the rest of the afternoon?" It was too early to start supper, but Cath wasn't sure she just wanted to sit in the living room together and talk.

"We could explore the cellar a bit more," he said, hanging both their jackets across the back of two chairs to let them drip on the floor as the snow melted. "Look for those journals you want to find."

"Okay." Cath wasn't as excited about exploring the cellar as Jake seemed, but she knew she'd much rather have him with her than do it on her own. Maybe in addition to searching for the journals, she could make a hasty inventory and get some idea of what would be involved in clearing the place.

On the other hand, if she did decide to remain, she would have years ahead of her in which to go through the items in the cellar and determine what to keep and what to discard.

She grabbed a tablet and pencil and headed down the steps after Jake. He seemed to relish the idea of wandering through the spooky place. Halfway down the door slammed behind her.

"Did you leave a window open?" Jake asked from the bottom of the stairs.

"No, but that door slams shut a lot. I forgot to prop it open. I think the house slants or something," she said, descending the remaining stairs. "When you think about it, a house that's two hundred years old and still standing is pretty remarkable."

"There speaks a child of modern America. I've been places where dwellings are several hundred years old, not just two."

"Mmm." She looked around. The dim lighting faintly illuminated the clutter. "Where do we start?"

"It's your cellar, where did you find the journal?"

"Over here." She retraced her steps from earlier and soon stopped by the old cradle. Nudging it, she watched it rock gently for a couple of moments. "I wonder how old this is? It's probably been in the family for generations."

Jake looked at the cradle, the tightness in his chest returning. Did all roads lead to children? A sadness swept through him. He wished he could see Cath when she was pregnant. See her holding a newborn, her head bent over him, her blond hair shielding her face. Then she'd look up and he'd see the love shining in her eyes.

Like he used to see it shining for him. Couldn't Cath see what they had was good? How could she throw it all away?

"Probably has dry rot," he said. He looked over the area. Other furniture was haphazardly stacked out of the narrow aisle. There were trunks and crates and boxes stacked two and three high.

"It does not have dry rot and with a little cleaning and polish it'll be beautiful. Carry it upstairs for me, would you?"

"Whatever for?" He looked at her.

"I can clean it up while I'm here."

"Cath—" He had nothing to say. It had all been said. "Fine." He pulled it away from the other furniture and lifted it. It was heavier than he expected and awkward, but he maneuvered it through the narrow space and to the bottom of the stairs. "Get the door," he said, motioning her to go ahead of him.

She passed him and ran up the steps.

"It's stuck," she said, pushing against it.

"Great." He set down the cradle and, skipping every other step, joined Cath at the top. He tried the door. It didn't budge.

"It didn't lock, did it?" he asked, twisting the knob.

"No. It sticks sometimes."

He pushed it with his shoulder. There wasn't enough room on the top step to get much leverage. Jake tried again. The solid door held firm.

He looked around the frame. "The hinges are on the other side, but maybe I can pry off the board on this side and get to them."

Just then the electricity failed and they were plunged into darkness.

"Jake?" Cath reached out and clutched his arm.

He turned and drew her closer. "It's all right. Just be careful and don't fall down the stairs. I guess the storm got worse."

"This place gives me the creeps," she said.

"It's only the underside of the house. Come on, take the stairs slowly and we'll get to the bottom. Do you know if your aunt had any flashlights or candles down here?"

"I haven't a clue. I never came here much when I was a kid. I know there are candles in the drawer in the kitchen."

"Fat lot of good they do us right now."

"Can't you pry off the frame and get the door open?"

"Sure. It may take a little longer in the dark, but we'll manage." He wasn't sure how, but she sounded nervous. He said what he could to ease her mind.

They reached the bottom, as Jake found out when his shins connected with the cradle. "Dammit," he muttered. If Cath had let the fool thing stay where she found it…

"So how can you work on the door when you can't see anything?" she asked, still holding tightly to his arm. "And where are you going to find any tools. I bet Aunt Sally had them all in the carriage house."

"If we can find a screwdriver or some kind of metal wedge to pry off the board surrounding the door, we'll be all set. There has to be something around here."

"I don't know where anything is in this place," she said. "How can you find anything in the dark?"

"Then we'll just sit down and wait for the power outage to end. It might not be long. Probably not as long as some of the places I've been."

"Or it could last a day or two," Cath said.

"Don't borrow trouble."

They sat on the bottom step. Jake looked off into the darkness. His eyes would have adjusted by now to any light. There was none. He could try to find some device that would work, but not knowing the layout, or what was even available, it sounded like a fool's errand. Plus, if Cath didn't turn loose his arm, he wasn't going anywhere.

He pried her fingers off, then laced them with his. "There's nothing to be scared about," he said. "It's just old furniture and boxes of stuff."

"Maybe ghosts."

He laughed. "I doubt it. Your aunt Sally lived here all her life, she'd have told you if there were any ghosts."

"Maybe."

"Tell me about Tansy. Isn't that the name of the woman who wrote that journal you're captivated by?"

he said, hoping to get her mind off her fear. "She may have been in this cellar herself."

"I wonder who she was. And what happened to them."

"How far have you read?"

"Just a couple of entries. They're lengthy, as if she had lots of time on her hands and poured her feelings out on the page. She talks about neighbors, and the cold, and trying to get the farm chores done on her own. I sometimes feel—"

Jake could tell she was holding something back. "What? There's more to it, surely," he said.

"She was lonely and afraid for her husband," Cath said in a soft voice. "It's uncanny how her words reflect my own feelings."

"What?" That startled him.

"Did you think I never worried about you when you were gone? You don't exactly have a routine, boring job, Jake. You put yourself in danger all the time and never give a thought to how those of us back home feel."

"Who else would care?" he asked.

"I bet your mother does," she said.

"Don't go there, Cath," he warned. He rarely thought about his mother. That was in the past and he planned for it to stay there. Cath knew he had nothing to do with his family, and why. Cath was all he needed.

For a moment he wondered what would happen if she went through with her plan of divorce. He couldn't imagine finding another woman to spend his life with.

"Okay, then we'll leave your mother out of it and talk about me. Us. You wanted to know why I want a divorce. Imagine the roles were reversed and I went to Bosnia in the midst of fighting, or to an earthquake area where the building codes are so laughable that the mildest aftershock topples whole buildings. No guarantees of safety. You wouldn't worry?"

Jake nodded, then remembered she couldn't see in the dark. "Of course I'd worry, especially someone like you."

"Leave that aside. I understand you think you're invincible, but you're not. Terrible things happen to journalists. So that's one part. The other is the loneliness. Jake, I don't like living alone. I don't like having no one to share my day with, or make plans for the weekend, or just talk about friends and co-workers. I miss having someone there to talk over situations that are new and different, to get some ideas for dealing with problem children, or gifted ones. I'm tired of sandwiches for dinner, but don't want to cook for one."

"I'm not a teacher," he said. "I can't stay in one place and do my job, Cath. You know that."

"That was an example. Honestly, you're not trying to see my side of it."

"I'm lonely, too, Cath," he confessed.

"Then why, for heaven's sake, aren't you home living with me?"

"You know my job—"

"No! Stop! I do not want to hear a word about your job. I want to hear about you. Why aren't we sharing a home, making a family, building a life together?"

"How do you propose I support this family if I don't report the news?" He was starting to get mad. Why was he the one at fault? She could travel with him. Granted, not to a war zone or disaster area. But she could move to London or Rome and be closer to where he usually worked. It would be easier for him to get to London than Washington.

"I don't have a suggestion, but I do think that's the crux of the matter. You like your job and it isn't in Washington. Or here. I'm growing to love this house. I don't know the neighbors, but maybe I'll make an effort to meet them and see if I could fit in. I think a complete break and change would be good," she said.

He hoped he wasn't hearing things that weren't there, he could swear he heard an undertone of sadness in her voice. Was there a chance she really didn't want to end their marriage? If so, she had a funny way of showing it.

"What changed?" he asked. "We've been married six years. What changed, Cath?"

"Aunt Sally's death made me look at things differently, I think. I only saw her a few times a year even though Washington isn't that far away. I should have visited more often. Having flying visits from you isn't enough. I see friends and co-workers going home to families each night, and I go home to an empty condo. I'm not getting any younger. If I want to find another man, to have a family, I need to do something now. I don't want to be old like my parents were when I have a child. I want to enjoy each stage of development from baby to toddler to teenager."

"You're around children all day," he said.

"Other people's children. And only a few hours a day. I don't hear the stories at the dinner table about what they learned in school, or what their best friend said. I don't make cookies or Halloween costumes, or Christmas decorations. It was hard being the only child of older parents. I want what I have never had."

"It's overrated," he grumbled.

"You should want what you never had, Jake. You said your mother turned to her new children by her second husband, virtually ignoring you. You missed as much as I did growing up. Maybe it was even worse since you witnessed it but couldn't participate."

"Don't psychoanalyze me, Cath. I did fine, got out as soon as I was eighteen. My mother is welcome to her second family."

"You know she was wrong to ignore you, or let your stepfather have the influence he had. You would make a great father—if you were home. You'd remember what your real father did and follow his example. But it's never going to happen, is it, Jake? We've been through this a dozen times before. You have your job and I have my dreams and they don't mesh."

He turned to her, finding her head in the darkness and covering her lips with his. This part of their marriage had always worked. She responded as she always did. Her kiss was warm and welcoming and so at odds with the words she spoke. This wasn't a woman who wanted to leave her marriage; he couldn't believe that. Yet if something didn't change, and soon, she'd follow through with her plan.

Could he show her how much they meant to each other?

His hands skimmed over her shoulders down to her back, pulling her into his lap and deeper into the embrace. She was like liquid silk, warm and pliant and sweet. He murmured words of wanting in her ear, brushing kisses against her cheeks, trailing them to her throat, feeling the rapid pulse at the base.

Her arms tightened around him, and he felt her breasts press against his chest. If the cellar wasn't cold and dusty, he'd make love to her here and now. He'd been gone too long. And it looked as if his strategy was backfiring on him. He didn't know if Cath was softening, but he wanted her more than ever. He couldn't bear the thought of her walking away forever. Yet the ending seemed inevitable. Why hadn't he seen that from the beginning?

"Hello, anyone home?" a faint voice called.

Jake and Cath sprang apart, turning as one to the door at the top of the stairs.

"Wait here," he said, standing and setting her on her feet. He climbed the stairs and pounded on the door. "We're trapped in the cellar. Are you in the house?"

"Dear me, I came to use your phone." The voice came from an elderly woman.

"I'll run home and get my nephew, maybe he can help."

Less than five minutes later Jake heard footsteps in the kitchen. Someone rattled the handle of the door.

"Is it locked?" a man asked.

"No, stuck only. I've tried pushing from this side," Jake said.

"Hold on. I've got hold of the handle. You push and I'll pull."

For several seconds they tried but the door wouldn't budge.

"Can you see the hinges?" Jake called.

"Sure. They look old as can be. Let me find something to pry them off," the man answered.

"There're tools in the carriage house," Cath called.

Within ten minutes the man had the hinges off and

together he and Jake were able to pry open the door. The stranger lifted it out of the way as Cath scrambled up the steps, glad to escape the cellar. She'd never again complain about the dim lighting—it was much better than total darkness.

"Thank you!" she exclaimed when she stepped into the kitchen.

An elderly woman and a handsome young man stood looking at her.

"You're welcome, Cath dear. I thought you'd come to visit me before now. How have you been?" the woman asked.

"I've been fine, Mrs. Watson. And we've been so busy cleaning and clearing out things I haven't had a chance to do any visiting. I'm glad to see you." Cath gave her a quick hug and then smiled at the young man beside her.

"This is my nephew, staying with me for Christmas. Bart Butler."

"Jake Morgan." Jake extended his hand and they shook. "And my wife, Cath."

"Sally and I were neighbors for more than forty years. I sure do miss her. I remember how very fond of you she was. Calling you the granddaughter she never had," Mrs. Watson told Cath.

She nodded, remembering her aunt telling her that. She considered Cath's father the child she never had, and had doted on him as well.

"My goodness, I came to see if you had a phone that worked. Mine is dead and I need to call to refill a prescription before Christmas," Pearl said. "I told Bart I could manage on my own in the snow, but didn't expect to find that door stuck. Sally used to say she was going to get it fixed. I guess she never got around to it."

"My cell works," Jake said, nodding to the kitchen counter where he'd left it. From now on, he'd keep it with him.

"I appreciate that," Bart said. "I don't mind driving into town, but if they can't fill it or there's a problem, I'd hate to drive all the way in this weather for nothing."

"Glad you needed the phone. We couldn't see a thing in the dark and I was wondering how we'd get out," Jake said, handing his phone to Mrs. Watson.

"We could have been stuck there all night," Cath said with a shiver. "I should have come over when I first arrived to tell you I was staying for Christmas."

"We saw the lights, so we knew you were here," Bart said as his aunt spoke on the phone. "I saw you out walking earlier. Too cold for me."

"You're not from here?" Cath asked.

"I live in Richmond. But I'm spending the holidays with my aunt this year. She didn't want to come to Richmond."

"No other family?" Jake asked.

"A boatload. My folks are taking a cruise this year, however. And two of my sisters are taking their families skiing. My brother and his wife are spending Christmas with her folks this year, so I was on my own. Aunt Pearl thought it better for me to come visit her than for her to visit me. I think she had some concern on the ability of a bachelor to fix a suitable Christmas meal."

Jake didn't like the smile Cath gave the man. Was she already sizing up Bart Butler as a candidate for her next husband? How convenient that would be, living right next door to Sally's house.

"There, it's all taken care of, dear," Mrs. Watson said to her nephew. "They'll even deliver tomorrow, even though it's Christmas Eve. So you don't have to drive in the snow."

"Good." He smiled at his aunt. "Not that I wouldn't have gone for you."

"I know, dear. We'd best be going back. It is colder than I thought it would be."

"Thanks for rescuing us," Cath said.

"Anytime," Bart said, turning his smile in Cath's direction.

"Do you have any idea how long the power will be out?" she asked.

"Not a clue. If our phone worked, we could have called the power company. They usually can estimate when it'll be restored. You can call, if you want to get an estimate," Bart said.

"Wait while I check." Cath retrieved Jake's phone and looked for the phone book. She remembered Jake's finding the Christmas Tree Farm in the book, and leaving it on the dining room table.

The power company estimated electricity would be restored within two hours. It would be full dark by then as it was already after four.

"Will you two be all right?" Pearl asked.

"Of course," Jake said, putting a proprietary arm across Cath's shoulders. He didn't need any more attention from the neighbors, especially Bart.

"Aunt Sally had oil lamps and we'll light them if we need light," Cath said.

"There's a gas stove, so you'll be able to cook," Pearl said, glancing around the kitchen. "Or you are both welcome to come over to our house for supper."

"We'll manage," Jake said.

"We'll be fine. Thank you for inviting us. I hope to see you again before I return to Washington," Cath said graciously, nudging Jake surreptitiously in the ribs.

"Oh, dear, you're leaving after the holidays? We were hoping you were going to stay. This house seems so lonely when no one is here," Pearl said.

"We live in Washington," Jake said firmly.

"Actually, I'm thinking of moving here next summer," Cath said, slipping from under his arm and moving closer to Pearl. "I'm a teacher. Do you think I'd have a chance of finding a job around here?"

"Sure thing," Bart said with a broad smile. "The area is growing and new schools need teachers. Aunt Pearl knows a couple of people on the school board, maybe she could put in a good word. It'd be nice for her to have a close neighbor again. The family on the other side of her house only visits on weekends."

Jake could imagine how nice Pearl would find it. Or was Bart more concerned about when *he* visited?

"No decisions have been made," he said, glaring at Cath. For every step forward, she seemed determined to take one back.

CHAPTER SEVEN

WHEN Mrs. Watson and her nephew left, Jake turned to study the door. The old house had settled over the years, and the door frame was no longer square. He had enough basic skills to plane the door so it would fit better, and shaving a bit of wood from it would insure it wouldn't stick shut again. Bart had offered to help, but he didn't need the young neighbor's assistance.

Jake planned to fix it right away if he could find the proper tools. He didn't like thinking what might have happened to Cath if she'd been caught down there alone with no neighbors needing the phone.

"If you're going to fix that now, could you bring up the cradle first?" Cath asked.

Jake nodded and brought it up. He placed it gently down in the center of the kitchen. It was old, yet had obviously been cared for through the years. How many babies had slept in its shelter? Cath's eyes were shining as she gazed at it. He felt a pang. Once she'd looked at him that way. Would she ever do so again?

"I'm going to the garage to see if there're any tools I can use to fix the door. It's too cold to let the cellar air come up into this level if we don't have to," he said.

Maybe he couldn't bring that shine to her eyes again, but he could keep her safe.

Cath nodded, already reaching for the rags she'd used for cleaning. She'd wipe down the cradle, give it a good polish to see what it looked like. Maybe there was even a small mattress for it somewhere and some bedding, though she couldn't imagine who had been the last baby to use it. Had it been her father? She didn't believe she herself had ever been put in it as her parents hadn't visited often, preferring Sally to come to their house.

The simple carving on the headboard was of flowers. She worked to get all the dust out of the crevasses and corners, wondering who had made it, who had done the carving. A proud father-to-be, she was sure. Maybe even Jonathan?

Jake returned with a handful of tools. He moved the door, placing it half on the table, half on the back of two chairs and started shaving curlicues of wood from the edge. Working on their respective projects kept both from feeling chilled in the cooling air. They'd really need the fire in a while if the electricity didn't come back on. While the heater was oil fueled, it needed electricity to work.

Cath brought out the wood wax she'd seen beneath the sink and began to work it into the old wood. Once finished, she sat back on her heels and smiled. The cradle was a beautiful piece of furniture. It was worn a bit on the sides, as if by many arms reaching in to pick up an infant, but that made it all the more special. The carving was as sharp and clear as if it had been done yesterday.

She pushed it to set it rocking. It continued on its own for several moments. How safe and secure it would hold a baby. Would one of her children sleep in it? She looked over to where Jake worked on the door. Together they'd make the world's most perfect baby. If he'd only be there for her.

Cath rose, cleaned up and pulled some milk from the refrigerator. "Want some hot chocolate?" she asked as Jake patiently shaved another thin sliver of wood from the door. "It's getting cold in here."

"Sure. I'm almost done. Then we can go into the living room and build that fire."

She put the pan on the gas stove and slowly heated it. She glanced from time to time at Jake, feeling odd. It was so domestic, wife in the kitchen fixing something for them both, husband working on a project. How many times had they'd done something like this? Too few. Looking around the old kitchen she could imagine Tansy preparing something for her Jonathan. Instead of the gas range Cath used, Tansy might have had a wood-stove, or even an open hearth. Had Jonathan sat in the warm kitchen, lovingly carving the cradle with flowers and designs for a baby's arrival? The modern kitchen faded and for a moment Cath could imagine how it might have looked two hundred years ago.

"Is it still snowing?" Jake asked.

Cath started, then looked out the window. "Yes." She had better pay attention so the milk didn't boil over. In only a couple of minutes, she had two large mugs of chocolate topped with whipped cream. She carried Jake's to him. He brushed her fingers when he took the mug and looked deep into her eyes.

"Thanks," he said. Taking a sip, he never let his gaze waiver.

Cath felt the touch almost like a shock. She returned his regard, lost in the dark brown of his eyes, the message clear. He wanted her. With effort she tore her gaze away.

"It'll be dark before long. Do you think I should get the oil lamps out and make sure they have fuel?" she asked, feeling flustered. She could almost grasp the tangible desire that flooded through her. She had loved Jake so much when they first married. In many ways, nothing had changed.

"It wouldn't hurt. Even if the power comes back, there's nothing saying it won't go out again later," he said, sipping the hot beverage.

"Better have candles in each room, then, with matches so we'd have light to get to the lamps," Cath said, glad for something to do. The spell was broken. She needed to remember to keep her distance.

The lamps were right where she remembered. Opening the cupboard she took stock of everything stored in them. She planned to leave the cleaning of the kitchen until last, able to make better inroads into the bedrooms and other rooms of the house first. If this cabinet was any indication, the room would take days to sort through and organize. Cath mentally revised her schedule. With both the cellar and kitchen ahead, not to mention the carriage house, there was truly no way she could complete everything this holiday.

Maybe she'd come down for the next few weekends and keep plugging away at the tasks. That way she'd be finished before summer.

It wouldn't be the same with Jake gone, she thought,

taking down the lamps and setting them on the counter. She had planned to work alone, but his arrival had changed that. Now she couldn't imagine doing all this on her own. What if she'd been caught in the cellar alone? What if Mrs. Watson had not needed to use the phone?

Taking down three lamps, she washed the globes. Then she raised the wick on each. Still plenty of oil in the base and the wicks looked trimmed. Lighting them, she soon had a bright, steady glow from each lamp.

"They work," she said just as the heater gave an *umph* and the lights came on in the cellar.

"Your timing is perfect. Maybe you should have lit them earlier," Jake teased.

"Maybe." She blew them out and put them on one side of the counter, just in case.

She glanced at the clock. It wasn't yet six o'clock.

"Do you think I have time to bake some cookies?"

"Why not, we're not on any schedule. And a warm oven will help bring up the temperature in this room."

Cath wasn't sure why she had a sudden desire to bake, must be the housework, nesting. Or maybe it was she wanted to do something for Jake, fatten him up while he was with her, so she felt she was doing something. She began to mix the ingredients for shortbread cookies. They were his favorite.

"There, I think that'll work," Jake said, sanding the edge of the door lightly, then wiping off the dust. "Help me put it back in place."

They rehung the door and it swung closed. She turned the knob and the door opened easily. Letting it go, it once again slammed shut. Again she opened it with no effort.

"That's perfect. Thanks," she said.

He gathered the tools and started for the carriage house. "I'll sweep up the mess when I get back."

"I can manage that," Cath said, "you did all the work." She quickly swept up the wood chips and sawdust and moved the cradle to the back wall, out of the way. The first batch of cookies was ready to come from the oven. She put in another batch.

Some time later Cath realized Jake hadn't come back from the carriage house. What was he doing out there? She glanced out the window, but the angle was wrong. All she could see was the river and the edge of the old building. He wasn't standing on the banks like she'd seen him before. Was he still in the carriage house?

Jake leaned against the back door of the carriage house and stared at the slow-moving river. He didn't see the silvery water as it drifted by, nor the snow that softly drifted from the sky. He was miles away in thought. It felt as if he was trying to hold a slippery eel or something. The tighter he held on, the more Cath seemed to slip away.

He wasn't ready to go back inside. Yet it was too cold and wet to walk along the river. So his choice was to stand here and freeze. He turned back into the carriage house. Another place needing to be cleaned. Had Cath allowed for that in her schedule? He walked around the old structure. It had gaps in the walls, but the roof looked sound. Obviously a catch-all place, it was stacked with boxes and old furniture. Either there'd been no more room in the cellar, or this furniture wasn't as treasured.

He spied an old carriage in one corner, too dilapidated to use. Once horses had pulled that carriage, maybe taking the Williamsons into Williamsburg or even as far as Richmond.

Walking over, he noticed how the barrel springs sagged, and how the spokes to the high wheels were broken in spots, making the carriage sag at an odd angle. Everything was covered in a thick layer of dust. The conveyance looked to be from the late 1800s, not that he was an expert on old carriages. He tried moving it, but feared the wheels would collapse after budging it only a little and having them creak in protest.

He kicked the dirt. Dry as dust. At least the weather was kept from the place. Glancing around, he saw signs of deterioration of the old building. It was not as in good a shape as the house. The gaps in the walls let the elements in if the wind blew in the right direction. He turned to head to the house when he spotted a small sliver of metal jutting up near the carriage wheel. The small movement of the carriage must have dislodged the dirt to reveal it. He looked closer, then scraped away some of the dirt and uncovered a small metal box. Had it deliberately been hidden, or had it fallen and been covered by dirt over the years?

Taking it to the workbench on the far side, he brushed off the accumulated dirt. The fastener was rusted. He tried to pry it open, then broke the latch to lift the lid. Inside were several coins and a gold pendant on a chain. Lifting it, he saw it was a locket, letters entwined on one side. How long had it been buried? To whom had it belonged, and why had it never been recovered?

"More mysteries for Cath to unravel," he murmured. He examined the coins, gold with an eagle on one side. Jake was startled to find the dates stamped on them from the 1850s. There were also two Confederate coins. Someone's treasure hidden from marauding Yankee troops?

He put them in his pocket, knowing they'd make the perfect Christmas surprise for Cath. She loved old things, and to get such a treasure from her own property would be special. He still lived with the fantasy of seeing her in that sexy nightie he'd bought. Maybe wearing this gold locket in the firelight.

Cath took out the last batch of cookies, setting them on a rack to cool. Where was Jake? She peered out the kitchen window again, but didn't see him. She was starting to get concerned. His jacket wasn't thick and it was cold enough inside to give her an idea of how cold it was outside. Should she go look for him?

She opened the back door. From there she could see into the carriage house. Jake was at the workbench, bending over something. She hoped he had enough sense to come in out of the cold before he caught a chill or something.

Reassured he was fine, she went into the living room. It still felt cool, despite the efforts of the heater. The fire they'd started earlier had died down. She added logs and stirred it to get it going again.

Feeling restless, she considered what to do. Maybe she'd read some more of Tansy's journal. Their expedition to search for more books had been aborted and she wasn't anxious to go back down in the cellar again. Next time, she'd make sure they carried flashlights. Of course the door wouldn't jam again, but she didn't want to be caught in the far corner if the power failed.

Or she could use Jake's computer to try to find out more about Jonathan Williamson. Had he fought in other battles leading up to Yorktown?

She watched as the logs flared and began to give off some heat. Satisfied the fire would warm things up, she turned on the laptop and began to search for more about the war Jonathan fought in. Knowing she had a great-great-grandfather fight changed how she viewed history.

A short time later she gave up on the war and began to look for Web sites describing life in the 1700s in America. Some were geared for elementary school level and she loved the sketches of clothes, houses, cooking utensils and early carriages. Maybe she'd make a special project for her kids when school started again.

The more she read, the more she appreciated the fine work that had gone into building the house, built before modern equipment. Two hundred years later it was still housing a member of the Williamson family.

Impatient to find out what happened to Tansy and Jonathan, she turned off the computer and went to find the journal.

The next entry began:

Tomorrow is Christmas,. It has begun to snow in earnest. Everything is covered and I hope my chickens survive. It is unusually cold. If I don't get the eggs right when they are laid, they could be frozen. It's hard to walk to the chicken coop, but I have a rope to use as a guide. Still no word from my husband. I hope he is planning a wonderful

*surprise and will show up tonight before I retire. I
would so welcome another night in his arms. And
Christmas won't be a special day without him here.*

*I miss my family. Maybe I should have gone to
stay with my parents, but I could not bear the
thought of Jonathan making his way home and not
finding me here.*

Cath gave a start. That was what she'd done, left
home when Jake said he'd made a monumental effort
to get home for the holidays. She bit her lip in remorse.
She should have at least let him know where she was.

Jake had figured it out. Jonathan would surely have
known if his wife wasn't home that she'd be with her
parents. How sweet of Tansy to wait alone and lonely
in hopes of her husband's arrival.

*Everything in the house is ready. I have boughs
of holly decorating the rooms, and a yule log
ready for the fireplace. I have mulled the cider,
which fills the house with a delicious fragrance.
I do hope I don't have to drink it all by myself. I'm
sure several neighbors will stop by to wish me a
happy Christmas in the afternoon. Last year
Jonathan and I drove to friends and neighbors to
raise a glass of cheer. It was so festive. I never suspected we wouldn't do it this year as well. Maybe
we shall, if only he gets home soon.*

The entry ended abruptly.
Cath felt a frisson of dread as she turned the page.
In stark letters the words—

Jonathan is dead. How will I go on?

The paper was smudged, as if by tears.

Cath's heart dropped. Slowly she ran her fingers over the long-dried tears. What happened? The entry contained only those blunt words, no date, no details, nothing.

Quickly she fanned through the remaining pages, but they were blank. That was all? She couldn't let it end there, she had to know! Were there other journals? Had Tansy thrown this one away after writing the horrible truth only to start another one when she could?

Cath jumped up and almost ran to the kitchen. Wenching open the door Jake had fixed, she flicked on the dim lights and hurried down the stairs, the door slamming behind her. She remembered where she'd found the first diary. Would there be more? Poor Tansy. Cath was almost as heartsick as Tansy must have been. She'd become involved with them, felt as if she knew Tansy and almost knew Jonathan. She'd so hoped he'd made it home for Christmas, instead, he had died. When? Where?

How had Tansy found out? How had she stood it?

Cath found the trunk and flung it open, rummaging around, but there were no journals.

She shut the lid and pulled down the box next to the trunk. Ripping off the tape holding it closed, she rummaged inside. Clothing. She felt through the stack to see if there were any books. None.

Tossing the box to one side she pulled down another. It almost fell from her hands it weighted so much. Opening it, Cath found the carton full of books. But a quick look and she knew there was no journal.

"Cath?" Jake called.

"I'm in the cellar," she yelled back, almost manic in her quest to find another journal. Tansy's story couldn't end with those brief words. What happened to her? Was she pregnant with Jonathan's child and didn't know it? Had she remarried, or remained a widow the rest of her life? Wasn't she a great-grandmother—therefore she had to have had a baby.

She pushed the heavy box aside, reaching for another.

"What are you doing?" Jake asked as he rounded the corner and saw her ripping into yet another carton.

"I'm searching for the blasted journal, what does it look like I'm doing?"

"Going through things like your life depended upon it."

She sat back on her heels and looked at him. "Jonathan died," she said sadly.

"Who—oh, the guy from Kings Mountain?"

She nodded, rubbing her chest. "I know it happened more than two hundred years ago, but honestly, I felt I got to know Tansy, she and I had a lot in common. Both our husbands gone on dangerous missions. Both of us lonely and alone. But I thought he'd come home. You came home. Instead the journal ended with 'Jonathan is dead.' I need to know what happened to Tansy."

Unexpectedly tears filled her eyes. She tried to blink them away, but the parallel was too strong. Tansy's husband had left never to return. That was the fear Cath had lived with for years. What if Jake had been killed at one of the skirmishes he covered? Or at the earthquake center when another trembler shook?

Yet she was planning to send Jake away, never to return.

How could she stand to have him out of her life forever? Was she certain that was the way she wanted things?

"Hey, honey, it's okay," Jake said, stepping over one of the boxes and squatting down beside her. He brushed away the tears that ran down her cheek. "Sad to know he died, but it's so long ago. You knew he was dead."

"But not like that. Not leaving Tansy behind. What happened to her? Oh, Jake, it's so unfair. People should fall in love and get married and live happily ever after. Not have one leave the other. I think she was only about twenty. They hadn't been married that long. What did she do for the rest of her life without Jonathan? Her love for him shone in every page she wrote." Cath couldn't help the tears, her heart ached for the couple of long ago. And for the couple of today. How had they come to this pass? She ached for love and family and a normal life with a husband safe at home each night.

Jake sat on the hard ground and pulled her into his lap, cuddling her as she cried. "We'll look and see what we can find. And if there's no other journal, we'll try the local historical society, or churchyard. We'll find out what happened to them."

"They're like us in a way," she said, burrowing closer, trying to feel safe, to have him wrap her in his arms tightly and never let her go. Her tears wet his shirt. Jake's heartbeat sounded beneath her ear, giving her comfort. His arms held her tightly, making her feel safe. The sadness was overwhelming. For Tansy and for herself. How had Tansy made it through? Cath didn't think she herself would want to go on if she knew Jake was no longer in the world.

Yet she was sending him out of her life.

Confused, hurt, sad, she didn't move. If she could stop time forever, it would be this very moment. Only, she wanted the ache in her heart to go away.

"It's getting cold, Cath. Let's go upstairs and sit by the fire," Jake said a little later when her sobs eased. "We'll have dinner and discuss how we can go about finding out about Tansy and her husband."

Cath didn't want to move, but she wasn't the one sitting on the hard-packed dirt floor. She pushed away and wiped her cheeks. Reluctantly standing, she surveyed the boxes and trunks stacked everywhere.

"I thought maybe Tansy started a fresh journal, one that didn't hold the bad memories the one I was reading did. She may never have written another word. I don't know. It was pure chance that I found that one."

Jake rose and looked around. "It could take a month to go through every box in this space. And, as you say, she may not have started another one. Let's try other means first."

Cath nodded. "If we can't find anything, I'll come back this summer and go through every single container in the cellar. I need to know what happened."

She needed to know that Tansy had moved on, found happiness and lived to be a grandmother who loved her family. That was the ending Cath wanted for Tansy—and for herself. She wanted some assurance that when Jake left, she'd be able to go on and find the family she so yearned for. She didn't want regrets or second thoughts. She didn't want to spend the rest of her life alone.

"Did your aunt do a family tree?" Jake asked when they went upstairs. "Maybe Tansy and Jonathan were on it and you'd have some indication of what happened."

"I don't know if she did or not. She talked about the family a lot when I visited as a young child. But not so much after I was grown. I think she felt she had told me all there was. I wish I had paid better attention. I don't remember hearing about a Tansy, though. It's an unusual name, I think I'd remember."

When they reached the living room, Jake added logs to the fire. The wood they'd brought in was dry and caught quickly. The room was noticeably warmer than the cellar. The lights on the tree seemed to grow brighter as the daylight faded into night. The snow continued, but the wind had died down.

"This beats the Middle East," he said, sitting on the sofa, and reaching for Cath's hand, lacing their fingers, resting their linked hands on his leg.

Slowly she leaned toward him, resting against his arm, her head on his shoulder. She still looked sad. He wished she'd smile, or laugh, or even get angry with him. He hated seeing her so unhappy.

Slowly she turned to look at him. "I should have made you welcome when you arrived. I'm sorry, Jake. I was just so set on ending our marriage, I didn't think about how you must have pulled some strings or something to get the time off. I'd much rather you be here than the Middle East. You could have been killed and never come home—just like Jonathan." Tears shimmered in her eyes again.

"No, Cath. I'd always come home to you." He had a sudden urge to give her the necklace, but held back. It would wait until tomorrow. Maybe it would cheer her up. Once he cleaned it, maybe the letters would reveal to whom it belonged. Wouldn't it be serendipity if it had once been Tansy's. Unlikely, however. The box was not from the 1700s. Probably someone had used it as a treasure box, hid it and forgot about it.

"This is a house made for a family, with lots of children," Cath said, gazing into the fire. "I hope Tansy found someone else to love, to share the farm with. Do you think she did?"

Jake couldn't get too worked up over a couple who had been dead for almost two hundred years, but he could see Cath was truly upset by her discovery. What could he do to take her mind away from it?

"I'm sure we'll find out. It may take a bit of time, but we'll find the answer. We can't do anything until after Christmas."

"I know. And it's probably silly, but I thought for sure I was going to read that Jonathan showed up in time for Christmas. I was counting on it," Cath said sadly.

His wife liked happy endings. He only wished she saw one for them.

Dinner was easily prepared and quickly eaten. Cath had little to say. Jake didn't push her. But he did watch her, conscious of the comments she'd made earlier about them not knowing each other well. They'd been married for six years, but he would never have expected this reaction to reading a two-hundred-year-old diary. He'd picked it up and scanned the last few pages. The death announcement was stark. Maybe seeing it written down had been the final straw for the young widow.

Or maybe she'd gone on to write a dozen more journals and they'd been lost or scattered over the years. He hoped they'd be able to find something out at the local historical society. Williamsburg prided itself on its history, surely the society would have information.

When they'd finished, Cath put a small plate of cookies on the table. "I should take some to Mrs. Watson, don't you think? If they hadn't come over today, who knows how long we'd have been stuck in the cellar."

"Take them tomorrow. It's pitch-black outside and treacherous to boot with the snow."

"Actually that'd be better. Tansy mentioned in her journal how they visited neighbors and friends on Christmas day. We'll be following an old tradition."

Jake could think of a new tradition he'd like to start. He rose and began to clear the dishes. Washing up took very little time. When they were finished, Cath looked at a loss.

Suggesting they go back to the living room, Jake found the Christmas records and put them on.

"Dance with me, sweetheart," he said, drawing her into his arms.

For a long time they danced to Christmas carols. She was sweet and soft in his arms. She made no move to end their closeness. Feeling bold, Jake began to give her soft kisses—first on her hair, then her forehead, moving down to her cheeks, and then capturing her mouth.

Cath sighed softly and encircled his neck, kissing him back.

"Come spend the night with me, Cath," he said softly.

She pulled back and gazed up into his eyes, hers soft and dreamy.

"I love you, Jake," she said.

Taking time to bank the fire, turn off the Christmas lights and shut off the record player, Jake leashed his impatience. He wanted to make love to her right then and there, but he wasn't some teenager unable to control himself. In bed, all night long, was better.

Hoping she wouldn't have second thoughts, he raced through the tasks and then walked with her up the stairs, fearing every step she'd change her mind.

"We only have the present," Cath said. "No one can see into the future. Would Jonathan not have gone to fight if he'd known he'd be killed? Would Tansy have married him if she'd known they'd have such a short life together?"

"Hush, Cath. It's in the past. Didn't the journal say they were happy?"

"Tansy missed him so much. I knew how she felt."

"I'm home now, sweetheart." Jake drew her into his arms and kissed her again. She responded almost feverishly. He started to ask where, but decided for the bed he knew was large enough for both of them. The door to his bedroom stood open. It was cooler inside without the warmth of the fire from living room. But he had no doubt they'd warm up quickly.

Slowly they moved toward the bed, hands touching, lips kissing, the soft sighs and rustling of clothing being shed the only sound in the silent night.

The sheets were cool but momentarily. He eased her down and followed quickly.

"Oh, Jake, I love you," Cath said, reaching eagerly for him.

CHAPTER EIGHT

HAD last night been a mistake? Slowly coming awake in the still dark morning, Cath took stock. She was wrapped in her husband's arms. She felt cherished and well loved, but confused. She'd clung to Jake during the night, afraid of losing him as Tansy had lost Jonathan. Yet hadn't she considered all the changes she needed to make?

Being with Jake clouded the issue. She had tried to turn him away that first night. If he'd gone, things would be different. But he'd refused. Now they'd made love again and she had to admit how much she loved her husband. Together she felt whole, as if some missing part had been restored.

Frowning, she wished last night had never happened. It would be doubly hard to bid him goodbye now. She'd psyched herself up and all her arguments had fled like the wind when he kissed her. Would this change the dynamics of their marriage? Would he finally realize how much being together meant to her? She could counter all his objections, if he'd only give them a chance. They'd make a wonderful family, she knew it.

Cath slowly slipped out of bed, snatching up her clothes and heading for the bathroom. Time to get up and dressed and start breakfast. And think about a different future than she'd planned when she arrived at the old house a few days ago.

When she left the bathroom a little while later, Jake was leaning against the wall of the hall, wearing jeans and a loose shirt. He smiled when he saw her, leaning over to kiss her.

"Good morning. Why did you get up so early?"

"I wanted to start breakfast," she said. It sounded like a poor excuse. She wasn't brave enough to tell him how confused she was. He'd pounce on her uncertainty and get concessions from her before she knew what she was saying. She needed to be careful, and make sure she knew what she was doing with her future.

"Make a big one, I've worked up an appetite." He kissed her again, then stepped around her and entered the bathroom.

Cath stood still for a few moments, relishing the embrace, fleeting though it had been. Her heart raced, her skin felt warm. For two cents, she'd turn and join Jake in the shower.

"Which would be totally dumb," she told herself. Putting yesterday's clothes in the laundry basket in her room, she headed downstairs. She went into the living room and turned on the lights. The sky was lightening, but remained overcast. It had stopped snowing with more than eight inches on the ground.

When she leaned over to plug in the tree lights, Cath saw two wrapped boxes, one larger than the other. She realized with a pang it was Christmas morning and she had not gotten Jake a Christmas gift! As his work could take him anywhere around the world at anytime, she'd had not bought anything due to the difficulty insuring the packages would reach him.

Yet there was the proof he hadn't forgotten her.

She tried to think of something she'd have that she could wrap and give him, but nothing came to mind. She'd have to confess she hadn't bought him anything. How sad would that be for Christmas?

Would he see her turning away similar to his mother? He'd lived with his mother's second family for nine years, but each year was more unhappy than the one before. He'd told Cath once how he'd felt like an outsider always looking in. And now she was going to make him feel like an outsider again. She'd bought presents for Abby and her family, even some of her friends. But nothing for her own husband.

What kind of woman was she?

Not that she would have minded yesterday or the day before. It would help cement her decision. But after last night, dare she hope things would be different? Maybe they could find common ground, start a family, find a way to have Jake work closer to home, or at least come home more frequently.

There was nothing she could do about it. She'd have to make it up to him in other ways.

Cath prepared a large breakfast of eggs, sausage, grits and toast, with orange juice and coffee for beverages. The last piece of toast popped up as Jake entered.

"My mouth is watering," he said, coming over to her and kissing her neck. "And not for the food."

She smiled and leaned against him for a moment, savoring the intimacy. She'd missed him when he was gone. She'd never get enough. "Eat, then we need to talk."

"Do you know how much I hate that phrase—we need to talk? It's never good," he said.

"What do you mean?" she asked as she served their plates and carried them to the table.

"It usually means a time to bring up bad news."

"Not this time. At least I don't think so. Sit down and eat."

"And then we'll talk, I know. So we remain silent during breakfast?"

She giggled and shook her head. "No." She sat and looked at him, biting her lip. "I'm sorry I need to tell you I didn't get you anything for Christmas. I didn't know you would be home."

"No problem. Actually the present I got you can be for both of us," he said easily.

"Oh." She gave a soft sigh of relief he didn't seem hurt. "Well, then, if you're not upset."

"No, Cath. After last night, I'm not at all upset."

She smiled in shy delight remembering.

"I have a ham I want to bake for dinner. I thought we could eat around one o'clock, if that suits you. Then later in the day we can take the cookies to Mrs. Watson."

Jake nodded.

His cell phone rang.

Cath groaned. "Not on Christmas!"

"It won't take long." He rose and left the room.

Despite last night, the scenario was familiar. Nothing had changed. Cath finished her meal alone, watching as his grew cold.

She cleared her dish and ran water over it, setting it aside until he finished and she would wash all the dishes at one time. Taking her coffee, she headed for the living room, passing Jake who paced in front of the window in the dining room.

"Not what I want to hear, Sam," he said as she walked through.

She started a fire, settling back on the sofa and sipping her coffee. Even though it was Christmas, she could still look through other boxes in the cellar for another journal. Or even for the family history her aunt had accumulated. If the Historical Society was open in the morning, she'd try there as well. She hoped they weren't closed until after New Year.

Jake came in sometime later.

"Sorry about the call, Cath. It was important."

"Your breakfast got cold."

"Still delicious." He stood near the tree, hesitating.

That was unlike him. Cath always thought of him as charging right in. Was he about to tell her he was leaving?

Stooping, he swept up the two boxes and joined her on the sofa. "Two for you. Merry Christmas, Cath." He leaned over and kissed her gently.

Offering the larger box, Jake sat back to watch her open it. He hoped after last night she'd be glad to get the filmy nightie. He hadn't been able to resist when he'd seen it in the window of a shop in the London airport.

"Oh my goodness." Cath held up the sheer gown— it was pale eggshell-blue, with lace at the top and bottom, and lace shoulders. "It's beautiful."

"You'll be beautiful in it."

She looked at him with a hint of mischief in her eyes. "Let me guess, this is the one we'll both like."

He nodded, watching warily for any hint she was

changing back into the freezing woman he'd found when he arrived. But she was as warm and close as she'd been last night.

"Thank you, Jake." She leaned over and gave him a sweet kiss.

"Want to model it now?" he suggested.

She laughed. "No. I know what will happen and I have to get dinner started before too long. The ham will take a while to bake."

"Later then, for sure."

She nodded, gently folding it and replacing it in the box.

"This isn't really from me," he said slowly, offering the smaller box. "I found these in the carriage house but thought they'd make a nice surprise."

She took the box, feeling something slide inside. Opening the paper, she lifted the lid.

"Oh." A gleaming gold locket lay on some tissue paper. Gently she lifted the necklace and held it in her hand. It was oval, about an inch in length. Initials had been engraved on the front with fancy curlicues.

"It's Tansy?" she asked, tracing a J and T. "Is this a locket from Tansy?"

"I thought of her when I found it. Jonathan and Tansy. It could be their initials, the engraving is so fancy it's hard to tell. Anyway, the locket looks old. Check out the fastener."

"It was in the carriage house?" Cath asked, lifting it gently, letting the delicate chain slip through her fingers as she gazed at the locket itself.

"In a metal box with some gold coin from the 1850s and a couple of Confederate coins. My guess is someone hid their treasure to keep it out of enemy hands and forgot it was there. Or maybe something happened to the person and no one ever knew what happened to the box. It wasn't buried very deep. I dislodge some dirt when I tried to move that carriage and found it."

"It couldn't have been Tansy, then. She would have died long before the Confederacy," Cath said. Slowly she opened the locket. A small curl of brown and black hair was tied in a faded ribbon, nestled in the tiny center of the locket.

"Or it was hers and passed down in your family," Jake suggested.

Cath touched the hair. "Whose, do you think?"

Jake looked at it for a moment. "Maybe both of them. There are two different colors there. Try it on."

Cath closed the locket, undid the fastener and presented her back to Jake, holding the ends in her hands.

"Fasten, please."

He brushed away her hair, fumbled with the unfamiliar connector, feeling her warmth radiating to his fingers. When it was hooked, he kissed the soft skin of her neck, moving around to her cheek as she turned to face him, ending at her mouth. It was a long time before Cath rose to check out the locket in the mirror.

Jake sat in the kitchen as Cath began preparing their dinner. She said she could manage everything when he offered to help, but would like the company. They still hadn't had that talk she'd mentioned earlier. Maybe he should open it up with his news.

"My call this morning was from Sam Miller, head of programming for the network," he began.

"And he wants you in some hot spot ASAP," she said without looking up.

"Actually I was getting feedback on my request for a stateside assignment."

She turned at that, staring at him in disbelief. "What?"

"I don't know if they can accommodate me. But I put in the request."

"You love your job."

"I'm not letting a job come between us. If it comes to the choice of my marriage or my job, I choose you."

Her face lit up. Jake felt his reaction like a kick. His desire flared. It was all he could do to keep from getting up and dragging her over to the table to make love with her again right then and there.

"That's wonderful. What would you do? Oh, Jake, this is the best present I could get." She wiped her hands on the towel and came over to give him a kiss. "You're really going to stay where it's safe? You'll be home a lot more, right?"

"Nothing's settled yet. But if they don't come through, I'll look for another network. I'm damn good at what I do. There have been other offers over the years. I'm sure I'll get something."

"There have?" She hadn't expected that, he could tell. Maybe he shouldn't be so forthcoming. But the comment she'd made about their not knowing each other rankled. He wanted to change that.

He'd never entertained moving from foreign reporting, so hadn't bothered to tell her when the offers had come before. Another mark against him. Cath was right, they weren't functioning as a married couple. That was going to change. If she'd forget her damn-fool idea of divorce, he'd do what he could to be the husband she wanted.

"One or two," he said casually.

She looked at him for a moment, then pushed away and went back to the food preparation.

Jake knew he'd blown it. He should have kept quiet about other offers. He spotted the cradle over to one side. Another topic he'd have to address sooner or later. Why had she fallen in love with that cradle? Maybe if he stayed home from now on, they could do enough together she'd forget having a baby.

"While the ham is baking, we could look again in the cellar for more journals," Cath suggested.

"If you want. This time we'll take flashlights," he said.

They spent most of the morning going through boxes near where Cath had found Tansy's journal. Nothing turned up. They moved deeper into the cellar, finding clothing from long ago. There were old shoes, the leather hardened and cracked. Another box had paper from early in the twentieth century.

"No sense in saving all this…it's all totally ruined," Cath murmured, as she rummaged through the mildewed pages.

"Clearing out this space is going to take longer than we have now," Jake said. It looked to him as if the job would take a month of steady work.

"When you asked for a stateside assignment, does it mean as much travel as you've been doing?" she asked.

"There won't be as much, depending on the job."

"Any chance you could work from here? I still think this would be a great house to raise a family in. I could look this spring for a teaching job to start in the fall, give my notice where I am now at the end of the school year. That would give us the summer to sell the condo. Or we could keep it as a place to stay when we go to Washington. Or if you need to work there."

"Early yet to know what a new job would entail. Let's leave that up in the air for the present," he suggested. He didn't have a firm choice yet. But had been very clear when talking to Sam about what he wanted.

"I hate for this place to sit empty for so long."

"It's been empty for four months, another few won't hurt it. We can come down every month for at least one weekend, to check on things."

"We could start fixing it up the way we want it," Cath chatted happily.

Jake felt impending doom at the direction of her thoughts. Just because he changed jobs didn't mean everything was changing.

She ripped the tape off another box and opened the flaps.

"I found them!" she called excitedly. "This box has several journals and I recognize her handwriting."

Jake joined Cath. She was fanning through different books, putting one down to pick up another. "I don't know the sequence, I wish she'd dated every first page just so I could put them in order. There are other journals here as well, different handwriting. Oh, this is so cool!"

"Let's take them upstairs and see if we can put them in some kind of order," he suggested. It was cramped in the narrow space between furniture and boxes.

"I hope she started writing after Jonathan died. The last one ended so abruptly."

"If not, maybe someone else wrote about her."

Jake carried the box up stairs and put it on the kitchen table. It was dusty and had cobwebs trailing from the base.

Cath wiped off the box, then opened it again and began to pull out the different books that housed thoughts of her ancestors.

The phone rang.

"Not again!" she exclaimed.

"It's yours, not mine," Jake said, pointing to the cell phone on the kitchen counter.

Cath dashed across to answer it.

"Hi, Abby, Merry Christmas!"

Jake continued to take out the books, opening each one to see if there were any dates. Some writers had dated each entry, but not the ones Tansy wrote. The dated ones he put in order. They were from the 1800s. The others had no dates. Maybe reading them would enable to determine approximate time frames.

"Things have changed for the best," Cath was saying. "I'll have lots to tell you when I get back. Are you having a good day? Yes, I want to talk to the kids. Was Jimmy thrilled with the bike?"

Jake turned slowly to watch his wife as she talked with Abby's children. She looked so happy. She loved being a teacher. She'd talked about it early in their marriage. She had that same glow now.

Jake turned back to the task at hand. Time enough to discuss a family later. For now, she was happy to find the journals.

Cath hung up and went to stand beside Jake. He explained the two piles, one with dates, one without. She skimmed the first few pages of each book in the undated pile. She'd gone through almost all of them, not finding one she thought was a continuation of Tansy's journal.

"Maybe she didn't write again," she said, setting yet another one aside and picking up a new one from the diminishing pile.

Jake was logging them into a file, with opening sentences for those that had no dates.

"Wait, this is it. I recognize her handwriting. Listen to this," Cath said. "'*I saw a robin today. It is the first sign of spring. And I was pleased to notice him. The winter was long and I still feel dark and chilled in my soul. I go to Jonathan's grave every day, but there is no comfort there. I've planted a rosebush and hope it grows. He loved roses.*

"'*The farm is too much for me to handle alone now that planting season is upon us. I've hired a man to work the farm and invited my cousin Timothy and his wife to join me. I do not wish to live alone and they are young and full of life. I'm hoping to find some joy in living and maybe they will give me that.*'" Cath looked up. "I wonder if this was written a few months after she learned of Jonathan's death. Sounds like it, doesn't it?"

Jake nodded. "Where is Jonathan buried?"

"I have no idea, maybe in the churchyard of that old church out on the Williamsburg road. We could go look."

He glanced out the window. "When the weather improves."

"Sissy," she teased, going back to the journal.

He continued his task while she read silently.

"Jake," her voice sounded odd.

"What?" He looked up.

"She's writing about the gold locket Jonathan had given a neighbor to give to her on Christmas morning, one with their initials entwined. It was her most cherished possession. You were right, Jonathan had entwined a lock from both their heads to show they were joined forever," Cath said, rubbing the necklace. "Do you suppose he had a premonition he wouldn't be coming back?"

"He could have just thought he wouldn't be home in time for Christmas," Jake suggested.

Cath shivered with the knowledge the locket she was wearing was Tansy's. She'd suspected as much that morning, but this added to her belief.

As she read the words of the woman who had died so long ago, she didn't find any mention of children. Tansy had not been pregnant with Jonathan's baby. Had she later remarried?

It was too soon after Jonathan's death for Tansy to be thinking along those lines. Yet Cath was impatient to find out what happened. She so hoped Tansy had found happiness—especially now when Cath found her own happiness. She couldn't believe Jake would change his career for her. For them. It showed how much he loved her. She'd be hard-pressed to give up her own job for him. Not that he asked her to—except to suggest she travel with him.

Did that mean he loved her more than she loved him? She felt odd with the idea. Why wouldn't she give up her career for the man she loved if he asked? Or even without being asked. Marriage was a two-way street.

One partner couldn't make all the sacrifices. Had she been selfish in demanding he change? She wanted her husband home every night, but maybe it didn't have to mean in Washington.

The thought was almost too overwhelming. Had she expected more than she should have?

She'd been so sure this fall that leaving Jake was the right choice. Now that they'd spent some time together, she couldn't imagine not spending the rest of her life with him. And if he found a job in the U.S., it would mean they'd have a normal family life.

A lingering sadness filled her. Was it for Tansy? Cath was getting the happy ending denied Tansy.

She tried to shake off the melancholia. Her own life did not parallel Tansy's. Granted both husbands had been gone for an extended period of time, and both she and Tansy had missed them terribly and feared for their lives. But unlike Jonathan, Jake was home and safe. She didn't wish to delve beyond that right now.

After their early afternoon dinner, Cath wrapped the cookies to take to the neighbor. She dressed warmly and was ready before Jake.

"I don't see why we need to do this," he grumbled. "They probably have a ton of food and won't even eat the cookies."

"It's tradition," Cath said. "Tansy mentioned visiting friends and neighbors at Christmas. I want to start some new traditions as well. And if we move here, we'll want to be on good terms with our neighbors."

"A friendly hello as we drive out of the driveway would work," he said, donning his own light jacket.

"Aren't you cold in that?" she asked.

"If I stay out too long, yeah, I get cold. But the weather feels good after the heat I've lived in for the last few months. I have a heavier jacket at home, but didn't think to get it before starting out."

Cath should feel guilty her letter had sent him hurrying after her without the rest he needed, or the chance to get appropriate clothing. She should, but she didn't. His decisive move in following her showed her how much he cared. It meant all the more to her after last night. She was buoyed with hope for their future.

The walk to Pearl Watson's house was difficult. There was no sidewalk, so they walked across the yards. The snow hid any obstacles and made it difficult. Twice Cath slipped and would have fallen had Jake not caught her. She didn't know how Pearl had made it the other day. Of course the snow hadn't been as deep then.

The clouds parted and the sun shone, giving the snow a sparkling look as if a thousand diamonds glittered. It was almost too bright to see.

The visit was all Cath had hoped. Pearl had welcomed them warmly and thanked them for the cookies, which, luckily, Cath hadn't dropped when she'd slipped. A fire burned merrily in the fireplace and the living room was decorated to the nth degree with fresh pine and holly and many ornaments and figurines that Cath guessed Pearl had collected over the years. Jake gave every indication he enjoyed the visit, talking football and sports with Bart and complimenting Pearl on her delicious mulled wine and fruit cake.

Cath knew he was being overly polite—he didn't like fruit cake. Still, she appreciated his efforts.

They didn't stay long, but Cath enjoyed the visit. It was fun, however, to return to their home together, closing out the cold. They'd eat dinner, she'd model the fancy new nightie and knew exactly where they'd end up. She could hardly wait.

CHAPTER NINE

As IF deliberately building the tension, when they entered the house, Jake suggested they watch a movie on television. Christmas favorites were playing all week, and he thought one was starting in a few minutes.

"The only television is in your room," Cath pointed out.

He shrugged. "So we watch it there." His eyes gleamed, belying the casual tone of his voice.

Her heart skipped a beat.

"Want to take up some snacks?" she asked.

"Sure. Make it a light supper and later we can come down for dessert, if we want."

She sliced some ham, added an assortment of cheeses, heated the biscuits and cut a couple of apples. The warm cider would round off the makeshift meal, she decided.

She wasn't sure where Jake was while she was preparing their evening meal. She didn't hear any murmured conversation, so at least he wasn't on the phone. She spotted hers still on the counter and went to turn it off. Not that anyone was likely to call her, but just in case. She just wished she knew where his was, she'd turn it off as well.

And maybe chuck it out into the snow. Let him find it come spring!

Carrying the meal upstairs, she was surprised to find Jake had brought in a bunch of pillows, building a seating area for them on the double bed. A chenille afghan lay at the foot of the bed, to cover legs if they got cool watching the movie.

Soft lighting completed the ambiance. Cath smiled, feeling her anticipation rise another notch. Was he planning to watch TV or seduce his wife?

Jake switched on the set. The Christmas movie was just beginning. They watched the opening scenes of the familiar story while eating the light supper. Once they finished eating, Jake put his arm around her shoulder and pulled her close, snuggling her next to him as the action unfolded. Cath tried to concentrate on the characters of the old black and white movie, but she was too conscious of Jake pressed along the length of her. His scent filled the air. His warmth kept the coolness at bay. She glanced over but he seemed absorbed in the film. She reached out to take his hand and threaded her fingers through his, feeling his palm against hers. This was a moment she'd remember forever. The two of them together in perfect harmony.

"If we decide to move here, I think we should put a fireplace in this room," she said at one of the commercial breaks.

He looked at the outside wall where the chimney ran. "I suppose it could be fairly easily done, tapping into the existing chimney."

"And we'd build the dock you wanted. Get a small boat."

"Build a gazebo near the water, where we could sit on summer evenings," Jake said.

Cath took it as a very positive sign that Jake was participating in her daydreams of what she'd have her ideal house be. Maybe they would move here and make it reality.

To Cath's amazement, they made it through to the end of the movie. It was getting late. After making a big push to get her in bed since he arrived, she was a bit surprised he hadn't rushed her tonight.

"Ready for bed?" he asked.

"I guess."

"Try on the gown I brought," he suggested.

She nodded, rising. Away from him, she felt the coolness of the air. At least the bed would be warmed from their bodies when they got in again.

"Let me get the dishes done first." Was she deliberately tantalizing him by delaying? She smiled mischievously and gathered the plates.

Together they went downstairs. Cath put the dishes in the sink and rinsed them off while Jake turned off the Christmas tree lights and made sure the fire was contained.

He offered the box with the gown when she met him at the foot of the stairs.

"I'll change in the bathroom," she said breathlessly. She felt as shy as a new bride.

The gown fit perfectly, if a floating froth of sheer silk that flowed from her shoulders had any fit to it. The pale eggshell-blue was almost virginal. Excitement brought color to her cheeks. She brushed her hair until it gleamed, studying herself in the mirror. She looked like a bride.

Her heart tripping double time, she wished she had a wrap or something to cover her from the bathroom to the bedroom. Head held high, feeling feminine and sexy, she almost floated to the room they'd share tonight.

Jake had turned back the sheets and shed most of his clothes. He wore only the dark trousers. One bedside light gave soft illumination.

He looked at her when she entered and Cath heard his breath catch.

"You are so beautiful," he said, coming around the bed to meet her.

She was glad he thought so. Forgotten was the pain of the past, the long, lonely times. She had tonight; and their future. Cath was sublimely happy as she walked toward the man she loved.

"You're beautiful," he repeated as he reached out to touch her soft shoulders, slipping the lacy strap down a bit and bending to kiss her warm skin. "Gold and lace, you should always wear gold and lace," he said as he drew her into his arms.

The light had been extinguished, the covers drawn over them. Cath lay in blissful afterglow, reveling in being in Jake's arms. Her breathing had returned to normal and she felt safe and happy. This was how their marriage should have been all along. How it had been every time he'd returned home. She had lived in fear of his safety each time he left. His staying would make a world of difference. The one thing to make their lives complete would be a baby.

She suddenly realized they hadn't used any birth control, and Jake knew she wasn't on the pill. It was surely a sign he was ready to start their family, despite his words to the contrary. She smiled in secret glee. Maybe they'd make a baby that very night.

"Tell me about the job possibilities," she said, feeling warm and sleepy. She wanted to know more. How did he feel about making the change?

"I'm not sure what they'll have for me. Ideally I'd like a position that allows some analysis and then on-air reporting. On the other hand, it's the analysis part I like. I can do that without being the one to report it."

"Won't you miss the travel, seeing all those exotic places?"

"Exotic only if that's considered foreign. War zones and disaster areas aren't exactly the place of vacations. I've been doing this for twelve years, Cath. I might have done it for another twelve, but you're too important to me. Time to let others get the fame, and for me to settle down and come home each night to my wife."

She smiled, rubbing her fingertips against his strong chest.

Her decision had brought this about. She hoped he'd never regret giving up his way of life for hers. She'd do all she could to make him happy and glad he'd made this change.

"It could be that by next Christmas, we'll have someone else to share the holidays with," she said dreamily.

"Hmmm?"

"A baby."

She felt him tense. Her euphoric mood vanished in a heartbeat. She realized they really hadn't discussed anything of significance. He said he'd look for a state-side job. But there'd been no mention of how soon. And what if he couldn't find the one he liked? Suddenly

Cath felt vulnerable and uncertain. They had not talked about starting a family. She'd told him she was ready. When would he be?

"What?" she asked, feeling constrained by his embrace instead of warmed by it. "If you get a job in the U.S., there's no reason we can't start our family. We're not getting any younger and I don't want to be old parents like mine were."

"Getting a job in the States is a long way from having a family. We need time to ourselves. Get to know each other all over again. I'm not sure I can live here. I might have to be in Atlanta or Washington or even New York. Too early to make firm plans until I know what I'll be doing."

"We've had time to ourselves. Six years' worth. And we will still have time for each other. It takes nine months to have a baby. And even after it's born, we'll make time for the two of us. I love you, Jake. I want to share in my life, share in yours. We'll always make time for us. But if you're home all the time, any arguments about having a baby disappear. It's time. Past time if you ask me."

"No."

"Hey, this is a two-way street. Are you telling me you don't want kids? Ever?" Just when she thought things had turned for the best, he was throwing her a curve. What if Jake never wanted children? Her decision made this fall would have to stand. But after the last two nights, she wasn't sure she was strong enough to walk away from love.

"We can't have children, Cath," he said a long moment later.

"Just because your dad died young and you got a

rotten deal with your stepfather doesn't mean you won't be a terrific father. I know you will be."

He brushed back her hair and kissed her. The darkness wasn't the cozy place it once had been. Cath wanted to see his expression. She wanted to rail against his stubborn stance. Why was he so adamant against having children? She knew he'd be a great father.

"Listen to what I'm saying, Cath. We can't have children."

"I don't see why you are so against it—"

"Dammit, *listen!* Cannot have children. Not won't, not delay. Can not."

She didn't understand. "Why not?"

He released her and sat up in the bed, drawing the sheets down with him. The sudden cool air against her skin didn't chill her as much as Jake's words.

She sat up, straining to see him in the dark.

"Dammit, what we have is good, Cath. We love each other. I'll stay with you, be with you. We'll do things like all married couples. We'll have a good life."

"As we would with children."

"I can't have children," he said heavily.

"What do you mean you can't have children?" she asked.

He sighed and got out of bed. She heard the sound of his jeans being pulled on. Afraid of what he would say next, she clutched the covers to her, trying to recapture the warmth.

"I cannot father a child," he said from the darkness.

"What?"

"I'm sterile. I had mumps when I was a teenager. There's no way I can ever father a child."

She stared at the place from which his voice came, picturing him in her mind, wishing the lights were on. The words echoed in her mind. *Sterile.*

Licking dry lips, she carefully asked, "How long have you known that?"

"Since I was seventeen and my younger sister gave me the mumps. The doctor had me tested afterward."

The words hit like a hammer. He'd wooed her and courted her and married her all the time knowing he could never have children. All these years she'd thought he was scarred by the experiences with his stepfather. That when they were ready, that when he was secure in her love, they'd start a family and he could finally experience how loving one could be. Instead she'd been kept in the dark. He'd always known they would never have a family.

"How could you not tell me, Jake? How could you marry me and not share this important fact? What were you thinking?" Her eyes were dry, the pain in her heart threatened to rip it apart. She was hurt beyond tears. He had to have known she would one day want children. All couples who married had children. At least all the ones she knew did. Yet he'd never given her a hint that they would never have a child together. Until tonight. Just when everything looked perfect, he'd hit her with this.

"There are lots of couples out there who have very happy lives without children," Jake said stiffly.

"Maybe if we'd built a solid marriage over the last six years, we'd have a chance. But this is more than I can deal with." Cath felt a part of herself die. "We've been married six years! You couldn't find a minute in all that time to tell me?"

"And have you say, sorry Charlie, I'm out of here? I've already had one woman turn on me, I didn't want another. We didn't discuss children at the onset. And over the years, we never talked about it. It was Sally's death that gave you the idea. Admit it. What we have is good, Cath. Don't turn your back on that!"

To her, having a family was fundamentally important. She was alone in the world except for friends, and for Jake. She wanted children and grandchildren and large family gatherings at holidays. She wanted love and quiet sharing times. Laughter and funny sayings of children to treasure. She yearned to share her life with offspring. Tell them about her parents and Aunt Sally, and even Tansy. To have continuity down through the ages.

But it was never going to happen. Jake had known that and not told her. In six years, he'd never shared that crucial fact.

She tried to absorb the magnitude of his revelation, but she was numb. She pushed aside the covers and rose. The nightie was somewhere on the floor, but she didn't even try to find it. It scarcely provided any covering. She went to the door and out into the hall and to her room. Closing the door, she locked it. Turning on the light, she quickly dressed in warm sweats and crawled into her bed. Her thoughts were in a jumble, but overriding them all was the knowledge that if she stayed with Jake Morgan, she would never become a mother. And he had known that all along.

Jake stood by the empty bed, listening to her walk down the hall, the closing of her door, the snick of the lock. He stared into the darkness, knowing his last hope had died.

It was only after several minutes, when he began to feel the cold, that he roused himself enough to get dressed. No point in getting back into that bed they'd shared. The memories would be more than he could deal with. He flipped on the light and found a sweat-shirt. Dressing quickly, he pulled on socks and his shoes. Maybe a walk would help.

Hell, nothing was ever going to help.

He'd suspected this day might come. From the first moment she'd begun to talk about having children, he'd known he'd have to tell her. It had not seemed important before. She had children at school, he was gone a lot. But all fall she'd talked about it on the phone calls and their e-mail.

Why couldn't she have been some woman all caught up in her career who didn't want to have children? Or the favorite aunt of dozens of kids, so having her own wouldn't be as important.

Why couldn't he be enough?

He'd deliberately stayed away these last few months, hoping to delay the inevitable. It had worked, sort of. He'd squeezed a few more weeks out of his marriage. It would end for certain now. Getting a job in the States had nothing to do with it. Even if he were home every night, she'd never stay.

How ironic that he was finally willing to change and it would do no good.

He went downstairs. The outline of the Christmas tree reminded him of the gift he'd given her. It had hurt a little that she had nothing for him. But she'd been coming from an entirely different direction. He'd not dwelt on it, but maybe he should have.

Yet, all he could remember was how beautiful she had been in the nightgown. At least he'd been given that.

Heading for the kitchen, Jake looked for the bottle of whiskey he'd had the other night. The way things were going, he was going to become good friends with alcohol.

He stopped and shook his head. He didn't need that crutch. The only thing it had accomplished the other night was to give him a headache in the morning.

He turned on the lights. It was two o'clock in the morning. Too dark to go for a walk, too early to be up, but he didn't feel a bit sleepy.

Mostly he felt lost.

Astonished, he sat down and gazed out of the dark window. He was a highly respected journalist. He had friends and acquaintances on three continents. He could write his own ticket for his career.

Yet without Cath, without their marriage, he felt adrift.

Like he'd felt when his father died. And when his mother had transferred her allegiance to her new husband virtually deserting her only son.

Anger took hold. If Cath only wanted a sperm donor, let her find one. If the bond they'd built over the years wasn't enough, so be it. He couldn't change that. He'd tried to rebuild their ties, to keep his marriage strong, but against this he had no defense.

Cath awoke late. She had been a long time going to sleep. The sun was shining, its glare reflecting off the snow, almost blinding in its brilliant light. Feeling groggy and out of sorts, she lay in bed wondering if she ever had to get up. Maybe she could just stay beneath the covers and not deal with life.

But she had things to do. Now more than ever she needed to decide if she was moving here, getting a divorce and moving on with her life.

Slow tears welled in her eyes. How could Jake have not told her? It spoke more to the flimsy strength of their marriage than anything. Granted, they had not discussed children before they married. Actually never discussed it at all. She'd said she wanted a baby this fall and he'd brushed it aside.

But she'd always thought they'd have children eventually. He had to know that.

Even if they didn't want children, wouldn't a husband have shared that major item of information with his wife?

Only if they had a strong marriage.

Which, obviously, they didn't.

The tears ran down the side of her face, wetting her pillow. It had been cruel of Jake to insist he stay for Christmas, for him to tell her he was returning to the States for good and then when her hopes were at their highest, to tell her the truth.

Her heart felt as if it were breaking. There would be no little boy with his daddy's dark hair. No little girl wanting to know the facts about everything. No children at all with Jake. Ever.

By the time Cath rose, she had a headache and was mildly hungry. She took a quick shower. Going downstairs, she was prepared to ask Jake to leave. If he refused, she'd leave. Abby would let her stay with her family until Cath could make other arrangements.

The house was silent. The Christmas tree wasn't lit, though its fragrance still filled the room. Cath barely glanced in. She went to the kitchen, gearing up to confront Jake. It, too, was empty.

Where was he? She looked out the window. There were prints in the snow, but nothing to tell her where he had gone. To the carriage house? On one of his walks? She didn't care.

She prepared a sandwich and ate it standing. Geared up to confront him, she felt let down he wasn't around.

Once she'd eaten, she went back upstairs, carrying her cleaning supplies. There was one more bedroom to clean and the second floor would be taken care of. The work gave her something to do, and the exercise would burn off some of the anguish, she hoped.

The afternoon passed slowly. As she worked she made mental lists of things needed such as curtains for all bedrooms. The rugs in the rooms had been taken out and would require a thorough cleaning. She wanted a night-stand for the room she was working on, there wasn't one. Maybe she should paint the bedrooms. She could use a different color for each one.

For the time being, she'd keep the furniture. It was functional.

And she didn't need baby furniture.

She blinked back the tears. Nothing had changed from the day she left Washington. Granted for a short time she'd thought her world had changed. She'd thought she and Jake would have it all.

Instead she was back to square one—end the marriage and find a man who'd love her, stay with her and give her children.

When she finished the last bedroom, she vacuumed the hallway, and wiped down the bath.

Tomorrow, if she was still here, she'd begin on the ground floor.

Cath carried all the supplies downstairs. Leaving them in the dining room, she glanced at the stack of journals. She wasn't in the mood to read about Tansy and her life. It had an unhappy ending, just like Cath's.

She frowned. Not like hers. Jake was still alive and well. Tansy had lost her husband to death.

Cath swallowed. In comparison, she had so much. Tansy would have given anything to see her Jonathan again. Cath and Jake had spent several wonderful days together.

Going into the kitchen, Cath realized it was after four and she still hadn't seen or heard Jake today. Had he left? She raced back upstairs to check his room.

The bed was tumbled as it had been last night. Her new nightgown was in a pile on the floor. Jake's duffel bag was opened on a chair. Some of his things were strewn about. He hadn't left.

So where was he? she wondered as she went back to the kitchen. The cradle seemed to mock her, gleaming in the light. She should never have had Jake bring it up. Never cleaned it up and dreamed dreams as she envisioned a baby lying asleep in it. Their baby.

CHAPTER TEN

CATH put the ham in the oven to warm again and began to heat some vegetables. It was growing dark and she still hadn't seen nor heard from Jake. Where was he? Despite her heartache, she was growing concerned. She'd checked the carriage house and found an excuse to go next door to see if he was there. On her way back from Mrs. Watson's, she realized Jake's car was not in the driveway. Had he left without taking his things?

She stayed in the kitchen, not wanting to be reminded of decorating the tree by using the living room. Christmas was over.

She heard the car in the driveway. Anger flared again. She wanted to rail against him for keeping her in the dark for so long. Why hadn't he told her long ago?

Though she couldn't think when the appropriate time would be. Had she told him about her appendectomy? She thought so, but maybe not. Still, it wasn't the same thing. He'd known she wanted a baby this fall. The first time she'd brought up the subject would have been an appropriate time to tell her.

He hadn't because she would have left. He explained that.

Tears welled again. She dashed them away and began to calmly slice the ham when he entered the kitchen.

She heard the slap of papers on the table and turned.

"Your aunt did write a family history and turned a copy into the local library. They had a genealogy section with lots of information. All you want to know about Tansy and Jonathan is in there."

"You went to research Tansy and Jonathan?" she asked in disbelief. He'd turned her world upside down and then gone off to do research?

"Wrapping up loose ends, Cath. I'll be leaving in the morning." He walked through to the dining room. A moment later she heard his step on the stairs.

No apology, no sign of regret. She stared at the thick stack of paper. He had flung them down and walked away. Tying up loose ends. She crossed to the table. Picking up the stack, she noticed several paper-clipped sections. One was a family history, another was the history of the house and a third looked like official documents from the county clerk's office. Jake had obviously spent all day locating this material. He knew she'd wished to know more, and had found what she wanted.

She sat at the table and began to read what her aunt Sally had written more than twenty years ago. When the buzzer sounded, it jarred her. She got up and turned off the stove and oven. Serving her plate, she went back to the table and picked up the pages. She'd read in her room.

Passing Jake's room, she hesitated by the closed door. What was there to say?

"Dinner's on the stove," she called, and turned for her

room. She closed that door and sat in the chair near the window. Reading as she ate, and then continuing when she was finished, Cath was fascinated by the history her aunt had unearthed.

Saddened, too, to learn that Tansy had never remarried. She'd mourned her Jonathan all her life. And it had been a long one. She had died in the 1830s, at the age of ninety-two. She'd lived in the house Jonathan had built—the large house built for a family to grow in—until her death. It had been filled with love and laughter and children. Her cousin Timothy Williamson and his wife had had eleven children. And Tansy had helped raise every one.

Cath looked away from the history, wondering how much of what Tansy felt would be in the later journals. For a moment a shiver of apprehension coursed through her. What if she were more like Tansy than she wanted to admit? What if she never found another man to love as she loved Jake? What if she mourned him all her life and lived to be in her nineties? She yearned for children, but not every woman who wanted a baby had one. Tansy had loved her cousin's children. How much must she have missed having her own with Jonathan?

The house had been in her family for years, but came down through Tansy's cousin, not Jonathan. Their last name had been White. It was Tansy's cousin Timothy who had been the first Williamson to live in the house.

Aunt Sally even wrote about the necklace, saying it had been lost during the Civil War, just as Jake had guessed.

Sally lamented the fact her nephew, Cath's father, had not wanted the old house. It should stay in the family. She hoped her grandniece would bring it back to life, and so she ended the history.

Cath could never sell it. Not after all this.

She might never fill it with children, but it was her heritage and she would hold on to it.

She didn't feel herself falling asleep, but woke with a stiff neck sometime later. It was almost 4:00 a.m.! She quickly dressed for bed and crawled into the cold sheets, going back to sleep. This time she dreamed she was an old woman, alone in a big house, with Tansy's necklace. She sat in front of a fireplace in the kitchen and lamented war.

When Cath awoke again, it was midmorning. She needed to talk to Jake before he left. She couldn't let things end like this.

He sat at the kitchen table, his duffel near the back door, when she entered a short time later. A hot cup of coffee held in his hand. He was reading one of the journals.

"Good morning," he said without looking up.

"Good morning. Ready to leave, I see," she said. Her heart raced. Sadness overwhelmed her. Six years of love and worry and loneliness and sparks of sheer joy crowded the memories of her mind. She saw a fabulously handsome, virile man sitting at her table, and her heart skipped a beat.

"It may be that I'm more like Tansy than I expected, though her blood doesn't run through my veins," she said, pulling out a chair and sitting before her knees gave way.

"No?" he asked.

"She never had children. She lived with her cousin and his wife and was auntie to their children. They were the ones to inherit when she died. She was Tansy White, not even a Williamson."

"You'll go on to have that family, Cath. Some smart guy will snap you up in no time and make sure you have a dozen kids if that's how many you want."

"Why didn't you tell me, Jake?" she asked.

"I figured you'd leave once you knew. I hoped against it, hoped you'd get enough of children at the school. I figured that's the way it'd play out if I ever had to tell you." He swallowed hard, studying her as if memorizing every feature. "Look at my mother. One child wasn't enough for her. She had to remarry and have three more. Then her life was complete. Only somewhere along the way she forgot about that first child. Her second family became her focus. Things would have been different if my father had lived. But he didn't. And children became the overruling passion of my mother. When you first brought it up, I was stunned. For once in my life, I thought I was wanted for myself. Not for some genetic donation to create a baby. Never once in five years did you mention having children. Then suddenly, wham, it's the most important thing you can think of."

Cath blinked. She had never thought about his feeling that way. She knew about his family. He had shared that, and it had been hard for such a proud man to admit how left out he'd been as a child. He'd overcome a great deal to achieve all he had. She wouldn't for one second want to diminish that. Or consider him only a means to an end. She'd loved him, wanted his children as a part of that love.

She'd never considered this point of view. If

someone thought that of her, it would hurt. After all that Jake had gone through, she regretted his feeling that way. She'd never wanted to hurt him.

For a long moment all she heard was the sound of water dripping from the roof as the sun melted the snow. The fragrance of coffee would forever be tied to this conversation. She stared at him, not knowing what to say.

Jake broke eye contact first. He lifted his cup and drained it. "I'll be on my way in a little while. Thought I'd take one more walk along the river. I called Sam last night and canceled the request to stay stateside. I'll be heading for London in the morning. Have your attorney send the papers to the office and they'll be forwarded to me."

He rose, shrugged on his jacket and headed out.

Cath sat as still as a statue, fearing if she moved an inch, she'd shatter into a thousand pieces. How cruel her actions must seem. His announcement had caught her unaware, but that didn't mean she didn't love him. She didn't only want him as a sperm donor. She wanted her husband!

I thought I was wanted for myself. His words echoed in her mind.

All she could picture was the bewilderment a young boy must have felt when his father died. And again when his mother remarried and started a new family. Always on the outside, never feeling truly wanted.

Cath loved Jake. She had from the first time she'd met him. She hadn't been thinking about children back then, but about the most wonderful man in the world. A man who seemed equally taken with her. Would she have left him if he'd told her at the very beginning? She began to think she wouldn't have. In the beginning it had been just Cath and Jake. It was only lately that she yearned for more. Aunt Sally's death had changed things for her and she had only looked at her own selfish desire. Was it a woman thing, wanting a baby? She frowned. She did not want to be labeled a woman like his mother. She'd harbored uncharitable thoughts about the woman since she'd first heard about her. Today's revelation made her even more angry at his mother. She should have cherished and loved her first child. Had her goal been to have children just to have them, or to love and raise them?

What was hers?

She feared she was more like Tansy than she expected.

The truth was Cath had never looked at another man after she fell in love with Jake. Even thinking she was ending her marriage, she couldn't summon up a spark of interest in finding another man. Everyone would be compared with Jake. And found lacking.

But could she give up her dream of a family?

Two was a family.

She wanted more.

Sometimes in life people didn't get what they wanted. Aunt Sally hadn't. Her fiancé had been killed at Normandy and she'd never found another to love. Cath shivered.

Were there other women in her family who were one-man women? What if she never found another man to love? Could she throw away what she had in the nebulous hope of finding love again?

She'd debated that in her mind all fall long. She thought she'd settled it. But seeing Jake changed everything.

"Cath!" A voice yelled from the yard.

She went to the door and opened it, stepping onto the back stoop.

Bart was running along the river, heading downstream, toward the McDonald yard.

"Bart?"

"Cath, get blankets and come a running. Jake fell into the river. I'm hoping to get him out at the dock."

She stood in shock for a moment—Jake had fallen into the river? He could freeze to death! She saw Pearl running from her house, two blankets in her arms.

"Cath, call for an ambulance. We couldn't get him out, the banks are too steep and it's so slippery with this slush," Pearl called, sliding as she ran after Bart.

Cath didn't hesitate, though she longed to cry out against the injustice of it all. He couldn't die! He'd been in wars and natural disasters, he couldn't die in her backyard. She whirled and went into action. As a teacher she'd been trained in emergency procedures. She called 9-1-1 and reported an accidental plunge into the James River. An ambulance was promised immediately. Cath flung on her jacket and scooped up the afghan from the sofa and dashed out the back door, running as fast as she could after Pearl and Bart. She could see them on the dock in the distance.

Over and over in her mind chanted the words, *wanted for myself.* She did want Jake for himself. For herself. *She loved Jake.* With a soul searing depth that frightened her. And gave meaning to her life. That would never change. How had she ever thought it would?

The slushy ground was slippery and sloppy. The sunshine belied the danger beneath her feet. Melting snow made it almost impossible to keep from falling.

Cath slipped and fell twice, soaking her jeans and scraping one palm. Keeping the afghan as dry as possible, each time she scrambled to her feet and kept going. Her heart raced, time seemed to drag by, each second an eternity. She had to get to Jake. Had to tell him he was all she wanted. He would be enough for her the rest of her days, if he only didn't die! God, don't let her end up like Tansy, losing the only man she loved!

The river water would be barely above freezing. How long would someone last in such cold water? Could he catch hold of the landing platform at the McDonald's dock? Was it still there? She hadn't used that since she was a teenager. Who knew what changes might have been made over the last ten years?

"Jake," she screamed, running as fast as the terrain permitted.

As she drew closer she could see Pearl on the dock that jutted twenty feet into the river. Bart had jumped down to the landing platform. She caught her breath. Jake had been stopped by the platform, but she couldn't tell if he'd caught it or slammed into it by the river current. Bart was struggling to pull Jake from the water. In only a moment both men were lying on the landing. Jake was streaming water, soaking Bart.

Cath reached the dock and jumped down beside the two men. Bart sat up.

"You okay?" he asked, and gently pushed Jake to lie on his back.

His eyes were closed, his lips blue, but, thank God, he was breathing very faintly. A scrape near his hairline bled sluggishly.

Cath unfolded the afghan and wrapped it around him, snuggling closer to share her own body heat. He was soaking wet and freezing cold.

"Jake, say something. Are you all right?" she asked frantically.

"Here, take these blankets, too. He needs to get warm. That water is freezing," Pearl said, dropping down the blankets she held. "Are you dry enough, Bart, or do you need to wrap up, too?" she asked.

"I'm fine. My slacks are wet, but I'll be okay for a little while. Get Jake warm first," he said.

Cath was trying. She rubbed his face gently, feeling the chill of his skin against her palms. She feared her hands were getting too cold to help.

"Why doesn't he say something?" she asked, rubbing his hands, they felt like ice.

"I think he hit his head when he was trying to catch hold of the landing platform," Bart said. "He was doing okay until then. Good thing we saw him slip in. He could freeze to death in that water in just a few minutes."

They wrapped the blankets around him, but Jake made no move to help himself. Cath pressed herself against him. "He will be all right, won't he?" she asked. He was still breathing but was so still, and his lips remained blue.

The ambulance siren could be heard.

"I'll go tell them where we are," Pearl said, hurrying toward Cath's house.

"What happened?" Cath asked as she and Bart chafed his limbs, trying to warm Jake.

"He was walking along the bank, too close to the

edge, hit a patch of slush and over the side he went. I ran out, he was holding on to a clump of grass at the water's edge, but we couldn't get him out. It's only about a three-foot drop, but the ground is so slippery with the slush. I couldn't get too near the edge, for fear of joining him."

Cath shuddered to think of both men in the water. Who would have fished them both out?

"He told me you spoke of a dock downstream, he said he'd try for that. Then he let go and drifted along the shore. I ran to tell Aunt Pearl and then headed for the dock. He was still lucid when he reached here, but wacked his head a moment later."

Cath held Jake tightly, saying everything she could to make him hold on.

"I love you, Jake. It doesn't matter about anything else. We're a family, you and me. And that's enough. Hold on, love. Help is on the way."

Cath had never felt so helpless. Jake was her rock, her anchor. What if he didn't recover? What if he did but had changed his mind and wanted nothing to do with a woman like his mother who put so much emphasis on kids to the detriment of everything else?

"I'm sorry, Jake. So sorry. Come back to me. Don't be like Jonathan and leave forever. Stay with me. Grow old with me. Jake, please wake up!"

The paramedics hurried to the dock. In less time than Cath could imagine, they had Jake on a stretcher and were heading for the ambulance.

"We'll come to the hospital with you, dear," Pearl said, when Bart and Cath climbed up on the dock.

"Can't I go in the ambulance with him?" Cath asked.

One of the paramedics looked at Bart and shook his head.

Cath saw the sign and almost collapsed.

"I'm going!" she said. "And you're going to make sure my husband is fine!"

The ride to the hospital was a nightmare. Jake was so cold they broke out warming bags and packed them around him. He never regained consciousness. Once at the hospital, he was wheeled away and Cath was left to answer the questions of the admitting clerk.

Pearl and Bart arrived a short time later.

"How is he?" Pearl asked when they found Cath in the small waiting room.

"I haven't heard. He has to be all right!" She couldn't voice her fear that she'd left things too late. She would not become another Tansy. This family story would have a happy ending! At least she hoped so. She prayed for Jake's recovery, glad Pearl and Bart had come to be with her. She felt alone and afraid. What if Jake didn't recover?

She knew Tansy's anguish. How would she go on?

A half hour later a young intern came into the waiting room.

"Mrs. Morgan?" he called.

"Yes?" Cath jumped up and almost ran over to where he stood.

"It looks as if your husband's going to be fine. He's being taken to a room now. We want to keep him over night. He has a concussion and his body temperature is still well below normal. We're warming him up slowly and will monitor the concussion. You can see him in about fifteen minutes, room 307. But just for a moment. Rest and warmth are the best things for him now."

"Thank you." Cath burst into tears, feeling as if the weight of the world had been lifted. She had to see him, to make things right.

"We'll wait here for you, dear," Pearl said, settling back down in the uncomfortable seat.

"Take your time. We'll drive you home when you're ready to leave," Bart said, sitting beside his aunt.

Cath almost told them she'd never be ready to leave, but knew the hospital probably wouldn't let her stay.

She found the room on the third floor. It was a semi-private room, but only one bed was occupied. Jake was bundled in blankets, one hand lying on the sheet, the rest of him covered from neck to toes. He had his eyes closed, and a white bandage on his head.

She entered. Had he regained consciousness?

"Jake?"

He opened his eyes and looked at her. Then he deliberately turned his head and closed his eyes, shutting her out completely.

"Oh, Jake, I'm so sorry," she said. Reaching out to take his hand, Cath was startled when he snatched it away, slipping it beneath the blanket, out of reach.

"You're going to be fine, the doctor said." She moved around the bed, but he merely turned his head the other way.

"Go home, Cath. There's nothing more to be said."

"Yes, there is. I was wrong. I'm sorry. I want our marriage to flourish."

"Get out."

"Jake, didn't you hear me?"

He looked at her then, his eyes bloodshot, his lips still faintly blue. "Did you hear me? Get out!"

"Not until you listen to me."

"Sorry, time for me to check vitals again," a nurse said in the doorway. "And I have some more warm blankets and a warm drink for you, Mr. Morgan."

"She was just leaving," Jake murmured, turning from Cath.

"I'll check on you later," Cath said tentatively.

"Don't bother. I'm only in here for observations. I'll be out in the morning."

"Then I'll come pick you up."

She left before he could say anything else. The nurse was already talking about seeing how much warmer he was.

Cath felt shell-shocked. He hadn't wanted to see her. She had apologized and he'd brushed it off.

She had to make him see she had a change of heart.

"How is he?" Pearl asked when Cath entered the waiting room.

"Cranky," she said, hoping it was the near death experience making him that way, not that she'd lost her last chance.

"Men do not make the best patients," Pearl said.

"I resent that," Bart said, rising. "Ready to go home?"

Cath nodded, feeling drained and tired. And immensely sad. Had she lost what she just realized was worth more than anything to her? How would she go on if Jake truly left?

When Bart dropped her off at the old house, he asked if she needed anything.

"Actually you could help me move something, if

you would." She'd had enough time to think between the hospital and home. She knew what she was going to do. She was betting her future on it.

"Sure thing."

They moved the cradle back to the spot in the cellar where Cath had first found it. Without a second glance at it, she left it behind and followed Bart back to the kitchen.

"I appreciate your saving Jake, if I didn't say so before, I'm sorry. He's all I have."

"He might have saved himself if he hadn't hit his head. Glad I saw him slip, or he'd have been in a real mess."

Or dead. Cath shuddered.

"Let us know how he does," Pearl said, giving Cath a hug. "Want to come over to our place for supper tonight?"

"Thank you, but no. I have a lot to do before Jake gets home tomorrow. And if he calls, I want to be home." Cath thanked them both for their help and watched as they drove the short distance to Pearl's house.

Cath went to the living room and sank on the sofa, gazing at the ashes in the fireplace. She hoped they didn't reflect the state of her marriage.

For a long time she sat in thought. All the arguments she'd had during the fall rose, but were dismissed in light of the knowledge she now had. Finally she rose and went to find Jake's computer. With only a small search, she found what she was looking for. Using her cell phone, she called Sam Miller.

It took her a few minutes to get through to the man himself, but she patiently used Jake's name at every stage and refused to tell anyone else why she was calling.

When they were finished, she brought up the boxes for the ornaments and began to disassemble the Christmas tree.

CHAPTER ELEVEN

JAKE walked up the driveway. He'd had the cab drop him at the curb. The snow continued to melt. Some of the asphalt was visible now. His car needed to be cleared. He'd load his duffel and head out. He'd missed his flight, but once he got to a phone, he'd square things with Sam.

His head still ached. The doctor had told him it might for several weeks. He'd given him some pain pills, but Jake hadn't taken any. He was driving up to D.C. as soon as he got his things, no sense risking that by getting dopey on drugs.

When he reached the back door, he noticed the Christmas tree leaning against the house. It still looked fresh and vibrant. In only a few more days, however, the needles would begin to drop until it was merely brittle branches.

Sort of like he felt, he thought wryly.

Opening the door, he stepped into the kitchen. His duffel was still by the door, where he'd left it yesterday. Beside it sat two suitcases—Cath's.

He should grab his bag and leave. But he couldn't resist telling her goodbye. He'd acted like an idiot at the hospital. He hated her seeing him down and out. Things had been bad enough without that. He'd rather her remember him standing on his own two feet than help-lessly shivering while trying to get warm.

Just then she breezed into the kitchen, carrying a heavy box.

"Jake! I was coming at ten to pick you up," she said, putting the box on the kitchen table. She ran over to him and hugged him. Involuntarily his arms came up around her and he buried his face in her sweet hair. Closing his eyes he focused on every impression, burning each into his memory. Her hair was soft and sweet and smelled like apple blossoms. Her body was feminine and curvy, molding with his. Her arms were tight around him, clinging like they'd never let go. Her voice was melodic, the prettiest he'd ever heard.

"I was so worried about you. I stopped back at the hospital last night, but you were asleep and the doctor said that was the best thing. They were checking you every couple of hours for the concussion, but it wasn't getting worse." She pulled back a little and looked up at him, her eyes full of concern.

"Should you be up and about so soon? How's your head?" she asked.

"It aches, but I was released with a clean bill of health. Just have to be careful and not bang it into anything."

She smiled, hugging him again.

"I came for my bag, Cath."

"Sure. Mine are ready. I did want to take the journals, though," she said, stepping away and moving back to the carton on the table. "Hold the door, will you?"

"What are you talking about?"

"Taking the journals?"

"No, that your bags are ready."

"I have to stop at the condo for my passport. And see about another set of clothes. Mostly I brought old things down here to do cleaning in."

"Where are you going?"

"Damascus," she said.

His eyes narrowed. Had the blow to the head addled his brains? What was she talking about?

"Damascus?"

She nodded. Picking up the carton, she carried it toward him. "Open the door for me, will you?"

He didn't budge.

"I'm going to Damascus," he said.

"I know, that's why I'm going," she said, standing in front of him with the heavy box.

"What are you talking about?"

"Get the door, this is heavy!"

He opened the door and followed her to her car, opening the back door so she could slide the carton on the seat.

"I just need to put my suitcases in and get the lunch I fixed for us and I'm ready. I would have had this all done before ten, when I planned to go to the hospital to get you."

"Damascus," he repeated, closing the car door and studying her.

"I talked to Sam Miller yesterday and asked for the safest place closest to where you were going. He said Damascus. I can stay there and you can come home whenever you get a break."

Cath watched him close his eyes and shake his head, then heard him groan softly.

Anxious, she reached out to grab his arm.

"Are you sure you should be up?"

He opened his eyes and nodded slowly. "I just shouldn't be making sudden moves. Cath, you are not going to Damascus."

"I am. I'm going wherever you go."

"You're a teacher in Washington, not a nomad like me."

"I'm changing that. I love you, Jake. I knew it before I almost lost you yesterday, but that was a scare I never want to live through again. It showed me how precious our love is. And how fleeting it could be. I don't want to end up like Tansy, mourning you the rest of my life. Or even Aunt Sally."

"Aunt Sally?"

"She lost her love in the Second World War. She never found another. I can't take that risk when I already love the world's most fantastic man."

"I thought you wanted children."

"I thought I did, too. But what I wanted was *your children*. Since that isn't going to happen, then I'll drop the subject."

"Just like that?"

She hesitated only a moment feeling the pang at losing the dream. But compared with what she'd learned yesterday when she thought she might lose him, it was a minor price to pay, the loss of a dream. She smiled at him with all the love in her heart.

"Just like that. I love you, Jake. You and only you are who I want to be my family." She held her breath. She'd put everything on the line, faxing in her resignation, leaving her friends, to go with this man. What if he turned away like he had yesterday? It would be no more than she deserved, but more than she could bear.

He didn't move for a moment. Just when Cath thought she'd explode he reached for her, pulling her into a tight embrace. His mouth found hers and he kissed her long and hard.

"You don't have to go with me," he said a minute later. "I can still ask for a stateside assignment."

"I want to be with you. I'm tired of being alone. And I want you to know beyond anything how much I love you. You were willing to give up your career for me. I want to show you I'm willing to give up my job for you. I don't want anything to keep us apart."

"You love teaching."

"I do. I love you more. Besides, I can find a job teaching English in Damascus, I bet. I want you to know beyond a shadow of a doubt that you are all I need to make my life perfect."

He kissed her again, holding her like she was fragile crystal. Cath reveled in being in his arms, longing to remain there all her life. She'd readjust her plans for the future. Nothing was as important as being with this special man.

"You don't have to leave everything to show me you love me."

"I want to. I've never been to Damascus."

"I'll ask for a stateside assignment."

"After this one, but only if you want."

"I want. Maybe even something close enough we can stay in this house. It's your legacy from the past. Don't sell it, Cath. It's got a great history behind it."

For a fleeting moment Cath regretted there would be

no children to leave it to when she and Jake no longer lived in it. But life was what it was. She'd already glimpsed what it would be like without Jake and what it could be with him. There was no hardship in that choice. She'd been fooling herself all autumn that she could leave. She could no more give him up than she could give up breathing.

"Whenever we're ready, we'll come back," she said. The future wasn't the one she'd thought to have, but with Jake it would always be more than enough.

EPILOGUE

JAKE paced the small room, stopping at the window, then turning to pace back to where Cath was sitting. The utilitarian furnishings were uncomfortable, how could she sit so calmly?

"How can you be so patient?" he asked. "Aren't you scared to death?"

She smiled and shook her head. "You've been shot at, almost drowned in the James River and had bricks fall on you from the earthquake last fall. What are you afraid of?"

"Messing up."

"You won't," she said with conviction.

"It's more than I can handle."

"It's not."

"You're sure?"

"Oh, yes. We'll make it—together." Laughter filled her eyes. He frowned and turned to pace back to the window, staring over the bleak landscape. Snow had turned dirty along the side of the street. The black tree branches looked stark against the gray sky. More snow was predicted that night. He hoped the storm would hold off until they were gone.

They'd signed the last of the papers earlier that afternoon. Everything was set for their flight home. It was the waiting that was getting to him. And the uncertainty.

Jake turned and looked at his wife. She smiled at him, obviously amused at his behavior. For a moment he felt silly. He was a grown man, had faced dangers most men rarely even thought about. He couldn't believe Cath had given up everything to follow him. The last couple of years had been fantastic. They were closer than ever. They'd visited every capital in Europe, stopped in exotic locales around the Mediterranean. Theirs was a strong love that would sustain him through anything. Even this.

He hoped.

The door opened. Cath jumped to her feet. Slowly Jake turned, his heart pounding.

"Here they are," the woman said in heavily accented English. "Anna and Alexander. We call him Sasha as a baby name." Her uniform was gray, the apron she wore was white. Her eyes were kind.

The two-year-old girl stared at them, her blue eyes bright with wonder. Cath knelt near her and held out a dolly.

"Hello, Anna. I'm your new mommy," she said softly. Then carefully she reached out and pulled the child into her arms. "I'm so happy to see you today," she said, her voice breaking slightly. She closed her eyes for a moment, but not before Jake saw the tears.

Jake took a deep breath and stepped forward.

"Here you go," the woman said, handing the baby to Jake. He hesitated a moment, then took the seven-month-old boy. The baby's blue eyes stared up into Jake's. For a moment panic took hold, then sanity returned. He'd wanted to do this. For Cath, and for himself.

Now he was a father of two children, orphaned by the fighting in their home country, alone in the world except for him and Cath.

The baby's fist waved and Jake caught it, feeling the tiny fingers wrap around his thumb. He said the words he'd never expected to say.

"Hello, Sasha, I'm your daddy."

Already he felt the tendrils of love wrap around his heart. He looked at Cath and smiled. They had discussed the option of adoption shortly after they arrived in Damascus. Cath had a heart full of love to share, and he wanted to be right there with her. She was right, together they could do this.

They were flying home tonight—to spend Christmas at the house beside the James River. He had a yard to fence, a dock to build and two precious children to love and raise. Their legacy to the future.

"Ready, Daddy?" Cath asked, picking up Anna and carrying her over to Jake.

He leaned over and gave the little toddler a kiss on the cheek, then one for Cath.

"We're ready, Mommy, let's get our kids home."

* * * * *

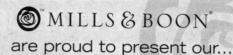

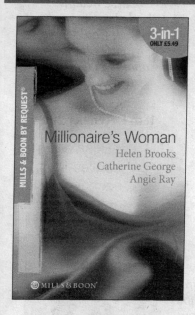

millsandboon.co.uk Community

Join Us!

The Community is the perfect place to meet and chat to kindred spirits who love books and reading as much as you do, but it's also the place to:

- Get the inside scoop from authors about their latest books
- Learn how to write a romance book with advice from our editors
- Help us to continue publishing the best in women's fiction
- Share your thoughts on the books we publish
- Befriend other users

Forums: Interact with each other as well as authors, editors and a whole host of other users worldwide.

Blogs: Every registered community member has their own blog to tell the world what they're up to and what's on their mind.

Book Challenge: We're aiming to read 5,000 books and have joined forces with The Reading Agency in our inaugural Book Challenge.

Profile Page: Showcase yourself and keep a record of your recent community activity.

Social Networking: We've added buttons at the end of every post to share via digg, Facebook, Google, Yahoo, technorati and de.licio.us.

www.millsandboon.co.uk

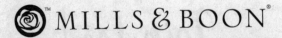